DEATH TOLL

ROBERT POULIN

DEATH TOLL
Robert Poulin

Printed in the United States of America.
Ghost Watch Publishing
Plattsburgh, New York 12901
Edited by Jaimee Finnegan

For more information about this book visit: www.ghostwatchpublishing.com
Edition ISBNs
Trade Paperback 978-0-9894469-3-8
E-book 978-0-9894469-4-5
Cover art and design by Hannah Carr
Book design by Christopher Fisher
PUBLISHER'S NOTE: This is a work of fiction. Names, characters, places, and events herein are either the product of the author's imagination or are used fictitiously. Any resemblance to actual persons, living or dead, is entirely coincidental.

Death Toll is dedicated to Tina, my best friend and soul mate. And to my uncle Wilbrod Poulin, who would have loved to have seen this work.

ACKNOWLEDGEMENTS

A project like this has many important contributors, hopefully I won't forget to mention anyone, I beg forgiveness if I do so. Thanks first and foremost to my Fiancée Tina Cook for her support and for putting up with me while the computer took up most of my free time. I can't thank my wonderful editor Jaimee Finnegan enough for her tireless work on this project, once again her input has given this book soul. Thanks to Hannah Carr, the cover artist for this book, she did an amazing job. Thanks to the team at The Editorial Department who did the interior layout, formatting, and conversions for the eBook as well as the print version. Thanks to Warren Middlemiss for helping with the proof reading and for his support. A very special shout of thanks to Beatrice Beguin and her colleagues at the New York State Commission for the Blind (NYSCB), without them Ghost Watch Publishing wouldn't have been possible. Finally, I want to thank my beta readers, Debra Piper, Karen Figary, Jessica Middlemiss, Justin Sharp, Don Sharp, Christy Hoke. I also want to put a good word in for the Writing Excuses Podcast and Publetariat.com, I learned a lot about writing from these online resources and continue to use them.

DEATH TOLL

Prologue

JEZEBEL WATCHED THE OLD CRONE with a mixture of disgust and fear. She had to suppress a growl of anger as the beast that lurked within her reacted to her fear. Two bitches of her pack stood at her sides; both of the tawny haired women were also watching the crone, but they didn't do nearly as well as she did in suppressing their fear. Their tense bodies vibrated with the desire to flee. Jezebel licked her lips and smiled predatorily as she momentarily pushed the crone from her mind and allowed her beast to feed on her companions' fear. The beasts within the other two women reacted to her hunger, and their own desire for blood, meat, and violence pushed the fear of their hosts aside. The three women began rubbing up against each other and growls of playful threat filled the Philadelphia night as they psyched themselves up for the coming hunt.

After a few minutes, Jezebel forced her mind back to the work at hand. She'd successfully distracted her subordinates who continued to rub their heads against her and grope her curvaceous body with their hands. More than sexual play, the contact allowed the suppressed beast within them to feel and comfort each other. The beasts were always wanting to fraternize with each other, and hyenas in particular needed it or they'd get quite grumpy. When you became a were-hyena, you left your inhibitions behind. This suited Jezebel just fine; she'd been a stripper in Vegas when she'd been offered the chance to become a were-hyena. She didn't regret her choice for one moment. She had power now: the beast within her was cunning and strong. The move to Philadelphia had presented many opportunities to grow in power, and one of those opportunities was a new ally. That's what had taken her and her pack mates away from her strip club this night; the crone was her new ally's avatar of choice for the moment. Judging from the power that the witch could wield, her ally was even more powerful than she'd imagined. At this point, others would be wondering if they'd gotten in over their heads, but not Jezebel. For her, there was no such thing as too much power. For her, the more power her ally had, the more there was for her to gain.

It took Jezebel a moment to spot the crone again, but she did so with little difficulty. Her night vision enhanced beast sight enabled her to penetrate the night shrouded city's darkest shadows. The old witch was tucked deep into an alleyway across the street from where Jezebel and her companions waited. She was surrounded by three menacing figures who towered over her and gave off a dangerous crimson aura that identified them as vampires. The crone stood against them unafraid, having lured them to the very spot that she'd desired. The vampires weren't the hunters this night, they were the prey. The witch that stood with them was short, maybe five foot two, and was draped in an unflattering robe of mud brown. Her hair was long, unkempt, and white, and her eyes were black and shadowed by bushy white eyebrows. The nose on her face was pointy and looked too long. The crone had called herself Bridget Bishop when she'd presented herself to Jezebel a few days ago. Jezebel had the uneasy feeling that the woman believed herself to be the very Bridget Bishop that had hanged in 1692: the first of the Salem witchcraft trial victims. After working with the woman for a few days, Jezebel wasn't at all sure that the idea was impossible. The crone was incredibly powerful, she talked funny, and she knew almost nothing about the modern world.

The witch made a sharp gesture and two of the vampires went suddenly rigid and unmoving. The third vampire glanced at her two male companions nervously, but her attention was redirected towards the crone who'd tilted her head so that her throat was bared. Jezebel's enhanced sense of smell caught the scent of fresh blood on the air. She shuddered as her beast suddenly roared to life, and it took all her strength of will to hold the hyena within her back. The vampire who was only a few feet away from that delicious smell was unable to hold herself back though. She lunged at the witch with blinding speed and plunged her fangs into the crone's neck.

Jezebel had to grab her two companions before they could rush into the alley and join the feast. She let her beast roll over them so that she could fully dominate the two lesser bitches and force their beasts back down. The two lesser beasts cowered in fear from her own dominant beast. She growled at them until they crouched low and pawed at her leather clad thighs in submission.

Meanwhile, the witch had begun to chant and the alley was beginning to fill with a nasty looking green fog. The blood lust quickly evaporated from all of their beasts as their hackles raised and dread suddenly filled them. Shapes were moving in the fog that now almost totally obscured the alley. A tentacle lashed the air at the border of the fog, and a scream of pure terror rent the night. Jezebel shivered as the air was filled with the sound of cracking and breaking bones and wet meat hitting the ground. The horrific symphony went on for what seemed like hours. The crone chanted the entire time. Jezebel's beast watched with her in fascinated horror, but she sensed that the other two's beasts had fled to hide in the deepest holes they could find, leaving their hosts huddled together in terror.

Finally, the mists began to clear and the movement of huge unseen monstrosities faded. The witch ended her ritual, and a sudden blast of wind cleared the alley of all evidence of green fog. The alley pavement and all the building walls around it were coated in glistening wet gore, yet the crone and the three vampires stood there apparently unscathed and untouched by the gore that covered everything else. The witch cackled in delight and began walking towards Jezebel. The three vampires followed in her wake. They moved like vampires, all graceful and predatory, but their auras were wrong now: their normal scarlet was now flecked with a corrupting yellow-green. The coppery blood scent that often accompanied vampires was also missing from these transformed creatures. Jezebel's work with the crone over the past few days had alerted her to the fact that the witch had some way of turning vampires to her master's service, but tonight's demonstration was the first time that she'd seen how it was done. For the first time in years, Jezebel wondered if she wasn't in over her head. Could this be done to her and her people, she wondered.

As Bridget Bishop drew closer, Jezebel's bitches began to whimper fearfully, and she turned on them in fury. She grabbed them both by the hair, and her beast launched its claws into them and pulled their beasts from their hiding places. The beast spirit residing within Jezebel wasn't able to leave her body completely, but as long as some part of it remained in contact with its host it could act against other spiritual creatures as it did now.

"Stop your sniveling," she commanded with a growl that carried her beast's scent and power. "You are bone-crusher hyenas. Stand up and stop acting like prey!"

The two women rose slowly, drawing heavily upon their pack leader's strength and courage. By the time the witch reached them, the trio was ready to stand together as a team. Jezebel had no illusions though. She would order a retreat before fighting against such odds as the witch and her three vampires. Hyena's fight best in large packs, and if the crone or her vampires threatened them, she would retreat and gather the others of her pack.

"I see you assessing your situation Jezebel," the hag chortled as she came to a stop a few paces away. The vampires fanned out around her and regarded Jezebel with cold hunger in their eyes. "Nothing has changed. Our alliance was hammered out by the Black Pharaoh himself. The turning is reserved for our enemies. Fulfill your end of the bargain and you have nothing to fear and much to gain."

Jezebel nodded curtly, angry that the witch had read her so easily.

"What now?" she asked.

"We leave for Providence immediately," the witch answered and turned towards the Ford Expedition parked at the curb nearby. "Our little strike team has business with the wizards of the Order."

Although Jezebel was aware of the mission, the idea of going up against the wizards caused a shiver to pass through her. The beast within her reacted by raising its hackles, and a soft growl escaped her lips. All creatures of the night knew better than to tangle with the wizards. Avoiding them was usually the best policy if continued survival was important to you.

"Don't fret girl," the old crone croaked at her. "The Order has grown weak, and the Old Ones fear them not. My master will trod upon the protectors of humanity."

"I ain't no damn child!" Jezebel growled; her fear of wizards was forgotten as anger flared up in her. She hated the old witch's patronizing attitude. "My sisters and I will feast upon the meat of wizards and snap their bones between our jaws this night."

The witch's answering cackle didn't do anything to improve Jezebel's mood. Her beast wanted to snap and crunch the crone's bones more than it wanted anything else in recent memory. Jezebel suppressed a sigh of frustration as she led her pack mates to the Expedition. She wished she could kill something before embarking on this trip; a little violence prior to getting into the vehicle with the exasperating witch would make the next few hours so much more bearable. Even better would have been some sex mixed in with the violence. There was nothing like fucking and getting ones claws good and bloody while doing it. Her head full of lustful, nightmarish fantasies, Jezebel got behind the wheel of the Expedition and revved the engine.

Mors Morta stared at herself in the wall length mirror of her personal bathing chamber. She stood totally naked except for the jewelry that glittered in the chamber's candlelight. A fire opal gleamed at her throat, dangling from a gold chain. Sapphires dangled from silver earrings, and diamond encrusted bracelets flashed at her wrists and ankles. Her nipples were pierced with blood iron, but her favorite piece was the ruby piercing her clit. She licked her ruby lips, and the diamond that pierced her tongue glinted brightly until her tongue disappeared back into her mouth. She was of average height, but nothing else about her was average. Her hair was raven black; it was long, hanging halfway down her back, and straight. Like her hair, her eyes were also black. Her face was perfectly shaped with perfectly pro-portional nose, lips, eyes, and chin, and her skin gleamed with perfect health: there were absolutely no blemishes. Her breasts were firm and well sized, not overly large. Her legs, hips, and but-tocks were what young women dreamed of when they imagined themselves to be movie stars or models. Mors Morta loved to gaze at herself in the mirror. There was no creature more perfect than herself except perhaps her mother, the Morrigan. Thinking of her mother displeased Mors Morta. Being the second most powerful fae and the second most beautiful woman in the world was just intolerable.

Mors Morta banished the thought of her mother from her mind with a shake of her head. There was an unannounced guest waiting for her, and he'd already been made to wait while she bathed. She pondered for a moment what she should wear and finally settled on just shadows. She enjoyed teasing men; it was great sport. Aside from that, she never knew before hand whether she'd take a man to her bed. It always depended on how well they played the game. A shiver of anticipation ran through her as she wondered how well her guest would play. Thraknir had warned her that the stranger exuded a mysterious power far beyond what he'd ever encountered. That was saying a whole lot since Thraknir had served in both her court and her mother's, and she'd have him flayed if he'd exaggerated the guest's power. She'd gone to great lengths to prepare herself for the man; he'd better be worth the effort.

As Mors Morta departed her bathing chamber, shadows gathered around her and formed into a diaphanous gown that both hid and revealed her most private parts with each movement. Her head was held high, and a small smile played across her features as she passed through her dominion and finally entered the sitting room that she'd decided to use for this audience. The room was dominated by a huge fireplace which blazed with a crackling fire. The red carpet was plush and sensuous on her naked feet. The chairs that dotted the room were elaborately gilded affairs made of rare woods and satin cushions. The walls were adorned with expensive original oil paintings and there were two oak bookshelves stuffed with leather bound tomes. The electric lights of the modern age were off. Mors Morta preferred the light of real fire.

As she entered the room, she felt the roiling power that came off of the stranger in waves. She knew immediately that he must be containing that power in order for her not to have sensed it miles away. It said a lot about his control that he could hide it until she was in his direct presence. He was standing near the fireplace and gazing into the fire as she walked in. He was tall, a little over six feet, and his hair was brown and shoulder length. His skin gleamed with health, with no visible blemishes, and was perfectly bronzed as if he'd lived his life in the equatorial regions of the world. His eyes were deep brown and were pools of bottomless knowledge when he fixed them on her. He had an eagle's nose and his body looked perfect and muscular. Mors Morta was filled with lust for the man as soon as her eyes met his; she would bed him whether he played the game well or not; it would be interesting to see if he could survive the ordeal. Only one man had ever done that.

"I am Mors Morta," she introduced herself to the stranger. Her voice was like an angel's and powerful compulsions rode upon it. Her shadowy gown moved with each word, revealing her secret places. "Who are you to demand an audience with the heir of the Shadow Court?"

"I am The Man with Many Names," the stranger answered quietly. He seemed to be unfazed by her beauty or the magic she was using on him. "I come to you as the avatar of Azathoth, the Lord of Chaos."

Mors Morta pursed her lips in displeasure. The shadows about her grew thicker and hid her body completely. She'd heard of the Old Cults; they worshiped old gods that supposedly predated the Nephilim. Azathoth was their chief deity. Anyone who worshipped the Old Ones was an enemy of the fae in her opinion. She wanted to banish this Man with Many Names immediately, but his power prevented her from ignoring him outright. He was a real threat. What was he doing in Philadelphia, she wondered.

"What do you want?" she asked coldly.

"One of your minions interfered with my subjects a few days ago," he answered without emotion. "I want to negotiate an alliance with you. I can make it worth your while. I can give you your fondest wish. Ally with me and I'll rid you of your mother and you can ascend to her place."

Mors Morta stared at The Man with Many Names in stunned silence. How could he possibly know what her deepest fantasy was? Visions of herself as the most powerful and beautiful fae in the world flashed before her in a vision that she often daydreamed of.

"No!" she croaked, shaking her head violently. Now he was

using magic on her. He might be able to dispatch her mother and elevate her to the highest ranks of the fae, but then she'd be the thrall of two new masters, and the little that she knew of the Old Ones told her that they would be far less pleasant than her mother.

The Man with Many Names sighed dramatically.

"Very well then. A truce. You and yours stay out of my affairs and I'll do the same."

"Why should I agree to this?"

"Because if you don't," he said taking a step towards her. "I'll kill you and your whole household right now."

His power rolled over her and drove her to her knees. The power was on the same level as her mother's, maybe even more. She trembled as she forced herself back to her feet. The negotiation was over. The terms were clear, and she saw no way around the truce that didn't involve her death. She would do what she had to do to save herself, but she was smart enough to realize that whatever this man was up to in Philadelphia, if he succeeded, she'd probably wish he'd killed her anyways. The best thing for now was to play along.

"Alright," she panted. "I'll sign a truce and call my people off. Who interfered with your affairs?"

"A troll," The Man with Many Names answered simply.

Mors Morta stifled a smile as she regarded her guest. The only troll that she knew that could garner the attentions of a power like this man was Alrik Solheim. Alrik was the king of trolls, and he'd signed a treaty with the Shadow Court in order to provide additional security for his nearly extinct race. If there was anyone in Philadelphia who could throw a wrench into the plans of a chaos cult, it was Alrik. Best of all, he could act independently without her getting the blame since he was technically an ally and not a minion.

"I'll have the papers drawn up in the usual manner," she said turning away from the stranger and exiting the room. The usual way was through a blood bond ritual. Thraknir would take care of the details. She was pensive as she returned to her chambers. A few hours in front of the mirror should calm her, she thought.

"Send for Alrik as soon as our guest has departed," she ordered her invisible servants. It had been some time since she'd had the troll in her bed. The memories of those three encounters flooded her, and she smiled wickedly as she studied her figure in the mirror. Not only was Alrik the only man to have survive her bed, he'd done it three times. She briefly considered not trying to kill him as he reached climax this night, she needed him to deal with The Man with Many Names after all, but she discarded the idea almost immediately. She needed a good fuck more than she'd needed it in a long time, and there was nothing like the thrill of your partner knowing that you would strike to kill at any time while you fornicated with him. Men were meant to enjoy her perfection only once, and of course they should never have another woman after partaking of her. Of the thousands of men she'd fucked in her three centuries of life, only Alrik had survived. To bed him again and not try to kill him would only be an insult to him. Besides, if he couldn't survive sex with her, how the hell was he going to survive thwarting the avatar of a god?

They attacked the Order's warehouse at 4:11 in the morning. They were a day late due to unforeseen circumstances, but they'd all fed well and rested during their delay. The city was deep in slumber with only a few trucks on the road heading for their early morning pick-ups or drop-offs so few would be around to notice what was going on. The warehouse was a rectangular structure with a flat roof and large double loading garage doors in the front. Jezebel had never been to Providence before, but the GPS gave her unerring directions through the small city's haphazard streets. She'd parked the Expedition a block away from their target and they'd gone the rest of the way on foot. The old crone had ordered them to stop when the wizards' storage building had come into view. Crouching, she'd slashed her wrist with an obsidian knife and used the blood to draw arcane symbols on the sidewalk. Jezebel and her pack mates had shied away as the witch began to chant in a soft voice. The hair at Jezebel's nape had risen as a light had suddenly flared around the warehouse. She thought she saw a huge tentacle beast beating at the magical wall surrounding the warehouse. The vision lasted only a moment and then the blue shimmering light exploded in a shower of sparks.

"Go!" Bishop had hissed at them. "We have scant time before the wizards send reinforcements."

The vampires had vanished entirely; their speed was incredible compared to Jezebel and her lackey's. Jezebel called on the beast within her to give her speed and launched herself towards the warehouse after the vampires. She followed their nightmarish scent where they'd crossed the street and gone down an alley between the wizard's warehouse and a furniture store. The door half way down the alley had been smashed open and lay on the floor twenty feet into the room. Jezebel smelled fresh blood and heard moans coming from the darkness nearby. She badly wanted to join the hunt, but that wasn't the purpose for which she'd been brought to this place. The vampires were here to do the killing: she was here to seek. It was a good thing their little delay had left her quite satisfied in the killing department otherwise her beast would have been very hard to control. As it was, it growled in frustration at being denied the opportunity to join in the killing.

"Spread out and find the jars," Jezebel growled to her two companions. "I want them found in less than two minutes. Go!"

Jezebel followed her own command by sprinting towards the back of the warehouse. She ignored a man who was stumbling down the stairs to see what was going on. The vampires would deal with him. She focused her attention on the smells of the room. The scents of blood, dust, wood, cement, rusting iron, and decay were a heady concoction that should have made it nearly impossible to track down one specific scent, but she picked up what she was looking for almost immediately. It was the scent of salt mixed with sulfur and copper. She found the jars packed in crates that were stored behind a chain linked fence. Snapping the chain that held the fence gate shut and locked was no challenge to Jezebel. Her pack mates had picked up the same scent she'd followed and they joined her as she yanked the gate open. She grabbed one of the large wooden crates and, with ease, hoisted the more than two hundred pound box and carried it towards the center of the warehouse. The witch had entered the facility and was standing in the center of the room. She was chanting again. Jezebel stopped and waited for nearly a minute as Bishop uttered her incantation. The air in front of the crone began to shimmer, and then a hole opened up and hung suspended in the air giving Jezebel a view of a lit room beyond. Jezebel almost dropped the crate she carried as she stared at the sight in wonder. The hole opened wider until it was more than large enough for two grown people to walk through together.

"Bring that here," Bishop snapped at her, and Jezebel obediently brought the crate to her. When the witch motioned for her to put the crate down, Jezebel did so and removed the lid by prying her razor claws between the seams and pulling the lid off with a screech of protesting nails. Jezebel and the witch peered into the exposed crate; there were large jars filled with a blue powder, and each was marked by a label with an alpha-numeric code on them.

"What's so important about these?" Jezebel asked with disgust. The whole trip suddenly seemed like a waste of time to her.

"The greatest alchemist of all time is within one of these crates," the witch said with a mad gleam in her eyes. "When I resurrect him, the secret lore of Yog Sothoth will once more be known to man, and the portals of the outer dark will open for our great god Azathoth. Now quit stalling and get all those crates to the other side."

Jezebel shivered, picked up the crate and, stepped through the portal. She didn't feel anything as she crossed the threshold. The room beyond was colder and damper giving her the impression that she was below ground, but nothing else happened. Her two companions deposited their crates in the room, and the three of them returned to the warehouse to pick up more. By this time, two of the three vampires had joined them, the third having been sent out to watch for possible trouble. Bishop watched them impatiently as they made quick work of moving the crates. She sent Jezebel back once more to make a quick sweep of the warehouse upstairs and downstairs to make sure that no jars were left undiscovered. Jezebel did in fact find a single jar locked away in an upstairs safe. She couldn't open the thing, so she ripped the entire thing out of the wall and carried it down to the waiting witch, who stared at her quizzically.

"Couldn't pass up the chance for some loot, eh?" the crone asked nonchalantly. "You're sure there are no other jars?"

"There's one in here," Jezebel said hoisting the safe for emphasis. "I can smell it, though it's very faint. It's lucky you sent me up there and it attracted my attention. See what avarice can get you."

There was a sudden crashing sound as one of the garage doors was blown apart. The third vampire regained its feet before Jezebel even had a chance to register that it had been hurled through the door. Standing on the sidewalk just outside the garage stood two angry looking men with blazing blue auras. One was tall, wearing blue jeans, a white tee-shirt, and a black leather jacket. He was pretty young looking and had a cocky look about him. The other man was short with graying hair and piercing blue eyes. He wore a black trench coat and sported a wooden staff. The younger man raised his hand to strike at the vampire again but failed to see the black streak of energy that shot from Bishop's outstretched hand. Meanwhile, the vampire turned its attention to the other wizard and leaped at the older man who shot a bolt of fire from his staff. The wizard's flame bolt struck the vampire, and it shrieked as its skin dissolved into a puddle.

Almost simultaneously, Bishop's black bolt struck the younger wizard, and he joined the vampire, screaming in agony as he fell to the ground and flopped about like a fish out of water.

"Noah!" cried the older wizard as he crouched down to check on his companion. He didn't turn his eyes from the vampire though, so he witnessed the big sack of blood filled jelly that wriggled free from the vampire's burned up body. The thing seemed to float upwards, and it had dozens of tentacles protruding from it. A look of terror crossed the older wizard's face as he once more raised his staff to send fire at his assailant. Before the fire could spring from the staff's tip however, a tentacle shot out from the floating blood sack and wrapped around his throat.

"Through the gate, you fool," the witch croaked at Jezebel and pushed her towards the portal. Jezebel did as she was told though she badly wanted to stay to see the rest of the fight. Bishop stayed on the other side for another two minutes then the blood sack appeared and passed through the gate followed by the witch and the two remaining vampires. The portal closed.

"What the fuck is that thing?" Jezebel asked nodding towards the floating jelly bag.

"It's a servant of our master," Bishop answered shortly. "There's a lot of work to be done. Get back to your club and start getting me some were-beasts to sacrifice."

Jezebel stared at the witch in consternation. She hadn't even gotten her breath back yet and Bishop was already moving on to the next task. At least the next part of the plan involved her working with her own people with no witch or vampire involvement. She looked around to get her bearings.

"Where the hell are we?"

"Byberry, the vampires can show you out."

1

THERE'S ONLY ONE THING more exhilarating than flying lei-
surely through the perpetually dark skies of shadow Philadelphia
and that is flying at breakneck speeds through the skies of any
metropolis while chasing a bad guy. There are few ghosts in
Limbo who can sustain flight for very long, so chasing bad guys
through the city's sky isn't an everyday occurrence. I wanted to
shout with joy as I dodged around a clock tower and climbed
rapidly at a ninety degree angle to avoid passing through the
building that lay a dozen yards beyond the tower. As a ghost, I
don't have to worry too much about hurting myself by hitting
buildings and other objects, but passing through them slows me
down and drains more power which I generally want to avoid
since flying uses up so much of it on its own. The bad guy had
gone through the building, so I knew I would get to the other
side quicker by going over it. He might double back and try to
go back the way he'd come but several members of the Ghost
Watch were following in my wake, and I fully expected them
to fan out to surround the building as we'd practiced in drills.

Either way, passing through the building would dramatically slow my prey down and cost him way too much power: what an amateur.

I wanted to be in a bad mood; the brazen attack on our celestial steel stores was hard to believe. Why would free souls engage in such activities when they knew that the city was in short supply of the valuable steel? Celestial steel is one of two substances that has a physical presence in Limbo, the realm of ghosts. The other substance is called devil's iron, and it is banned in Philadelphia due to its unpleasant qualities. When I'd successfully led a rebellion nine months ago and Philadelphia had become a free city, I didn't expect that our troubles would only grow from there. The blighted ghosts that ruled the rest of Limbo weren't pleased with our revolution, and the city has endured several assaults and a celestial steel embargo as a result. While the flames of revolution have spread to other parts of Limbo, we've had a difficult time in providing assistance to them as we've been too busy trying to hold things together at home. Our enemies are quite willing to give us devil's iron, which goes to show that our banning of it was the right move, but celestial steel is forbidden to us. The steel is critical because it is what our armor and weapons are made of. We can't fight our devil's iron equipped enemies without the celestial steel as doing so would be disastrous. Fortunately we started out with a good supply, so we've been ok up till now, but then the smugglers started attacking our soldiers and police to get their celestial steel from them, and then just a little under an hour ago, I was summoned to the US Mint building where an assault was under way. The mint is where we keep our remaining steel supply. We defeated the attackers of course, but it is very worrying that our own populous is turning to smuggling devil's iron into the city, and now they're attacking military supply depots. Some members of the Assembly, in particular those who are trying to legalize devil's iron, have tried to imply that the entire population is turning against the ban, but I personally think it's a relatively small group of folks who think they can get something out of a changed policy.

The bad guy came out of the other side of the building and tried to speed off. I pounced from where I was hovering at the top of the building and grabbed him from behind. He grunted in surprise, whirled around and clumsily tried to stab me with a celestial steel knife. I smiled and willed the knife to become a flower. The steel moved like liquid and became exactly what I pictured in my mind. It's a really cool effect kind of like the new kind of Terminator in Terminator II, the one that could change its shape at will. The bad ghost stared in shock at what used to be his knife. I winked at him; on days like this I'm so happy to be me. I'm a banshee who can shape celestial steel with a single thought, and I can fly: what's not to like about that?

"Oh, thanks for the flower," I said with a sneer. "But pretty gifts aren't going to get you out of trouble today."

My bodyguards arrived within seconds and the smuggler was unceremoniously pulled to the ground where we could question him without having to expend the enormous amounts of power that were required to fly or hover. All ghosts have a limited amount of power; the tank size if you will is different for every ghost, but we all go into deep hibernation when our tank gets empty. I have a huge tank, but I also tend to run into a lot more trouble than most ghosts, so I like to be conservative at times like this. Waste not, want not.

Once my men had the ghost bound in celestial steel cuffs, I approached him once more. He flinched from my gaze apparently now aware of who had captured him. I'm rather famous in these parts; I'm the girl that led the revolution that overthrew the Master of Philadelphia. I'm also the captain of the Ghost Watch, shadow Philly's police force, and I'm a banshee. The banshee part is what really scares people, as it should. Banshees are a really specialized kind of ghost that are made when a woman is tortured to death. The torturer must be a master at his craft and must set out to make a banshee on purpose. Since most living people don't even believe in ghosts, it is exceedingly rare for a banshee to be created. A year ago however, the Master of shadow Philadelphia manipulated a serial killer into terrorizing the living city by torturing and killing his female victims. By the time the PPD put an end to his reign of terror, with my help I might add, ten women had been killed, and I was one of them. Although I hadn't been tortured like the other victims, I somehow ended up as a banshee anyway as did all of the serial killer's other victims. Being murdered and then enslaved in the ghost world is what had led me on a course of leading a rebellion. The rest is history as they say.

"Do you know who I am?" I asked the prisoner in a mild tone.

"I know you," the ghost replied with a little defiance in his voice. "You're the captain of the Ghost Watch, Veronika Kane. Everyone knows of you."

"What's your name? Did you fight in the Battle of Philadelphia?"

The ghost nodded reluctantly and I waited patiently for an explanation.

"I'm Simon. I was among those freed by Marshal Jonus at Grey's Ferry. I didn't see much action then but I did at the Battle of Statues when Black Maria assaulted us."

"Then why in the name of all that is holy did you attack the Mint?" I asked in frustration. "We lost twelve souls in defense of that precious celestial steel supply. You killed souls that were with me from the very beginning. Why would you betray us like this?"

"It's because of you and your moralizing about the devil's iron," Simon spat out at me. "We need it to survive. We can use it for weapons, currency, and so many other things, but you keep dumping it into the river. Everyone knows that you are the voice that is keeping it illegal in our city. This is your fault."

"You were at Grey's Ferry you just said," I retorted, my own anger flaring up. "You wore a devil's iron collar. Not only is it the sign of our slavery but it is a corrupting and malignant substance.

The fact that our enemies would gladly give it to us should be warning enough."

"That's just moralizing nonsense," he shouted at me. "You promised us liberty but instead you rule over us like a queen."

"Watch your mouth!" one of my guards growled angrily.

I stared at the ghost in disbelief. The members of my guard unit and the Ghost Watch patrol that had joined us muttered among themselves and shot unfriendly stares at the prisoner. No one was used to seeing me treated like this; after all, no sane ghost would talk to a banshee like this. For my part, it was his words that hurt. I thought I'd gone out of my way to avoid becoming 'a queen': I'd turned down the Governorship and the position of Marshal of the army to avoid just this kind of accusation. All I wanted to do with my ghostly existence now was to protect humanity from the many supernatural predators that they mostly didn't know existed, and to help ensure that ghosts in Limbo didn't prey or manipulate living people. I'd suffered terrible things at the hands of Philly's old masters: some of them had left scars on my soul that would likely be with me for all eternity. But even those pains paled in comparison to what I was feeling every time I saw and heard of a free soul embarking down the dark path. This of course is the natural progression of things when you give people free will. Some will choose a path that doesn't serve the greater good. Our enemies were using human nature in order to weaken us, and yes, ghosts are still subject to the influences of human nature.

I sighed heavily and shook myself; the best way to avoid self pity and thinking too much is to stay very busy, and that's exactly what I do. We won our liberty nine months ago, but that was just the beginning of a greater war being fought all across Limbo now.

"Enough of this," I said while walking towards the man. I drew the long celestial steel knife that hung at my right hip. A katana was sheathed at my left hip. The man's eyes went wide as I raised the blade. I called the wind to me, and with supernatural speed and precision I sliced the prisoner's shirt down the middle without touching any part of his body. I could simply have over powered Simon's will and made his shirt disappear since clothes are really just a figment of our imagination held in place by our will, but I wanted to scare the man. I signaled one of my guards, and he came over and pulled the shirt open so that we could all stare at the smuggler's torso. He could have willed the shirt whole again, but he was apparently too stunned to think of it. As I'd expected, where the man's right nipple should be, there was a three inch celestial steel disc imbedded into his ghostly flesh. The blue disc was marred by a diagonal squiggly line of devil's iron that bisected it.

"You're a member of the Styx Cartel," I said gesturing at the token on his chest. "You are going to give me something or this is going to get extremely unpleasant for you."

"I'm a citizen of this city," the man scoffed. "You are required by law to turn me over to the magistrate for trial. I wonder which magistrate I'll get. I've been hearing that a few of them have been rather lenient towards smugglers."

I smiled bitterly. The anger at the pit of my stomach was becoming a raging furnace. There did appear to be judges that felt that way lately, and a growing number of Assembly members were supporting the bill to legalize devil's iron.

"You attacked a military installation," I growled. "That makes you a traitor and an enemy combatant. I have the authority to do whatever is necessary to protect this city. You led that attack. I want to know who you took your orders from."

"Go ahead then," Simon said quietly. "I'm ready to die for the cause. I won't give my brothers up."

I sighed dramatically and turned to a female Ghost Watch officer.

"Take this scum out into the wilds and hand him over to Thor. I'm sure the furies will know what to do with him."

"Yes ma'am," the officer replied and moved to take charge of Simon.

"Wait!" the ghost cried out desperately as Ghost Watch agents began to drag him away. "You can't do this! You have to put me up for trial!"

"Wrong," I answered. "I can summarily execute you. I can torture you. And I can give you over to our allies. Our enemies have continued to prey on the furies who've just about had enough of the unwarranted attacks on their packs. I'm sure they'll be happy to receive such a gift as yourself."

"Look," the ghost pleaded. "If I tell you where I got my orders, will you let me go?"

"This is not a negotiation," I told Simon. "You will answer my questions or I will send you to the furies. Choose quickly, I've got other business to attend to."

The prisoner struggled with indecision. The fear of the wild lands and especially of the furies had been instilled deeply in all of shadow Philly's citizens by the Master. Most free souls of the city had been saved and had fought alongside the furies in the battle of Philadelphia, but the primeval fear was deep and unshakeable in some. The furies were like the boogey man to many.

"Alright!" Simon shouted when I nodded to the agents that held him. "I'll tell you what I know."

"Who ordered the attack?"

"I took orders from Reverend Creed."

"Where can I find the Reverend?"

Simon once again seemed to struggle with himself but when he saw my expression he made up his mind to push on.

"He runs a casino in the First Unitarian Church of Philadelphia."

Casinos were popping up all over the city. They were the popular gambling dens where the coin was almost always made of devil's iron and where rumor had it shades could be won or lost.

"How is all of this devil's iron getting into the city?" I asked with fury blazing in my eyes.

"I don't know, I swear!" he answered as he cringed away from me. "It's a closely guarded secret of the cartel. Only those in the upper echelons know that secret. Please, I'm telling you the truth."

"And you will continue to do so," I told him. "While I go shut down this casino, you are going to tell my people the locations of all the other casinos in the city that you know about. If you lie, I will make sure that you fall into the hands of your Cartel friends. Something tells me that they are far less lenient than I am. We'll use a siren to find out all that you know, so any lies you try to feed us will be discovered."

I gave orders for Simon to be transported back to HQ and for word to be sent to my second, Melanie Baker, to meet me at the First Unitarian Church of Philadelphia. Then with another sigh, I set off for the church. All of this intrigue was really starting to grate on my nerves. I prefer fighting to politics or James Bond style espionage, and I much preferred to fight darklings then these slinking agents of the Styx Cartel.

2

THE FLIGHT TO THE FURNESS, the short name for the First
Unitarian Church of Philadelphia, wasn't long, but I felt the
passage of time acutely. I had an important appointment with
private detective Frank Cooper in the living world, and I
couldn't afford to be late. The church complex lay on the corner
of Chestnut and Van Pelt Streets in the affluent neighborhood
of Rittenhouse Square. Like many other buildings in the city,
the Furness was an architectural wonder. It had been designed
by Frank Furness, a famed architect of the nineteenth century,
hence its nickname. The structure featured a six arch cloister
with a porte cochére at one end that was topped by a pyramidal
tower. An iron cross tops the steepled sanctuary at the center of
the building. I landed just inside the portico at the front of the
church where a pair of arched doors stood barred.

Eight members of my personal guard landed at my back
followed by four officers of the Ghost Watch. I hate having a
personal guard, but the Assembly had passed a law requiring all
banshees in the city to have one. They claim it's to keep us safe

because we are high value assets, but I think it's to keep an eye on us in case we go crazy. At times like this though, it was useful to have extra armed ghosts at my back. Normally, I'd have waited for my second, Melanie Baker, and the Ghost Watch back-up, but with twelve able bodied fighters with me and little time to spare, I decided to go for it. Doing so wasn't going strictly by the book, but what's the point of being the captain if you can't be creative with the rules?

I signaled my backup to hold their positions while I moved forward to the double doors. My guard wasn't pleased about me taking the lead, but I'd trained them to follow my orders. I don't put up with anyone who doesn't. I know it sounds foolish, but the fact is that I can do a lot more stuff than any of my guards. I need to be free to do what must be done. In this case, I slid my hand through one of the double doors and quickly encountered a barrier of celestial steel on the far side. It is a common practice in Limbo to employ celestial steel and devil's iron as a security measure against unwanted ghostly intrusion. Because of the preciousness of both metals, security measures usually took the form of a netting of the steel or iron that was draped over the walls and ceilings of a structure. There are few ghosts in all of Limbo that can penetrate such barriers. It is incredibly uncommon to find a door or whole structure sheathed in either of the metals. Someone had gone to great lengths to ensure that unwanted ghosts were kept out of the Furness. Unfortunately for them, I was one of the few ghosts in Limbo who could penetrate any barrier made of celestial steel. I'm a well known celestial steel shaper; the fact that it was being used here meant that either there were other surprises in store for us, or that those within were depending on me not finding out about this place. Whatever the case, I willed the blue metal within to part for me, leaving a large opening so that my friends could follow me through.

I didn't wait to see if the celestial steel would do as I willed it; I knew it would. I waved at my backup to follow and pushed my way through the door and emerged within a vestibule whose walls were indeed sheathed in celestial steel. Just ahead, an archway opened into a towering sanctuary that seated up to seven hundred parishioners. As I moved forward towards the archway, I caught a glimpse of movement ahead. At first I didn't see anyone, but then a clean shaven man in a dark suit suddenly appeared three feet in front of me. I froze in surprise.

"Captain Kane," the man said in an oily voice. "Welcome to the Furness. I am Reverend Creed. I don't believe that we've met personally before now, but your reputation precedes you. We are closed right now otherwise the doors would have stood open for you. Is there something I can help you with?"

His eyes widened slightly as my guard and the Watch began to fill the vestibule behind me. He didn't seem pleased to see us, but he did do a fairly good job of keeping a blank face. I was very curious to know how he'd suddenly materialized in front of me without any warning. Were there others hidden nearby?

"We are investigating an attack on the armory today," I answered coolly. Something about the guy gave me the creeps. "A lead has brought us here."

Reverend Creed made a show of looking at the walls.

"As you can see," he said slowly, as if explaining something to a child. "We have no lack of celestial steel here. What reason would a spiritual organization have for attacking an armory?"

I stared at the man for a moment and then pointed at the just barely visible ceiling of the sanctuary beyond him.

"Is that devil's iron?"

Reverend Creed half turned his body so that he could follow my pointing finger and still keep an eye on me. The magnificent cathedral ceiling was indeed sheathed in devil's iron while the walls were covered by blue steel. It was an extravagant display.

"You know it is," he answered in a tight voice as he turned back to face me. "It's all decorative and has been here since before the changes. We've been grand fathered in."

"I'm afraid you've been misinformed Reverend Creed," I

told the ghost. "There is no grand fathering when it comes to devil's iron. We'll have to confiscate it so that it can be properly disposed of."

People always volunteered to dispose of the devil's iron for us. The stuff had such an enormous street value now that I entrusted the task mainly to the city's gargoyles; they at least were incorruptible.

"This is an outrage," Reverend Creed growled angrily. "I'd heard that you were an insufferable moralist, but this…this goes too far. I have friends in the Assembly. I'll make sure they stop you!"

"An insufferable moralist," I said incredulously. "What a strange insult coming from a reverend. Tell me Creed. Did you run this church during the old order?"

"I have run this church for more than a century girl," Creed answered. "I have seen many powers come and go. You have become too big for your skirts and need to be taught humility."

The guards at my back muttered angrily but quieted when I raised a hand to forestall them.

"And did you wear the collar?" I asked. "Were you a slave shade running this place, or were you a darkling working for the Master?"

Creed suddenly went still and the anger that had flashed across his features vanished behind a blank mask.

"I will say no more," he said finally. "You are trespassing. Don't come back without a warrant."

"That's not the way this is going to go down Creed. I'm investigating an act of sedition. Our sources tell us there is a casino here. We are going to search this complex. You will be taken to Ghost Watch Headquarters for further questioning."

"You can't do that!" Creed roared in defiance. His hand vanished into his suit jacket.

"If you withdraw a weapon Creed, I'll blast you where you stand."

The man froze and I nodded to my guards without taking

my eyes from his. Two members of the Watch ran forward and grabbed the reverend. Once he was bound in celestial steel cuffs, one of the Watch searched him and found a devil's iron dagger in his jacket. He and I had a mental battle of wills for a few moments as I forced his shirt and jacket to be torn away so that I could get a look at his torso. He had a strong mind, but in the end my will was stronger and his shirt and coat were torn asunder. Like Simon, Creed had a celestial steel disk implanted on the right side of his chest. His disc however had three wavy red lines bisecting it.

"A high ranking member of the Styx Cartel," I commented. "It's odd that you used celestial steel instead of devil's iron on your doors considering my talents."

"The devil's iron is more valuable as a tool to crush your supporters Kane," Creed said arrogantly. "Those we don't crush we'll seduce and corrupt. You are a child. You may have begun the toppling of the old order, but the new order won't be you. We've been preparing for this for centuries. You've helped us enormously, but now you're in the way. Continue on this path and it won't end well for you."

I stared at Creed in stunned amazement. He had all but confessed his sedition in front of a room full of witnesses. It frightened me that he seemed totally confident and unconcerned about his situation. Under the law, I could execute him right here and now. I really considered it for a moment, but Creed was the first high ranking member of the Styx Cartel that we'd been able to apprehend. Given some time with a Siren and we'd be able to learn a whole lot of secrets. Another scary thing was that Creed was implying that he'd been part of a seditious organization plotting against the old order far before I came along. What were their goals? Would they be better or worse than the old order?

I shook my head. I didn't have time for this. I left three of my guard and a Watch officer with Creed and took the rest with me into the complex. There was nothing of note on the first floor, so I chose to go down into the basement instead of going up. At the bottom of the stairs we encountered a devil's iron door which I destroyed with a blast of my banshee wail. The banshee wail is one of the most destructive powers in Limbo or the living world. It is fueled by fury that is released in a destructive sonic blast that few things can withstand. As the door shattered, we found quite a surprise on the other side. The room was packed full of specters and darklings. Fortunately, my blast had destroyed a good dozen or so of the bad guys. Rather than rush into the room, me and my backup held the stairs. The specters charged us three times, and I annihilated them with my banshee wail. The darklings tried to cast black bolts of energy at us, but I blocked these with a shield that I made with the ever present mists of Limbo. Yes, I'm a one ghost army; that's why I don't like my guard getting in my way.

Eventually Melanie arrived with the reinforcements and we rushed the cavernous basement room. Melanie is also a banshee; with two of us and a score of the Ghost Watch and our two personal guard units, we were far too much for the enemy to handle. We destroyed them to the last. We had Creed; we didn't need any of them. Besides, none of them tried to surrender. They all fought to the final death.

A search of the room did turn up all the paraphernalia of a casino. Celestial steel cards, devil's iron coins and tokens of all sizes, tables and dice made of the two metals, and other odds and ends. We also found a large cache of devil's iron weapons. What we didn't find is how the enemy had gotten into the building. It was one thing to have smugglers and traitors among us, but it was quite another for nearly fifty specters and darklings to be so deep into the heart of the city. How had they gotten here? The army patrolled the city's borders heavily and the furies helped us. We had a major security breach somewhere.

The final room we searched left us with the largest mystery so far. It was devoid of any furnishings. The only thing of note was the huge pyramid painted into the center of the floor. On closer inspection, I found that the pyramid was actually transposed over top a circle with squiggly lines of devil's iron. The pyramid also featured an eye at its apex.

"I hate geometry and occult lore," I muttered. Melanie was standing at my side, a dissatisfied frown on her face. "Have any idea what it means?"

"Not me," she answered quizzically.

"Alright," I said with a sigh. "I've got to get going. Get some scholars down here once this place has been cleared out. See to it that Creed gets locked up at HQ till we can get Amber to do her mojo on him. I'll give the Governor a full report when I get back, and be sure to let Jonus know about this breach. He's going to be pissed."

Melanie nodded and the two of us headed back upstairs.

"You still need backup for tonight right?" Melanie asked me as we reached the sanctuary.

"Yes," I answered. "Frank's been investigating the disappearance of some were-creatures and the trail has led him to some vampire owned property. We're going to check it out."

"Alright," Melanie answered. "I'll lead the team myself if I can. I'll see you in a couple of hours."

I nodded and watched her lead the team that took Creed back to HQ. The bastard had the nerve to look back and grin at me as if he didn't have a care in the world. I sighed unhappily wishing that I could just cut the guy's head off and be done with it. I hated to leave enemies alive. I gave my guard some final instructions and then I translated into living Philadelphia right outside the First Unitarian Church. In modern days the building looked slightly different than in Limbo: the porte cochére had been torn down in order to save the money that it would have cost to renovate it. My guard didn't come with me. Living world operations were only for the strongest and best trained ghosts, and none of them could operate here for a quarter of the time that I could. The late day sun was shining brightly and my mood changed quickly. The oppressive mists of Limbo were gone and the city of brotherly love lay unveiled before my eyes in all its glory. I hummed quietly to myself as I made my way to Frank Cooper's PI office.

3

THE PHILADELPHIA STATE HOSPITAL is a massive complex encompassing more than fifty buildings on over one hundred acres of verdant farmland. The architecture of the various structures ranges from colonial revival to art-deco depending on the architect that built it. The facility had once housed more than seven thousand patients and workers at one time, though its documented safety capacity was less than four thousand. Byberry, as most locals called the asylum, had housed men, women, and children with varying degrees of mental illness. The institution had become an expensive pariah that the public wanted to forget about while various politicians had used it to line their pockets with continual building projects that went to their biggest campaign contributors. Meanwhile, the inmates of Byberry had suffered from neglect, abuse, and medical experimentation which the general public had turned a blind eye to. By all accounts, Byberry was an American nightmare.

Vampires are attracted to nightmares as are darklings and other evil beings. In the case of Byberry, the vampires had been there from the beginning. They had been behind the scenes manipulating Philly's political leaders to establish the farm for the mentally ill that later became a full blown institution. They chose the site at Byberry because it was on the very fringe of the city in the Northern most neighborhood: far enough out of the way, but still close enough to the lights and vibrancy of Center City. The founders of Byberry were proud to adopt the teachings of Dr. Benjamin Rush, founding father and resident of Byberry township. His teachings declared that mental problems were a disease that could be treated. Part of that treatment relied on isolation, so Byberry was built as a complex of buildings rather than a single monolithic structure as other facilities of the day had adopted. It wasn't surprising that the city's vampire population used the institution as its own farm. Byberry was the perfect slaughterhouse for them; the human cattle were penned up and isolated. After all, no one listened closely to the screams of crazy people. Countless victims of the vampires disappeared, shoddy record keeping covered up the trail, and many cases were blamed on other insane patients or scapegoat staff that wouldn't play ball with the powers that be. Though the public despised the horrors that they knew were taking place within the complex, they found it easier to curse Byberry and then turn a deaf ear to the screams of its wretched inhabitants rather than deal with the problem of mental illness in an open and humanitarian way.

The end of the vampire farm did come eventually, but altruism played a very minor role in its demise. Advancements in psychotropic drugs and new treatment methods led to a more community oriented service model that allowed some patients to leave the institutions. For every one of these, however, three more were admitted as the state began to dump some of its criminals into the asylums as prison populations became overcrowded. The real death of Byberry came because of the downsizing of government. The loss of industrial jobs and the rise of healthcare costs forced government to move away from large, expensive programs, and the Willowbrook scandal gave them the impetus to shut down most of the state run asylums. Byberry itself did not close down until 1990, and it has lain abandoned until recently. At least that's what the vampires want the good citizens of Philly to believe.

The huge complex became overgrown with trees and natural growth making it a favorite haunt for the city's homeless and gang populations to party, shelter, and carry on nefarious activities in its underground tunnels and ruined buildings. The buildings were looted, vandalized, and repainted in urban art. The PPD attempted to patrol the complex, but the sheer size of the grounds made this effort nearly impossible. Meanwhile, the vampires had continued to feed well in this chaotic environment. They fed on bums and crack addicts alike, and the horror that had been Byberry continued. Demolition of the site proved economically unfeasible for the state as asbestos removal would have cost billions of dollars. Finally, after nearly two decades of this urban blight, a development firm came to the state's rescue and bought the property for cheap with the promise that it would be cleaned up. An elaborate public ceremony, attended by city and state leaders, saw the sign "Philadelphia State Hospital" be taken down as the first step in demolishing the dark legacy of the Byberry asylum. Barbed wire fences were erected around the complex and hundreds of construction trucks came and went for many months, yet true demolition never occurred. Instead, Byberry got a face lift. An industrial park and other businesses occupied several newly renovated buildings, but this was a mere facade. The decrepit and evil core of the asylum remained intact. The development company was of course part of the vampire syndicate, and the Archbishop of Philly's vampires had now claimed the nightmare grounds for himself. Byberry was far from shut down; the evil that had manipulated and fed upon it had come to make it its home.

It was a dark, moonless night as Frank Cooper and I approached the facility from the South. We had ditched Frank's car a half mile back in favor of making our run afoot. Frank was dressed all in black including a black mask with night-vision goggles. He wasn't exceptionally tall, but in the past nine months he'd been working hard with weights, and he'd become quite buff. He carried a blue steel Desert Eagle pistol in his right hand and moved with the obvious caution and assuredness of a cop. His gun wasn't standard issue of course. I'd made some modifications to it, having coated it in celestial steel. The bullets chambered in the beast were also coated in celestial steel, and I'd made him a fine celestial steel mesh armor that he'd had stitched into his tactical vest. These modifications to weapons and armor were what allowed Frank, a normal human, to be able to fight monsters with a reasonable chance of hurting them and maybe even the chance to survive a blow or two from them.

I'd spent the last few hours with Frank at his Rittenhouse Square office. He'd filled me in on the history of Byberry including the vampire angle which he and a small team of Ghost Watch agents had uncovered in the course of their investigation. Frank had been hired by Marcus, the city's were-beast pack leader, to find some missing pack members. Over the past six weeks, many of the pack's weakest members had vanished without a trace. The pack had tried to deal with the problem on its own, but even their heightened senses couldn't make much headway with the evidence left at the various scenes. By the time Frank got the case, the trail had gotten quite cold. Fortunately, with the assistance of the Ghost Watch, Frank was able to discover the involvement of the vampires along with what appeared to be were-beast involvement. Frank was operating under the assumption that either there were traitors in the local pack, or outsiders were attempting to muscle their way into Philly. Whichever the case, there were at least some were-beasts working with vampires, and the trail ultimately led to the Byberry asylum. I'd agreed a few days ago to personally participate in a raid of the facility hence my presence here tonight.

"I wish we could do this during the day," I told Frank as we made our slow progress towards the asylum grounds. I was very concerned for Frank's safety against a congregation of vamps operating in their own element. The sun isn't a threat to vampires; that's just Hollywood crap. They just prefer the night because it's easier to cloak their deeds in darkness.

"We've fucking been over this," Frank growled. "The vamps have fucking turned Byberry into a legitimate industrial park. The place is full of fucking innocent people that come to work during the fucking day. We can't risk that kind of fucking exposure."

I nodded my understanding, but something about this entire case made me uneasy.

"What I don't fucking like," Frank said. "Is doing this without fucking backup."

I agreed completely. Melanie and the squad of Ghost Watch agents that were supposed to meet us for this mission failed to appear at the appointed time. We'd delayed for over an hour, but finally Frank had insisted that we move without them. He was worried that the kidnap victims were in mortal peril. Melanie's absence worried me tremendously; the continuing turmoil in Limbo was most likely to blame, but it would take something pretty serious to prevent my second from sending me backup. I'd seriously considered returning to Limbo but didn't because I was worried that Frank would try to enter Byberry on his own.

"There's been lots of trouble in Limbo as I've explained. It's likely that another crisis has struck and the personnel can't be spared."

"I'm sorry," Frank replied in a serious voice. "If I wasn't so fucking worried that lives could be hanging in the balance, I'd hold off so that you could go check. I fucking appreciate you covering me on this one."

"No problem Frank. The Ghost Watch is well trained and there are nine other banshees besides myself. If they can't deal with a crisis without me, then the city is doomed, sooner or later. I can't always be there."

"It's been a fucking while since the two of us have worked in the field together. This will be like old times. Though come to fucking think of it, I hope there aren't any fucking ghouls. I hate those creepy bastards."

"Don't worry Frank, I've got a bad feeling about this one. After all, Vamps are way scarier than ghouls. I'll go in first to get a look around and assess the situation."

"You know I don't like being fucking left behind," Frank said. "I can take care of myself."

I sighed heavily; everyone always underestimates vampires thanks to Hollywood. The most obvious problem between movie vampires and the real thing is that real vampires aren't vulnerable to things like garlic, holy water, or silver. Even sunlight isn't an issue for them, which, quite frankly, isn't fair. Yes, vampires are nocturnal creatures. What evil, nefarious being isn't? But the sun doesn't burn or weaken them in any way. They can be harmed by the same things that will kill most living creatures. The difficulty is that their undead bodies are powered by a human soul that has merged with a demon, making the vampire supernaturally hard to destroy. Bullets, swords, and especially fire can be effective weapons against them, but it takes a lot of damage to put them down, and in the meantime, the vampire isn't likely to stand still while you try to kill it. It's gonna come at you with a vengeance.

"I know you can handle yourself," I told Frank. "That's why I didn't call this mission off when the backup team failed to show. But you're not a ghost. The vamps will hear and smell you a mile away. We don't want to take on the whole congregation. We will find your missing were-beasts and get them out as quietly as we can. I should be able to locate them without being detected. Once we know the situation, we can devise an appropriate plan."

Frank Cooper had been a fourth generation Philadelphia cop before he'd been kicked off the force last year. That had been all my fault; I'd used his crusading personality to help me catch the man who'd murdered me: a serial killer nicknamed the Tormentor. It turns out that the evil wraith that ran Philly's shadow city in Limbo was using the serial killer as a tool in its own power struggle. Frank's tenacious efforts to bring the Tormentor to justice exposed the PPD's commissioner as an interfering fool who had the city's entire law enforcement apparatus looking for the killer in the wrong direction. Frank's failure to obey a direct order led to the Tormentor's capture but also resulted in his summary dismissal from the PPD.

Defeated, Frank let out a sigh and pointed to a patch of thick underbrush by the side of a quiet, one lane road.

"I'll wait for you there."

Fifty feet beyond the patch of tall vegetation, a twenty foot tall barbed wire fence blocked access to the Byberry facility. A hundred yards beyond the fence, three six story monoliths rose darkly into the night sky. These buildings were new additions to the complex. They were the core structures that made up the new industrial park, and not coincidentally, they blocked the public's view of the central grounds of the facility. The structures were alien in appearance and were made of black stone that somehow seemed organic in nature. The dread inspiring buildings had no windows and only a single set of great double doors in their North facades. Hailed as the newest architectural wonders of the city, it was obvious to anyone who knew what to look for that they were intended as havens for vampires.

A flapping of wings brought my attention back to Frank as a great white owl with glowing yellow eyes descended out of the darkness and landed on the detective's shoulder. The spirit tethered itself to the living world giving itself enough physical presence to become visible to the living. Frank gave a start of surprise when the owl suddenly appeared on his shoulder.

"How many fucking times do I have to tell you not to do that?" He said, glaring at the owl.

I smiled as my ghost familiar, Sebastian, began to preen.

"It's not my fault you're blind as a bat," sneered the owl. "You look ridiculous in those oversized glasses. What good are they if you can't see me coming?"

"Stop harassing him Sebastian," I told the owl. "The goggles help him see in the dark, they don't help him see an insubstantial ghost. You know that. Let's skip the foreplay and go straight to your report."

"Yes mistress," the owl answered sheepishly. "Aerial surveillance is complete. I saw only one patrol consisting of two armed thralls, one dampyre, and a large dog of the German Shepherd breed. There was something odd about the way the dog moved. I suspect that it may be darkling possessed, though I didn't risk getting close enough to find out for sure."

A chill went through me at this news. What was a darkling doing here? They were outlawed in shadow Philly, and the Ghost Watch hunted them vigorously on both sides of the veil. But as recent events in Limbo had shown, the darklings appeared to have found a way to circumvent our sentinels.

"What the fuck does that mean?" Frank asked looking from the owl to me. "Is he talking about dogs like the ones we fought in the yard at Primal Cuts?"

I nodded. Primal Cuts had been the slaughter house owned by James Paul Saunders, a.k.a the Tormentor. The old masters of shadow Philly had tried to protect him by sending a pack of darkling possessed dogs against Frank and his contingent of PPD officers. The attack had failed thanks to my intervention and Frank's big ass gun, but no one who'd been there would ever forget it.

"Son of a bitch," Frank exclaimed.

"Stay with Frank," I ordered Sebastian. "Hold the fort Frank, I'll be back shortly. Send Sebastian if there's any trouble."

Without pausing to hear their responses, I strode towards the Byberry Asylum.

4

I STRODE THROUGH the industrial strength barbed wire fence without really noticing it. Normally, passing through physical barriers like walls require a ghost to expend a bit of energy; it's the price you pay for breaking the laws of physics. In this case however, the fence was so thin and had so many gaps that the energy I expended in passing through it was negligible. Fortunately for me, I hadn't expended too much power during the assault on the Mint. My power reserves were still well above half filled, so I should be able to deal with whatever trouble we encountered here.

I headed East, skirting the three new vamp buildings. Though they had been my original targets, the news about the darkling dog made me want to scope the complex out more thoroughly before I acted. Something was going on here that didn't add up. Was this some kind of trap aimed at catching me? I paused, suddenly disquieted by my train of thought. Had someone back home betrayed me and diverted my backup knowing that I would go on with the mission anyways? If so, I was extremely vulnerable right now. I shook the dark thoughts from my head. Events back home with the Styx Cartel were really beginning to make me paranoid. My people in the Ghost Watch were good, reliable ghosts; I needed to trust them. I couldn't let malcontents affect the bond that had developed between me and the agents of the Ghost Watch.

I continued on, moving with more caution now, until I worked my way around to the back of the monoliths that squatted like sentinels protecting the secrets of the inner yard. Each of the three buildings had a recessed double doorway that was the only feature to break the smooth surface of the edifice. The doors were like gaping maws in a black featureless face. The arched portals were nearly twenty feet tall, as though giants might issue forth from their depths, and they were made entirely of brass. The buildings featured an architectural style that I'd never seen or heard of before. It was as if a mad scientist had taken up architecture; the non-Euclidean angles and shapes of the structures played havoc on one's senses. A strange feeling of vertigo would hit you if you stared at them for more than a few seconds, or if you moved your head too quickly while staring at them. They were utterly alien, and a sense of dread and power hung around them like a cloak.

I turned away from the buildings and looked around at the vast complex that lay revealed before me. Straight ahead was the ruin that had once been the morgue, and immediately North of it lay a vast warehouse building. This was the West colony, and more than seventy percent of it was still in ruins. Beyond the West colony, I could make out several structures that were part of the C section of the facility and comprised the administration buildings, staff dorms, and patient dorms. Here and there I spotted dark openings in the ground that could only lead into the dank tunnels that connected the various buildings to each other. Far beyond the C buildings lay the North colony with its sanitarium and maximum security dorms. The South colony along Roosevelt Boulevard was the public face of the new Byberry which featured modern office buildings and warehouses. It lay hidden away from the rest of the complex by a well tended hedgerow.

A noise caught my attention, and looking around, I spotted movement to my left. I darted forward and passed through the wall of the ruined morgue. I slid through the maze of corridors that made up the structure's interior until I found a flight of stairs. I quickly climbed them, being careful to remain tethered to the floor. Ghosts are subject to the laws of gravity. This can get tricky for us since we are incorporeal; we generally fall right through floors until we reach the earth's outer crust. In order for a ghost to go up stairs or use an elevator, we must tether ourselves to the environment, making ourselves solid enough so as not to pass through the floor. It doesn't require a whole lot of solidness, a grain of sands worth is enough, but it does require concentration and practice. I'd been trained in living world operations when I'd been drafted into a Sowing Team during my first weeks in Limbo, back when the Master had tried to recruit me. I accepted the training, but rejected the foul work they'd expected of me. Consequently, I had learned how to tether with little effort, and the concentration was now pretty much automatic with all of the practice that I'd had in the past nine months.

Once I reached the third floor, I found a window and watched the patrol pass by. The two thralls were unremarkable: men armed with clubs and pistols hidden in the small of their backs. The dampyre was a woman that moved with the grace of a cat. She wore jeans and a black tank, showing off her pale skin. Dampyres are thralls who've earned their master's favor. They are offered diluted vampire blood, which they quickly become addicted to, but in return they gain some of the vampire's power. They are faster, stronger, and tougher than normal humans but are not possessed by a spirit or demon. Dampyres are one hundred percent mortal, though they may as well have sold their soul to the devil. New vampires are usually selected from among the ranks of the dampyre; to understand the dampyre, one must understand the vampire.

Vampires are chief among the preternatural beings that prey on humanity. Their numbers in Philly are quite astounding, and yet they have maintained secrecy through a combination of mental domination and gaining power over influential institutions. One thing the movies did get right about vampires is their need to feed on blood. The thirst for blood is a result of the merging of a human soul with a demon. The human instinctively needs physical sustenance while the demon craves violence which is made manifest in the spilling of blood. The desire for sustenance and craving for violence are merged into an unholy thirst for blood that makes a mockery of holy communion which symbolizes the transformative power of the blood of the Lamb of God. Vampires are vile creatures through and through. No one can become one by accident or by force. A human soul must willingly merge with the demon through the drinking of the blood of a master vampire. The demonic blood of a vampire is poison to a living being; consuming it drains the life from the body while at the same time merging soul and demon into one evil being. The body dies, but the creature that remains is both immortal and powerful beyond human comprehension.

The dog that accompanied the dampyre and the thralls was what interested me the most of the trio though. It was indeed a German Shepherd, but its eyes glowed red, giving the darkling within it away. It took all of my self control not to immediately leap down there to kill it on the spot. Here again was an example of the enemy operating within our borders with apparent impunity. How were they doing this without the army or the Ghost Watch noticing?

I untethered myself and dropped through the intervening floors until I reached the first where I once again tethered myself before I could slip into the basement below. Hey, it's one of the perks of being a ghost; you don't have to leave the same way you came in. I exited the morgue through the East wall and began my exploration of the ruins of the C section of the campus. The buildings were empty and devoid of life. Even the area's aura felt desolate which was unusual for a place that had seen so many horrors for so many decades. Three alien structures loomed over the entire complex, their baleful auras blanketing everything around them with cold dread. It was as if the decades of growing horror that had settled over the grounds of Byberry were but a pale imitation of the malice that emanated from the new buildings.

A furtive movement in the nearby bushes brought me to a halt. I stared for a few moments confused. The telltale glow of a green aura announced the presence of a were-creature, but the thing was so small that for a moment I thought I must be imagining it. Was this one of the victims or was this a member of the pack snooping around on its own? A tiny, black and grey ferret darted out of the bushes I was watching and ran for the shadow of a nearby ruin. I stared at it in bemusement. A were-ferret? Really? How cute.

I followed the creature's stealthy journey into the North colony of the facility. The small animal seemed to know that it was operating in a dangerous neck of the woods and used all of its skill to stay hidden. There was no way I could have followed it if its aura hadn't been such a neon sign for me. I wondered if it knew how visible it was to spirits. If the darkling possessed dog got a good look in its vicinity, the ferret would be dog food. The thing seemed to sense my presence. Maybe it even saw my aura; I wasn't doing much to keep out of its sight, but it could neither smell nor hear me and must have thought I was a mere ghost. No one should be surprised to encounter a ghost or two in a place like Byberry.

The were-ferret continued its nervous trek until it reached a particularly dense copse of overgrown trees and vegetation along the side of a poorly paved road that separated Furey Ellis Hall from the N-8 building, the former female maximum security dorm. It looked around to make sure no one was watching and then slipped into a patch of tall grass. I moved in closer to see what it was doing. It gave a sudden squeak, and I nearly screamed myself when a full grown, naked woman seemed to pop out of the ferret like it was a jack-in-the-box. I stared at the woman in shock as she rose to a crouch, her green eyes looking everywhere. She was small, maybe 5'2, with a slim waist, and perky little breasts that any woman could be proud of. Her hair reached to her shoulder blades and was dirty blond. Her features were dainty: a small nose, smiling mouth, and narrow eye slits with alert, green eyes that gave her a mischievous look. She moved with the precision of a dancer and held herself with the poise of a trained assassin. Her body was wreathed in the green aura of a shifter.

The woman reached carefully into the brush at her feet and lifted a small black nap sack from the brush. She nodded with satisfaction, opened it, and withdrew a 9mm pistol. I think it was a Glock, but I really don't know that much about guns, so I couldn't say for sure. She withdrew the clip and checked it quickly before sliding it back in place. When she was sure that the ammo hadn't been tampered with, she gingerly withdrew a black catsuit from the bag.

"What?" she snarled, glancing my way. "You've never seen a naked chick before? You aren't a gay ghost are you? Not that I have any problem with that, but I've got work to do and you're making me nervous. Go haunt someone else."

I stared at the woman in consternation and embarrassment. She ignored me and began dressing. The tightness of the form fitting outfit didn't slow her down; she slid into the thing as easily as if it were a glove. As far as I was concerned, she needn't have bothered dressing at all. The suit left so little to the imagination that she may as well have stayed naked.

"What are you doing here?" I answered in a huff. Who was she to dismiss me so casually? "Shoo, little ferret. Run along home. I'm sure you have a nice safe cage somewhere with a wheel to exercise on. This place is too dangerous for you."

That got her attention. She turned on me, her mischievous green eyes blazing with anger.

"Everyone always underestimates the ferret. Get lost or make yourself useful, though I can't see what good a ghost could be other than to provide information, and ferrets are good at uncovering secrets on their own."

I stifled an angry retort and studied the dainty woman more closely. It suddenly struck me that she knew exactly where she was and how dangerous a place this was. She had come in stealthily, dropped her gear in this thicket, and gone exploring in her ferret form. While her fashion sense wasn't anything to write home about, it was actually practical considering what she was doing. I mean, you can't expect a ferret to lug a gym bag around. It isn't an issue of weight since shifters have supernatural strength, but rather of size. Ferrets are tiny creatures and pulling a gym bag around would have made stealth nearly impossible. Instead, a small waste bag with the pistol and catsuit were perfect for infiltration work. Her composure and the ease with which she handled her pistol bespoke of practiced skill. I knew she wasn't a cop; she didn't have the tell tale bearing of law enforcers. No, she was something else: probably a thief.

This was my first meeting with an actual shifter, although I'd seen plenty of them about in the city. I'd determined early in my tenure as Captain of the Ghost Watch that Philly's were-community was well behaved. They were more likely to help out than to threaten the ordinary people of the city. I'd learned that shifters were created through a complex ritual in which a fury, the spirit of an animal that had been violently killed, merges with the soul of a living human. The human soul can be forced into this merger, but the fury itself must come willingly. The ritual cannot guarantee what kind of fury will respond to the call of union, so were-communities tend to be a Hodge-podge of different creatures. Philly's were-pack had a policy against forcing any human to merge with a fury; it was all voluntary, and so I'd left them alone. Gazing at this tenacious ferret woman though, I wondered if I'd made a mistake. These creatures might make valuable allies, especially if the vampires had grown as powerful as I was beginning to fear. Still, what the hell was a ferret doing out here on her own? Why would the pack hire Frank and then turn around and send their own people into the lion's den? Was she a spy for the pack? It seemed more likely that she was acting on her own.

"I can do a lot more than give you information," I told the ferret. She waited, watching me with distrust in her green eyes. "I'm working with Frank Cooper, the detective that Marcus hired to find your missing pack mates. I'm guessing that you're here to find your friends, right? It just so happens that our backup failed to show up tonight, so it seems providential that we should meet at just the right time, don't you think?"

5

THE FERRET GIRL GAPED at me in amazement.

"Are you serious? Are you truly willing to help the pack?"

"Yes," I said. "I'm Veronika Kane, Captain of the Ghost Watch. It's my mission to protect humanity."

"Well I'm not human anymore. None of us are" the young shifter replied turning away from me and heading towards the N-8 building.

"Wait!" I called after the were-ferret. "You can't do this alone. You'll just end up like the rest of your friends. The only thing you'll do is alert the vamps and make it harder for Frank and I to do our jobs. Please come with me and I promise I'll help rescue your friends."

The woman froze and slowly turned back to face me, a look of fear and indecision played across her pretty face.

"My companion says that your kind are nothing but trouble. What is your angle here?"

"If you are referring to the fury within you when you speak of your companion," I answered. "Then I understand your fear, but things have changed in shadow Philly. The Master has been destroyed and the new city government has an alliance with the furies of the wild. The ghosts of Philadelphia no longer manipulate things from the other side. We want to help protect humanity from our kind and from other preternatural beings that would prey on them."

The tension slowly drained from her, though her eyes remained wrathful.

"I've got friends who are in trouble," she said after a moment of visible internal struggle. "If you're on the wrong side then I'm already screwed, but I'm fresh out of options that will save my friends. I guess I'll have to count on my luck. I just don't know how a ghost is going to be of any use in this situation."

"You'll be surprised at what ghosts can do actually. Take me for instance. I'm a banshee. I can level this entire complex in a matter of minutes if I wanted to," I answered and shook my head in negation at the sudden look of hope that filled her eyes. "But I'm not going to. Doing that would start a war, and the consequences would most likely be dire for everyone involved. Humans would bear the brunt of it I'm afraid."

"So how can you help me then?" she asked dejectedly.

"Well, let's hear everything that you know, and how about starting with who you are."

The ferret girl stared at me for a full minute, clearly trying to decide whether she should tell me anything.

"I'm Brianna Martin."

"I wish we were meeting in a different place and under different circumstances," I replied. "But it's a pleasure to meet you Brianna Martin. We don't have much time before the patrol comes this way, so give me the cliff notes. Do you know for sure that your friends were taken to this place, and do you know what building they are being held in?"

"The vamps have kidnapped four of our people in the past month," she began. "The last one they took was two nights ago. Sarah is an Abyssinian cat, and she's my best friend. I tracked the blood suckers to this place and have been casing the complex for the past day and a half. I was going to try to go in yesterday, but this red eyed dog keeps chasing me off."

"That's a darkling possessed dog," I told Brianna. "It has all the senses of the dog and of a ghost. Your aura stands out like a neon sign to us ghosts. That's why you're having trouble staying off of its radar."

"Damn it!" Brianna swore. "I can't just leave her. What can we do?"

"Did you see where they brought her? Is she in one of the new black buildings?"

"No. I didn't see where they took her, but the trail went towards the N-10 building before I lost it. There's something very rotten there. It smells like death."

I didn't like the sound of that. Why in the hell would vampires be messing with shifters? That seemed risky and out of character for the fiends. Philly's were-community might want to avoid an open confrontation with the vampires, but like any other cornered animal, they could be provoked into fits of rage that not even the vamps would want any part of. And what were they doing at N-10, way at the opposite end of the complex from where they'd built their power base?

Brianna waited impatiently as I pondered my next move. If I helped her I would be putting her into more danger, and the vampires would know that we'd invaded their territory. On the other hand, we lacked the necessary back up to attempt a full on assault, and there was a very good chance that if we didn't act soon the missing pack members wouldn't survive the night. The vampires weren't just allied with shifters, they clearly had darklings on their side too. Whatever they were doing with the shifters, it couldn't bode well. I needed to stop whatever was going on and put a big wrench in their plot, whatever it was.

"Alright," I told the tense were-ferret. "I'll help, but you'll have to wait here until I return with my partner."

Brianna looked relieved but also impatient. Nervous energy

pulsed from her, and she bounced up and down on her toes ready to spring into action.

"How long? They could be hurting Sarah."

"As long as it takes to get us all together without being detected. It's odd that the patrol hasn't come by yet."

"That's why I chose this location. The patrol doesn't come into this area of the complex. What do you suppose that means?"

"I don't know," I said, a new feeling of dread filling me. I really hoped that we weren't going to find Brianna's friend already dead. "A friend of mine will join you in a few minutes. He's my ghost familiar Sebastian, an owl. Until then, stay out of trouble. I'll bring Frank as quickly as I can."

I waited until she acknowledged my orders, and without further comment I sprang into the air. I called the wind to me and shot straight up, going much higher than usual as I didn't want to be detected by anything below. Flying in the living world is a big energy drain on any ghost, and I generally avoided doing it. The need for speed was what led me to go aloft though; I wanted to get Sebastian over to Brianna as quickly as possible. I didn't trust the girl's patience one bit. I made a wide circuit of the creepy black buildings, and then sped down to scare the shit out of Frank. Fortunately, he didn't fire that big assed gun of his. He might startle easily, but he had nerves of steel and amazing self control.

6

"ARE YOU FUCKING KIDDING ME? A were-ferret? Tell me this is some kind of fucking joke."

Frank and I were skirting the edge of the complex making our way to its far side where the patrols failed to go and where Brianna waited for us with Sebastian. I'd just finished telling the incredulous detective the whole story of my encounter with Brianna. The naked girl part hadn't gotten his attention half as much as learning that she was a were-ferret.

"No, I'm not joking Frank. She's an honest to god were-ferret. I saw her transform with my own eyes."

"Ferrets are fucking cute and all, but what the hell good is she going to be to us? You should have sent her home. I mean, why don't we recruit a fucking were-chicken while we're at it."

"Admittedly I'm not an expert in the gun totting club," I said dryly. "But the way she handled her pistol and carried herself made me believe that she can handle herself in dangerous situations. I'm going with my gut on this. She'll be fine."

Frank grunted noncommittally, clearly not wanting to question my professional competence but still unconvinced.

"A ferret isn't as impressive as a wolf or a bear, but they certainly have their own interesting capabilities," I went on. "Neither a wolf nor a bear could have discretely breached the security of this facility. The bigger beasts wouldn't have been able to evade the security, and while they would have put up a better fight, they would inevitably have been captured or killed. The ferret on the other hand was able to escape such a fate. Once she was aware of the danger, Brianna was able to penetrate the security a second time and tracked down where her friend had been taken to. She's bold and enterprising, two very valuable traits. Besides, we don't have any other back-up, and beggars can't be choosy."

"I don't fucking like it," Frank grumbled halfheartedly.

"I understand," I answered with a twinge of regret. "If the vampires are truly preying on the shifters, we need to step in before a war breaks out. Besides, it'll engender more trust between us and the pack if we let one of their own participate in the rescue, won't it?"

Frank was silent for several minutes as we continued to make our slow progress around Byberry. He finally nodded in grudging agreement.

"You're fucking right, I guess."

"Whatever the vamps are up too, it's big," I said pensively. "They've bargained with some big time power brokers, maybe even a corrupt wizard, and they've made quite a fortress for themselves here. I'm gonna have to get a look at this place on the other side of the veil. Hopefully if we save the shifters, we'll have new allies to help us deal with whatever shit they're up to."

"Alright, let's fucking rescue some shifters then," Frank said cheerfully. "We should be reaching the area around N-7 in a… what the fuck?"

Frank came to a sudden stop and raised his big assed gun, pointing it towards a nearby thicket. Two things happened simultaneously before I could react. A blue, glowing energy cage dropped over me, and a disembodied hand of blue energy yanked Frank's gun from his startled grip. I knew that Frank couldn't see the lines of energy that pulled his hand canon away from him as he stared after it in surprised shock.

"You want to go get my fucking gun for me?" Frank asked through gritted teeth. He was really pissed off.

"I can't," I told him. "The son of a bitch has me in a ghost net. I'm sorry."

"Shit!"

"You are one difficult ghost to catch up too," said a male voice from the thicket.

A tall, lanky man wearing blue jeans, a white tee shirt, a jean jacket, and brown construction boots stepped out of the copse of trees. He had a long face with stormy grey eyes, and long black hair that was bound in a ponytail. He was grinning widely; his white, perfect teeth gleamed in the darkness. By the way he was gingerly holding Frank's gun I could tell that he was clearly uncomfortable with it.

"You!" I choked in recognition. Rage filled me and I seriously considered blasting the ghost net with a banshee wail, but I knew that the net itself would be unaffected while everything else in the attack's path would be demolished. While that would be satisfying, it would only bring more trouble.

Frank began cautiously stalking towards the wizard, his muscles coiled and ready to spring into action as soon as he got close enough.

"That's far enough detective Cooper," the wizard warned Frank in a tone that resonated with power.

Frank paused for a moment, shook his head, and started moving again towards the man who held his gun.

"It seems you've got me at a fucking disadvantage asshole! You know my name, but I've got no fucking clue who you might be."

"Interesting," mused the wizard. "Your aura says you're plain human, but you resist my suggestions. A powerful will is useful if you're going to be playing with the preternatural."

"Back off, Frank. This is Nathaniel Carter, Philly's lone wizard. He's been trying to catch me for months."

"And now I have," Nathaniel smiled at me again. His stormy eyes remained alert however, and he tracked Frank's every movement. Frank heeded my warning and halted, though he remained poised and ready to spring into action at a seconds notice. "I must say, you've led me on a merry chase."

"What do you want with me?"

The wizard looked around and frowned with distaste.

"We'll discuss that in a less haunting location. I mean really, Byberry of all places? I guess it shouldn't surprise me to find you here though."

"What are you insinuating?" I asked angrily. "I have some important business here. It could prevent a street war between the shifters and the vampires."

"Sorry, but I don't let ghosts operate in the living city if I can help it. Particularly banshees," Nathaniel said. "I'm gonna close down the net. Don't worry detective Cooper, your ghost friend won't be harmed. She'll be in a pocket dimension until I release her. You can come along if you like."

The sound of a gun being cocked interrupted us, and Brianna stepped out of the shadows of a nearby tree. Her pistol was aimed directly at Nathaniel's head. Although her presence meant that she'd disobeyed my orders, at least she'd had the sense not to try to rescue her friends alone. Her initiative in coming to look for us might prove useful in this instance.

"Release the ghost, now!" she commanded coldly; her stare was green ice and her hands were rock steady.

The wizard cocked his head towards Brianna and his eyes flared with blue lightning for a second. Brianna's pistol fell to the ground as did her suddenly empty catsuit. Brianna had completely vanished. In her place a ferret struggled to get untangled from the human clothing. Once it did, it chittered indignantly at the wizard.

"Oh, isn't that cute. I love ferrets," the wizard said turning his gaze back towards Frank and me.

Frank chose that moment to launch himself at the man, but

before he had closed half the distance between them, Nathaniel wriggled his fingers at the headstrong detective. A complex net of blue beams shot from the wizard's hand and wrapped themselves around Frank's entire body, bringing him to a sudden stop. He panted in fury, but apparently was unable to move.

"Don't worry detective, we can bring the ferret along too," the wizard said. He turned his electric gaze on me. Interest flickered in their calculating depths. "You have interesting and loyal friends Veronika Kane. I think our conversations will be most enlightening."

"Release me now wizard or know my wrath," I warned him. I considered using my siren's song on him but dismissed the idea as it was unlikely that it would work on a being of his power; he was a wizard after all. I was going to have to use a less conventional method to escape my bonds: one that he wouldn't expect.

"I know that you're a resourceful girl," Nathaniel said. "But ghost nets are fool proof. No ghost, once captured, has ever escaped from one without outside aid. Please come quietly. I promise not to hurt you or your friends."

"Nothing is fool proof," I said as I drew my celestial steel katana from its sheath.

I filled the katana with my will, envisioning it cutting through the ghost net. Nathaniel watched with interest as raw power drained from me and imbued my blade, giving it a magical energy. I raised the blade and struck at the ghost net. The celestial steel blade sheered through the ghost netting as if it were made of silk thread. The wizard gaped in astonishment as his spell cage collapsed in on itself and vanished. Before he could regain his wits, I sprang at him, calling on the wind to lend me supernatural speed. Before he could blink, I had the katana at his throat.

"Drop the gun and release Frank and Brianna at once," I ordered the wizard. I shoved my face into his own so that our eyes were only inches apart. I let him see the controlled fury that burned just below the surface. He saw that I could be a cold blooded killer when I needed to. I saw in his own eyes that he could destroy me, even now as I held my blade to his throat. I felt the incredible power within him, a power that glowed like the sun and gave him a golden aura that he'd masked from me until now. We both saw in each other's eyes that there was no evil intent on either of our parts. His eyes pulled at my soul, and I felt a deep connection snap into place between us. I didn't understand what was happening, but a thrill of strange feelings surged through me, feelings I'd thought lost to me with my death. Carter himself stared at me in stunned disbelief; the emotions I felt were clearly mirrored in his own blazing eyes.

Nathaniel wordlessly dropped Frank's gun, and a second later Frank himself was free to retrieve it. He dashed to his big assed gun, snatched it from the ground, and leveled it at the wizard's head.

"That won't be necessary Frank," I said as I stepped away from Nathaniel. "I think that Carter and I have reached an understanding, haven't we?"

"Indeed we have, Miss Kane," he said formally. I watched with a fluttering heart as he regained his composure. I knew at that moment that I was in big trouble. A fluttering heart is a ridiculous thing for a ghost to suffer; it can only mean trouble.

"What the fuck are you talking about?" Frank growled still not lowering the gun. Nathaniel stood still but remained uncowed. "Did you see what this freak did? Didn't you say a wizard was working with the vamps? I'd say it's an incredible coincidence that we find him here. What do you say to that warlock?"

Nathaniel said nothing, though his eyes blazed with anger for a moment. It seemed he didn't like being called a warlock.

"He's ok Frank, trust me. I've looked into his soul and he's clean. He means us no harm."

"You looked into his fucking soul? What the hell does that mean?" Frank argued. "What if he's wearing some kind of soul camouflage? Look, he hasn't changed that lady back."

The idea of soul camouflage hit me hard. I knew without a

doubt that Carter was ok, but was such a thing as a soul cloak possible? If it was, and the bad guys had one, they might be able to disguise themselves as free souls in Limbo.

"She can shift anytime she wants to," Nathaniel Carter answered Frank, bringing me out of my dark musings.

"You shut the hell up."

"Where did you get this emotional windbag, Veronika?" Brianna asked springing back into her human shape. "I hope he isn't the backup you were talking about."

Frank turned towards Brianna's voice and froze, gaping in abashed wonder at her gloriously naked body. She stretched languidly, revealing all of her curves and hidden parts. A mischievous gleam danced in her sultry green eyes.

"Hi Frank, nice to meet you. I'm Brianna," she said in a Jessica Rabbit voice. "The wizard smells clean. Now, put that big gun away before you get arrested for indecent exposure."

Frank tore his gaze from her and fumbled with his gun, seeming unsure of himself. His skin was pink around the ears, and the eyes he turned towards me begged for help. I glanced at Nathaniel and saw that Brianna's nakedness hadn't phased him a bit.

"Get dressed Brianna," I said smiling inwardly. It was nice to see the stalwart Cooper squirm for a change. It seemed to me that Brianna would be good for him. "The night is getting old and we've got shifters to rescue."

7

FIVE MINUTES LATER, we breached the perimeter of the Byberry facility near the N-7 building. Brianna, once again dressed in her black catsuit and armed with her 9mm pistol, led the way. I followed the were-ferret, Nathaniel Carter came next, and finally Frank brought up the rear. More arguments had ensued when the wizard had announced that he would be coming with us. Frank angrily proclaimed that he didn't trust the man, but in the end I over ruled him. A few moments later, when I'd tried to take Brianna's pistol in order to plate it with celestial steel as I'd done with Frank's monster gun, she'd refused until Frank told her she was being a baby, and the two proceeded to get into a shouting match. Carter had watched the exchange with a bemused expression on his long face. Personally, I was exasperated. It would be a miracle if all the noise we'd made had gone unnoticed. I finally shut the two up by telling them that I would leave them both behind if they didn't start acting like grownups about to embark on a dangerous mission. After I'd gotten my way with Brianna's pistol and ammo, we'd set off at a brisk but quiet pace.

As we approached the N-9 building, Brianna slowed her pace and hunched her shoulders in distress. I enhanced my senses by burning off some of my stored energy and was immediately assaulted by the stench of death and rotting things. My ghostly innards convulsed involuntarily, and I began to gag. I turned down the volume on my sense of smell until the odor was so faint that it was barely perceptible: it was just another perk of being a ghost. Carter seemed oblivious to the offensive smell that clung to the area like a wet blanket. The only hint that he was aware of the stench was the sense of hyper alertness that he suddenly exuded. Although Frank was clearly bothered by the rancorous smell, his cop training and experience helped him keep his composure. Sebastian was nowhere to be seen as I'd sent him aloft to see if there was any activity from the patrol or the vampire monoliths. Our little group pressed on even as the smell got worse.

The N-9 building was a six story stone structure whose purpose had been to contain the most dangerous and violent male inmates the facility had to offer. The building had survived the test of time and it appeared that it had recently been renovated. The rusted bars that had hung like rotting teeth in the windows had been removed and new heavy duty plexiglass had replaced them. As we drew nearer, I noticed that the ground we were walking on was newly turned earth as if the grounds crew had prepared it for a new planting of grass. A set of double brass doors were the only visible points of entry along the southern face of the edifice of the building. Brianna paused, clearly considering whether entrance would be more easily attained via a window or the doors. She made a quick decision and headed for the doors.

"I'd normally go into ferret form at this point and find a pipe to crawl in through," she whispered back to me. "But with Tweedledum and Tweedledee back there, we'll have to do this the hard way."

Frank's face colored with anger, but Nathaniel ignored the quip; his head was cocked as if listening.

"Run!" he roared suddenly and followed his own advice by springing forward, his long legs carrying him past me in two strides. The ground all around us erupted in geysers of dirt and stone, and the source of the foul stench was revealed. Scores of rotting and dirt covered human bodies rose from the ground and began a cacophonous moan of hunger. I stared at them in horrified recognition, shocked to the core at how right on Night of the Living Dead had gotten zombies. These beings were in varying stages of decay, but they all had three things in common: they were universally in agony, uncontrollably hungry, and they were all walking dead.

Carter snatched Brianna up in one arm as he dashed towards the entrance of N-9, dodging outstretched arms as the slower zombies continued to struggle onto their feet. Brianna was too shocked to react, allowing herself to be carried towards the double doors. The doors were fronted by a small covered porch with six concrete steps leading up to them. It was the only part of the grounds on this side of the building where zombies weren't erupting from the earth. Carter unceremoniously dumped the were-ferret onto her behind in front of the doors when he reached the top of the stairs before whirling around to face the oncoming zombie horde.

A roar of thunder brought my attention back around to Frank. His face was ashen and he hadn't moved from where he'd been standing when the zombies had broken through the earth. His Desert Eagle was pointed down at a corpse whose head was gone; brain matter was splattered all around it. Frank took aim at another zombie, and its head exploded in a shower of putrid gore. He continued a steady barrage of head liquefying shots that left a pile of broken limbed, headless bodies before him. He destroyed five of the lurching dead in less than ten seconds, but a small horde of them had gathered at his exposed back and were preparing to charge. Frank knew that he was exposed, but he continued to fire upon the ones in front of him clearly trusting that I'd have his back.

I stepped up to the detective's side facing the oncoming zombies at his back and timed my scream with the roar of his gun. The banshee wail struck the dozen or so zombies and shredded them. The savageness of the attack made me want to spew, and tears welled up in my eyes as I surveyed the carnage that I'd wrought. In Limbo my screams pulverized my enemies into torn bits of mist, but in the living world, the devastation was far more gruesome. Arms, legs, heads, hands, feat, and internal parts lay strewn across the yard, some blown as far as fifty feet away. There were exposed organs, blood, and other bodily fluids soaking the broken ground. Most horrifically, many of the zombies continued to move; those that had not lost a head were still animated. Though I'd put more of the zombies down in a single attack than Frank had, his at least were out of their misery. I'd left many of my victims more broken but still trapped in a horrible existence.

A bright light followed by a whooshing sound brought me around to face the N-9 building. Nathaniel Carter was standing at the top of the stairs his right hand held before him in a fist. At least twenty zombies in a thirty foot cone in front of the stair were on fire. Brianna stood besides the wizard, her pistol held high, but at the moment she was gaping at Carter. The wizard's eyes were fierce with concentration; lightning seemed to flash in their stormy grey depths. Sweat beaded his forehead as the burning zombies continued to shamble towards him, their moans of agony drowning out all other sounds.

"Ajilv!" shouted the wizard unclenching his fist and stretching his fingers wide. The burning zombies exploded in a momentary blaze that would have challenged the sun for brightness; the flames died as quickly as they flared. The smoking things that remained were nothing more than piles of ash. None of the piles moved. The battlefield was eerily silent for a moment. Even the remaining zombies seemed taken aback, though that was probably just a trick of the mind.

"Get your asses over here," roared Nathaniel to Frank and me.

Frank needed no further urging; he immediately strode forward towards the steps, only pausing long enough to blow the head off of a single zombie that blocked our path. The moans of the zombies resumed, and a quick glance around showed me that there were still dozens of them remaining and still more were pulling themselves out of the ground. Where had all the corpses come from, I wondered. Surely they hadn't been buried here over the centuries had they? And if this wasn't the site of a mass graveyard, then that meant someone had dug them up from somewhere else and brought them here. Ick!

"Veronika, you go inside and clear the entryway of any threats," ordered the wizard when we'd reached the landing at the top of the stairs. "And don't use the wail against zombies, it's too damn messy. If you can handle that katana as well as I think you can then that should work just fine. Brianna, you work on getting these doors open. Frank and I will keep the zombies at bay."

I stared at Nathaniel in consternation for a moment wondering how I'd lost control. A look into his storm wracked eyes told me that this man was used to command. I was in his territory, so I guess I would just have to deal. Carter had both the experience and power to back up his authority, and I knew that every good commander must also be able to take orders. In this situation, it was right for me to follow Nathaniel's lead.

"Hey!" exclaimed an indignant Brianna. "First you manhandle me like I'm a sack of potatoes, and then you insult me by assuming that I'm some kind of thief with the know how to break into a secure facility. Do I look like a burglar to you?"

"Yes," said Frank and Nathaniel in unison. Frank was eyeing the girl appraisingly and he flashed a smile towards Carter before adding, "now that you fucking mention it, you definitely remind me of a thief I once busted."

"Hah! You wish," Brianna harrumphed turning away from the two men. She stepped up to the door, a pouch of tiny tools appearing in her delicate hands. As I phased through the buildings doorway, I wondered where she'd hidden them in that tight outfit. The look on Frank's face said he was wondering the same thing.

8

I stepped into a dimly lit foyer and found four zombies quietly lurking in the shadows. I paused a moment to study them, looking for any signs of the demon or spirit that must lurk within their rotting flesh. These zombies were apparently newly dead for there was very little visible decay, and they were still bloated from the embalming fluids used to preserve them during the funeral process. The creatures had a very faint, sickly grey aura that flickered, and the spirits that animated them were shriveled beyond recognition. Whoever was responsible for raising these horrors had to be shut down quickly.

The sound of Brianna's tampering at the door's lock mechanism seemed to wake the zombies because they suddenly began to moan and shuffle towards the closed portals. If Brianna opened those doors at this moment, she'd be getting up close and personal with four ravenous zombies. The sound of Frank's gun going off at regular intervals reminded me that my friends needed to get inside ASAP. It was time for me to do my part.

I drew my katana and pushed ghostly energy into it, willing

the celestial steel blade to become solid. The really cool thing was that I didn't have to make myself corporeal in order to wield the sword. I'm not sure how I can do this. I guess it's the manifestation of my complete control over celestial steel, but it sure does come in handy when I'm dealing with corporeal threats. I made quick work of the zombies, dancing among them like the lady of death incarnate. I decapitated each of the zombies with a single fluid stroke. It was messy but not as bad as the banshee scream had been.

I checked the hallway beyond the foyer and found a confusing array of dark hallways with scores of doorways at regular intervals. There was a wide stair case leading upward just outside the foyer. I found a pair of zombies lurking near a second, smaller stairway that led downward. I relieved them of their heads and headed back to the foyer just in time to see the doors slide open.

"Ghaaah…!" Brianna exclaimed. "Did you have to leave your mess right at the door, Veronika?"

"I could have let them eat you," I replied in a matter of fact tone. "Besides, if you want a cleaner, it's best not to call on a banshee. Everyone knows we're messy."

"I'm glad to see you two ladies getting along so nicely, but we aren't out of the woods yet," said Nathaniel as he pushed past Brianna. As if to punctuate his mild rebuke, Frank's gun roared once more before the detective ducked into the relative safety of the foyer. Brianna slammed the door shut behind him and locked it.

"Holy fuck!" said Frank. He was breathing heavily and sweating profusely. "Someone want to tell me what the fuck we just walked into? It's like the fucking set of The Walking Dead out there."

"Eloquently said my friend," Nathaniel replied with a half smile. I was surprised to see genuine respect for the detective reflected in the wizard's grey eyes. "I'm not sure what we're dealing with here other than to speculate that the world's most powerful necromancer has come to Philly; though, it's more likely that a convention of lesser necromancers has been persuaded that Byberry is so much better than the Holiday Inn. I trust you've secured the immediate vicinity Ms. Kane?"

"This place is huge, with a whole mess load of rooms," I answered with a nod. "I only found two more of these things near a stairwell going down. What are these things anyways?"

"What do you fucking mean, what are these things?" Frank scoffed incredulously. "They're fucking zombies aren't they?"

"Indeed they are detective Cooper," Nathaniel answered while sticking his head through the nearby archway and looking down the corridor beyond. "But I think Veronika is asking a more profound question about the zombie's nature, are you not?"

"Yes."

"Zombies are created in much the same way that shifters are created."

"Are you freaking kidding me," Brianna spluttered angrily. "You're comparing me to a zombie? On second thought Cooper, go ahead and shoot the wizard. Obviously he's an idiot."

Frank snorted derisively, but he watched the were-ferret with obvious interest.

"I wasn't comparing you to zombies noble ferret. Anyone who has seen you in your birthday suit could hardly mistake you for a zombie," the wizard said in an amused voice. "I was speaking of the binding ritual that is used to summon a fury to merge with a living human host."

"Shut up wizard!" Brianna said in a threatening tone. "It is forbidden to speak of this. How did you come by this information?"

"Peace Brianna," the wizard commanded, and I felt the power of his words slide over Brianna like a glove. She immediately relaxed, tension going out of her. Frank looked askance at the wizard, not knowing exactly what had happened but aware that something had happened.

"It's ok Brianna, we're all friends here. We'll keep your secrets," I told the young woman before turning back to Nathaniel. "How do you know all of this stuff?"

"I'm a wizard," he replied, as if the answer was self evident. "Now, if I may continue. The fury that responds during a making ceremony comes willingly and chooses to join with the human vessel."

He paused a moment for dramatic effect.

"The necromantic ritual of making, however, is far more brutal. Spirits that wander Limbo are grabbed by the magic and forced into a rotting corpse. The force of the spell destroys the essence of the spirit, blasting it into a shriveled and hungry thing that no longer remembers what it was. It rises as a ravenous zombie."

I stared at the wizard in shock, my mind racing and tying my thoughts into knots.

"Tell me Captain, have there been an unusual number of missing ghosts in your domain lately?"

I nodded slowly, tears blinded me as I tried to focus on the mangled corpses of the zombies that I'd destroyed. These had been free souls. I'd destroyed my own people.

"Is there anything we can do for them, any way to set them free?" I asked looking towards the doorway going outside, where the moans of my hungry people could still be heard.

"I'm sorry Veronika," Nathaniel said with compassion in his voice. "The only thing you can do to help your people now is to set them free with your blade. They are already gone."

"After all that we've been through, why would God allow this to happen to the free souls?" I whispered, my heart breaking. I'd assumed that the reports of missing souls were tied to Cartel activity. I couldn't have imagined something as horrible as the truth that Carter had just revealed.

"This is not God's doing," Carter answered me. "This is the work of his true enemy. Not the one you call Satan. That one was of His own creation and was merely a rebellious servant that He chose not to destroy. This is the work of chaos. The one named Azathoth is behind this magic."

"Well, if I can't save the ones they've taken," I said, anger rising from the depths of my being, "I'll save others from being taken by killing the assholes who did this. You can tell me about this chaos stuff later, right now we have business to attend to."

9

I LED THE STALWART GROUP through the maze of halls until we reached the downward staircase where I'd taken out the two guard zombies. From there, I signaled the group to wait while I scouted out the room below. Before I made my descent, I untethered myself so that I wouldn't be visible, at least not to most beings. The stairs ended in a large, dark room with two open doors leading into different corridors. One of the hallways was lit, providing the dim light in the landing room. The room was devoid of furnishings, and the walls were painted in lurid scenes of alien vistas populated by monstrous beings that defied description.

I was momentarily mesmerized by the alien landscapes depicted in the murals; they looked so real that I imagined that I could step into them and find myself in those strange places. The thought of going there and being in the presence of the terrible beings that populated them sent a shiver through me. When one of the creatures suddenly moved, I saw with horror that it was actually not part of the painting at all. It was real and in the same room as me! The thing was froglike, but it was covered in lidless eyes, and writhing tentacles swarmed from its crouching leathery body. It was the size of a pony, and its hundreds of eyes glowed: each one a different color. The thing had no aura that I could discern, and I felt myself wanting to crawl away and hide where the monster couldn't find me. I shook off the dread that filled me and turned away from it; I was invisible to it after all. I moved over to the lit corridor to peer down its length so that I could ascertain what other threats might be lurking nearby.

I gasped as a searing pain suddenly shot through my left shoulder and across my chest. I looked down at myself and found a tentacle with serrated bone protrusions latched onto me. I tried to pull free from it, but its grip was like a vice and I felt myself being pulled backwards. I'd assumed the creature couldn't see me; well you know what they say about assumptions right? I maneuvered myself around so that I could see the frog thing that was attacking me. I watched in sick fascination as a clump of its eyes near the top of its head split open and a huge mouth gaped in their place. It let out a screeching sound that paralyzed me. A monstrous tongue covered in dripping, thorny protrusions lashed out and struck me across the face. The agony that the attack provoked was so intense that I found myself swooning. I wanted to let forth my banshee scream, but I couldn't. I felt my mind going numb and insanity threatened to overwhelm me as I was inexorably pulled towards that alien maw. I felt the mental defenses that I'd built over the last nine months begin to crumble. I relived my own murder and the helplessness that had filled me during my first hours in Limbo. The memories flared through me, and I was again reliving my worst nightmare: my captivity and torture at the hands of Delilah and Freak. Rage, fear, and self loathing flooded me till I felt as though I'd burst if I couldn't find an outlet to pour my emotions through.

A shout followed by a blinding light suddenly cleared my head of the growing madness that had paralyzed me. The monster stopped dragging me towards its mouth, though its tentacle did maintain a hold on me. Nathaniel Carter stood at the foot of the stairs; a glorious golden light shown around him, bathing the entire room in warm light. The beast hissed at the wizard. Clearly it didn't like Carter's light.

"What the fuck is that?" cried Frank in a tremulous voice.

"It's the face of chaos and madness," answered Nathaniel. "It has a hold on Veronika. Shoot it in the eyes."

I saw that both Frank and Brianna had accompanied the wizard. Both stood a couple of stairs above him and aimed their pistols at the hideous chaos monster. A pair of the beast's eyes exploded as the detective and the shifter opened fire. Rage at my own folly suddenly filled me, and I re-tethered myself and willed my blade to take on physical form once more. I sent the blue katana into a wide arc that struck the tentacle that held me and instantly severed it.

The chaos monster let out a scream that filled my head with a momentary feeling of slimy things crawling all over me. Just as quickly as the feeling came, it was banished by Carter's comforting golden light. I stared at Nathaniel Carter in awe as I realized that it was his power that was pushing back the drowning madness that the chaos beast invoked with its cries. The warmth of his light made me feel safe. It reminded me of how his soul felt when we'd shared a lifetime of experiences in a single gaze less than an hour ago. Warmth caressed me and other emotions threatened to distract me from the ongoing battle. It was amazingly fortuitous that we'd been waylaid by the wizard on this night of all nights. Without Nathaniel, we might well have perished down here.

The creature's tongue lashed out at me again, but I sliced a good foot off of it with a defensive stroke. I considered charging it but didn't want to get in the way of Frank and Brianna's withering fire, so I stayed back and played defense.

A tentacle lashed out and struck Nathaniel in the forehead; he staggered and blood poured from the wound, but he didn't lose his hold on the light ward that he was protecting us with.

Before I could react, more tentacles lashed out at my three companions on the steps. They were all struck several times, leaving them bloodied and momentarily staggered. The firing faltered, and madness hammered at all of us for a second as Nathaniel's ward slipped. The wizard got control of his spell through sheer force of will, driving the madness back once more as the ward shone brighter than ever. Regaining my own composure, I called the wind to me and in less time than it takes a person to blink, I was standing before Nathaniel, my back to him and my sword raised. I howled my defiance at the chaos beast and met every tentacle that it thrust at my friends with my celestial steel katana. The thing roared in its own mad rage as all of its attempts to get through my guard met with a steel curtain that left its appendages shortened. Frank and Brianna resumed their deadly assault on the creature, giving it an entirely new reason to scream.

"Hold your fire!" I yelled when most of the creature's eyes on the side facing us had been obliterated by the hail of bullets. The thing was a mass of gory meat that madly flung too-short tentacles in all directions. Trusting that they'd do what I asked, I leaped forward. My speed enhanced body moved faster than what a normal human eye could track. I followed Frank's last bullet as it slammed into a glowing purple eye. My sword slid into the gaping wound as I drove my blade in up to my elbow. The chaos beast only had a half second to shudder as I twisted the katana and sliced upwards. A quarter of the beast's grotesque body rolled away, leaving a gory trail in its wake. I didn't pause to see if the thing was dead. I swung again and again until I felt a firm hand grasp my uninjured shoulder. I paused, startled, looked at the hand, and followed it up until I stared into Nathaniel Carter's stormy grey eyes.

"That's enough, Veronika," he said gently. "It's quite dead."

"Jesus Christ!" exclaimed Frank. "You're one crazy bitch Veronika. You chopped it into salsa."

I stared at Carter, seeing the blood pour from a deep gash on his forehead and cheek. I looked over the rest of him and saw blood soaking through his shirt and jeans in at least a half dozen places.

"We need to get you to a doctor," I said huskily, my eyes once more drawn to his. A strange feeling settled over me; it felt like butterflies flopping around in my stomach. I'd felt this a time or two in my short life, but come on, I'm a ghost now. I can't fall in love, can I? The thought was ridiculous. I was dead, and he was a powerful wizard. He couldn't possibly be interested in me, even if I'd been alive. He was out of my league, and besides, he was old enough to be my dad. I shook my head, trying real hard to push the emotions away. There was too much work to do; love was best left to the living. "Thanks for coming when you did. That thing really surprised me."

"I'll be fine," he said quietly. "We don't have time for doctors right now. Whoever called this thing up is still around here, and we can't let him go causing this kind of mischief, can we?"

"No," I agreed, staring at the hand that still held my shoulder. "How can you touch me? I'm tethered, but my whole mass is less than a grain of sand. Your hand should pass right through me." His hand felt warm and real on my shoulder. It must be some kind of illusion.

Carter withdrew his hand with an embarrassed expression on his face.

"I'm a wizard, all things are possible to us," he answered with a gleam in his stormy eyes. He was a bloody mess, but I suddenly found this mysterious stranger to be the most beautiful man I'd ever met. He made me feel alive. That's a magic I'd love anyone for, but of course the Captain of the Ghost Watch didn't have time for silly little girl dreams. There was a necromancer to destroy and shifters to rescue.

I took stock of my surroundings noting that both Brianna and Frank were also bleeding from open wounds, but both seemed determined and eager to continue. Of the beast there was nothing left but chunks of meat strewn about the room, black ichor splattered the walls, and I was drenched in the gore. I shuddered at my own murderous ferocity and untethered myself long enough to let the gore slough off of me. Re-tethering myself, I led my friends into the lit corridor.

10

THE CORRIDOR ENDED AT A closed wooden door. Its surface, covered in runic symbols, made me pause.

"Let me see," said Carter, as he moved up to my side and slowly extended a hand toward the door. His hand began to glow with a golden brilliance, and when he was just an inch from the doors surface, the runes suddenly flared to life and began glowing a malevolent red. "Just as I thought. It's warded. Not even a ghost could get through it without risking serious magical backlash."

"What do we fucking do about that?" asked an increasingly stressed Frank Cooper.

"I'll have it down in a moment," the wizard said, his brow furrowed in concentration. A bandana was wrapped around his head, staunching the flow of blood from the cut on his forehead. The golden glow around his hand intensified until it blazed like a mini sun; the glowing runes on the door began to flicker and finally went out. He dropped his hand away and leaned tiredly against the corridor wall. "The ward has been disabled. Brianna, you'll need to unlock it. Veronika, we need you to look through the door and see what's lurking on the other side. Take caution. Whatever is beyond isn't likely a friend."

"Are you alright?" I asked him.

"I'm a wizard, I'll be fine," he said with a grateful smile. "Just a little fatigued, that's all. Overcoming magical wards is difficult work."

Brianna shook herself and stretched her graceful body provocatively before slinking her way from Frank's side. She produced her lock picking tools as she approached the door. I shook my head in mock disgust at her teasing of the detective, and with a reassuring smile cast towards Nathaniel, I stuck my head through the door.

My head passed through the door without any problems. Not that I doubted Carter's skill, but I must admit that I'd been a little worried that something would go wrong. That's the kind of day I was having after all. The room beyond was large and well lit with flickering candles. Like the landing room, the walls were painted with scenes of alien vistas. Rather than strange landscapes though, the murals depicted a city constructed of black stone that appeared to absorb light. The cityscape was nightmarish; it teased the mind with the promise of everlasting laughter and screaming. The buildings were cyclopean, as if built for titans, and the architecture defied human reason with its non-Euclidean geometry. I shuddered as I recognized the material and architecture as being similar to that used in the construction of the new Byberry vampire fortresses. What mad powers had the vampires allied with, I wondered as I continued to survey the room.

The rest of the chamber was as frightening as the painting of the mad city. In the center of the room, a massive pentagram had been drawn on the floor. A black candle flickered menacingly at each of the star's points. An altar, seemingly made of the same alien black material in the mural, was centered in the pentagram. The body of a naked young woman lay splayed upon it, her life's blood still dripping and pooling at the altar's base. Throughout the chamber, crosses had been erected, and upon each of them hung the body of a dead man or woman. A mound of bloody flesh and bones was piled into a corner while an antique desk was pushed against the wall opposite of me. A flicker of movement drew my attention to the left corner of the room nearest to me, and I saw someone disappear through a hole in the floor there.

"It's a mess in there," I told the others after pulling my head back into the corridor. "Lots of dead people; looks like they've been sacrificed. I saw someone disappear down a hole in the floor in the left corner of the room nearest us, so be careful. They know we're here."

"Oh God, not Sarah, please!" moaned Brianna as she redoubled her efforts to get the door open. Her eyes brimmed with tears and her hands shook.

"Tell me everything you saw," the wizard commanded. He was alert and full of energy all of a sudden. Adrenalin is a great thing in a pinch.

I began to describe what I'd seen starting with the black city mural then moving onto the pentagram and finally the ghastly crucifixions and sacrifice. I was interrupted by the clicking sound of the lock mechanism being turned, and before any of us could object, Brianna pushed the door open and sprang through it into the room beyond. She paused for a moment, her eyes darting about the room as her mind tried to make sense of the carnage before her.

"No Brianna, stay back!" roared Nathaniel, but she wasn't listening.

"Sarah! No!" the distraught ferret woman screamed in horror when her eyes alighted on the altar. She sprang towards the naked figure on the altar totally oblivious to Nathaniel's warning shouts. The rest of us followed her into the room, but she had too much of a head start for any of us to stop her. As soon as her body broke the plane of the pentagram, the candles at each of its points went out, and a monstrous bell began to toll. Brianna stopped dead in her tracks, sudden fear breaking through her grief. A light breeze began to blow in the basement chamber, and a black smoke rode upon it, blotting out the room around us. The ominous ringing of the bell filled my senses, seeming as if it were drawing closer. There was a sudden lurching sensation, and the physical tether that I held was wrenched from me.

The light breeze became a strong wind, and the curtain of smoke surrounding us was carried away. The bell rang one final time, and a crawling silence took its place.

"Holy shit," whispered Frank in a voice filled with awe and dread. "I don't think we're in fucking Kansas anymore."

We stood in a small plaza of the black city from the mural. Cyclopean buildings loomed all around us. Though the sky above us was moonless, thousands of stars shone brightly, providing an ambient light that was both comforting and terrifying. Everything in the city, its buildings, roads, and monuments seemed to be made of the same black alien material that the vampire monoliths were made of. The square was dominated by a colossal statue of a monstrous being whose very shape was surely designed to elicit endless nightmares that would finally result in blissful madness. I couldn't tear my gaze from the bat-winged monstrosity. Its head was bestial with protruding tentacles that reminded me of a giant squid. It was humanoid in shape with two legs, several arms, and a single head on its squat shoulders.

"We have to get out of here or we're doomed," Nathaniel Carter said through gritted teeth. "Everyone gather around. I'll need your help Veronika."

I tore my gaze from the nameless god monument and went to stand by the wizard, who once again was bathed in golden light. A shriek pierced the silence of the black city, and I shuddered as the call was taken up by thousands of beings throughout the city.

"Is that who I fucking think it is?" asked Frank in a quavering voice. I followed his gaze back to the statue I'd been staring at before Nathaniel distracted me.

"Probably," Nathaniel answered grimly. "Everyone get in a circle and hold hands. I need Veronika holding one of mine."

We did as he commanded, a sense of urgency filling all of us as the screams, shrieks, and hoots continued to grow closer. I wasn't surprised that I was able to hold Nathaniel's hand, but I gaped in astonishment when Frank grasped my hand without passing through it.

"What the hell? I'm not tethered, how can you do that?" I asked. Frank looked momentarily surprised then shrugged.

"We aren't on the material plane, nor are we in the lands of the dead," answered Nathaniel. "This place has many names, the Dreamlands, the Black City, Ry'lah, Yuggoth, but the Order calls it Pandemonium. This is the boundary realm between all other realms and the outer chaos. If we remain here long, we will be taken, devoured, and ultimately given to Yog-Sothoth. None of our physical bodies are actually here. They lie sleeping in the basement room with the pentagram."

The names that the wizard mentioned seemed to have a profound impact on Frank. Each time one was mention he jerked as if punched. They meant nothing to me. The only thing that I understood was that we weren't in the living world or in Limbo anymore, and we were definitely in deep trouble.

"In that case," Brianna said in a quavering voice. "Get us the hell out of here."

"I'm working on it," Carter replied in a pensive voice. "I've never done this sort of thing before. Talking keeps me calm while I work out the formulas."

"Why don't I open a gate to Limbo?" I suggested. "If you're all spirits, you should all be able to follow me, and I could guide us back home."

"That would be unwise," Nathaniel answered. "Only a trained adept like myself can travel Limbo without suffering final death. Living people who enter Limbo in any form have their life's essence drained from them the moment they enter the land of the dead; their bodies age rapidly and death from old age can occur within hours. The soul of one lost in this way becomes a lost spirit. Only those versed in proper warding techniques can prevent this outcome. Though I do know the warding spell, it cannot be extended to others. If we tried to pass through Limbo, both Brianna and Frank would die. Besides, you don't want to weaken the veil here. Azathoth's avatar, the Man with Many Names, has long sought supremacy over the dead. I doubt you want to give him a back door into Limbo."

"No," I agreed with a shudder. "How can I help you?"

"I need to borrow power from you. Most of my own power is bound to my physical body."

"Great, now I'm a battery eh? You really know how to make a girl feel special, Nathaniel."

Nathaniel stared at me in abashed surprise. He started to say something but stopped before the words came out. His face looked a little pink.

"Oh come on!" Frank said in exasperation. "I'd tell the two of you to get a fucking room but we're about to die, remember? Let's get the fuck out of here, and then you can do all the flirting you want. Hell I'll even spring for a room if you want."

Nathaniel shook his head as if clearing it and his expression changed to one of focused concentration. He squeezed my hand and closed his eyes.

Monsters of all shapes and sizes began to pour into the square, but they all halted just outside of the growing golden light that blazed from Nathaniel. The power that the wizard drew from me was small at first, and the feeling was almost sensual. I wondered momentarily if this feeling was akin to what people experienced when being fed upon by a vampire. The milling mass of creatures surrounding us suddenly grew still and silent as a grinding sound reverberated throughout the city. A roar shook the dark metropolis, and upon its sonic wave was carried every imaginable horror that has ever plagued the mind of mortal man. All of us in the circle, including Nathaniel, were shaken to our cores. Silence followed and it seemed like all of creation labored to get its breath back. Before we'd fully recovered, a new sound sent icy tendrils of terror down our collective spirit spines; a rhythmic tread shook the nightmare city as if a titanic elder god was walking its streets. Carter maintained his focus through sheer discipline, though he drew power from me more swiftly now. I began to grow more tired and our connection was much less comfortable now.

Silence descended once more, and I strained to see what the darkness hid. When I finally saw it silhouetted between two buildings, I found that terror really did have a face. It gazed down at us with glowing green eyes, its dark shape a titanic version of the statue in the square near us. Nothing has ever terrified me more, and the urge to run was so strong that I felt my hand hold on my friends beginning to loosen.

"If we live through this," Brianna said in a choked voice. "I'll take you up on that offer of a room Frank. I don't think we'll ever be able to sleep again. Lots of sex seems like a good way to stave off insanity."

"Get us out! Now!" I shouted desperately to Carter. I opened myself fully to him and shoved nearly all of my power into him.

"Gorthosba!" Nathaniel cried out and the plaza exploded. It was as if ten thousand suns had suddenly appeared. The gargantuan god roared, and I felt its power beat at us, trying to keep us from escaping, but it was too late. There was a lurching sensation and then we were back in the basement of the men's maximum security building in Byberry. We had been dragged out of there in a black fog, and we returned in a blaze of glory that both surprised and blinded our earthbound enemies.

11

Brianna was nowhere to be seen, but both Frank and Nathaniel had been bound, gagged, and dragged to the corner of the room near the hole in the floor. Two women of extraordinary beauty were crouching defensively nearby, having been momentarily stunned by the sudden blinding light that had heralded the return of our spirits. The green aura that hung about the two pin-up models informed me that they were both shifters of some kind. They wore tight fitting brown leotards and black, knee high stiletto boots. Although they appeared to be soft and voluptuously weak, nothing could be further from the truth. The way their eyes darted about the room as they crouched in perfectly balanced defensive stances indicated that they were combat trained, and the hardness of their eyes bespoke a willingness to kill.

Before either of the women could do anything but take up a defensive posture over their captives, I unleashed the siren's song on them. I sang "Dust in the Wind" by Kansas. The shifters and to my chagrin, Frank, were immediately mesmerized by my siren power. Nathaniel however, wasn't; he nodded at me in approval. I went to him and cut his bonds with my off-hand short blade which I infused with power in order to give the celestial steel a physical presence. He nodded in thanks as I continued to sing, holding the shifters at bay until they could be properly bound. It was gratifying that my abilities went beyond mere destruction. Sometimes I was capable of not killing my enemies. Nathaniel removed the gag from his mouth, his stormy grey eyes never leaving my own. I couldn't read his expression, but I was pretty certain that he was impressed with the range of my powers.

The wizard rose gingerly to his feet, and tearing his eyes away from mine, he went to each of the shifter women, placed a hand on their foreheads, muttered a single word that I didn't hear, and they both slumped in apparent slumber. I cut Frank's bindings and brought the song to an end. I suddenly felt very drained; a quick internal inventory revealed that Nathaniel had used a majority of my strength in getting us back here. I wasn't complaining or anything, but soon I'd have to return to Limbo to recharge.

"Holy shit," Frank muttered, rubbing at his wrists. "I fucking dreamed that we were in a black city where fucking Cthulhu lives, then we escaped, and an angel was singing to me. I need a fucking beer."

"It wasn't a dream," I said. I peered down the nearby hole. A rusty old iron ladder dropped into the darkness below. "I don't know what a Cthulhu is, but we were in a black city. At least your spirit was. When Nathaniel got us back here, those two bitches had you tied up. I mesmerized them with the siren's song, and Carter put them to sleep after I freed him. Brianna is missing though. My guess is that they took her down this hole."

Frank looked up in alarm and gave the room a quick glance. His eyes narrowed when he saw the two sleeping ladies.

"What the fuck are they doing down here?" he asked in confusion. "Let's wake them up, maybe they know where Brianna went."

"I don't think that would be a good idea detective," Nathaniel said. "Those ladies are were-hyenas, and I suspect that they work for those responsible for the atrocities we've witnessed tonight. If so, they are very dangerous femme fatales, and you'd do well not to underestimate them."

"Where the fuck is my gun?" Frank asked patting himself down with a panicked expression on his face.

"It's over here," answered Nathaniel from the other side of the room. He bent down and lifted Frank's gun. "I think they've taken the ammo though."

"Mother fucker!" Frank swore. He moved towards the sleeping women, obviously intending to search them.

"We don't have time for this," I said. "Brianna could be in serious trouble. I'm going down after her. Follow when you can."

Without waiting to hear a reply, I leaped down into the darkness below, letting gravity pull me down the shaft. I gave myself more mass so that I'd fall like a pebble rather than a feather. In any case, it wasn't enough to make the landing uncomfortable. I found myself crouching in an old, rough hewn tunnel; its walls were covered in graffiti and there was about an inch of stagnant water covering the floor. This must be one of the old service tunnels that connected various buildings of the complex.

I cocked my head for a moment, listening for voices or other sounds that would clue me in to which direction Brianna's captors had taken her in. I heard someone laboring on the ladder above me and muffled voices coming from the right hand tunnel.

"Go right," I called up to my companions and took off like a bat out of hell.

I reached a four way intersection where the water got to nearly a foot deep. A faint flickering of light caused me to take the right hand passage, and I soon came to an opening in the wall through which the glow was emanating. The room beyond the opening was large, once having been a storage room, and was lit by several torches. What caught my immediate attention was the shimmering portal that stood open in the middle of the chamber. Beautiful young women like the ones in the sacrifice room above were carefully carrying huge crates from the chamber through the portal into the wooded area beyond. An ancient, bent-backed crone with a pointy nose and shriveled chin stood by the gate watching the proceedings with a critical eye. She was dressed in a shapeless brown robes, and her aura was as black as I'd ever seen. Beside her stood another of the voluptuous, tawny haired females; this one was taller than the others, and instead of wearing a leotard, she wore a skin tight suit of spotted brown leather. Her aura was green as was that of the other shapely women in the room. She looked right at me as I stood in the doorway surveying the room.

"Ghost," she warned and stalked towards me.

"I see her Jezebel, leave off," the hag croaked. "This one is far too dangerous for the likes of you. I'll deal with her myself. We've got enough now. Get everyone through the gate. The wizard will be here soon, and we do not want to be here when he arrives."

"Who are you?" I asked stepping into the room. My eyes darted about searching for any signs of Brianna.

Jezebel snarled at me before turning away towards a corner of the room where I glimpsed a form sitting on a crate. The man rose slowly as she approached him, and the black hood of the robe that draped his entire body fell away revealing golden hair that flowed below his shoulders; his skin was covered in patches of green and brown rot. His studious eyes, however, returned my own gaze with sardonic arrogance and malice. Jezebel took the tall man's arm and led him towards the gate.

"Clear out everyone, and grab the ferret on the way," Jezebel commanded. The strange man that she guided moved slowly and with apparent pain. Though he allowed himself to be led, the aura of black power that shimmered around him told me that he was likely the one in charge of the entire operation.

"Who I am is no concern of yours, ghost," the hag croaked in answer to my question. Power suddenly flared around her, and for the second time this night, I found myself caught in a ghost net. I sighed in exasperation.

"Hmm…you're right," I replied. "I don't need to know your name in order to put you down."

I put more power into my sword and swung the blade at the threads of the ghost net. The blade clanged as it met physical resistance, and then it shattered. I stared in shock at the shards of celestial steel as they fell to the floor and evaporated before my eyes. The crone cackled at me as my arm went momentarily numb.

"I wish I could spend some time with you girl," said the witch as she shambled towards the gate. "You are very interesting. We'll meet again I think."

I saw the last two shifter women carrying a shape between them, and I went cold when I recognized Brianna's still form. I let go of my tether allowing myself to become totally incorporeal. Then, I tried to pass through the net. The thing wasn't called a ghost net for nothing though, and this one was particularly nasty. It had tendrils of black energy that I'd never seen in such a trap. Upon contact with the net, my very soul was assailed by such powerful nightmare visions that it felt as if I should surely die of fright on the spot. The warm place at my heart where the siren's song is fueled reacted to my deadly plight by filling my mind with a song that countered the vile madness that was engulfing me. With a strangled scream of effort, I pulled myself away from the net's touch and panted heavily as I tried to control the panic that threatened to overwhelm me. I was completely trapped and powerless to help Brianna.

Just as the shifters reached the gate however, I saw Brianna twitch, and then she shrank. Her captors were left holding a mostly empty catsuit and a squirming ferret. Before either woman could recover from their surprise, Brianna disentangled herself from the clothing, bit one of the women holding her, and leaped to the ground when her captor reflexively let go of her.

"Let her go," ordered the old witch, pushing the shifters

towards the gate and following on their heels. She turned back to face me once she'd crossed into the forest beyond. She cackled and waved a hand over the portal, and it winked out of existence. As soon as the gate vanished, the ghost net holding me collapsed; its master was apparently too far away now to keep it active. I heard footsteps coming down the corridor behind me, and a moment later Nathaniel appeared in the opening behind me. Frank was at his back trying to peer into the room over the wizard's shoulder.

"You're too late," I told them. "They escaped."

"Brianna?" Frank asked in a trembling voice, and the ferret skittered across the floor to them and chittered indignantly. "Oh…there you are," the detective said with evident relief. "What's wrong?"

"I think she's pissed because they stole her clothes," I answered.

"Where did they go?" asked Nathaniel striding into the room and looking around.

"They went through a portal, into a forest," I answered. "There was a powerful old witch who used what I'm guessing was chaos magic. She put this nasty ghost net around me, and when I tried to cut through it like I did with yours, the fucking threads shattered my katana. There was also this yellow haired guy with them; he looked sort of like a zombie, but his aura was stronger than the witch's. About a dozen of those hyena bitches were here too, led by a woman named Jezebel. They carried a couple dozen of those crates over there through the portal that led into the forest that I mentioned."

Carter looked grim as he surveyed the room and finally went over to one of the crates. He studied the outer shell of several of the big boxes before choosing one to open. Frank moved over to assist, and within a few moments they'd pulled one open. The crate was full of packing material that cushioned several objects that when uncovered proved to be glass jars filled with a blue powdery substance. Each of the jars was marked with a series of numbers scrawled in black ink.

"What the fuck is this shit?"

"It's bad news," answered Nathaniel, his stormy eyes distant for a moment. "I'll have to do a chemical analysis of this stuff, but I think these jars may contain the essential salts."

Frank gaped at the wizard incredulously.

"You don't fucking mean the essential salts from *The Case of Charles Dexter Ward* do you?"

"I do indeed."

"Who's Charles Dexter Ward?" I asked in confusion. I wasn't aware of the pair of them having worked together on a case before.

"Haven't you ever read any fucking Lovecraft?" asked Frank turning to me in exasperation. "Don't they teach anything in school anymore?"

"I've heard of him," I answered defensively. "Isn't he one of the authors that influenced Stephan King?"

"He is," Nathaniel answered before Frank could. "He was much more than a writer though. He was a seer and a prophet which means the things he wrote about are real."

"Fuck me!" swore Frank. "All of his protagonists go insane! Is that what's in fucking store for us?"

"Not all of them," corrected the wizard, his eyes flashing with lightning. "My grandfather, John Carter, survived well enough without going mad. Now let's get out of here before more trouble comes."

As if to punctuate his words a flapping of wings announced Sebastian's arrival. The white ghost owl flew down through the ceiling and alighted on my outstretched hand.

"Vampires are coming. Lots of them," he said without preamble.

Nathaniel went to the center of the room, muttered something and waved his hands in a slashing motion. A golden aura surrounded him for a moment, and then a portal opened up revealing a cozy, fire lit room beyond.

"Help me with the crates Frank, we don't have much time."

Frank stared at the portal for a moment, shook his head and set about helping the wizard move the crates into the distant room. The work got done quickly, but even so they had barely finished moving the last one when we heard the sounds of voices in the tunnels beyond the room we were in.

"Time to go," Nathaniel said. Frank picked up Brianna and strode through the gate. Nathaniel waited for me expectantly.

"I've got to return to Limbo for a while," I told him. "My responsibilities as Captain of the Ghost Watch demands that I look into certain matters that have been revealed this night. I will return after I've rested and I've seen to my duties."

"Very well," answered the wizard. "But don't be too long. I've still got questions for you about your activity at City Hall. Look for me at the Grand Lodge. In the meantime, we'll look into things on this side, but be very careful. Where chaos lurks not even the spirits of the dead are safe."

"I will," I told him, mentally making a list of things to look into as soon as I translated back home: There was a traitor in the Ghost Watch, possibly more than one, free souls were vanishing, probably due to the work of a necromancer, and Byberry in Limbo needed to be investigated, darklings were prowling its grounds, and chaos structures had been built on its soil. There were still too many questions to answer, and adding to my rising frustration was the fact that there didn't seem to be enough time to do all the work that would get us those answers. To top it all off, I was bloody tired.

12

I watched Nathaniel Carter pass through the portal, and I sighed heavily as the all too familiar feeling of loneliness returned. My living friends helped me forget that I was all alone, and as the portal closed, I fervently wished that I could stay with them forever. I shook the feeling aside and steeled myself for the work that lay ahead. Vampires suddenly flowed into the room, their bodies moving with inhuman speed and grace. There were three of them, two males and a female, and they saw me immediately. Vampires are creatures of the living world, but the demon in them can both perceive and cause damage to ghosts. Three vampires didn't worry me though. Even without my katana, I still had my banshee wail, but rather than waste my time fighting them, I called the wind to me and flew up through the ceiling where they couldn't easily follow me.

Once I reached the surface, I flew around the compound. There were scores of vampires out, and they were covering up the zombie mess that we'd left in our wake. Flashing police lights in the vicinity of the main gate told me that the PPD had responded to local complaints about the noise coming from the facility grounds. It was likely that the vampire public affairs team was holding the cops at bay by feeding them a heaping plate of bullshit lies. I had no doubt that they would concoct a viable story and send the men and women in blue on their way. I fully expected the headline in the morning's Inquirer to read "Disturbance at Byberry Due to Continued Demolition". The important thing for now, though, was that the situation was contained. Satisfied that the zombies wouldn't spill into the community at large, I turned away from Byberry and sped my way towards Center City. I'd made an agreement with my personal security team that I'd only translate at my haunt in Franklin Square or at Ghost Watch HQ at the Pennsylvania Hospital if at all possible. My guards didn't like me wandering about Limbo without protection. They hated not being able to cover me in the living world as well, but the fact was that no one in shadow Philly could operate half as long here as I could save for a few of the city's other banshees.

A faint light in the East announced the approach of dawn as I landed in the empty courtyard that is the remnant of Benjamin Franklin's old home in modern times. The basement still survives; tourists can visit the courtyard to go down a flight of stairs to view some of the American icon's surviving possessions. I concentrated for a moment, and a wall of mist began to form. Once enough had gathered before me, I stepped into the mist and passed through the veil that separates the living world from Limbo. As the energies of Limbo coursed into me, I immediately felt better. The wall of mist had become a blanket that hung across the cityscape. The courtyard was no longer empty: Franklin's two story colonial home stood as it had two centuries ago. Because Limbo is a place of memory, the stronger and longer lasting a memory is the more likely it is to have a physical representation here. More than being a simple historical site though, Franklin Court is a place of power for me. It is my haunt: my ghostly home where I can rest and recharge.

Movement all around me announced the deployment of my

guard detail as they became aware of my presence. Sebastian landed on my shoulder and watched intently as a short, stocky man with dark eyes and a balding pate stepped forward.

"Glad to see you Captain," he said. "You were out longer than expected, and when we got word that your backup got diverted, we got worried."

"I'm ok, Lieutenant Bird," I told the former PPD detective who now ran my security team. "There was a lot of bad mojo tonight. Sebastian, go tell Melanie that I need to speak to her. Don't tell anyone other than her that I'm back."

After Sebastian hooted in ascent and flew off, quickly disappearing into the mist, I walked to the front door of my haunt and willed the celestial steel portal to swing open. As far as I know, I'm the only one in Limbo who can command celestial steel with just a thought. It's a gift from God. It has to be, considering how often the ability has saved my ghostly life. I followed Bird and two other members of the detail into the house, then I closed the door behind us, leaving the rest of the guards outside to patrol the grounds.

I went straight for the basement where my own personal armory was stashed. The basement door was made of celestial steel, and the rooms below had been stuffed with piles of raw celestial steel ore the first time I'd come here. Along with the ore there had been a cryptic message written in celestial steel on the wall of the furthest chamber; it had warned of a coming apocalypse and had been signed by "BF". A fact unknown to the average American is that Franklin was one of the most powerful wizards to have walked the planet. According to my sources, Franklin had been on par with Merlin on the power scale. Franklin had seeded the city with magical wards, guardians, and who knows what other surprises, many of which had been a thorn in the side of Philly's old masters. These magical artifacts had been pivotal in helping the free souls of Philly win freedom from the Master. His gift to me was the ore which I'd turned into weapons and armor. I'd given most of that arsenal away to help the city's defenses, but I'd kept a reserve for myself. On the back wall of the last room in the basement now hung a celestial steel rack with half a dozen katanas and other oriental style weapons. I retrieved a katana and then went back upstairs to rest on my celestial steel bed. Aside from making a useful weapon, the ore itself has healing and restorative powers; it's why I require my banshee sisters to wear celestial steel jewelry: it helps keep their madness at bay.

As I rested, I thought about the message that Franklin had left behind. Could this business with the forces of chaos be what he'd been warning about? Coming from a Judeo-Christian background, my mind had immediately assumed that the enemy that would bring us the apocalypse was Satan and his demonic horde. I'd assumed that the book of Revelations would hold answers to what was coming and maybe provide clues on how to stop it or at least mitigate its effects. If Nathaniel was correct though, I should have been reading HP Lovecraft instead. The idea that my Christian upbringing could be wrong troubled me, and I made a mental note to talk the matter over with Jonus. Jonus was the Marshal of Philadelphia's army, and he was also a luminary: an angelic ghost with the power of heaven at his fingertips. I'd rescued him from slavery aboard a celestial steel train used to transport shades from Philadelphia to the Devil's Forge in Centralia, and since then he'd helped me win the battle for Shadow Philly and become my best friend in Limbo and a great advisor. Being very wise and knowledgeable, he'd taught me most of what I know about unlife and Limbo. My previous instructor, Delilah, had also played an important part in teaching me, though on the opposite end of the spectrum; I'd learned living world operations from her, but much of her tutelage had been full of propaganda and outright lies.

A flapping of wings informed me that Sebastian had returned. He would enter the house through the chimney, which I'd left free of celestial steel mesh for the exact purpose of giving the owl access to the house. No one else could enter without my assistance. Well, that's not entirely true. Plenty of ghosts could break in; busting through celestial steel meshing would take a lot of effort, but it could be done. I sat up, feeling about fifty percent restored, which was quite a bit more power than any five average ghosts have at their combined disposal.

"She's on her way," reported Sebastian coming to a perch on the windowsill of my room.

I nodded and went into the kitchen where there was a table and several chairs all made of celestial steel. Detective Bird waited for me there while the two other guards stood sentry at the front door. I seated myself and waited patiently for the knock that came roughly two minutes after Sebastian made his announcement. Not bothering to leave my seat in the kitchen, I willed the front door to open. I counted to five and willed the door to close again. Melanie Baker, my second in command, entered the room. She looked haggard. She'd been the oldest of the Tormentor's victims and had been a beautiful mother of three children before her death. Melanie was my most loyal and trusted friend outside of Jonus.

"I'm sorry Veronika," she said. There was pleading in her voice as she crossed the room and knelt at my feet. "I didn't want to leave you without backup, but we got a call in from HQ. More than a score of free souls vanished last night, and we busted up another devil's iron smuggling operation. Did everything go ok with the shifters?"

"No," I said, seething with sudden anger. The Cartel again! "The mission was mostly a failure. We found the missing shifters, but they'd already been brutally murdered. In the process of the investigation, we stumbled upon a plot that's threads are complex and deadly. It may be that many of our recent problems are connected. Get up Melanie, I'm not mad at you. You followed procedure as we laid it down. The fault is with the one who used it against us. Who was the watch commander last night?"

"Rebecca Stern," Melanie answered rising to her feet with a concerned look in her eyes. "What's going on?"

"I need you to summon the entire Ghost Watch," I said without answering her question. "Everyone. Recall all field teams. No exceptions are to be granted. Anyone who fails to obey will be hunted down as a deserter under article five. Everyone is to gather in the auditorium in one hour."

"You're invoking an article five?" Melanie stared at me in shock. Detective Bird was suddenly very alert. "What do we tell the other services?"

"Send word to the Governor and army. Inform them that we are holding a drill," I answered grimly. "We'll resume our duties within two hours."

Melanie stared at me for a moment longer then stood straighter, determination giving her purpose.

"I assume deadly force is to be used if anyone fails to comply or acts in a suspicious way?"

"Yes," I nodded unhappily. "Where's Reverend Creed?"

"I'm…sorry, Veronika", Melanie stammered. "He was released an hour after you translated. Rebecca Stern was senior officer at HQ when the magisterial order came. She claims that she had no choice but to uphold the lawful authority of the court."

I nodded my understanding, not at all surprised by this turn of events. Melanie waved a goodbye and departed. I willed the front door open once more, leaving it that way an extra minute while I gathered up my own gear and headed out in Melanie's wake.

"Off to HQ," said detective Bird to the security detail as we exited the house. The door closed behind us.

"We'll be stopping at the Walnut Room first," I said, taking the lead. Lieutenant Bird looked surprised, but he didn't argue with me. It was a quality that I really liked about him.

13

THE WALNUT ROOM IS A lounge in Philadelphia's Rittenhouse neighborhood located among the posh boutiques and erudite eateries of Walnut Street. The lounge isn't a place that you find accidently; you really have to know what you're looking for. It is located on the second floor of a quaint cafe called the Buttercup Bakery and is only accessed via an unmarked door in an alley-way between the bakery and another shop. The place has a good reputation as a solid example of Philadelphia's vibrant nightlife. It's also one of the few bars that isn't owned or frequented by vampires or some other preternatural being.

The Walnut Room is also Amber Morgan's haunt. Amber is the youngest of the city's banshees; she was only fifteen when she was tortured to death. Of all of my sister banshees, I was proudest of Amber. She had unleashed her full potential and become the most powerful siren in the city, surpassing even my own abilities with the siren's song. The power of her voice had given her purpose, and she had unlocked the gift in many other ghosts. Because of her efforts, shadow Philly had a score of lounges where ghosts could go for entertainment. Being a ghost is very lonely. Regret and anger are constant companions while daily life is relatively boring, often meaningless, and seemingly unending. To combat this, the Assembly had passed laws requiring all citizens to join one of the city's service organizations: army, Ghost Watch, or a government agency. The law was intended to give structure to our city and provided jobs for ghosts who would otherwise have nothing to do but wallow in their misery. Forgers and sirens were the only two groups of citizens who were exempt from joining a service organization. Their time was considered too valuable to waste on common activities that any other ghost could do. Sirens and forgers were expected to open their own shops and lounges in order to sell their services to the community at large. Even they, however, had to serve the greater good and could be compelled to provide their services to any organization that legitimately needed it. The siren lounges were especially popular as the ghosts of the city were able to relax with friends after a day's work.

A twinge of panic hit me as I stepped into the alley leading to the Walnut Room. I hate alleys, mostly because I was murdered in one. I don't feel claustrophobic or anything like that; I just get a really bad feeling and memories of being trapped fill me with dread. Today, I ignored the unsettling feeling and strode towards the two ghosts guarding the entrance to the bar.

"I need to speak to Amber," I said as one of the guards stepped in front of the non-descript door.

"Let her go Peter," said the second guard who continued to lean against the wall unconcernedly. "Welcome to the Siren's Den Captain Kane. You won't need your whole contingent up there; take whoever you want, but I assure you it's secure."

Detective Bird stiffened when I told him to remain behind with the rest of the team, but he didn't argue. We are among friends here, my eyes told him before I went on up by myself. The Siren's Den is what the city's denizens had come to call the Walnut Room. Amber herself was known as The Siren and was the most loved of all the city's citizens. The girl was shy and humble though and hadn't allowed all the attention to go to her head. She was also fiercely private and her guards were very firm about preserving it.

I passed the guards, opened the door, and went up the stairs pausing at a second door at the top. I put my hand through the door till I encountered the celestial steel mesh that I'd personally placed there. Satisfied that the barrier was still intact, I withdrew my hand and knocked on the door. Most things in Limbo don't have a physical presence, but they act the way we expect them to anyways. Ghosts can generally pass through any objects other than celestial steel or devil's iron, but if we treat an object the way we think it is supposed to be treated, then the object will respond in kind. So though I can put my hand through the door, I can also knock on it without my hand passing through it, and the expected noise and vibration occurs as it would in the living world. It just requires a little concentration to do.

The door opened revealing a large room full of celestial steel tables, chairs, a massive bar, chandeliers, and a stage. Two huge wall to ceiling windows dominated the front of the room, giving customers a picturesque view of Walnut street, at least what you could see of it through the ever present mists of Limbo. Amber stood at the door, her dimpled smile welcoming me. She was a petite girl with a gymnast's body. Her eyes were green and her hair auburn.

"Hi Veronika," she greeted me. "Come in."

I smiled my thanks and entered the lounge. She closed the door behind me, and we hugged and then she led me to a table overlooking Walnut Street.

"I wish this was a social call," I said. "But it's not. I need your help. I think the city is in great danger."

I quickly told her about everything that had happened earlier in the evening, and in particular about my fear that our enemies might be using some kind of soul camouflage to mask their presence among us. Amber listened intently and nodded with understanding when I'd finished.

"You're hoping that the siren's song can cut through their disguises."

"Yes. I've enacted an Article Five. The entire Ghost Watch will be assembled in the HQ auditorium. I think we should start with our own security detail before we move onto the Watch."

Amber nodded, and ten minutes later both of our twenty man details were assembled in the Walnut Room's main hall. Amber began to sing "*I Would Do Anything for Love*" by Meat Loaf; her hauntingly beautiful voice filling the room with waves of power that made you want to worship her. Amber's audience was immediately and totally dominated. Besides myself, only Amber could completely charm hundreds of the most powerful of ghosts, but though my siren's song matched hers in raw power, her control of the ability far surpassed my own. She had the ability to elicit any emotion that she desired from her audience, and she could exercise complete control over them if she wished to. The Assembly had tried to limit the use of the siren's song through legislation. They feared the siren's controlling influence, and it's power was deemed dangerous to freedom. Amber's legion of fans had descended on Independence Mall in the first mass demonstration against the Assembly's legislation. The governor had asked me to speak to Amber, and the ghost teen had agreed to take full responsibility for all of the city's sirens. She'd established an academy and a licensing system with regulations and a code of ethical conduct. Under the rules, no siren could use her abilities unless licensed. If the code was broken by a siren, her license was revoked, and if the offense was great enough the Ghost Watch's Siren Squad would be called in. Under the agreement with Amber, a squad of sirens had to be provided to both the Ghost Watch and the Army in order to help deal with situations much like our current one.

Today, Amber was eliciting emotions of honesty and truth. In particular, those who meant harm to the city in any way or who were subverting its laws should make their confessions to Captain Kane immediately. The compulsion was carried on her voice and presented in mental images that were irresistible to the average listener. By the time Amber had reached the beginning of the second verse, three ghosts were standing before me, confessing their sins. One guard was from my unit, a free soul named Terrance Small; he'd been a Vietnam vet in life. He'd committed suicide when he'd come home and found himself unable to cope with what he'd seen and done overseas. The ghost that wore his guise revealed himself to be a darkling named Daniel Webb from Trenton. He and a team of darklings had murdered the real Terrance more than a week ago according to Daniel. Under further questioning, I found that Daniel didn't know where his fellow team members had gone, but he reported regularly to Sergeant Rebecca Stern of the Ghost Watch. The other two ghosts that came forward were members of Amber's team and both confessed to being members of the Styx Cartel. These last confessions struck me harder than the darkling infiltration did. The fact that free souls with respected positions would risk everything to join a traitorous secret society bothered me immensely. A thorough search of the three ghosts revealed that they all had the Styx Cartel discs somehow embedded into their ghostly bodies, though the darkling's was in the palm of his hand rather than his chest like the cartel's acolytes. The palm disc was smaller and easily removed which, when accomplished, removed the soul cloak that disguised the darkling's nature.

Once I was certain that I'd learned everything I could from Daniel, which included his mission goal to assassinate me at some opportune time, I drew my katana and without ceremony removed his head with a single smooth swing. I know it's pretty damn harsh to just kill someone on the spot like that, but we're at war with the darklings. We don't compromise with them; they're outlawed in Philadelphia on pain of immediate execution, and the son of a bitch had participated in the murder of one of my personal guards, and he'd also been planning to murder me. Amber brought her song to a close when she saw that I'd dealt with the darkling. All that remained of him was quickly dissipating into mist leaving no evidence that he had ever existed. The two Cartel cultists we bound with celestial steel manacles and took them with us as we departed for Ghost Watch HQ. We had to get there as quickly as possible to purge it of darklings before whatever plot they were planning could be set fully into motion.

As Amber and I left the Walnut Room, I whistled and Sebastian flew down to land on my shoulder.

"Go tell Jonus that I need him to meet me at HQ as soon as he can," I told the owl. "Also tell him to put a cordon around Byberry Hospital, but warn him to keep his troops off of the facility grounds. Tell him to treat it like a quarantine zone."

Sebastian hooted and flew off. I turned to Amber.

"I think we're going to need all of your licensed sirens to purge this infiltration."

Amber nodded grimly, and a sharp whistle from her brought the sounds of wings to us once more. What emerged from the mists wasn't an owl, however; it was a squat, red eyed gargoyle that you'd expect to see decorating the edifice of a gothic cathedral. That was exactly where it had come from. The former masters of the city had leashed the spirits of animals to stone statues throughout the city and used them as guardians and spies. This gargoyle had attacked us during the Battle of Philadelphia, but Amber and I had tamed it and others with our siren's songs.

"Rex," Amber said to the creature as it hovered before her. "Call out the sirens, the city is in danger. All the apprentices are to report to the academy and remain there until the danger has passed."

Rex growled in ascent and flew off to do his mistress's bidding. We continued our journey towards HQ in grim silence. We all knew that the enemy would attack sooner or later, we just hadn't expected them to be so subtle. Was this going to be the first act in a second battle of Philadelphia? The dread that had been building in the pit of my stomach since my little jaunt to the black city left me feeling that there was a lot more at stake than just shadow Philly this time around. I had a sneaking suspicion that the real threat was on the other side of the veil and that whatever went on here was just meant to distract us from the true threat. Even if that were true though, this threat was dangerous enough that if not dealt with it could topple our regime. Then it hit me: this was all about sowing chaos.

14

GHOST WATCH HQ IS LOCATED at the corner of Pine and Eighth Streets in America's oldest hospital. The Pennsylvania Hospital was founded by Benjamin Franklin and Doctor Thomas Bond in 1751. Amazingly, it is still operating today and continues to be one of the top hospitals in the country. Many ghosts had looked at me askance when I'd chosen it as the HQ for the Ghost Watch, but I had my reasons. Chief among them was the fact that Franklin had been involved in its creation, and such places were feared by Philly's enemies. Secondly, it was a stark reminder of what we were fighting for. Lives were being lost and saved in this group of buildings every day, and the Ghost Watch would be there to harvest those that died and rejoice for the saved. The modern hospital is also renowned for its maternity ward: a sight that I wanted my people to be constantly reminded of. We were fighting for the living. Our purpose in death was to protect humanity from the monsters that prey on them, and to make sure that people who died and passed into Limbo would have good guidance. Every member of the Ghost Watch must repeat the hospital motto "Take care of him, and I will repay thee" during their swearing in ceremony. The words are engraved on the hospital seal and have their origin in the parable of the Good Samaritan found in the Bible, and they echo exactly what the Ghost Watch stands for.

The oldest part of the Pennsylvania hospital is the East wing on the corner of Pine and Eighth, while the West wing was erected soon after and occupies the corner of Pine and seventh streets. The center building, called the Great Court, was built in the early eighteen hundreds and is where most of the Ghost Watch has its offices including the duty room where assignments are handed out.

I led Amber and company through the Northgate, passing under the eaves of the Treaty Elm and entered the Preston Welcome Center. This is the modern day reception entrance for the facility. It features a gift shop, cafeteria, and the Zubrow Auditorium. Baron, my own gargoyle friend, was waiting for me just inside the gate. The ten foot tall stone creature that had once been a dog grabbed me in a hug of welcome and danced about in glee.

"Whoa boy!" I laughed. "Put me down before you squish me to death. I'm happy to see you too."

The gargoyle put me down with a chagrined look plastered on his stony face. I laughed at him and gave him another hug.

"Its ok Baron, but we've got some serious work to do now. Are you ready?"

Baron growled menacingly and fell in behind Amber and myself. Both our guards wisely gave way to the huge stone monster. We strode into the Welcome Center where Melanie and Rebecca waited for us.

"An Article Five, Veronika?" Rebecca said with a sneer. The woman was of medium height and build, with stringy brown hair, and a face like a bulldog. She had acquitted herself well in the Battle of Philadelphia and had proved to be a competent leader, though she was somewhat too ambitious for my tastes.

"What's this all about? The governor isn't going to be happy when she finds out that you've gotten the city in a stir for no good reason."

"Baron, seize that woman," I said pointing at Rebecca. It was very possible that the darkling Daniel had lied about reporting to Rebecca, but I was confident in Amber's power. "You can snap her neck if she says another word without my permission."

Rebecca Stern's eyes went wide, and she tried to back away, but Baron leaped over us and grabbed the Sergeant before she'd moved more than three steps. He yanked her off her feet and growled in her face, showing her his huge pointed stone fangs. Sergeant Stern went still and fear shown in her eyes.

"What you did at the Walnut Room was perfect Amber. We might as well weed out all the troublemakers while we're at it."

Amber nodded in agreement and began to sing the moment I pulled the door to the auditorium open. She began with "*Don't Know Why*" by Norah Jones; her voice burst into the noisy auditorium before anyone saw her. The place went instantly still. Amber went up onto the stage, her guards encircling her as she went. I stayed with Baron and my own guard at the foot of the stage waiting for the first confessors to come forward. It wasn't a long wait, and my heart sank as two score out of nearly three hundred agents came forward. As had happened at the Walnut Room, the majority of the confessors proved to be acolytes of the Styx Cartel involved in the smuggling of devil's iron. Six confessors identified themselves as darklings, and two claimed to be free souls though they admitted to working for a foreign power.

I turned to the Sergeant and ordered the enraptured Baron to put her down and let her speak. The gargoyle did this gladly and went back to mooning over Amber. The gargoyle was a sucker for a pretty voice.

"Who do you serve Rebecca? What have you been up too?"

"I serve the Crawling Chaos" she answered, voice devoid of emotion.

"What the hell is that?" I asked terrified of what the answer would be.

"He is Azathoth's avatar."

My bloodless body went cold at the mention of that name; it was the second time I'd heard it this day.

"Where is this Crawling Chaos," I asked.

"I don't know."

I stared at the woman in frustration.

"Are you a darkling Rebecca?"

"No."

"How can you serve evil and not be a darkling?"

"I don't serve evil," came the wooden reply. "I serve myself. I serve chaos. Only through anarchy can we truly be saved. Law is a tool used by evil to control what it doesn't understand."

"Who do you report too?" I asked with exasperation. I drew my katana, ready to strike the offending ghost down if I didn't get a straight answer.

"Delilah."

"Delilah Mourne?" I spluttered. Red hot hatred surged in me at the thought of my old nemesis.

"Yes."

Damn! Delilah had promised to wreak vengeance on me for my betrayal of her. Would she really have gone to the lengths of selling herself to chaos in order to achieve that goal? I knew without doubt that she would. Her heart was as black as any beings, and my victory over her master nine months ago would only have added to the hate that burned within her soul.

"Where is she?"

"I don't know."

"Where do you make your reports?"

"Delilah finds me when she wants one."

That was all I needed to know. Delilah was a trained and cunning agent. She'd covered her trail as best as she could. I checked the traitor for any signs of the Cartel discs implanted in her body, but there was none. Rebecca being of no more use,

I executed her with a single slice of my katana, sending her head flying to dissipate into mist. Amber continued to sing while I moved on to interrogate the darklings. They all admitted that they were under Delilah's command, but none of them knew where to find her or anything about a Crawling Chaos. The acolytes of the Cartel, however, did know about this entity and admitted to being members of a splinter cult within the Styx Cartel. The cultists called themselves the Scions of Twilight and were led by none other than Reverend Creed. The cultists claimed that the cult had more than a hundred followers in the city and that smuggling devil's iron and something called mania stone was part of their mission to bring chaos to the city. Further questioning revealed that mania stone was a black stone often having red flecks or green striations in it. According to the cultists, touching the stone produced hallucinations and psychic breakdowns. The mania stone was being used in some large scale construction projects, but none of the cultists knew where or for what purpose. The cartel discs that each cultist wore seemed to provide some resistance to Amber's song for no information about the whereabouts of Creed, the cult's safe houses, or what living world operations were in progress could be pried from them. Cutting the discs out of the cultists resulted in immediate destruction as an inky black substance was released from the black edges of the artifacts. The ooze seemed to devour the ghosts where they stood. Removing the smaller discs from the darkling's palms on the other hand only resulted in their true natures being revealed.

Once the questioning was done, I executed the darklings and gave strict orders that the remaining cultists be put into our most secure holding cells. They were to be kept apart from each other and have no contact with anyone. I wanted to execute them all on the spot as well but didn't have the legal authority to do so. As for the foreign spies, we would send them to the governor for her judgment. Amber brought her singing to an end, and I ordered everyone else in the auditorium to stay put until

I'd consulted with Amber, Melanie, and Danielle privately. The four of us went into a nearby conference room where I briefly summarized what I'd learned from the interrogations.

"Even more alarming is the fact that three of us banshees had darklings in our guard contingents. I think Delilah is going to try to take us all out in one fell swoop."

"Oh my God!" whispered Danielle in shock. "What do we do?"

"We've probably uncovered this plot before they expected us to," I answered. "They'll have to act before they wanted, but Delilah isn't just a crafty bitch. She's decisive and will act as soon as she realizes we're onto her."

"We'll deploy Watch units accompanied by sirens to every high value target in the city at once," Melanie said. "The rest of our people will begin a grid search for both cultists and darklings. You can request that the Governor declare a state of emergency, and the army will lock the city down and help us with the search."

"Good," I told Melanie. "You and Danielle organize the effort here. Amber and I will go to the Governor and secure her and Bridget. I've already sent a message to Jonus, and I'm sure the Governor will sign off on the order of emergency."

We ended the meeting and headed off to our assignments. As Amber and I led our guard retinues towards the HQ exit, we were met by High Marshal of the army Jonus who was just arriving with his own retinue. Jonus is a creature of pure beauty, bathed in an angelic light that makes his blue eyes and handsome features even more appealing. At the moment however, he looked angry.

"Veronika, what in the name of God is going on? There are strange new structures on the Byberry property. I've locked it down and left Quinn in command there, but something really feels wrong there."

Amber began to hum as I gave Jonus a quick update on what we'd learned. The luminary was unaffected by the siren's song, but the rest of our retinues were enraptured and unable to follow our discussion. When I finished explaining the situation to him, Jonus asked Amber to check his team for possible threats. Two of his guards proved to be darklings, and Jonus dispatched them himself after confirming that they worked for Delilah. Once the unpleasant duty was over, we headed straight for the Governor's office in Old City Hall.

15

THE ATTACK CAME WITHOUT WARNING and with such a brutal ferocity that it left us momentarily stunned. We were on Sixth Street heading North through Washington Square when a dozen reapers and two score darklings seemed to materialize out of thin air. The mists of Limbo were fairly thick once more, having been replenished since I'd used it all up during the Battle of Philadelphia, but even with the cover of the mists a force of this size shouldn't have been able to penetrate this deeply into the city without raising the alarm. An ominous and familiar sound of peeling bells shook the city as the enemy struck.

The free soul guards surrounding myself, Amber, and Jonus were among the finest soldiers in the ranks of Philly's army, but five of them fighting in concert were no match for a single reaper. I hadn't ever seen so many reapers in one place, not even during the Battle of Philadelphia. The tall skeletal ghosts wore hooded black robes and twin points of fire glowed in the empty eye sockets of their skulls. All of the darklings and reapers carried swords made of a black alloy instead of their usual devil's iron weapons. The speed that the reapers moved at was too much for our free soul guards, and a dozen of them were cut down in the first seconds of the assault before we even had a chance to draw our own weapons.

The reapers came directly for Amber, Jonus, and me; anyone who stood in their way went down. Too many of our guards went down at the mere touch of those terrible black blades. Normally, ghosts can take incredible amounts of punishment before falling apart into oblivion. Now however, half a dozen souls lay on the ground screaming and thrashing about wildly like dying snakes. The reapers did encounter one obstacle that wasn't so easily moved however. Baron roared in challenge and met the first two reapers to break through our screen of guards. The reapers used their superior speed to their advantage, striking the massive gargoyle several times, but their blades simply bounced off of his stone hide, and the madness that seemed to affect the free souls at the merest touch of the black blades had no affect on the gargoyle. One of Baron's massive arms suddenly lashed out, and one of the reapers found itself clutched by the throat. Baron flexed his hand and a cracking sound was followed by the creature's head popping off its shoulders like the cork in a Champaign bottle. The gargoyle tossed the body into its oncoming companions, though it dissolved into mist before it could trip them up.

Amber began to sing, and her melodious voice locked down the darklings before they could do much damage with their black bolts. That left Jonus, Baron, and myself with only the reapers to deal with as the siren's song had no affect against them. A beam of white light shot forth from Jonus's outstretched hand, catching a charging reaper in the chest. It stopped, momentarily stunned, then began to scream as white flame began to consume it from the inside out. I called on the wind for speed and leaped to attack, my katana and short sword dancing through the air in blinding arcs and thrusts that left one reaper without a sword arm while another's skull shattered into a thousand pieces as I shoved my celestial steel blade through one of its eye sockets. Once I'd danced my way clear of free soul guards, I let loose with my banshee wail catching three reapers in its sonic blast and annihilating them in a single heartbeat. Baron was at my back, keeping the remaining reapers off of me.

The remainder of the battle was a blur; Baron and I worked together, aggressively taking the fight to the reapers while Amber continued to lock down the darklings with her singing, and Jonus covered her back and blasted reapers with beams of holy light. Finally, after two minutes of intense, hard fighting, the ominous ringing of bells stopped, and the remaining two reapers withdrew from the battlefield leaving their mesmerized underlings under Amber's control. In all, out of fifty four guards, we lost thirty one with my own unit having suffered the worst losses. We didn't bother questioning the darklings; we slew them without mercy and headed straight for the Governor's office in Old City Hall.

Independence Square is the center of government on this side of the veil, and it was in chaos when we arrived. Free soul soldiers encircled the square, keeping everyone out. Jonus and I were allowed through of course, but the Marshal had to pull rank before Amber was allowed to accompany us. The square itself was mostly an open yard with some trees and a statue of Commodore John Barry, father of the US Navy, stationed at an intersection of paths. It was here in this square that the Declaration of Independence was first read to the public. The Northern end of the square is dominated by four grand structures; Independence Hall, Old City Hall, Congress Hall, and Philosophical Hall. Independence Hall is where the United States was born and is where the ghost Assembly meets. It's a brick structure built in the Georgian style and is dominated by the famed bell tower and steeple. Old City Hall is a brick box of a building that lies to the East of Independence Hall, and it is the current office space used by the Governor and Army Command. It was to this building that we now headed.

My ghostly heart thudded as we witnessed the chaos continue unabated. Though there were many soldiers around, there were very few commanding officers to be seen.

We pushed our way into Old City Hall and finally reached the Governor's office on the second floor. Everything seemed quiet here, though the guards were tense. We were immediately passed into the main office where we found Governor Rachel and Speaker Jully locked in quiet conversation. Governor Rachel was a radiant luminary while the Speaker was a free soul; both were beautiful, strong, and competent leaders that I respected.

"Thank the Lord you're alright Marshal Jonus," said the Governor coming to her feet as soon as we entered. "You too Captain Kane. I'm declaring a state of emergency, effective immediately. We have come under attack in the most cowardly and vile way imaginable. Reports are very sketchy at this point, but I'm hoping one or both of you can tell me how reapers and darklings were able to penetrate our security without raising the alarm."

"I'm glad to see you safe as well Governor," Jonus said. "Veronika uncovered the plot just a few hours ago. Unfortunately, the enemy seems to have been further along in their plans than we'd hoped."

The Governor turned her blue eyed gaze on me, and I began giving her the details of everything that had happened to me during and since the Byberry operation in living Philly. Half way through my retelling, Bridget entered the room looking more angry than usual, and the Governor interrupted me to ask the captain of her guard for a full report.

"They took out at least twenty three members of the Assembly including Sonya Taylor. A member of her own guard assassinated her."

The room fell into a shocked silence. Sonya Taylor was one of Philadelphia's ten banshees. Besides losing a valued member of the city's legislative body, we'd lost one of our most formidable weapons. More heart wrenching for me though was the knowledge that I'd lost a sister.

"Marshal Jonus will have to confirm this, but from the slim reports that I have received so far, most of his officer corps was wiped out," Bridget continued. "Among your personal guard Governor, we lost eight including four traitors among them."

"Thank you Captain Bridget," the Governor said heavily. "If it hadn't been for your swift actions during the initial assault, the city would have been short two banshees and a governor. Jonus, I'm sure Veronika has filled you in on everything you need to know for the moment. Go assess the damage to the army and plug the holes as best you can. Send scouts out to be sure we aren't facing eminent invasion. Captain Kane, you may proceed."

Jonus saluted the Governor and departed while I resumed my story. Both the Governor and Speaker occasionally interrupted me in order to ask questions while Bridget listened intently without saying a word, but her eyes betrayed the furnace of rage that burned within her.

"This is a strange picture you paint for us," the Governor interjected when I'd finished reporting the full story. "I've never heard of this Azathoth nor the Crawling Chaos. News that there may be a cult among the free souls is incredibly disturbing though. The Ghost Watch will have to make that a priority investigation. We've seen the effects of the mania alloy during the attack and how devastating it is to our soldiers. I want Reverend Creed and all members of the Cartel arrested. The Ghost Watch has authority under the state of emergency order to search everyone within the city's borders for signs of collaboration with the cult. These discs they imbed into their bodies should make them easy to find."

"Indeed. We'll have to add the black ore, what did you call it? Mania stone? To the list of outlawed substances," the Speaker added. She was a pretty, petit blond who had served as my aid de camp during the Battle of Philadelphia. "You'll need to give the Assembly a full report on this business. Maybe we can kill this movement to legalize devil's iron once and for all by laying the blame for this attack on the Cartel. Reverend Creed has a lot of friends in the Assembly, and they won't be happy with your orders Governor."

"Amber," the Governor said. "Can you provide a siren for each of the banshees guard details? It seems you are our best defense against these soul camouflages. We'll also need some sirens for the Assembly and other important assets."

"Including the Governor," Bridget chimed in.

"This will put a significant strain on my people," said Amber with a worried frown. "Most of them despise government and want nothing to do with politics or military stuff."

"I know Amber," said the Governor with a sigh of her own. "It's always been the way of things that artists create while warriors and politicians spend and destroy. I wish we could do this without you, but our very survival may depend on you."

"I understand Governor," Amber replied gravely. "My people are good. They will respond to the city's need. I should go attend to these matters if you don't need me anymore."

"Of course dear," the Governor said with an affectionate smile. "Bridget, will you see to it that Amber returns to her haunt safely?"

Bridget nodded reluctantly and led Amber out of the office. I poked my head out for a moment to ask Baron if he'd go along to make sure that Amber got home safely. The huge gargoyle barked in ascent, and I watched the trio disappear down the hall.

I closed the door behind me and turned to face the Governor and Speaker.

"So, you know Delilah better than any of us," the Governor said. "What is her next move? What is she up too?"

I thought about the question for a full minute before I answered.

"Delilah is a follower. She's extremely competent and cunning, but only as far as her master's goals allow. She isn't particularly creative, but she'll use every tool at her disposal. If my suspicions are correct and Sergeant Stern's information is right, then Delilah has changed teams and now follows Azathoth. Her orders will almost certainly include causing chaos with the ultimate goal of tearing the veil between Limbo and the outer chaos. How she can accomplish this I'm not sure, but I believe that the new buildings at Byberry are an important part of the plan. The cultists told me that they were using the mania stone to build several structures in the city. What purpose these structures serve I don't know, but having been near one myself, I don't think it's good for the city. It's my opinion that the wizard Nathaniel Carter may be our best hope for spoiling Delilah's plans."

"We've always been warned to stay away from wizards," said the Governor; the Speaker also nodded her head in agreement. "But like so much we were told by the previous regime, we must hold this advice in doubt. We are sailing through uncharted waters here, and it seems the wizard may know these seas better than we. I know that we made you the Captain of the Ghost Watch Veronika, and you have excelled at it, but you are also the city's best field agent, particularly in living world operations. We need you to investigate this matter and do everything in your power to prevent the success of our enemies' plans. Melanie and Danielle will jointly command the Ghost Watch until you are finished with this assignment. All of the city's resources are at your disposal."

I nodded excitedly. I really hated all this talking and politicking; I was a woman of action and long meetings bored me. The chance to work with Nathaniel especially excited me in a way that shouldn't have been possible for a ghost. Nathaniel thrilled me; he was alive and yet he could touch me. He was powerful, mysterious, and full of answers that could save the city. Being demoted to field agent was ok with me under the circumstances. I thanked the two leaders and headed for the door.

"And Veronika," the Governor called after me. "I'm giving you a direct order to retire to your haunt so that you can rest for a full cycle before you begin your mission. There is no room for sloppiness in the coming days. You have fought in several battles today and traveled to an unknown place of power. You need to recover your strength."

I nodded reluctantly and left the room before they could give me any more orders.

16

I SLEPT FOR NEARLY FIVE HOURS, which is a relatively short span for a ghost of my power. Typically, most ghosts need eight to twelve hours of rest to fully recharge their strength; the more powerful the ghost the more rest that is required to refill the battery, as it were. I, on the other hand, have never slumbered more than six hours, except when badly wounded. No one had been able to come up with a good theory as to why I was able to break the normal rules; it was just another oddity about me in a long list of them. Once up, I went down into the armory and dressed in full battle gear. Recalling what had happened to my katana yesterday, I grabbed a back-up for each of my blades.

When I was fully equipped, I went back upstairs and gathered my entourage which included Baron and my guards. There were many new faces on the team; I'd met these before going to sleep last night, and we'd all shared in a short ceremony of mourning for our fallen comrades. Now I led the grim group towards Ghost Watch HQ. I found the place mostly deserted except for Melanie, her guards, and a few assisting agents. Melanie eyed me worriedly and gave me a quick report. Scouts had come back from the hinterlands with reports that there was no evidence of imminent invasion from our neighbors. The Governor had also called on our friends, the furies, to keep an eye out for any massing or movement of armies in the wild lands. While our borders were being secured, the Watch had been dispersed throughout the city; most of them were organized into hunting teams looking for darklings and cultists. Amber had come through with the sirens, and now every hunting team, as well as the critical assets like the Assembly and governor's office, had one siren assigned to the guard detail. The army was providing additional security for the sirens, and it was patrolling the streets as well as holding the city's borders. In the time that I'd slept, the entire city had been mobilized. Reverend Creed had vanished without a trace, and there were still no clues as to how the reapers and darklings had entered the city.

"I sent Danielle off to rest an hour ago," Melanie continued. "She'll relieve me in about nine hours. We did have an incident about three hours ago. At least twenty free souls vanished. There were multiple eye witnesses to it. Fifteen of the missing are Ghost Watch agents who were in this very building at the time of the incident. The other missing free souls were taken from the surrounding neighborhood. We mounted a search of the entire area but couldn't find a trace of them."

"Damn it!" I swore, mind racing. "That's the necromancer's work, it has to be. I want you to move HQ to the Philly International. Put the word out to everyone that they should stay as far away from cemeteries as they can until we can shut this necro down."

"Ok," Melanie answered with a dubious look on her face. "That's gonna be a little difficult though."

"I know. The whole freaking city is practically a cemetery, but it's the only advice I have for trying to avoid becoming a victim of the necro. Hopefully the magic requires a ghost to be pretty close to the body being resurrected to work," I said in disgust.

Throughout Philly's early history, people had been buried in parks, church yards, gardens, and even in basement catacombs. Huge cemeteries had been placed at the city's edge only to have the city expanded around them; there was no telling where you might find a grave in the city of brotherly love. Philadelphia was practically a necropolis: a big fat amusement park for a sick necromancer.

"Do what you can, I'm sorry to leave you in such a big mess, but I really think the answers that are alluding us are on the other side," I told Melanie. I gave her a hug. "Watch your back. Better yet, Baron will do it for me, won't you big guy?"

The gargoyle barked his agreement and swept Melanie into his protective arms. I'd asked Baron to send his other gargoyle friends to watch over some of my more vulnerable sisters as well. Amber had her own gargoyles, and Bridget was the one banshee that I didn't worry too much about; in an even up fight, she might be able to take me. I'd also asked Sebastian to stay in Limbo so that he could assist the Ghost Watch. I smiled at Baron, gave Melanie a wave, and left the building. I led my guards to the Treaty Elm and gave Lieutenant Bird orders to wait for me at my haunt. I then translated into living Philly where an overcast sky threatened to weep rain upon the troubled city.

17

I HEADED WEST ON PINE STREET until I reached Broad where I turned North. I would have gotten to my destination much quicker by flying, but I decided that conserving power was more important than speed, at least for now. Even on foot though, it didn't take long before I reached the grand tower of City Hall. Across the street on the corner of Broad and Filbert sprawled the architectural splendor that was The Right Worshipful Grand Lodge of the Most Ancient and Honorable Fraternity of Free Masons of Pennsylvania where I was supposed to find the Grand Master: the wizard Nathaniel Carter. The building had two grand towers and was built in the Norman style with some of its hewn stone and marble coming from as far away as Egypt. The Masons enjoyed a rich history in America, and Philadelphia in particular. Many of the nation's founding fathers had been part of the brotherhood, including George Washington, Thomas Jefferson, and good old Benjamin Franklin. Franklin was known to have been the Grand Master of a Masonic temple in both Paris and Philadelphia.

Fortunately for me, I'd spent a lot of time exploring this amazing temple back when I was alive, and therefore I was able to swiftly pass through the seventeen foot tall Grand Entrance Gate and the Norman porch beyond it without wasting precious time gawking. I did, however, pause along the inner steps of the temple to salute the two large bronze sphinxes. These two titans had been among the many guardian gargoyles of the city that'd fought in the Battle of Philadelphia nine months ago. Beyond the entry steps was the Grand Foyer which runs the length of the building from the Grand Entrance to the massive bronze portals of the Benjamin Franklin Room. The floor of the foyer was a black and white checker board marble while the walls were adorned with life size oil paintings of past Grand Masters. Doric columns and the Grand Staircase, which is made of Tennessee marble, add to the architectural majesty of the Grand Foyer. Except for a small tourist group near the Franklin Room, the building was otherwise very quiet.

I headed straight for the Grand Master's Conference Room to the left just inside the Grand Entrance steps. I passed through the ornate double doors and found Nathaniel Carter waiting for me; his stormy grey eyes tracked me the instant I entered the room even though I hadn't tethered myself to the living world yet. The room was beautifully furnished with comfortable look-ing chairs and sofas. Everything was handmade with expensive woods and fabrics; lamps of porcelain and fixtures of bronze and gold added to the splendor of the chamber. The walls were adorned with masterpiece oil paintings while the ceiling was re-splendent with a mural depicting a scene from ancient Masonic legend.

"It's about time," Nathaniel said. "I expected you hours ago."

"Sorry. We were attacked, and then I had to rest."

"Bad?" He questioned, his long face creasing with worry.

"Very bad," I answered and quickly gave him the six o'clock news version of the events in Limbo.

"This is worse than I'd feared," he said once I finished

recounting the tale. "The fact that the Man with Many Names has already gained a cult following in Limbo, one apparently strong enough and well organized enough to pull off the chaos that you describe in Limbo, is extremely bad for us. Your Governor was right to prioritize this investigation and put her best on it. The enemy has put his plan in full motion now, and all we know so far is that we have an enemy."

"Enemies," I corrected. "The necromancer that raised those zombies in Byberry was at work last night in Society Hill. At least a score of ghosts have gone missing, including some of my own agents. They vanished right in front of witnesses."

"Detective Cooper called an hour ago to tell me that the PPD had responded to a call about vandalism at the Micvey Israel Cemetery along with a break-in at the Church of St. George. He and Brianna should be here shortly to fill us in on what they were able to learn."

"The Micvey Israel Cemetery is right across the street from HQ. That can't be coincidence can it? But why would this necromancer target the Ghost Watch, and how would he know where to strike?"

"I think all of our problems are connected," Carter said. "The witch you encountered at Byberry is probably the necromancer, and the power she showed off to you indicates that she is in league with the Man with Many Names. It seems likely that your Delilah has had contact with one or both of them. The Crawling Chaos is but one of the Man with Many Names many avatars."

"Ok," I said. "Let's assume that these forces are all linked in some way. Other than bringing chaos to both the living and dead city, what are they truly up to?"

A firm knock at the door prevented Nathaniel from answering right away. A bald headed man dressed in a tailored suit stuck half of his body into the room and half bowed towards the wizard who was standing in the center of the room apparently talking to himself.

"Ah! Your Right Worshipfulness," The newcomer said with a disapproving air about him. "You have two guests who have requested an audience. I offered to set up an appointment for them, but the gentleman was quite firm in his insistence that he see you right away."

"Send Mr. Cooper and Ms. Martin in right away Jamison," Carter answered with a sigh. "And thank you."

"Of Course, Your Right Worshipfulness," said the man as he withdrew from the room.

"Your Right Worshipfulness?" I inquired of Nathaniel. "Isn't that a little pretentious."

"The Fraternal Order of Freemasonry is ancient, Veronika," the wizard answered earnestly. "Few people know just how old. It is a secret guarded by the order, passed down from Grand Master to Grand Master. King Solomon, son of King David of Judah was the greatest of us; he was our founder. Our titles come from a time when our leaders were actually kings."

"If this is such a big secret, why are you telling me?" I asked.

"I trust you Veronika," the wizard said, his roiling eyes boring into me. "I sense in my being that the fate of mankind rests on your shoulders. The more you know and understand, the better equipped you are to deal with our enemies. Besides, since you aren't alive I'm technically not breaking my vows."

I nodded thoughtfully, not liking the implication that mankind's existence rested on my shoulders, but I wasn't going to argue with destiny; that would be a waste of time. After finding Franklin's mysterious note to me in the basement of his house last year, I've come to learn that being a hero mostly involves getting your ass kicked at regular intervals. Destiny was going to beat the shit out of me whether I liked it or not, no point in complaining about it.

"You're the wizard Your Right Worshipfulness. Shouldn't you be saving mankind? I'm just a dead college student."

"This temple and the world wide order of Freemasons were created for that very purpose," said Nathaniel in answer. "We have prepared for centuries for the apocalypse foretold by the Prophets. We've held back the darkness for eons and suffered great losses and persecution in our efforts to guard mankind. Our numbers are fewer now and our power greatly diminished from our golden age, but we are still a formidable ally and bastion of strength. Grand Master Franklin left word that a banshee that isn't a banshee would rise up to cleanse the shadow city by awakening the ancient guardian. I assume that you were the one who awakened the guardian within the statue of William Penn?"

I nodded, mesmerized by his earnest and sure manner.

"Franklin warns that the Gate Master, Yog, would awaken on the day that the Ancient Guardian does battle in the city of the dead. Yog is the gateway to all worlds and dimensions; he gives the lord of chaos the means to invade our world once more. In saving the city of the dead, you have brought doom to the living. That is why it is your destiny to stand against the roiling chaos. My vow to the order requires me to assist you in all ways possible, but even if it did not, I would do so without hesitation."

"You're saying that it's my fault that this Yog has awakened? This current mess is my doing?" I said with guilt stabbing at my guts. But what else could I have done? Without the guardian and its army, Black Maria would have subjugated us and living Philadelphia would have paid a heavy price. The phrase "the road to hell is paved with good intentions" suddenly came to mind. Despair threatened to suffocate me; was fate so cruel that all choices led to a bad ending?

"This was foretold in prophesy," Nathaniel said. "If you hadn't acted as you did, things would be worse now. Prophesy cannot be denied or avoided. One way or another, the chaos lords were going to come. You have built a force in Limbo that may be able to fight chaos in a way that the living cannot hope to do."

The door opened before I could say anything else. Brianna entered first followed by Frank. The door closed behind them with a click. Brianna was wearing blue jeans with a black tee shirt and black boots. Her hair was done up in a ponytail. Frank wore black slacks, a white button up shirt, and black blazer that did a poor job of concealing his big ass gun. Frank was battered and bruised while Brianna seemed to have come out of last night's fight unscathed. They both looked tired but full of energy. Electricity passed between them when they looked at each other. The casual way in which they touched each other spoke volumes about why neither of them had gotten much rest in the intervening hours since last night's action.

"Is everyone around here so fucking tight assed?" Frank grumbled looking back towards the entryway.

I tethered myself just enough so that I would become visible to Frank and Brianna. The were-ferret gave no indication of surprise at my sudden appearance, but Frank almost jumped out of his skin.

"Fuck! I hate it when you do that," he snarled.

"Would you prefer that I stay invisible and just project my voice instead?" I asked, grinning at him.

"Fuck no; that would be creepy," he growled. "You could at least give some kind of warning before you just pop in like that though."

"What kind of warning?"

"I could pinch you whenever I know there's a ghost around," Brianna chimed in helpfully, confirming my suspicion that her animal spirit could sense my presence whether I was tethered or not.

"If you girls are done teasing the good detective," Nathaniel interrupted before Frank could reply. "We have some important business to discuss."

The wizard asked me to start the meeting by telling the others about the events that took place in Limbo upon my return there. We all took seats in plush chairs around the coffee table while I spoke. By the time I was finished, everyone was grimmer than they had been; their faces were creased with concentration and worry. Nathaniel ordered tea from the temple staff, giving everyone a few moments to ponder the news I'd brought. The temple secretary himself delivered the tea, and the look he directed my way was both startled and bewildered. Either he couldn't figure out how I'd gotten in without his noticing me, or he was gifted himself and could see that there was something supernatural about me.

"He's a warlock," Carter said, answering my questioning look. Jamison had left four steaming cups of black tea, along with a bowl of sugar cubes and a pitcher of cream, all neatly arrayed on the coffee table.

"Aren't warlock's evil?" asked Brianna, sitting forward nervously.

"No. Sorcerers are evil. Warlocks and witches are simply lesser talents in the arcane arts. Many thirty second degree Masons are warlocks. It's virtually impossible to reach the upper echelons of the brotherhood without some talent with the arts."

"Are all Grand Masters wizards?" asked Frank. He was looking around the room with a thoughtful frown on his face.

"We've got more important matters to discuss than the secrets of my order," Carter answered tersely. "Why don't you tell us what you've learned about the Mikveh Israel Cemetery incident?"

Frank stared at Nathaniel for a moment, their eyes locking in a test of wills. In the end, the detective nodded with a sigh as he tore his gaze from the wizard's stormy stare.

"I spoke with Wendi Kopudo a little over an hour ago, and she relayed to me that Mikveh's wasn't the only fucking cemetery in the region to be hit last night." He paused long enough to let this revelation sink in. "The Old Pine Street Church cemetery and St. Peter's Church in fucking Society Hill were both hit. The crypts below each of the churches were also vandalized and fucking looted. The religious community is up in arms, and the PPD is under enormous fucking pressure to solve this case before it blows up into a full fledged fucking political nightmare."

"This has Delilah's signature all over it," I said quietly. "She loves to cause political turmoil. Besides the public chaos though, the big worry for us is what they intend to do with the corpses they've taken. It sounds to me like they took more bodies than they actually resurrected."

"Those are some really old cemeteries aren't they?" asked Brianna. "I mean, they won't get very effective zombies out of them, will they?"

"You are correct," Nathaniel said. "Most of the corpses taken last night won't make effective zombies. The problem is that I don't believe that we are dealing with just a necromancer like we were at Byberry. I believe that the witch that Veronika encountered managed to reanimate a true menace of chaos: the Reanimator himself, Joe Curwen."

The room was silent for a moment and then Frank exploded out of his seat.

"You've got to be fucking kidding me! That's just a fucking story, it can't be fucking real."

Brianna and I both came to our feet, bewildered expressions mirrored on our faces.

"Who's Joe Curwen?" we both asked at the same time.

"He's an eighteenth century alchemist, and an acolyte of Yog," Nathaniel said, still sitting calmly in his chair.

"He's a fucking character in a work of fiction. He's not fucking real!" Frank yelled. His face was contorted in rage and fear.

"Frank," Brianna said, quietly putting a tender arm around the former cop's waist. "You're standing next to a ghost, you had wild sex with a were-ferret last night, and now you're arguing with a wizard. Seems like anything is possible, don't you think?"

Frank stared down at the petit woman for a long moment then he sagged in acquiescence.

"How do you fucking know it's him?"

"I don't for sure," Carter answered. "But I told you last night that Lovecraft was far more than a depressed writer of pulp horror fiction. He was a prophet who saw directly into the abyss of chaos. It was his curse to see the future as the Old One's dream of it. Furthermore, I've traced the crates we took from Byberry back to Providence, Rhode Island. The Masonic lodge in Providence was attacked two months ago. All of the brothers were killed. The temple's warehouse was looted, and I've since confirmed that some of the items stolen were among the crates that we recovered at Byberry."

We all stared at Carter, our breaths held in fascinated terror at what he would reveal next.

"What did they steal?" asked Brianna.

"The crates contained jars full of the essential salts of life recovered from Curwen's underground laboratory," Carter answered. "The most vital treasure that the temple guarded was a jar of essential salts collected from a Providence asylum where Curwen vanished from in the 1930's. The jar was labeled JC002."

"Let me guess," I chimed in. "The tall guy with the long blond hair matches Curwen's description."

Nathaniel nodded.

"Shit!" Frank whispered.

18

"So what's so bad ass about an eighteenth century alchemist, and what are essential salts used for?" I asked.

"The essential salts are the alchemical components that make up a living being," Carter began. "Combine a person's essential salts with an extremely dangerous ritual and it is possible to reanimate the person with its own soul. Remember that zombies are corpses that have had a random soul shoved into them. Curwen's reanimated zombies have their original soul which means that their memories and skills are intact. They are a much more advanced zombie than the ones created by a necromancer. In fact, Curwen's zombies look like normal people, particularly if properly fed. The age of the corpse doesn't matter either when it comes to reanimation. Once broken down to its essential salts, the body can be returned to a more normal state. All it takes is the proper ritual."

We all stared at Carter in fascinated horror.

"You're saying that this guy can raise an army of zombies that can move among the populous without anyone being able to recognize them as being monsters?" asked Brianna.

"Not quite that bad, but close. The reanimated corpses still have a stench about them, and they will have an almost uncontrollable hunger for raw meat. But with the right precautions taken, these creatures could operate among the general populous for a short time without much risk of discovery. These zombies also possess supernatural abilities: they are faster, stronger, and smarter than normal zombies. I'm sure you'll agree that allowing our enemies to reanimate an army of Philly's dead would be a very bad thing."

"This can't possibly work every time," I objected. "Surely the souls that have gone through the Celestial gates are immune from being dragged back into their bodies, and I would think that Satan wouldn't give up his prizes either."

"You are most likely correct," agreed Nathaniel, his stormy grey eyes flashing. "But this ritual calls upon the power of Yog who is the Gate between all realities. If there is any being capable of snatching souls from heaven and hell, it would be Yog."

"If your fucking Order had possession of Curwen's essential salts, why didn't you fucking destroy him in the manner proscribed by Lovecraft?" Frank asked angrily.

"I wish I had an answer for that, detective Cooper," the wizard answered, a hint of fatigue creeping into his voice. "Grand Master Franklin left strict commands for how the essential salts of Joe Curwen and other beings like him were to be handled. For whatever reason, the writ was ignored by the Providence temple. Curwen and Franklin have a long secret history of animosity that culminated in Curwen's attempt to reanimate Franklin back in the 1920's. He failed, however, when the police intercepted the truck in which Franklin's remains were being transported. There's some ambiguous evidence that Franklin may have been accidently reanimated by an investigator looking into the case of Charles Dexter Ward. If so, things didn't work out quite the way Curwen envisioned they would. In fact, whoever the accidental reanimated zombie was, he completely destroyed Curwen's European network."

"This son of a bitch was running around in the 1920's?" I asked incredulously. "How was he defeated?"

"He tried to use a ritual that would have turned a living man into the essential salts. Fortunately, that man knew the counter ritual and Curwen himself was reduced to his essential salts. Unfortunately, no action was taken to destroy his salts, and instead they were collected and put into secure storage. The warehouse where he was stored was hit a few months ago and here we are today."

A sudden thought hit me and I was momentarily over-whelmed with terror.

"Could they do this to me?" I asked.

The room fell silent as three pairs of eyes turned to regard me. For the first time since I'd met him, I saw fear in Nathaniel Carter's eyes.

"Oh shit!" Frank breathed.

"Where are you buried?" asked Carter regaining control of his emotions. Without waiting to hear my answer, he walked over to a closet and withdrew his leather duster, placed a brown fedora on his head, and grabbed a rune carved staff.

"Woodlands Cemetery," I said numbly as sudden dread threatened to crush me.

19

THE WOODLANDS CEMETERY is located on the Western bank of the Schuylkill River in the University City neighborhood. The Woodlands was originally a two hundred and thirty acre estate belonging to famed Philadelphia lawyer Andrew Hamilton who purchased the land in 1735. A villa, built in the federal style, its grand two story portico overlooking the river, graces the cemetery grounds to this day along with its matching set of carriage house and stables. Over the years, the Hamilton family turned the property into an idyllic English landscape with more than ten thousand plant species from around the world. The estate was purchased in 1840 by local investors who quickly transformed the grounds into a rural cemetery with the manor and its supporting structures at its heart. Even though Philadelphia's sprawl spread across the Schuylkill, the Woodlands Cemetery maintained its rural charm hidden behind a wall of trees.

By the time we pulled up to the front gates of the cemetery it was late afternoon. It was immediately obvious that something was very wrong when we found the gates closed. The grounds were normally open from dawn to dusk every day. The cemetery was a recognized National Recreation Trail that people jogged, biked, and walked their dogs on every day, so it made no sense that it would be closed at this hour. A makeshift sign on the gate proclaimed the cemetery closed for emergency maintenance. Frank pulled his car up a couple hundred feet from the cemetery's entrance and parked on the side of the road. I untethered myself from the back seat and walked through the car door heading straight for the ten foot tall brick wall that surrounded the graveyard. The others were delayed by the normal procedures of unbuckling their seat belts and opening the car doors before they could climb out and join me. Being a ghost is so cool sometimes. You don't have to bother with those trivial tasks that waste so much time.

I paused in front of the brick wall and surveyed it for a moment, focusing all of my senses on it and searching for any signs of magical warding. I felt a slight crackling force at the edge of my senses, so I slowly pushed my left hand into the wall until it encountered a wall of force that blocked further progress.

"I could have told you it was warded," said Carter blandly as he came to stand beside me. Frank and Brianna waited a few paces back, both of them scanning the road and local environment for signs of trouble. "Someone punched a great big hole in the ward up at the gatehouse. We can go in that way or I can open a door here."

"If you can do it quickly, let's go in here," I said.

"I can do this in less than three seconds," the wizard said frowning at me. "If I do it that quickly though, any practitioner within five miles of us will be aware of our activities here. Give me two or three minutes and I'll open a portal that no one else will detect unless they're within thirty feet of me."

"Do it the quiet way then," I said with nervous exasperation. Somewhere in this graveyard, my enemies were digging up my body so that they could make a zombie slave out of me. Nathaniel nodded, his stormy eyes conveyed the message that he understood my anxiety and that he wouldn't let anything happen to me. As he bent forward in concentration, I silently thanked God for putting the wizard on my path. He was a comfort to me; not only did his power allow him to actually touch me, but his knowledge and quiet confidence filled a deeply buried lonely place at the core of my being with warmth. Frank and Brianna's presences were also comforting; they guarded our backs and exposed themselves to great danger on my behalf, but what I felt for Nathaniel was different though my damaged mind had difficulty defining it. All in all though, I was extremely fortunate to have such good friends and support on both sides of the veil. I knew that not many ghosts could claim as much.

It seemed to take forever, but it was actually less than two minutes when Carter looked up and nodded to me. Without pausing to get an explanation, I plunged through the brick wall and emerged into the silent, wooded cemetery beyond. As I surveyed the landscape, I drew my katana and prepared for battle. I moved deeper into the gloomy graveyard as the sound of scrabbling boots on the brick wall behind me proclaimed that my friends were following. It was eerily silent; not a single bird chirped and even the crows were quiet. We were West of the "I" section of graves in a heavily wooded area that wasn't used for anything. My own grave lay a distance to the South East in the "K" section. I continued forward until I reached a paved road across from which lay row upon row of tombstones broken up here and there by an obelisk or spired monument. I waited for a long two minutes until the others caught up to me. Brianna led, moving gracefully and completely silent while the two men following behind were surprisingly quiet even with their heavier footsteps.

Although I desperately wanted to follow the road South and get to my grave as quickly as possible, I also knew that this route would take us near the gatehouse and the trap that surely waited there for intruders. Instead, I followed the road West until it turned Southward between "G" and "I" sections. There was absolutely no movement or sound except for those made by my companions. As twilight approached, fog began to rise from the surrounding landscape.

Nathaniel Carter suddenly stopped and waved to me frantically. I sprinted over to him, eyebrows raised in silent question.

"Someone is performing a ritual off in that direction," he whispered pointing to the Southwest of our current position. "If the necromancer isn't stopped in the next three or so minutes, this entire graveyard is going to be raised. If that happens, Frank, myself, and Brianna will be joining you shortly in Limbo."

I stared off towards my grave with longing, and with a sinking feeling I nodded my understanding. I was fairly certain that Carter's declaration of certain doom was merely hyperbole, but I understood the importance of his message; letting the entire cemetery be raised would be a bad thing. I was the only one who had any chance of getting to the necromancer in the short time before he or she completed the ritual.

"We'll meet you at your grave," Carter said as I called the wind to me and sprang into the sky, flying Southwest as fast as I could manage. Although the rising mists obscured my vision of what lay below me, I had a pretty good idea of where to go. The Hamilton Mansion lay in the direction that Nathaniel had pointed to as did several mausoleums belonging to prominent families. I landed on the roof of the two story mansion and focused my senses as Sebastian had taught me. I wished that the familiar was with me now, but he was needed more back home. Only half a minute had passed since Carter had warned me that the necromancer must be silenced before he finished his ritual. I still had two minutes to find and stop him. I cleared my mind of all thoughts and worries and concentrated on what I could hear. Slowly, I became aware of chanting and soft weeping sounds coming from somewhere very near. Another thirty seconds had passed.

I let my eyes rove over the nearby grounds until I saw what appeared to be torchlight streaming through the open door of the Drexel Mausoleum. The Drexel's were one of the most influential families in Philadelphia, being prominent in the financial sector and having founded the well connected Drexel University. Several generations of Drexel's lay entombed in the mausoleum, and today it was being desecrated by a necromancer.

Rage filled me, and I squeezed it into a tight ball of power and stored it at the core of my being. I launched myself from the mansion's roof and sped through the evening sky heading straight for the mausoleum's entrance. As I approached, I noticed that the door was being guarded by two beings that glowed with a sickly bright florescent green that reminded me of radiation or Mountain Dew. I'd never seen creatures with that color aura before, but the stench that wafted up from them reminded me of zombies or ghouls. I zipped right through the space between them before they could react to my presence. The crypt was dimly illuminated by torches showing me a scene straight out of a Conan the Barbarian movie. A robed man was chanting and holding an obsidian knife poised to plunge into the heart of a naked and thrashing blond headed girl. I flew straight for the unsuspecting necromancer, and when I was only two feet away from him let loose with the tightly controlled banshee wail that I'd prepared. The poor girl was screaming as the knife descended towards her and became even more frantic when her assailant suddenly exploded in a shower of blood and bits of bone, drenching her naked body in gore that would probably leave her mentally scarred for life. I flew through the cloud of gore that had once been the necromancer and continued on through the mausoleum's back wall and out into the evening sky. Once I exited the crypt, I shot straight up, going about forty feet, before whipping around and diving straight for the mausoleum's roof. The girl was still in grave danger; I couldn't leave her to those Mountain Dew zombies.

I plunged through the shrine's roof and immediately willed my upper body along with my celestial steel katana to manifest as physical objects. As I'd anticipated, the zombies were closing in on the bleating sacrificial lamb. They never saw me coming so intent on their screaming victim were they. I used the momentum of the dive to carry me right between them. As they jerked up in sudden surprise, I swung my katana in a lightning circle sweep that took off both of their heads in one fell swoop. Unfortunately, the girl was further traumatized by two heads bouncing off of her naked body before they rolled away to land on the floor. Two gouts of black blood shot up from the headless bodies, spraying the girl with more gore before they toppled to the ground. I looked around for more danger but saw no other threats in the immediate vicinity.

I wanted to rush to my grave, sure that all the noise that I'd made here would have alerted my enemies to my presence, but looking at the hysterical girl, I couldn't bring myself to leave her here to fend for herself not even to save my own unlife. The problem, of course, was what to do. The sudden appearance of a ghost wasn't going to help the young lady's mental stability, but I needed to quiet her down and get her out of the tomb before the reinforcements arrived to finish the job. A squeaking sound brought my attention to the entrance just in time to see Brianna slip into the crypt. She was in her ferret form, but once inside, she shifted back into her human form. She wore only a nylon pistol belt. Unabashed by her nakedness, she strode over to the alter and began trying to calm the girl.

"I'll take care of her," Brianna said to me as she worked at freeing the girl from her bonds. "Frank and Nate should be reaching your grave any minute now. Go help them."

"I can't leave you alone out here with just a pistol and a frantic girl," I protested but wished that I could. "We need to get her out of here. There should be some cars near the mansion. I'll hot wire one of them and the two of you can get the hell out of here."

"Geese…Veronika, couldn't you have made a little less of a mess?"

"I'm not used to dealing with physical things," I said defensively.

"In Limbo there aren't any messes. Besides, when something is trying to kill you or someone you're trying to protect, you don't worry about how messy the surviving is."

"True I guess, but this poor girl is gonna need some serious therapy after this."

"At least she'll be alive."

Brianna grunted her agreement and continued to try to sooth the girl. I decided to fly back up through the roof to get a look around. The fog had continued to thicken until the whole cemetery was blanketed in it, making it impossible to see for any distance beyond ten feet or so. I made a quick circuit of the mausoleum and returned to Brianna to find that she'd worked a miracle. The girl stood shakily on her own; she shivered and trembled with terror, but Brianna's comforting hand on her shoulder seemed to give her strength.

"Veronika," Brianna said. "This is Lindsay. I told her that you are a guardian angel that is going to help us get out of here. Isn't that right?"

I stared at the were-ferret incredulously for a full twenty seconds before replying. Was she trying to break the girl's brain even further?

"Hi Lindsay," I said finally, projecting my voice so that she would be able to hear me clearly. I tried to put as much friendliness as possible into my voice. Even so, I thought Lindsay might bolt for a second as her eyes bulged in fear at the sound of my disembodied voice. "It's true Lindsay, I'm going to help you get out of here. Would you like to do that?"

"Yes…please…I'm…cold," she said, teeth chattering.

"Take Brianna's hand and let her guide you," I instructed. "I promise I'll be nearby protecting you, ok?"

"Ok," the girl answered reaching out and taking Brianna's proffered hand.

I led the way out of the mausoleum and headed East up along the Southern side of the Hamilton mansion. There were two cars parked in front of the building and I immediately chose the blue Buick. I slipped through the front door and into the driver's seat where I tethered myself and then sent a surge of electricity through the ignition bringing the vehicle to life. A tapping on the passenger window reminded me that Brianna wasn't a ghost; she needed the doors to be unlocked. I willed my hand to take physical form again, and at the cost of a bit of power, I was able to unlock the doors. Brianna opened the passenger side door and pushed Lindsay into the seat belting her in before coming around to the driver's side. I untethered myself and stepped out of the car as Brianna opened the door.

"I'll be your hood ornament until you hit Woodlands Avenue. Don't worry about the gates. I'll take care of them; just keep the pedal to the medal."

"Good luck, Veronika," Brianna said as she sat in the driver's seat and belted herself in. "Please take care of Frank. He's got a foul mouth, but I've become fond of him."

"I will," I promised. "Frank likes you too, though that shouldn't come as much of a surprise with you flashing him your tits and ass all the time."

"Well, how else is a girl going to compete against sword wielding ghost bitches and flame throwing wizards? A girl uses whatever tools she has in her arsenal to get her man. You might think about that when dealing with that wizard of yours."

She gunned the car forward before I could reply, and I was forced to fly after the speeding car, catching it up within seconds, and tethering myself to its hood. What a sight we made: two naked women, speeding along in a cemetery with a banshee riding as hood ornament. Anyone who got in our way was in for a bad day.

20

THE CLOSED IRON GATES came into view as Brianna banked the Buick around the final turn leading to the cemetery's entrance. Four Mountain Dew zombies armed with submachine guns poured out of the Paul Philippe Cret Gatehouse and moved to intercept us. Yeah, freaking zombies with machine guns; that just isn't fair. There should be some kind of cosmic law against that sort of thing.

On a whim, I reached out to the fog, calling upon it to do my bidding as it does in Limbo. I was astonished when it responded to me. Instead of drawing from my own power reserves, I burned off the fog to fuel four small tornadoes, which I created with the force of my will, and sent them plowing towards the zombies as they raised their guns to fire on us. The hail of bullets was intercepted by the miniature vortexes as they rapidly closed with the undead monsters. The surprisingly quick and agile zombies attempted to evade the oncoming threat but only managed to get some of their bullets past before they were caught in the tempests that proceeded to tear them to pieces.

We sped by the unfortunate zombies, and I let my banshee wail loose on the iron gates when we were a mere ten feet away from them. Unlike the tightly controlled burst that I'd used in the Drexel mausoleum, here I let the rage flow out of me in a wide cone that blew the gates into bits of flying debris. Fortunately, traffic was light at the moment and no vehicles were caught in the blast of shrapnel and sonic waves. I turned to Brianna who was banking the car into a right turn onto Woodland Avenue and gave her a thumbs up. She nodded, and I untethered myself from the Buick's hood and sprang aloft calling the wind to me and speeding my way back into the cemetery.

Once inside the cemetery, I got my bearings and sped off South East towards where my grave lay. I reached the "K" section in less than a minute and came to a landing near the community garden near where my grave lay. My heart sank though as I reached plot 436 only to find an empty gaping hole. There was no sign of Frank or Nathaniel as I turned in a circle to survey my surroundings. No other graves in the vicinity had been disturbed. A sudden movement from the nearby carriage house caught my attention, and I sprinted towards the building. As the fog parted before me to give me a better view, my heart sank even further. Delilah stood upon the roof of the carriage house. Two dark, leathery skinned creatures that looked like harpies with tentacles stood on each side of her.

Delilah was a perfect specimen of the colonial era maiden. She was incredibly beautiful with lustrous black hair that fell in ringlets to her waist and framed her perfectly oval face. Her eyes were deep pools of blue and her lips were plump and red. She wore a long black dress with a plunging neckline that exposed her curvaceous bosom to devastating effect. She had been my patron and trainer when I'd first arrived in Limbo. She was also an evil bitch that had intended to corrupt me, and when I'd had the audacity to thwart her plans, she'd tortured me for weeks. There was a lot of bad blood between us. In the end I'd destroyed her master and forced her to flee into exile, but she'd left me with mental wounds that had nearly driven me mad. If I'd had the opportunity, I'd have killed her.

"You're too late, Veronika," she called to me as I approached the carriage house warily. "We've taken your body, and soon we'll animate you, and you'll be my eternal slave."

"You fucking bitch, why don't you come down here and we'll settle this once and for all!" I snarled back at her.

Delilah added insult to injury by throwing her head back and laughing.

"Really now, is that what you want? You amuse me Veronika. Don't you know that strategists like myself are too valuable to waste on the likes of you? But you've proven yourself to be a competent warrior, so it pleases me that I will have you as my favored slave. I'm sure you remember all the fun we had at the Walnut Prison. How would you like to repeat our little lessons but this time as my little assistant? With those powers of yours, I'm sure you'll excel at the task, and if you don't, well, I'm sure there might be some way you can further serve my amusement."

Calling on the wind to lend me speed, I leapt into the air while drawing my katana. Delilah jumped back behind her two chaos minions who sprang aloft to meet my attack. The things were agile and nearly as quick as me. They attacked aggressively with more than a dozen tentacles each lashing at me from multiple points. Even with my wind aided speed it was all I could do to fend off their assault. Each of their tentacles was wickedly barbed and dripped a black ichor that I suspected would affect even my ghostly form.

"I'm certain you'll handle the night hags, Veronika," Delilah called out to me. "In the meantime, I have pressing business to attend to. The next time we meet, you'll be wearing your own flesh once more. Don't worry, the reanimation process will take away most of the rot. You'll still be quite attractive on the outside."

And with those final words she was gone.

"To hell with this!" I snarled. I blasted one of the night hags with a banshee scream that it seemed to resist for a moment. Then the creature exploded into black tendrils of viscous matter that tumbled to the ground below. I charged the final flying hag, parrying three tentacles, ducked under a fourth, and thrust my katana through its hideous face. Black blood sprayed from the gaping wound as I ripped my blade free just in time to sever two more oncoming tentacles with quick defensive slashes. Tendrils of mist rose from several places on my body where the night hag's blood had splattered on me. It soon became obvious to me that the mist pouring from my wounds was in fact my power reserves bleeding out of me. If I didn't find a way to staunch the wounds, I'd be out of power in a few hours. On the other hand, it looked like the night hags had some kind of super regenerative powers; the gaping wound in the face of the one I was fighting was rapidly closing, and it was moving to attack me once more. It really wasn't fair that the bad guys had such cool healing powers. I met its charge with a full throated scream of rage that ripped it into thousands of black gooey tendrils that plopped to the ground. Looking down at the black oozy puddles that were the remains of the first night hag that I'd put down, I noticed with astonishment that the small puddles of black gook were actually moving towards each other. Was the thing trying to reform itself? If my banshee wail couldn't permanently destroy these things, they were nigh invincible.

An explosion off to the East of me tore my fascinated attention from the slowly regenerating night hags. They wouldn't be an issue for several hours, and that blast sounded a lot like Carter's work. As if to confirm my suspicion, several blasts from a large caliber gun reverberated throughout the cemetery. Clearly Frank was in trouble. As I sped towards the battle I saw a dozen night hags circling the area near the Hamilton Mansion. As I approached, a small ball of fire shot up and struck a night hag. It exploded with such force that even I was pushed back by the wave that followed. More shots rang out and a second hag went tumbling to the ground. Forks of lightning suddenly began to strike from above, and I decided it was time to get to ground.

I hit the ground running, heading in the direction from which I'd heard Frank's gun being fired. I found the detective and wizard crouched under the eaves of the old stables building. An engine was being revved somewhere nearby.

"What's going on?" I asked and almost laughed when Frank nearly jumped out of his skin.

"Stop fucking doing that," he shouted over the roar of the lightning blasts. "There are a couple of fucking zombies with god damned machine guns around the corner. They've been loading a truck with fucking coffins. The flying monsters are preventing us from getting to them."

"I'll take care of it," I said. "They're not getting away with my body."

I pushed myself through the wall of the stable and ran to the other side of the building. The truck was just beginning to move when I poked my head through the wall facing it. A couple of Mountain Dew zombies had their backs to me, submachine guns pointed towards the corner of the building where Frank and Nathaniel crouched. Dozens of bullet holes attested to the fact that the zombies had tried to shoot them through the building's walls, but Nathaniel must have had some kind of ward up to protect them from such an attack. It was a standoff between the two groups, but the zombies had the upper hand since they clearly were just there to hold us at bay until the truck could be loaded and make its escape. I was about to make their mission a complete failure.

I let loose with a full throttled scream that struck the slowly moving truck from the side. I didn't care if my body was shredded into millions of pieces; stopping the truck was all that mattered. I didn't need a body anymore. It was now a liability that my enemies were trying to take advantage of. The sonic blast shattered the truck's windows and sent it careening out of control. It flipped a half dozen times before coming to rest on its ruined side. As the Mountain Dew zombies turned towards me, Frank anticipated their reaction and stepped out from behind his cover and plugged them both with a single shot each to the back of the head. And just like that it was over. I started towards the truck but paused when Nathaniel called to me.

"Hold up Veronika," he said jogging up to me. His stormy gray eyes were blazing with battle rage, but his body was showing signs of the strain he'd been putting on himself with all of the spell slinging he'd unleashed in such a short time. "I need your help. Christ Church Burial Ground is under attack."

I stared at him uncomprehendingly.

"I need to secure my body before Delilah can get it back," I said turning away from him and taking a step towards the ruined truck.

"Curwen's trying to get Benjamin Franklin's bones again," the wizard said, and I froze. "He's tried before. Franklin has knowledge that The Man With Many Names wants. You're the only one who can get there fast enough to prevent a breach of the wards. Frank and I can secure your body. We'll meet up again in Center City."

I sighed. There was no way I could let the enemy have Franklin, even if it meant losing my body again. I nodded my agreement to help.

"Good. The burial grounds are heavily warded, that's how I know that they're under attack. The wards won't hold long under sustained assault however. Do your best to drive them off or at least hold them at bay. I'll have every mason in the city converge on the site. We'll need about an hour before reinforcements can back you up. Can you do it?"

"Just make sure you secure my body. I'm gonna be pissed if I have to serve that bitch Delilah as a zombie. I'll probably come for you first if that happens, so don't screw up," I said and prepared to fly off to Center City.

"We won't. Now, hold on for a moment longer," Carter said and he reached out and touched me with a glowing hand. I was momentarily stunned by the feel of him; I actually felt his skin on my own bare arm. It felt amazing, warm, comforting, and I felt alive for a moment. His hand glowed with the light of the sun, and I saw my wounds close up and felt power pour into me from him. His eyes blazed with something that startled me even more than his touch. Could that be genuine affection, maybe even love showing in his stormy eyes? I wondered what it would feel like to have his entire body pressed against mine, preferably with the both of us naked. The thought sent a shudder through me, and a vision of Freak intruded on my thoughts; I nearly pulled away from Nathaniel as flashes of my torture at Freak's twisted hands ran through my mind. As I fought the urge to withdraw, I told myself that Freak was no more. I'd seen to that myself. Besides, I couldn't let the memory of him continue to haunt me. The sick bastard would have wanted nothing more than to know that he'd permanently dashed all of my future relationships.

"Love is the most powerful magic in the universe Veronika," Nathaniel whispered, distracting me from my thoughts. "Don't underestimate what you can do with it. Satan and his crew always do, as does Azathoth. They don't understand what keeps us going when all hope seems lost."

I stared at him in wonderment for a moment, wondering if he could read my thoughts. My whole body tingled with the feel of his simple touch. I tore my gaze away from his, fighting to regain my composure. This wasn't the time for emotional entanglements.

"Jesus H Christ! We're in the middle of a warzone and the two of you are behaving like star crossed fucking lovers," Frank blurted in disgust. He was watching the night sky nervously. "Just get a fucking room later on when we've cleared out of here will you."

"I'd better go," I said. "Uncle Ben needs my help."

Carter bent forward and placed a gentle kiss on my lips. The magic that passed between us was enough to fuel ten thousand suns. A part of me wanted to scream in horror, to cringe away from the sudden physical contact, but I grabbed that sickened part of my mind by the throat and shoved it into a dark place and focused my thoughts instead on the warm feel of Nathaniel's energy. He wasn't Freak, I told myself, hoping it would shut up that little terrified voice in my head. I was damned if I was going to let that bastard's memory stop me from enjoying this moment. I stepped back from Nathaniel and gave him a shy smile.

"I have to go."

I called the wind and sprang aloft. The storm of lightning had passed, and it appeared that the night hags had either been wiped out for the moment or they'd decided to find shelter elsewhere. Thus unimpeded, I sped towards Center City; my heart was a little lighter despite the terrible danger that loomed over us all.

21

CHRIST BURIAL GROUND is located on the corner of Arch and Fifth Streets in an area known as America's most historic square mile. The cemetery was established on what was then the edge of the city in 1719, but now it lies in the heart of Philly within walking distance of such famous attractions as Independence Hall, Constitution Hall, The Liberty Bell Center, the US Mint, and a score of other museums and historical sites. It occupies a space of two acres of land and is surrounded by a seven foot tall brick wall. The graves of Benjamin Franklin and his wife as well as other Franklin relations rest here along with more than a thousand other residents, many of them from the revolutionary era.

As I approached Center City, I was astonished to see a massive storm engulfing the central district. The rain was so heavy that I could barely see the glittering lights from the city's skyscrapers. Lightning flashed and the wind blew at near gale force. I pushed my way into the storm and found that I had to use up twice as much energy to fly through it which told me that this storm was anything but natural. As I approached the burial grounds, I was surprised to see lightning surging up from the ground itself and arching into the sky rather than the other way around. I landed on the Independence Visitors Center roof across the street from the cemetery in order to get a better view of the situation.

The sky above Christ Burial Ground was thick with what I at first thought were crows but quickly realized were night hags masquerading as natural birds. Of course, there's nothing natural about birds cavorting in the sky during a heavy rain storm. Lightning was actually emanating from the cemetery at various points, arching upwards and striking night hags who got too close to the protected air space above the cemetery. The normally steady traffic that would be encountered at this time of night had practically vanished in the face of the drenching rain. The storm had a supernatural feel to it that probably contributed to the empty streets more so than the actual rain or lightning did. There was an oppressive feel to the night; a sense of danger and unease permeated Center City's atmosphere. Besides the danger that the night hags represented, there were things even more terrible crawling upon Philadelphia's streets this stormy night.

The nightmares emerged from what looked like a sewer access manhole in the middle of Arch Street almost exactly between my position and the front gates of Christ Church Burial Grounds. The manhole had a black aura that was flecked with flashes of red fire. Obviously this was some kind of dimensional portal since normal manholes don't have auras. The first creature that squeezed through the portal was impossibly huge for the small opening that it emerged from. It was a spider the size of a Pinto. Like most things of chaos, the thing had dozens of lashing tentacles and thousands of glowing eyes of all colors covering its whole body. As soon as it was free of the portal it turned to the cemetery and leaped for the top of the brick wall that surrounded the grounds. A bolt of lightning suddenly lashed out from thin air within the cemetery and caught the chaos spider full in the torso in mid jump. The arachnid horror was flung forty feet and landed on its back on the sidewalk below me. Unlike the night hags, however, the chaos spider was not destroyed by a single strike; it wriggled for a bit before righting itself. Meanwhile, another spider had emerged from the portal and the night hags continued their assault from above. As I continued to watch and assess the situation, I noticed that the lightning strikes from the cemetery were becoming less potent. If I was going to prevent the desecration of this historic burial ground, I was going to have to act quickly. The problem was that I hated spiders.

Seriously, I'm a ghost. I shouldn't have to deal with spiders anymore. And these freaking things were as big as cars and had tentacles, how gross is that? The problem of course was that there was no one else around to do this job. I was beginning to understand what Batman must feel like: never any shortage of bad guys in the big city, but only one of me to fight them all. I decided that I might be able to avoid the spiders for a short time by going after the portal's creator first. Maintaining a portal between the living realm and wherever the spiders were coming from had to be costing the caster a great deal of power and concentration.

I surveyed the area once more and noticed a City Water Department van parked on the Northwest corner of Arch and Fifth streets. What really made the van stand out was the two lovely women who were crouched in the van's shadow. They were both wearing tight leather spandex and brandishing submachine guns. They also had the tell tale green auras of shifters. It seemed pretty likely to me that the power behind the portal was hiding within the van.

I called the wind to me and launched myself towards the van's roof. The shifters were apparently mesmerized by the horrific troops that chaos was calling upon to assault the ancient graveyard for neither of them was watching the sky too closely. I hit the van's roof head first and performed a mid air back flip as soon as my head pierced the vehicle's compartment. The maneuver saved my life as a reaper stabbed at me, expecting my momentum to carry me forward. I was able to get a quick view of the interior of the van before I kicked back and performed the back flip. The reaper misinterpreted my maneuver and sprang through the van's roof in pursuit, but I was already on my way back through the van's roof, this time a few feet from my original entry point and coming in feet first. The brown robed witch from Byberry was squatting behind the driver's seat, gazing fixedly through the front window shield and chanting softly. Even deep in concentration she felt the danger and managed to roll away from a killing blow that I launched at her. Instead of taking off her head, I got her hand. She screamed in agony and rage as a fountain of blood sprayed from the stump of her arm and drenched the van's window shield. Knowing that my goal had been achieved, I sprang skyward just as the reaper lunged through the van's side.

A group of night hags had broken off from the assault on the cemetery and were waiting for me as I rose into the night sky. I was ready for them though. I let loose with a full throated banshee wail that shredded the entire group, leaving only black tendrils drifting upon the stormy winds. I knew that they would reconstitute themselves eventually, but that would take hours. The battle for Christ Burial Ground would be decided by then. What I hadn't anticipated, however, was that the chaos spiders would have the capability of shooting ghost binding webs.

As I veered away from the temporarily destroyed group of night hags, I was suddenly struck by something heavy and sticky. The weight of the black webbing caused me to drop from the sky like a stone. I hit the ground and instinctively rolled with the fall. Though the hard landing jarred me, it caused no real damage. The roll, however, resulted in me getting tangled in the web even more tightly. I drew my celestial steel knife from my belt and slashed at the webbing, only to find it highly resistant to damage from the weapon. A mad cackle brought my attention back around to the van that lay behind me now. The brown robed witch was leaning against the van. Her handless arm was wrapped with towels.

"You have meddled with our plans for the last time," she croaked. "Destroy her."

I heard a heavy clicking sound and turned to watch as one of the massive chaos spiders approached me. Its clawed legs were actually tearing fist sized holes in the street's blacktop surface. As it came closer, I saw that the dozen or so tentacles were barbed and dripped an oozing ichor just like the night hags'. Making matters worse, the creature's maw was as large as a car door and its mandibles the size of butchers knifes; they too dripped with poisonous ooze. I frantically tried to cut my way out of the web, but it was clear that the spider would be upon me before I could even cut one strand of the web. I tried with all my might to phase through the web, but to no avail. I was left with very few options: try to fight the horror with both my hands and feet literally tied behind my back, or flee. I was very certain that if I tried to fight, the chaos beast would destroy me. It was clear to me that its chaos laden body was fully capable of harming me. To flee, I was going to have to translate back into Limbo, leaving the field and probably Franklin's bones in the enemies hands. The thought of failing Nathaniel was what made me decide on the third option.

"Come on you fucker! Come and get me!" I yelled at the spider in defiance. "Let me send your master a message he can't fail to understand!"

The spider chittered back at me with a voice that sounded like nails on a chalkboard. Then it leaped at me. I lay still as its tentacles lashed out and struck me in half a dozen places. The strikes hurt like hell, but no more so than what I'd endured during my battle with the master wraith of Philadelphia nine months ago. I held my ground in the face of the assault until the spider loomed over me, its fetid breath making me want to puke, and then I let loose with my banshee wail; the scream held all the rage and desperation that I could muster. The fear of losing Nathaniel when I'd just begun to accept the possibility that I might have a chance of being with him was laced into that scream. Most of the web that held me shriveled and fell to dust in the wake of my terrible wail, but astonishingly the spider seemed momentarily unaffected by the blast. It was only when a second scream joined mine that it began to disintegrate. I stared in confusion for a moment, and then whirled to face the witch. Unfortunately, the van was pulling away. The old crone sat in the passenger seat staring at me, her face was contorted with hate and malice. I momentarily considered going after her, but the cemetery was still under attack.

"Veronika!" called Bridget as she moved to join me; it was her wail that had combined with mine to destroy the spider. "We've got a bag of weapons and a platoon waiting to come through. I took care of the reaper while you were testing the spider web. Sloppy of you to leave yourself open to a captain of Limbo."

"Thanks," I said with a sigh. It was nice to see that the systems we'd put in place over the intervening months since our liberation of shadow Philly were working in spite of the crisis on both sides of the veil. Center City was a major point of focus in shadow Philly's defense strategy, and we'd set up warning systems and operational plans in case of major supernatural activity on either side of the veil. The assault on Christ Church Burial Grounds had set off the alarms in Limbo, and the Ghost Watch had acted according to plan. Bridget's presence wasn't part of that plan, but I was guessing that she'd been sent when the Watch's observer reported my plight to the Governor. After myself, Bridget was the most skilled and ruthless warrior among the city's banshees.

"I'll run interference until you get back," Bridget said. The gleam in her eyes conveyed the excitement she felt at the prospect of battle.

"Watch out for the webs," I told her, noting that only three of the five spiders that had gotten through the portal before I'd shut it down remained active. Apparently the lightning had taken its toll on one of the beasts, but there would be no such luck with the other three. It was obvious that the wards on the graveyard had weakened significantly. Some night hags were actually beginning to survive the lightning strikes. "I wasn't expecting it to work on me. It's like some kind of super ghost net webbing. Also don't underestimate the night hags. They're fast and tough."

Bridget nodded her understanding, and I wasted no further time translating back into Limbo.

22

I LEFT THE RAIN OF THE living world and stepped into the mists of Limbo emerging onto the same street that I'd just been on, though in Limbo the buildings were older. Gone were many of the more modern structures that occupied Independence Mall in the living world. In Limbo the first official Presidential residence still stood along with a half dozen other colonial style houses and mercantile buildings that no longer stood in the living world. The roads here were cobbled instead of paved and there were far more trees in the landscape of the dead city then there were in modern Philly. The things that have a presence in Limbo are those that hold the strongest memories in the minds of the dead, and as a result Shadow Philadelphia is a hodgepodge of the old and new.

A platoon of the Ghost Watch stood in ranks of four columns with eight ghosts in each for a total of thirty two watch-ghosts. Danielle stood at their head, and four celestial steel bags filled with weapons lay at her feet. I loped over to her and scooped up two of the heavy bags. She picked up the other two and handed them over when I was ready. This task was solely mine because I was the only one in the city who could translate celestial steel from Limbo into the living world.

"Let's go," I said and translated back into the living world.

Danielle appeared at my side just a second after I arrived, and the platoon materialized a few seconds later. One agent from each column ran forward and took a bag from me. As they began distributing the weapons to their lines, Bridget appeared out of the curtains of rain that seemed to have gotten worse in the minute or so that I'd been gone. She grabbed a sword from a proffered bag, tossed it to Danielle, and took one for herself.

"Let's go kick some ass," she said. The vicious looking wounds she was now sporting hadn't diminished her enthusiasm for battle one iota.

"Delta team with the Captain," shouted Danielle. "Bravo your with me, Echo go with Bridget, and Alpha hold here in reserve!"

I surveyed the battle field and noticed that the remaining three spiders were attempting a group assault on the front gates of the burial ground. I launched myself into the air, rising to about thirty feet and dove for the spider on the left flank. The thing saw me coming of course; it was covered in eyes after all. It reared up and shot a web towards me. I was ready for it this time, and before the web could open up to engulf me, I let loose with a banshee scream that destroyed the streaking web and dazed the spider that had launched it.

I slammed into the beast, driving my katana deep into its torso. My Ghost Watch companions came down all around the creature and began hacking at its legs. It shrieked, lashing out with its tentacles. One of them scored a critical hit that decapitated one of the attacking free souls. The others stared in horror as they watched one of their own dissipate into mist. I focused my revulsion and rage into a tight blast scream that I aimed directly at the deep wound that my blade had left in the spider's body. I shrieked and the chaos spider exploded, showering the entire vicinity in black gore.

Up above, I heard Danielle scream and knew that her team had engaged the night hags. Bridget had led her team against the spider on the far flank. They were hacking the thing into bits, but they hadn't come away unscathed either. At least two of their team had been destroyed in the short but vicious fight. I looked around for the third spider and saw it straddling the brick wall of the cemetery. It showed signs of having been wounded by the wards, but the lightning had completely ceased now indicating the collapse of the burial ground's defenses. Before I could move, it leaped into the cemetery grounds and vanished from view. I knew where it was heading however, so I called the wind to me and sprang onto the brick wall and then onto the spider's back as it furiously dug at Franklin's grave which lay right beside the wall.

The spider saw me jump for it and used its tentacles to try to fend me off while its clawed legs continued to tear clumps of dirt from the ground. The headstone that marked the grave had been carelessly tossed aside. Night hags had descended into the grave yard and were joining the spider's efforts to dig up the ground heedless of the danger posed by the spider's scrabbling legs. I severed three of the spider's tentacles with a single swipe of my katana following up the defensive maneuver with two tightly focused screams aimed at the exact same location on its torso. The spider's chaos infused carapace resisted the first blast but crumpled under the second. The beast screamed, and with incredible effort of will it struck at me with all of its remaining appendages. In the skies overhead, bravo squad was locked in a battle of attrition with the far more numerous night hags. I swung furiously, hacking off two of the spider's legs and a tentacle, but in the end it got a hold of me.

Three of its barbed tentacles stabbed into me; one of them wrapped itself around my body and prevented me from swinging my katana. I tried to scream, but another tentacle wrapped around my head and mouth with such force that it gagged me and prevented me from doing anymore damage with my sonic attacks. As the chaos spider fell to the ground thrashing in its own death throws, the tentacles that held me pulled me towards its gaping maw. I thought I was a goner for a second, but then alpha team arrived. Its members fell on the spider and hacked its limbs off before it could pull me into its deadly mouth. I was dragged away from it and was able to rip the tentacle from my mouth. I hyperventilated for a few seconds until I could get through to my brain that I no longer needed to breathe. The only thing that the tentacle had been truly able to do was stop me from screaming.

Bridget and Danielle had led their teams down into the cemetery. The Ghost Watch had firm control of Franklin's grave though the night hags continued their assault until the first of the masons started arriving. The Grand Master's secretary, Jamison, led the effort. He had keys to the grounds, and as soon as he and his underlings gained access to the graveyard, they began deploying basketball sized pyramid artifacts throughout the grounds while chanting in Latin. I led the Ghost Watch to the roof of the Independence Visitors Center where we watched until we were certain the cemetery was properly warded once more and that the night hags had given up.

"So that's it then, eh?" asked Bridget with a sigh. "What was it all about?"

I grunted and led my sisters over to where we could talk privately without the other members of the Ghost Watch hearing us. Danielle and Bridget weren't really my sisters of course, at least not in the blood relationship way, but they were banshees like me. They'd been murdered by the same psycho that had killed me, and that made them my sisters in my book. All three of us had taken a good pounding in the battle, and we'd all expended a lot of power. We'd lost eight members of the platoon: a fourth of what we'd started with. Those weren't good numbers. Surprisingly Limbo's population isn't as large as you would think. Only those who die in an act of violence end up in Limbo. Everyone else goes somewhere else.

"They were after Benjamin Franklin's bones," I said in a conspiratorial tone.

"No shit Sherlock," Bridget replied. "But why?"

"One of the bad guys knows a ritual of reanimation."

My two sisters stared at me blandly.

"What does that mean? Is it different from normal necromancy?" Bridget asked.

"It's very different from normal necromancy. First of all, it's more alchemy than necromancy. The corpse that is targeted for reanimation must be broken down into its essential salts before the ritual is performed. The ritual is so powerful that it forces a dead person's spirit back into its original body. As long as the spirit is fed properly it will be an improved zombie that can almost pass for a normal person. The real scary part is that the reanimated zombie is a slave to whomever created it. It must obey all of its master's commands. Its skills and memories are also intact."

The two banshees stared at me, shock playing across their faces.

"They...they were going to do that to Benjamin Franklin?" Danielle asked in a choked voice.

"Yes."

Bridget stared hard at me. I could almost see the wheels turning in her head.

"They can do this to us," the captain of the Governor's guard said, turning away from me so that she could look over the city. "You were wise to not say anything within ear shot of the others. This kind of news could cause a panic. You will keep your mouth shut Danielle, do you understand me? Don't even tell Melanie or any of the others. We need to keep a lid on this."

Danielle was gaping at the two of us, her eyes huge with incredulity.

"That's an order from not only the Governor's guard captain Danielle, but also from me," I said with an edge of hardness that mirrored Bridget's. "This is a need to know security matter, though I would recommend that Jonus, Melanie, and Amber be told Bridget."

"I can understand Jonus and Melanie, but why bring Amber into it? She's a little young for this kind of responsibility."

"If word of this gets out, and chances are good that it could," I said. "I'm sure you'll recall that the enemy has already infiltrated our ranks and as a result should easily be able to disseminate any news or rumors that it desire. In such an eventuality, it will fall to Amber and her sirens to control the panic. She'll need to prepare a contingency plan. Don't underestimate her. She is young, but she knows her business. The worse mistake we can make at this point is to handicap our leadership by withholding vital information. They must have foreknowledge so that they can react appropriately."

Bridget nodded in grudging agreement.

"What are you doing to contain the situation, and how widely known is this ritual?" she asked, changing the subject.

"The wizard, Nathaniel Carter, tells me that the ritual has only been learned by less than a handful of people in the history of mankind." I answered, recalling the grilling I'd given him as we drove out to the Woodland's Cemetery. "Apparently it requires such a high level of skill to perform that most who attempt it are themselves annihilated. Carter believes that there are only two people in the world today who can perform this ritual, and both are in Philly right now."

"What about the wizard, can he do the ritual? How do you know we can trust him?"

"I trust him," I said simply and truthfully. "He does not know the ritual nor does he believe that he would be sufficiently skilled to perform it. He says that he's far too emotional for that kind of controlled spell craft."

"Sounds like an interesting man this wizard," Bridget said with a smile playing across her normally rocky features. "You should introduce me to him sometime."

A pang of jealousy assaulted me and I had to press the mute button on my tongue before it gave me away.

"What's been going on at home?" I asked, quickly changing the subject.

"There have been more disappearances," Danielle chimed in nervously, clearly uncomfortable between Bridget and I. "Moving our people away from the cemeteries has helped, but like Melanie says, the whole damned city is practically a graveyard."

"There have also been incursions of chaos creatures," Bridget reported impatiently. "We've tracked their starting points to Byberry. Anyways, you should come back with us and make a full report to the Governor."

"I can't afford the time right now," I told Bridget. "I will most likely have to return soon to recuperate, but right now we have leads that must be followed up. So far we've been relegated to reacting to everything the enemy is doing. We need to strike a decisive blow soon or all could be lost. Tell the Governor what I've told you, and tell her that killing the two reanimators is at the top of my list of things to do."

"Very well, Veronika," Bridget said with a respectful nod. "It was nice waging war with you again. Be safe."

After Bridget had translated back to Limbo, I turned to Danielle.

"Leave a full squad behind to keep an eye on things in the burial grounds until this thing blows over. Be safe."

"Yes, Captain," she said in reply. "Be safe."

I called the wind to me and headed for the Masonic temple.

23

"WHAT DO YOU MEAN it wasn't there?" I asked, terror threatening to throttle me. "You promised that you would secure my body! I protected the cemetery for you, the least you could have done was get my body back!"

Nathaniel Carter flinched away from my accusing gaze while Frank's head was bowed and his hands were clenched tightly into fists. Brianna Martin sat calmly on a plush couch. She was thankfully dressed once more. We were in the lavishly furnished Franklin Room in the Grand Masonic Temple. Two huge double doors made of pure bronze opened up onto the chamber which was dominated by the portraits of past Grand Masters and eleven murals. Though the room was meant to be a place where the brotherhood could relax with their guests, I in no way felt relaxed. I felt like screaming; I wanted to bring the whole building down around me. How could this have happened? Delilah had my body, and now she was going to make me into a zombie slave!

"Calm down Veronika," Brianna said quietly but firmly. "It's not their fault. They searched the entire graveyard once it became clear that your body wasn't on the truck that you blasted. What we need to do now is figure out where they've gone with it. I'm guessing this reanimation ritual takes time to prepare, right Nathaniel? What's the earliest they could do anything to Veronika?"

The wizard shot a grateful look to Brianna, and then seemed to do some mental calculations.

"Assuming that they started immediately, it would take at least twenty four hours to break her remains down into the essential salts. After that, with the proper sacrifices available, it would be another hour or so."

"Is there a good reason why they wouldn't start immediately?" Brianna asked.

"I'm sure there are a couple," Nathaniel answered. "For Curwen, Veronika is a side show. I think the only reason he'd even bother with her is for an ally's sake. No offense Veronika, but you're young. Your worldly knowledge and experience is slim compared to the minds that Curwen has been aiming for. You don't fit his target profile."

"She does now," said Frank quietly. He was looking at me now. "She thwarted his plans to get Franklin's bones, and she injured a key ally of his. Lovecraft was pretty clear that many of Curwen's targets were purely for vengeance sake. He came away with almost nothing tonight. That was a lot of fucking effort for nothing. But he has her, so we have to assume that he's already started the fucking process."

Nathaniel stood frozen for a full minute; emotions battled across his features until he clamped down on them and composed himself with obvious effort. When he looked back at me, the storm that raged in his beautiful gray eyes was so terrible that it was my turn to flinch away from him. That look told me that he would tear this world apart before he'd let anyone enslave me. Though I felt helpless and more frightened than ever, I also remembered his words. Love is more powerful than any force in the universe. It makes us fight even when all hope is lost. Looking into those eyes, I knew that he would fight for me, and I sure as hell wasn't going to give up now.

"We have twenty four hours," he said encompassing Frank and Brianna in his gaze. "Any ideas on where to start?"

"There will have been fucking clues dropped at the various cemeteries that were hit in the last fucking day," Frank said. "A witness will have fucking seen something, and surveillance cameras will have recorded small details that will lead us to the perpetrators. It's fucking tedious work, but I've got friends on the PPD that will provide me with what I need. I'll get on it right away."

Frank headed for the door but was intercepted by Brianna. The two exchanged an awkward kiss, and then Frank departed to do some detective work.

"The were-hyenas have been involved in this from the start," I said thoughtfully. "Do you know where we can find them Brianna? I think their leader was a woman named Jezebel."

Brianna's green eyes blazed with hatred at the mention of the woman. After all, she'd been partially responsible for the death of many of the were-ferrets friends.

"Sure, Jezebel runs a strip club in Penn's Landing. Funny enough, it's called 'Jezebel's'. Her entire pack works there. They probably live there for all I know."

"Let's go," said Carter, grabbing his staff and heading for the door.

"Not so fast big guy," I told him. "I think we should use the stealth approach first. Jezebel doesn't strike me as the type that will be intimidated into turning on her allies. Am I right Brianna?"

"You're right V. She's gonna be a hard nut to crack. I'd prefer trying to infiltrate her lair first."

"That's what I was thinking," I said. "Do you know any spells that could hide our aura's Nathaniel?"

The wizard thought about it for a moment, then nodded.

"I can give Brianna a human aura and make your own unde-tectable for a short while. I'm not sure I like this plan though. It sounds too dangerous. Who knows what chaos beings they may have lurking in their den."

"It will be ok, Nathaniel," I told him. "Brianna and I can take care of ourselves. Believe it or not, we did just fine on our own before meeting the big bad wizard."

"You can't depend on luck your whole existence."

"What?" I asked in a dangerous tone, though I was smiling faintly at him.

"Nothing, I didn't say anything."

"Good answer."

"What am I supposed to do while you're having fun at a strip club?"

"I need you to figure out why the forces of chaos are build-ing structures made of mania stone," I said. "There have been incursions of chaos creatures into Limbo. Our scouts in Limbo have tracked the incursions to these structures. Are these some kind of portals to the chaos realm? How do we safely shut them down?"

Nathaniel looked intrigued and worried at the same time.

"Tell me everything," he ordered, and I did, relaying the scant information that Bridget had passed on to me at Christ Church Burial Ground.

As Brianna and I prepared to leave ten minutes later, Carter pulled me over to him with his warm, soul touching hands. He held me for a moment, and then he surprised me by putting his arms around me and kissing me passionately. My first reaction was to stiffen up, to cringe, but if Nathaniel noticed, he didn't show it. After a moment of uncertainty, I gave in to the feel-ings that I'd been harboring for the wizard since we'd shared in that amazing soul gaze. I wanted the kiss to last forever; it was beyond magical, but after a long moment, I forced myself to pull away. I smiled at him and headed for the door.

"By the way," I said turning back to face him. "What the hell was up with those zombies we encountered at the Woodlands? Since when can zombies use machine guns? That shit isn't fair."

"Those were reanimated bodies," he answered grimly.

A chill went down my spine.

"No way am I gonna be a Mountain Dew zombie, Nathaniel," I said to the wizard in a quavering voice. "If we fail to stop them in the next twenty-four hours, I want you to destroy me. I can't bear the thought of becoming a slave to evil."

24

I STARED AT *JEZEBEL'S* in consternation. Brianna and I were standing across the street from the strip club which was situated on Front Street just South of Market. It was still raining out, though only lightly. The streets continued to be oddly quiet with the exception of the area surrounding Jezebel's; the place was absolutely hopping. People were literally waiting a significant amount of time in the rain before ever reaching the front entrance. It was so busy that the only way you got in was when someone else left. The bouncers that commanded the entrance were large and moved with the grace and confidence of professionally trained killers. It was apparent that they had total control over who went in. The security wasn't what was upsetting me though. It was the building itself that troubled me.

Jezebel's was in a structure that defied descriptions. It was massive, taking up nearly half a city block, and it was made of what appeared to be a single block of mania stone. The architecture of the monolith was similar to those located on the Byberry complex. The edifice was completely alien, and its non-Euclidean geometric shape made my brain want to jibber in terror. There were no discernable windows and only one gargantuan portal stood at the front as if it were meant to admit some monstrous god from the beyond. Above the great portal, a neon red sign declared the establishment's name, *Jezebel's*. The sign bathed the entire area in front of the club in a terrifying red glow.

"Our plan isn't going to work," I told Brianna. "We didn't know this place was so heavily connected to chaos. I mean, it was obvious they were working with them, but this is way more than a working relationship."

Brianna shrugged. She was wearing a black mini skirt, red tank top, and red stiletto pumps. She was an absolute knock out with her green eyes and red wig. The plan had been for her to enter the club as a job seeker. The way she looked and the grace with which she carried herself would make her an A list candidate in the world's most famous gentlemen's clubs, let alone a new establishment like *Jezebel's*. We had seriously underestimated the place's popularity, and more importantly, its security and threat level. I'd hoped to be able to slip into the club unnoticed while Brianna kept the staff busy. The structure being entirely made of Mania stone made my entry into it far too risky though, and Brianna was likely to be left cooling her heals with the rest of the crowd in the rain for hours. Jezebel must have had the tits and ass part of her business well covered with her own pack.

"We'll have to go with plan B, then," Brianna said.

"We didn't discuss a plan B," I replied.

"I know. I'm so disappointed in you. A ghost on your pay grade should have had a contingency plan. Luckily, the agency taught me to be a plan B, C, and D kind of girl."

"I don't get paid," I said indignantly.

"The perks and benefits package must be out of this world then."

"Not unless you consider fighting for your existence every waking hour a perk," I snorted.

"Your job really sucks," Brianna said. "Remind me to never die."

We both chuckled, and some of the tension drained out of me.

"So what's plan B?" I asked.

"I go ferret and sneak in. You cause a distraction."

"I don't like that plan. It's too dangerous for you to go into that place alone. What's plan C?"

"We storm the evil castle."

"D?"

"D is a bad plan, we should go with plan B," Brianna said. "I'll be fine. I've infiltrated more dangerous places than this in my lifetime, and I didn't have the furry guy with me then."

"The ferret fury is a male?" I asked.

"Yup."

"That must be interesting."

"It is," Brianna said with a serious expression on her face. "Come on Veronika, we don't have much time. You being a Mountain Dew zombie is unacceptable. We need to accept some risks here. This is one of our best and only leads. I can do it."

"If something happens to you Brianna, I won't be able to face Frank again," I said. "It's only been a very short time, but I think that he loves you."

"Give a man sex and before you know it he's in love," Brianna said with a fond smile. "Don't worry, that man has more than one big gun, and he knows how to use both. Getting more of that is an incredible incentive for me to come out alive. Besides, I'm not gonna die until some kind of union is formed in Limbo. Volunteering is nice and all, but I've got expensive taste in shoes."

I laughed. This petit woman knew how to embarrass me and put me at ease at the same time; a rare skill indeed.

"I really didn't need to know that about Frank," I said. "As for shoes, you don't have to worry about that. You can wear anything you want with a single thought. The same is true for your appearance. Go ahead, I'll provide the distraction. And don't get caught; there are a lot of worse things than death out there."

Brianna looked at me with wide, mocking eyes.

"You can wear anything you want and change your appearance at will and this is the best you can do? Veronika, you really need to spend some time at Victoria's Secret instead of at the medieval reenactment fair. Do it for Nathaniel's sake."

"If you're going to do this, get going," I growled. "Before I change my mind."

25

IT TOOK ME MORE THAN AN HOUR to set up the diversion. Considering the security that Jezebel had at her disposal, it was going to take a full blown supernatural assault to get her full attention. Since Bridget told me that the Governor was considering an attack on the Byberry complex, I figured she'd be even more concerned about a chaos base so close to Center City. It turned out that I was correct. Governor Rachel quickly approved my plan and ordered Marshal Jonus to provide me with whatever military resources that I needed. Once the politics of getting what I wanted was out of the way, it really didn't take me long to get things assembled.

"Let's do it!" I ordered and stepped out of a dark alley a block South of the strip club. Behind me, a squad of gargoyles roared with battle lust and poured out of the alley after me. A quarter of the Fury possessed statues flew on stone wings while the majority of the group was made up of big lumbering monstrosities, most bearing the semblance of some great beast like a bear, rhino, elephant, and even a dinosaur. My old friend

Baron led the gargoyles, and behind them came two of Amber's best sirens: Nightingale and Rhapsody. Each of the sirens had her own contingent of free soul guards whose sole jobs were to keep the valuable sirens alive at all costs. A full brigade of the Philadelphia Free Corps waited in Limbo in case we needed them. This, however, was merely a diversion. I wasn't trying to take or destroy the place; some instinct told me that the cost to carry out such a venture would involve more ghosts than what I was willing to pay at this point.

As we swiftly approached the mass of waiting customers outside of *Jezebel's*, the two sirens began to sing 'Homeward Bound' by Simon and Garfunkel. The reason that these two particular sirens had been chosen for this mission was for their ability to project their voices and power into the living world. The message that was carried by the siren song resulted in the immediate desire of the living listeners to go home. The line before the club suddenly dissolved as the crowd flowed away, the sudden urge to be home overwhelming all other desires. Not even the bouncers were immune to the effect. All four of them at the entrance to the club abandoned their posts and headed home without bothering to clock out. Only one of Jezebel's scantily clad hyenas resisted the song, but she was mesmerized long enough for one of the flying gargoyles to sweep down and smash her head with a stone fist. The blow probably would have caused a normal person's head to pop like a balloon. The shifter, however, only suffered from a broken neck. I felt no remorse as the sultry woman collapsed to the ground. Given time she'd recover; such are the regenerative abilities of shifters. I'd given my troops the order to show no mercy. In Limbo there was no Geneva Convention. Neither the forces of evil or chaos gave quarter, and it was generally our policy to do likewise. It's generally bad practice to let your enemies live to fight another day on purpose.

The gargoyles surged forward in glee trying to be the first ones through the cavernous portal that was the door of the alien structure. I started out uneasy, and the ease with which we were succeeding only set off more warning bells.

"Hold!" I shouted before the majority of the gargoyles had gotten in. Baron bellowed, and the four flyers who'd made it inside turned to retreat as ordered. Before they could get out however, the door suddenly slid closed without making a sound, trapping the gargoyles within.

I stared in horror at the black wall where the front entrance had been. There was no sign of there ever having been an opening in the wall. It was completely smooth and featureless. Panic began to well up inside of me; not only were four gargoyles trapped in there, but now Brianna was too.

"Baron," I shouted to the gargoyle leader. The huge stone beast lumbered over to me and gazed down at me with adoration in his green eyes. "We have to get that door open."

Baron cocked his head at me, warbled something, and then began bellowing orders to the other gargoyles. The creatures seemed to understand each other in a way that would indicate an intelligent language was being used, though all they did was growl, roar, and bark at each other. Of all of Limbo's denizens, gargoyles fascinated me the most. They lived in both Limbo and the living world at the same time and could interact with both at will. A strange psychological haze clouded the perception of any mortal man who saw them, shrouding their ability to perceive the gargoyles as anything other than statues even when they moved. It was these unique abilities that had led me to ask them for their help for this particular mission.

Baron led the T-Rex and elephant gargoyles to where the door had been, and the trio began to pound away at the mania stone building. Nightingale and Rhapsody began singing 'Eye of the Tiger' to motivate the gargoyles to fight even harder. Though the gargoyles pounded the wall with the force of a speeding eighteen wheeler, not even a chip of stone was scoured from its surface. Just as I was about to take the gargoyles' place and give the banshee wail a shot, I noticed that the sounds of the blows that the gargoyles were raining down on the edifice had suddenly changed. Instead of the sound of rock smashing into rock, it sounded more like rock smashing into soft ground.

The building suddenly shuddered, and I saw a ripple run along its length from ground to soaring rooftop. Then glowing eyes popped open all over the building's surface. The eyes were the size of basketballs, and there were thousands of them all of different colors and hues. Before I could shout out a warning, scores of tentacles the size of oak trees sprang forth from the living chaos building. They smashed, grabbed, hurled, and squeezed everything in their sight, and ghosts weren't immune to them. Both Rhapsody and Nightingale were destroyed in the first ten seconds of the onslaught. Rhapsody was grabbed by one tentacle, and her head was twisted off by another. Nightingale was smashed by a tangle of tentacles that also wiped out her entire guard in one fell swoop. Baron grabbed a tentacle aimed at him and literally ripped it out of the now organic wall, leaving the first scar on the thing's surface. His companions didn't fare so well though. Both the t-Rex and elephant were smashed to powder by tentacles that grabbed them and proceeded to smash them together. I called the wind to me and with unnatural speed was able to barely avoid the building's attacks on me.

"Fall back!" I yelled to the few remaining ghosts and gargoyles.

"Mistress," called Sebastian who had been assigned back to me for this mission. "Shall I call in the cavalry?"

"No!" I shouted back. "This thing will eat us for lunch. Get word to the Governor now. Tell her that a direct assault on these structures will result in utter defeat. We have to find another way to deal with this threat. I've got Nathaniel Carter working on it."

Baron and I did our best to aid the others in escaping the monstrous building's reach, but even so, we lost more than half of those who'd survived the initial onslaught. In the end, only eight gargoyles came out along with four ghosts including myself. We had just lost more than half the city's gargoyles and two of our best sirens. This was a disaster of such monumental proportions that my mind reeled. How could chaos be fought if it could bring this kind of malevolent power to bear? It seemed that at every turn it introduced something new and more terrible than the time before.

I stood across the street from the building staring at it in a shocked state of mind. As the minutes ticked by I watched the building return to its normal state, including the reappearance of an open door and neon sign. I was beginning to lose hope for Brianna when a chittering sound brought me around to find a drenched and smelly ferret scampering from across the road towards me.

"Thank the Lord," I breathed as Brianna shifted back into her beautiful naked self. "I thought we'd lost you for sure."

"Never count a ferret out," she said with a relieved smile of her own; her eyes were haunted though. "It was touch and go there for a few minutes. Fortunately, even buildings that turn into monsters are subject to municipal sewer laws. It's a hefty fine for a public entity to have no operating bathrooms during business hours. Hurray for bureaucracy."

"What about all the people in there?" I asked dreading the answer.

"Some were eaten by the building when it first woke up," Brianna said with a shudder. "The staff moved the majority of the people to safer locations throughout the structure. Things were so crazy in there that no one noticed me. That was a hell of a diversion Veronika. Do you ever do anything small?"

"That diversion was far too costly," I said quietly, turning away from her. My heart ached for what we'd lost, and the souls that would never make it to the celestial gates. "Please tell me we got something in return."

"Where are my clothes?" Brianna asked. Baron answered with a loud rumble and dropped her knapsack into her hands. "I didn't have as much time as I'd like to have had, but I did come up with an interesting bit of information that may be an important lead."

"What?" I asked turning back to face her. I had to hold on to hope.

"I found a file with contract information and brochures from the builders of *Jezebel's*. It's a company called Arkham Enterprises. They have a major facility in Brewerytown. According to the flyers, they specialize in "fantastical architecture". There were pictures of buildings made of similar materials as this one and those at Byberry."

While clearly not what we'd hoped to get, this was indeed very important information. If we could infiltrate the Arkham Enterprises facility, we might be able to learn the purpose and weaknesses of the chaos buildings. We should also be able to learn what other structures have been built in town. It was very likely that Delilah, Curwen, and my body were holed up in one of these secure locations.

"Well done Brianna," I told the shifter as she slipped into her usual tight skinned catsuit. "Let's go get the boys, and then we'll go to Brewerytown."

"Can we stop to get a shower first?" Brianna asked. "I don't want Frank to see me like this."

"Frank's a cop. He's seen and smelled worse."

"Not from his girlfriend," Brianna said indignantly.

"I forgot to mention that perk to you earlier," I told Brianna. "No matter how many sewers I slop through, I never have to worry about smelling or looking bad. I guess being a ghost isn't so bad after all, eh?"

Brianna glared at me with disapproval for a moment then we both burst out laughing. It was a good moment, and it hurt inside not to be able to give the petit woman a hug, at least not without expending too much power. While Sebastian led the survivors of our effort back to Limbo, we walked the three blocks to Brianna's car in pensive silence. Baron came with us, though he had to fly in our wake because he was too big to fit in Brianna's

Mercedes. We stopped at her apartment in Rittenhouse Square so that she could freshen up before we regrouped with Frank and Nathaniel at the Masonic temple.

26

BREWERYTOWN IS A MOSTLY POOR residential neighborhood in modern North Philly. Once upon a time, the district
had featured nine city blocks with each dominated by its own
lager brewing complex, and a central square that was the center
of community activity. In an era half forgotten, it had been a
vibrant community of working class German immigrants who
lived in row houses and worked in the nearest brewery. People
lived and played within sight of the grand buildings that gave
them their livelihoods. In those days, money flowed like beer,
and the great captains of industry took pride in the structures
that represented their companies. Architects were let loose to
practice their art without care of cost, and they produced wonders that the modern world could only marvel at. The brewery
complexes of that golden age were distinctively Germanic and
Romanesque Revival in their architectural style. These buildings
were so well made that the US military rated them as able to
survive nuclear attack. By 1920 when Prohibition became law,
Philadelphia had over seven hundred breweries, but by 1933

when the law was repealed, only four remained. And so began the long decline of the great neighborhood of Brewerytown, and with the decay came the abandonment and eventual demolition of most of the great breweries. Today Brewerytown is a place of lost industry and forced gentrification.

I stood on the Southeast corner of Jefferson and Thirty First streets looking at one of the last behemoths of the lager industry. I was pleasantly surprised and pleased to see that the new occupants of the building hadn't done something as sacrilegious as coat the building in mania stone. The sign on the top of the old F.A. Poth Brewery building now read "Red Bell Brewing Company Welcomes You to Historic Brewerytown". Sadly the return of brewing to this building had been short lived. The new occupants had a small free-standing sign just outside the arched front entrance; it simply read, "Arkham Enterprises". Though it was after three in the morning, lights shone brightly in most of the building's windows.

I called the wind to me and flew around the huge building to make sure there weren't any surprises waiting for us. There was a large parking lot in the back of the building. It was full of trucks and tractors of various types: pretty much what you'd expect a construction firm to have in its lot. What was unusual however was the level of security surrounding the large warehouse building that connected to the lot and was part of the facility. Besides the usual cameras and padlocks, there was a patrol consisting of two vampires and a darkling possessed German Shepherd. The new warehouse was made of mania stone and shared the weird architectural qualities of the other structures made of the chaos stone. I idly wondered if one of the properties of the stone was that it could only be shaped into alien patterns that seemed to play havoc on the human mind. Fortunately, the storm that had hit the city so hard earlier had weakened to a light misting rain that provided me with enough ambient fog that I was able to create a mist cloak out of. Neither the vampires nor the darkling dog detected my presence allowing me to continue my surveillance of the main building without interference. Once I determined that everything was quiet outside the target building, I headed back to the alley a few blocks away where my friends waited for me.

"No perimeter guards outside the main building," I said, suddenly materializing right in front of Frank. He jumped, and then glowered hotly at me. "There's a warehouse made of mania stone in the back, and there are vampire and darkling guards patrolling the back lot."

"How many fucking times do I have to tell you not to do that?" Frank growled at me.

I gave the detective my best 'I'm sorry daddy' puppy dog eyes and he threw his hands up in resigned exasperation.

"Anyways, it looks like there could be activity in the main admin building. There are entirely too many lights on."

"I've been looking into Arkham Enterprises," Brianna said, still staring at her IPad tablet. "They're a privately owned company with extremely deep pockets. They've got their hands in an awful lot of pots. I've been having trouble tracking down exactly who the primary owners are, and that's pretty unusual for me. I'm good at hacking my way into that kind of information. It's the kind of thing you see with drug cartel or vampire owned businesses. They're good at creating false fronts. Arkham Enterprises is very old though. It seems to have been a subsidiary of the East India Company. Who knows, maybe Arkham actually owned that infamous company instead of the other way around."

"Fucking great!" Frank exclaimed as he fiddled with his big ass gun nervously. "It's not fucking bad enough that we have to deal with zombies, chaos nightmares, and buildings that turn into tentacled monsters, now we have to deal with fucking vampires too!"

"Frank's right," Brianna said. "Let's hit this place in the morning when the vamps are more likely to be sleeping."

"We can't assume the vamps will be sleeping," Nathaniel said. "Veronika doesn't have much time, and we're already here."

Silence fell over the alley as all eyes turned to me for a decision. I saw fear and determination in Brianna and Frank's eyes. Carter's were filled with concern and something else: love perhaps?

"We'll hit this place at ten AM," I said decisively, and nodded at the shifter and detective. "You two get out of here and get some rest. I need to talk to Carter alone."

Frank looked doubtful, as if he thought the wizard and I would go in without him. Brianna smiled however; she had a look of understanding and approval in her eyes. She kissed Frank on the ear, whispered something to him, and tugged him towards the mouth of the alley. Carter watched them go and turned back to me once they'd disappeared around the corner; his eyes raged with disapproval.

"We don't have time for this," he said quietly.

"Tomorrow is going to be a hard day for all of us," I replied. "I sense that an even bigger storm will break over the city. I'm tired, I need to recharge, and so do you."

"So you're going back to Limbo?"

I stared into his blazing eyes nervously. Tomorrow I might die; it was time to be bold. The problem is that I've always been a chicken when it came to relationships. I've had far fewer boyfriends in my twenty-one years than most high school students have in their senior year alone. Add to that the horrors of my experiences with Freak, and it shouldn't be any surprise that I'd be a little gun shy. But again, tomorrow I might die, and I really liked Nathaniel.

"You said that love is the most powerful force in the universe," I said quietly. "I felt the truth of those words in your touch, in your kiss, and I was hoping that we could make love if that's possible. I was thinking that maybe we could fuel each other."

I stopped, embarrassed by my rambling forwardness. The hurricane of anger and worry in Nathaniel's eyes changed and instantly became a tornado of love and lust. I didn't feel lust in the traditional sense of the word. I don't have hormones racing through my body after all, but Nathaniel showed clear signs of being quite aroused. His reaction sent a thrill of anticipation through me, and I smiled at him nervously.

"Anything is possible," he repeated huskily. "Come."

I turned to the silent Baron and ordered him to hide on one of the nearby rooftops where he could watch the Arkham Enterprises building, and then I followed the wizard to his car.

27

NATHANIEL LIVED IN A SPRAWLING mansion in the Chestnut Hill neighborhood of Northwest Philly. Normally I'd be paying attention, watching the scenery pass by as we drove through some of the city's more affluent areas, but I was a little too preoccupied to notice much of anything. Part of me was on fire, filled with hope and expectation. Another part of me was terrified, screaming at me to get the hell out before disaster struck. It was insane for me to expect this to work between a ghost and a living person; I was setting myself up for humiliation. And even if it did work, how would Nathaniel react to what had been done to me by Delilah and her pack of maniacs? I was damaged goods, and Nathaniel deserved better. These two sides of me warred within me the entire trip to the wizard's house; I felt incredibly nauseous by the time we got there.

We turned down a wide driveway and approached a closed gate with a pair of hulking lion gargoyles posted atop the brick walls on either side. I gave a start when I realized that they were truly active gargoyles with furies attached to them. Nathaniel mumbled a few words in a language I didn't recognize and the gates opened silently. We passed under the watchful gaze of the gargoyles and drove up a long access road that was bordered by a forest of trees. At least a half dozen more gargoyles lined the road on either side. They watched us pass with impassive stares that gave me the willies.

"Why do you keep so many gargoyles?" I asked the wizard, momentarily forgetting the turmoil within me.

"I've been helping the furies for many years now," he answered. "They loan me the gargoyles to provide security for my residence. I keep wards up of course, but one can never be too careful. The life expectancy of a wizard is quite short these days."

"Hmm...," I mused thoughtfully.

We came around a bend in the drive and a large gothic style mansion complete with an actual tower came into view. It was constructed of black marble with streaks of sky blue that reminded me of celestial steel. There were more gargoyle sentinels posted liberally across the building's edifice.

"Holy crap," I breathed. "Isn't this a little stereotypical for a wizard? It's kind of creepy."

"I was going for foreboding," Nathaniel said, eyes darting over his house in pride. "I call it Orthanc."

He said the name as if I should recognize it; I didn't.

"The Lord of the Rings," he said in disgust. "It's what the tower in Isengard was called."

"I read the books and saw the movies," I said proudly. "I don't know the names of all of those places and people though. It was good and all, but I didn't geek out over it."

"Wait here for a moment," he said as he parked the car and got out. He came around to the passenger side, opened the door, and held out his hand to me. My heart fluttered, ok it really didn't but it felt like it did, and all of the turmoil that had roiled through me while we traveled here came back in a flood. I reached my hand out and paused before taking his. Should I tell him about Freak? Seeming to sense my internal struggle, Nathaniel reached further until our fingers touched. The dam within me broke, and I began to weep. His hand was so warm and alive. He bent over me and put a comforting arm around me.

"It's ok Veronika," he said to me quietly. "Nothing is going to happen here tonight that you don't want to happen. I love you and respect you, and I want you to feel comfortable and safe with me, not afraid."

"But…you don't…know," I wept in misery. "I'm damaged. I'm only good for killing now. I'm good at that."

"You're right," he answered gently. "I don't know what you've been through, but I do know that you are an amazing woman. I saw that when I looked into your soul. Veronika, you have the courage of storybook heroes. You are generous and selfless, you are filled with compassion, and you are a true leader. Your path has been lonely and you've suffered greatly, but you've persevered. You are not used up or unworthy of love; you are the most amazing person I've ever met, and though we've only known each other for a scant few hours, I feel a soul deep connection to you that I doubt I'll ever have with anyone else."

I pulled away from him so that I could look into his eyes. They were gentle pools of liquid compassion. He was the first person to think of me as a person. He didn't refer to me as a ghost; he called me a person, a woman even. Wonder filled me at this. Could he truly feel the way that I did about him? Could he really accept me for what I was despite what had been done to me?

"Can we stay in the car for a bit?" I asked pensively. I didn't want him to be disappointed, but I wanted him to know everything.

"Of course," he said gently. He released me, closed my door, and came back around to the driver side and got in. He put the radio on and took my hand. He then waited patiently for me. I started slowly from that terrible night in that dark alley. I told him everything. When I got to the part about my capture and subsequent torture, I broke down. He held me hard as I wept like never before. He held me and listened to it all. Finally drained, I rested in his arms quietly for a time and then looked up into his eyes fearful of what I'd see.

"Do you hate me?"

"No," he said and kissed me on the forehead. "I love you more. Most people would have broken or given up. Not you. You decided to end everyone's suffering. Tell me, do you believe that Amber, or Bridget, or Melanie aren't deserving of love?"

"No!" I answered indignantly. "They are all amazing people. Anyone would be lucky to have them as friend or lover."

"Then why not you? The tortures and indignities that your sisters suffered at the hands of the Tormentor have made them no less worthy of love than anyone else. It's not their fault what happened to them, just as it isn't your fault. If the banshees are worthy of love, then so are you. You are no more damaged goods than they."

And there it was; the words rang true in my soul. All of my sisters and most of the free souls had suffered unbelievably; all of them deserved love, including me. A weight was suddenly lifted from my shoulders, and I let my love for Nathaniel Carter settle deeply into my soul where it could keep working its healing magic.

"I think I'd like to go inside now, if you still want me that is."

"I want you more than I've ever wanted anyone, my lady."

"Then stop wasting time and get over here and open the door for me."

Like the gentleman that he was, Nathaniel once again exited the car and came around to usher me out of the car; he closed the door behind me with a single word of magical command and then led me up to the front entrance, which passed through a recessed Norman portico flanked by a small tinkling fountain on one side and a mean looking gargoyle on the other. The double doors that confronted us at the end of the portico were made of the silvery blue material that streaked the marble building and reminded me of celestial steel. They were covered in runes. I hadn't had a chance to take runeology in college before I was murdered, so I couldn't read any of them. Like all the other doors around his sanctum, these portals opened silently at a word from Nathaniel.

Unlike the outside of the house, the inside was warm and friendly. The entry foyer gave way to a massive living room furnished with black leather couches and reclining chairs, a fifty-two inch flat screen television equipped with Blu-ray player and full theatre surround sound system, two end tables with fine porcelain lamps, and a large fireplace that promised cozy warmth in winter. The floors were tiled with white marble and several expensive Chinese throw rugs were scattered in strategic locations. Off of the living room through an archway lay a game room complete with pool table, fully stocked bar with stools, and an exercise area with plush mats and a punching bag. A huge kitchen, formal dining room, and two large bathrooms completed the tour of the first floor. Nathaniel let me explore a little while he went about ordering the lamps to turn on and put some mellow jazz music on. I wasn't surprised to find that the music reached every single room through tiny little, nearly invisible speakers.

"Jeez!" I exclaimed. "Wizards sure make a lot of money."

"It's not really my money," Nathaniel said quietly, coming to stand beside me as I surveyed the living room for a second time. "It's money that's been saved and invested for centuries by Arch Mages of the Order. By policy of the Order, any wizard reaching the rank of Arch Mage must maintain a domicile that is both impressive and defensible. In bygone ages this meant castles and wizard towers. Today it means castles or mansions. There aren't many castles in the United States, so I went with the mansion that looks a lot like a castle."

I considered this for a moment and nodded in understanding. As humanity's greatest protectors, wizards were number one on the hit list of any supernatural baddie who had malevolent plans for mankind. Wizards had a pretty low life expectancy, even in modern times, even though they were said to be unnaturally long lived under normal circumstances. The Order of Magi, or whatever they called themselves, would want their most adept members to be as protected as possible, particularly when those wizards were resting or studying. It spoke volumes of the Order's commitment to its primary goal that it hadn't become insular and had resisted the instinct to pull back its members into a few strongly guarded fortresses. Considering the threats they faced, who could have blamed them if they'd retreated behind safe walls? The perks of a lavish house equipped with all the best toys seemed like a only a small benefit considering the hazards that wizards faced daily, and they did so alone.

"How many Arch Mages are there in the United States?" I asked curiously, not really expecting to get an answer.

"In normal times there are always thirteen," Nathaniel answered without hesitation. "One Adept and five Seekers are assigned to each state. If an Adept proves skilled enough to pass his final test to become an Arch Mage and the thirteen slots are occupied, he is assigned to another country. There are more slots than can be filled these days I'm afraid. In fact, there are presently only seven Arch Mages in the United States. We haven't been at full capacity since the 1970's when the Great Malaise hit the country."

I knew that the Great Malaise was an important period in the supernatural world; it was a time in which mankind seemed to withdraw into itself, and worldwide, evil supernatural forces triumphed over humanity's protectors. In the living world the period was understood to mean the decade of economic stagflation, political corruption, and weak Presidential leadership in the United States. Mankind was tired from the century's two world wars and the ongoing Cold War. In its state of depression, humanity didn't notice when evil got the upper hand. Like a cancer, it snuck in and began to corrupt all facets of life; in politics the statesmen dwindled away to be replaced by the ultra partisan, and in business the philanthropic industrial robber barons were replaced by moguls who gambled with their money preferring to invest in unsafe high yield financial instruments like derivatives rather than invest in job creating ventures that the old robber barons had built the nation on. Even worse was the decay in moral values. Most notably, greed and selfishness became accepted norms. Just thinking of mankind's decline and how it had so empowered the forces of evil and chaos depressed me, and I didn't want to think about it anymore.

"Make love to me, Nathaniel," I pleaded, turning to him.

As if sensing my fears, Nathaniel wrapped his arms around me and pulled me close until my head rested against his chest. I could feel the warmth of his hand rubbing small, soothing circles on my back. "It will be alright" he whispered, comforting my unspoken fears.

"Thank you," I told him quietly. I rested in his arms for a full five minutes or so until I felt safe and warm: two things I haven't felt since becoming a ghost. "As nice as cuddling is though, I want you to make love to me."

"I don't know if this is a good time," he hedged, the storm returning to his gaze. "You've got a lot of emotions going through you. I don't want to take advantage of you."

I pushed myself out of his embrace, stepped a pace back from him, and with a single thought changed from my normal skin tight celestial steel mesh battle armor into a sleek, lacy blue negligee with matching pumps and gartered hose. The only thing I altered in my body's appearance were my nails. As a dedicated martial arts practitioner, cultivating long, lustrous nails was highly impractical. I'd occasionally used the fake ones when I'd felt it necessary to impress a date or something, but in general I didn't pay attention to my nails. Now however, my nails were long and painted black like my hair and my toe nails. The rest of me I left normal. I like myself, not in a narcissistic way, but in a healthy, humble, accepting way. I'm not the most attractive girl in the world, but I've got my parents' good looks coupled with an athletic build forged by years of hard work in the dojo.

"That's not fair," Nathaniel groaned.

"Hasn't anyone told you that life isn't fair," I answered bending over to touch my toes and give him a good view of my cleavage.

Nathaniel's eyes were now truly stormy, and he leapt forward and swung me into his arms before I could dodge him. I laughed in pleasure as he carried me up the wide circular staircase that led to the second floor. I craned my head around his shoulder in order to get a glimpse of the rooms we were passing on the way to his bedroom. I saw what must be two guest rooms, another large bathroom, and a library filled from floor to ceiling with books. The floor up here was covered in a plush carpet of white, while the walls were decorated with magnificent tapestries.

The two oaken doors at the end of the hall swung open at his command, and he carried me into his master bedroom. The room was dominated by a four poster bed and an antique oaken wardrobe. A large table filled with tools and scrolls took up a corner of the room, while a fireplace occupied the wall near it. Two windows and a set of French doors leading onto a veranda provided a breath taking view of the English style gardens below. There was a door leading into the master bath and another into a walk-in closet.

Carter unceremoniously plopped me down onto the bed and straddled me. Tendrils of fear and loathing wrapped themselves around my heart, and for a moment it was Freak straddling me. I opened my mouth to scream but fought back against the nightmare. This was Nathaniel, the man I loved. His face hung right over mine, and he looked deeply into my eyes and waited for me to calm. I forcefully pushed all of the fear and loathing into the small place that fuels my banshee scream to use later when I'd need it. Then, I gave Nathaniel what I hoped was my best flirty smile.

"Didn't your daddy ever warn you about teasing wizards ghost girl?" he said huskily.

"My daddy would kick your ass if he saw you right now."

"You are so beautiful," He said gazing down at me with a serious expression on his face.

"Those are just words. I'm a ghost. I can look pretty much like anything you might desire."

"But you are yourself," he said quietly and kissed me.

"How do you know?" I asked breathily when he pulled up to look at me again.

"I'm a wizard. It's my job to know."

"You use that line entirely too often," I said with a shake of my head. "You need a new line."

"You are amazing," He said looking down the length of my body. It's a pretty good body: long legs, firm abs, and shapely boobs that aren't so big that they get in my way. I have a lot of other things going for me too; my long, straight black hair, bright blue eyes, a smile that was known to melt my dad's heart, and a brain that could keep up with most intellectual conversations.

"Stop talking and make love to me, now," I said insistently, my eyes pleading.

"It will be better if you manifest fully," he said.

My heart sank. I couldn't justify that kind of power usage under any circumstances. Full manifestation would result in me having a physical body, but its power costs were huge. Disappointment seeped into me, and I closed my eyes to hide the tears that threatened to well up in them. It had been silly for me to think that I could make love to a living person without manifestation. The fact that he could touch the incorporeal me had given me false hope that he could make it happen somehow.

"It's ok," he said, his lips brushing mine and sending a jolt of electricity through me. "I'll be feeding you energy to replace what you lose. We could do this without you manifesting, but I thought you might like the full experience. Both our spirits and bodies can entwine. The pleasure can be enjoyed on both levels at the same time."

Hope sprang in me like a flower, and I opened my eyes and gazed into his.

"I love it when you talk dirty to me," I quipped. "Can you seriously keep me charged through this? Manifestation is quite costly."

"I'm sure. I learned the technique from a private Franklin journal," the wizard answered. "The old master knew a lot about ghosts. I suspect that he may have done this with one of his lost loves."

I was momentarily intrigued until Nathaniel bit my neck sending warmth and waves of pleasure through my limbs.

"Do it now," he said biting my ear. "It will be twice as pleasurable."

I concentrated, willing my body to manifest fully. The world around me became more vibrant, the colors sharper. My senses were assaulted by things I barely noticed in ghost form: the silk sheets of Carter's bed beneath me, the feel of the negligee on my body, the smell of burning wood from Carter's fireplace, and then his touch on my breasts. That last sent a convulsion through me, and I cried out. Nathaniel chuckled and let his hands glide over my body, slowly tearing more moans from me. I let my own hands rove, and I felt my own pleasure rise when he reacted with his own moan of pleasure.

The foreplay went on for what seemed like hours. We teased each other and ferreted out every pleasure center, exploring each other's physical and spiritual bodies. I played around a little when I was living, but there's no way it could even approach what Nathaniel and I were experiencing now. It was nothing short of magic. And when we finally got down to the love making, well I'm thinking that once you have a wizard you'll never want anything else.

We ended up in a tangle of naked arm and legs both having reached climax at nearly the same moment. We were both breathing heavily, and Nathaniel was covered in a sheen of sweat. His tall, naked body glistened beautifully for me, and I wanted him again, but I knew he wasn't ready for it that quickly. I myself felt rested. I was flush with power, and I felt sexier than ever.

"Can we do that again?" I asked cupping him with my hands, and feeling thrilled when I got a moan out of him.

"You bet," he said lowering his lips to my breast and taking the nipple between his teeth; he bit me lightly, sending shivers down my spine.

The Imperial March, a Star Wars theme song and ringtone on Nathaniel's cell phone, interrupted us before we could get through the second round of foreplay. Nathaniel groaned in disgust, but nevertheless reached for the phone buried in his pile of clothes on the floor.

"Sorry," he said sheepishly. "That ringtone is reserved for very important people."

I shrugged in acceptance and kissed my way down his belly. Just because he was busy didn't mean I couldn't find something interesting to do.

"Its Brianna," he said, and I pulled away from him with sudden trepidation.

"What's up Brianna," he said into the phone after pressing the green button on his display. The time read 5:33 AM.

"We need you and Veronika at the zoo ASAP," the shifter said without preamble. "The pack is under attack."

28

I WATCHED NATHANIEL PUT ON a fresh set of clothes. From his walk in closet he retrieved black jeans and a brown Levi button up shirt which he deposited on the bed next to me. He then fished out a pair of boxers and white low cut socks from the dresser. As he sat down next to me and began getting dressed, I leaned over and kissed him lightly on the cheek and let go of my manifested form.

"Thank you," I said to him as the world returned to its spectral shabbiness and my senses shifted back to normal, which is to say that I lost my sense of smell and touch.

"Hey, no need to thank me," he said earnestly while reaching out with a glowing hand to grasp my own. "I love you. Whatever happens, nothing will change that."

"You make me feel alive," I said. "And I love you too."

"We need to get to the zoo quickly," he said squeezing my hand then letting go of it and pulling on his jeans and tucking in his shirt. The socks and black sneakers followed. After this he went to the wardrobe and selected a black leather duster from a row of them; next came a black Stetson. My man really looked hot as he finished off his wizard costume by choosing a staff covered in blue runes from a rack by the door.

"Open the veranda doors for me," I told him, not daring to try to pass through them. I was fairly certain they'd be heavily warded. "I'll get there in a few minutes on my own. Can you use a broom or something to fly with me?"

"I'm not Harry Potter," he growled. The French doors opened silently when he uttered a single arcane word. He grabbed me and pulled me into his arms for one final kiss before letting me go. "Be careful."

I smiled at him in acknowledgement then called the wind to me and shot through the veranda doors and into the pre-dawn sky. This was what it was like to have someone love you; it was something I had thought lost to me forever. It felt good to have someone worry about me and to feel the same way for him.

A heavy curtain of fog was hanging over the city; fortunately the misting rain had come to an end. I flew Southeast reaching Girard Avenue in Germantown and followed it until I arrived at the Philadelphia Zoo at 34th street. I landed on the roof of the main entrance gatehouse overlooking Zoological Drive. The structure was two stories tall, made of brick, and had a steep cross gabled roof. The zoo was part of Fairmount Park and had been originally designed as a picturesque Victorian garden. The Philadelphia zoo was the oldest zoo in the United States having been established in 1859, and it currently held nearly thirteen hundred animals of various species on its forty two acre campus. It specialized in the breeding of endangered species and was widely respected as one of the best facilities for this kind of sensitive technical work.

The sounds of the park's hundreds of animals as they responded to their keepers' morning rituals of feeding, cleaning, and whatever other task that needed to be done at the crack of dawn was a symphony of sound that only animal lovers can fully enjoy. My dad loved animals, and he passed that love down to me.

He used to give money to the zoo in my name on my birthday. We had both adopted residence of the zoo, being sponsors for especially endangered creatures who needed expensive medical care to give them a chance to survive. The sounds that floated on the air filled me with nostalgia and sorrow. It was a reminder of my past and a place I couldn't let my new ghostly reality touch.

The chorus of natural sound was shattered by the roar of gun fire. It sounded like Frank's big ass gun, and it was coming from inside the park. I drew my katana and leapt into the air calling the wind to me as I flew Northeast towards the sounds of battle. The air was immediately filled with tension and the harmonious sound of nature was replaced by a cacophony of discordant screeches, roars, and cries of terror and rage. The speed at which chaos descends and destroys order is truly mind numbing. Its effects are instantaneous and long lasting, while order requires hard work and vigilance to maintain. This singular reality means the cards are heavily stacked in chaos's favor. It was no wonder that God had locked the enigmatic force that was chaos away from his creation. Nathaniel had explained that God, or the Supreme Being as he called Him, only allowed a sliver of chaos in the form of entropy to touch this world. Now chaos was trying to push itself fully into the living world, and I was afraid that its agents had come to the Philadelphia Zoo.

I flew over a mixture of lush habitats with their myriad pools and varied vegetation and the public access facilities such as snack bars, bathrooms, and pavilions where people could engage in various activities. The park was of course closed at this hour, though the majority of the day-time work force was arriving for the early shift. I passed Bird Lake to the Northwest: a large aviary and bird sanctuary that was among my dad's favorite locations at the zoo. The birds were strangely quiet now though. The shooting was continuing pretty steadily and my heart sank even further as I zeroed in on its location. Big Cat Falls was my personal favorite of the animal habitats followed closely by Bear Country. Though I favored dogs over cats as a pet, I loved watching the curious cats at play. The big cats of this habitat ranged from lions to snow leopards and tigers. There was a beautiful black jaguar and the amazingly fast pumas; all were beautiful and graceful. They were my chosen animal to emulate in combat. That was something my dad had made me choose way back when I was just six years old and just beginning my training in Kendo and Ju-jitsu. We spent hours at the zoo watching and studying every animal, observing their movements and habits. After a full year of this study, dad told me to choose one and to learn how to emulate its habits and movements when practicing my forms and katas. This was not a traditional way to teach either Kendo or Ju-jitsu, but it was something that he passed on to me personally. It gave me my own distinct style and flourish that had made me a champion on the tourney mat. Now my big cats were under attack, not to mention my friends of course. Frank had better not be shooting my lions.

Big Cat Falls is a series of habitats connected by overhead caves that the cats can traverse in order to reach other parts of the habitat. Each area features lush African style vegetation, pools of water, and rock outcroppings. At the very center of the habitat is a fourteen foot waterfall and public pavilion. I tracked the sound of combat to this central tourist spot. The scene that greeted me when I shot over the last tree was horrific. Frank was indeed shooting my lions; already three females were laying at his feet in pools of blood and gore. The male lion that was menacing Brianna and Frank was a huge beast with a full mane that crowned him king of the beasts. The roar that issued from the beast was anything but natural though. Its voice was too high and almost birdlike. It was then that I noticed the tentacles shoot out of its mane as they actually deflected the fresh round of bullets that Brianna unloaded on it with her pistol. Looking more closely, I also noticed that the lion's tail which was lashing back and forth was barbed and oozing a black fluid that sent tendrils of smoke rising when it hit the stone of the walkway. Frank opened up with his big gun and though the fifty caliber bullet was deflected, the mutated lion lost a couple of its tentacles in payment. Apparently my friends had run out of celestial steel rounds because the ammo they were using looked standard. The beast screeched again and moved forward making inexorable progress under heavy fire. I saw Frank urging Brianna to flee, but she would not leave him to face the monster on his own. It was clear that if the lion reached them it would likely kill them both. They were pouring everything they had into it, and it was batting their bullets aside as if they were Nerf balls. For every tentacle that Frank destroyed, two more grew in its place. Steeling myself, I prepared to come to the defense of my friends.

I adopted the cat's tactic of striking unseen from the high ground. I swooped down, launching myself at the chaos lion, and manifested myself and my sword at the very last second before I struck. I could have merely manifested my arm and katana, but I wanted the full strength and momentum of my body behind the blow. The chaos lion's tentacles had eyes of their own however, and they detected me a split second before I struck. Half of its tentacles were instantly diverted to parry my blow, but these tentacles were no match for my celestial steel blade and the katana sheered through them and struck deeply into the lion's neck. The tentacles had slowed the momentum of the blow however, and though the lion was severely wounded it was not a mortal blow.

The beast's head turned one hundred and eighty degrees around to glare malevolently at me. I saw now why it had sounded like a bird. A huge kraken-like beak marred its normally regal lion's face, and a single radiant green eye dominated its forehead.

"The Black City comes!" it croaked at me and then it tried to eat me with that nasty beak. I gracefully dodged its charge and shoved my smaller celestial steel knife into the glowing green eye as its lunge carried it past me. It bucked away from me, tearing my katana from my hand and almost taking the knife too. It shrieked and thrashed for a moment before Frank put it out of its misery with a clip of bullets to the head.

"Are you alright?" he asked coming over to me. I was staring at the scene. My whole body shook with fury and sorrow.

"No, I'm not fucking alright," I shouted. "I'm going to kill whoever decided to throw this party at the zoo. I like fucking lions."

"I'm sorry," Frank said quietly. "I never fucking killed an animal before I met you."

That brought me to my knees, and I couldn't stop the sobs that poured out of me. I was constantly being reminded of how my whole ghostly existence had been consumed by killing. I had become a killer of man and animals, and I was dooming my friends to the same existence. Memories flashed through my mind in rapid succession: the slaughter of darkling possessed dogs at Primal cuts, the sacrifice of an entire free soul unit led by Captain Bret, the massive losses at Christ Church Burial Ground and Jezebel's. All of them were my fault.

"Way to go jackass," Brianna yelled at Frank as she leaned over and tried to comfort me, though it was hard without being able to touch me. "I'm sorry Veronika. Don't listen to the jerk off behind me. You save people: that's what you do. Unfortunately the bad guys don't play fair, and a lot of innocent bystanders get hurt and you're forced to do some very bad things that no one else can or will do in order to save the greater population. I know it hurts, but you have to keep going."

"I'm tired of all the killing," I said still sobbing.

"I know, but if Delilah succeeds at her plan to reanimate you, you'll be doing a lot more killing and it won't be people or things that need to be killed."

That brought me up short. Brianna was right. If I didn't stop Delilah, she would use me to kill every sort of innocent that she could imagine. The thought made me shiver, and I wiped the tears from my face and began to compose myself.

"What you do Veronika is necessary. I know it's unpleasant but someone has to take out the trash."

"What happened here?" I sniffed, getting back to my feet

and feeling mildly embarrassed about breaking down. This was no time for weakness. The bad guys were up to something that could have dire consequences for the entire world; we were going to lose people and animals in this fight. That's the nature of war.

"I got a call from Cynthia Shepherd about forty five minutes ago," Brianna replied. "She is a member of the pack and works here at the zoo. She said that Jezebel and her hyenas had invaded the pack's territory. She was afraid that something bad was going to happen."

"Like what?"

"She probably was worried about a dominance fight for pack control," Brianna said. "But knowing Jezebel's connection to chaos, I worried that something far more sinister was afoot. I called Nathaniel immediately."

"The necromancer at Byberry fucking sacrificed shifters," Frank interjected. "We were concerned that they might be after more of them in order to reanimate you and power whatever other evil they fucking have planned."

I nodded in agreement.

"So what brought you to Big Cat Falls, and what happened to the lions?"

"Cynthia is a big cat expert and mostly works this part of the park," answered Brianna. "When we got here, four of Jezebel's bitches had Cynthia subdued and were carrying her off. When we tried to stop them, they threw a couple of vials of black liquid into the lion habitat. The transformation was nearly instantaneous. The tentacles on the big guy smashed right through the safety barriers as if they were made of tinfoil."

"Alright," I said. "I'll see if I can track down the hyenas who took Cynthia. Are there any other shifters who work here?"

"Half the pack works here," said Brianna.

"Judging by the brazenness of this attack, I'm guessing the enemy is moving into the final stages of its plans," I said. "That means they'll go after the most powerful shifters in the park."

"That would be Bruno in Bear Country, Cynthia here, and Martin the pack master works at the Solitude."

"Go after Bruno. I'll see if I can free Cynthia and then I'll check the Solitude. Call Nathaniel and tell him to meet you at Bear Country."

"What about this mess?" Brianna asked waving her hands at the carnage around us. "Frank and I could get blamed for this."

"I'll have a cleaning team take care of it," I said. "Don't worry, the Ghost Watch is very good at making evidence disappear."

Brianna nodded her thanks. Her green eyes showed relief. The detective and the ferret took off at a jog while I flew off towards the nearest parking lot.

29

THE ONLY REASON I FOUND ONE of the trucks Jezebel was using in her operation was because it had the Arkham Enterprises logo on its doors. It was parked in a service lot backed right up to a loading bay. I landed on the roof of a gift shop that overlooked the small service lot and surveyed my surroundings. The only vehicle in the lot was the truck, and its driver sat behind the wheel nervously fiddling with the seat belt as the engine idled. The back of the truck was almost up against the building, and a ramp was barely visible as it hung off the back end of the truck and disappearing into the gift shop below.

The driver's aura was radioactive green, marking him as a Mountain Dew zombie, so I didn't feel bad about landing on the truck's cab and driving my katana down through the roof and into his head. With a single thought, I caused the spirit blade to fully manifest. The zombie was killed instantly as six inches of celestial steel suddenly appeared in its head and exploded its brain in an instant. I let the katana go back to its ghostly form and silently thanked God that neither celestial steel nor devil's iron could commonly be used in such a way in the living world. Any ghost who could do what I just did would be an unstoppable assassin. The problem of course was that if I could do it, someone else could too. It might be a rare ability, but it was both arrogant and foolish to think that I was the only ghost with this talent.

I dropped down into the cab to make sure the zombie was dead. The green aura was gone, and it slumped against the wheel. A trickle of blood flowed from one eye and its mouth. I was disquieted by my own growing skill at killing; it was so much cleaner in Limbo, almost cartoon like, but this was real, and it made me loathe myself. I passed through the back of the cab into the cargo trailer. It was dark back here but nothing that my ghostly senses couldn't overcome. I found Cynthia manacled to the trailer's wall. She was naked, and the bruises that covered her body bespoke of the beating she'd taken. She was conscious though, and her yellow-black eyes regarded me with feline defiance. I liked this woman already.

"It's ok," I told her quietly. "I'm a friend of Brianna's."

She said nothing but watched me curiously as I moved to her side to inspect her bonds. They were made of mania stone as I'd feared. I stepped back a moment to ponder the problem. My celestial steel weapons were weaker on this side of the veil while the mania stone seemed stronger. Cutting through the manacles might not work at all, and in any case it would take too long. I could just drive away with the truck and get Cynthia to somewhere safe, but then I'd be abandoning the others. Not to mention, if there were any hyenas close by they would hear me pull away and would likely catch up to a truck with their supernatural speed. I decided to try the trick I'd employed when rescuing my banshee sisters from their iron maiden prisons in the Walnut Street Penitentiary. Uncertain how well this would work outside of Limbo, I called the fog of Philadelphia to me, not all of it, but enough to fill the trailer with such a thick mist that it was impossible to see your hands even when they were practically touching your face. I then willed the fog to compress and fill the space between Cynthia's wrists and the manacles. The fog was strangely reluctant to touch the mania stone, but with a push of my will it complied with my wishes. I then forced the mist to take on a physical form and to push outward on the mania stone. I watched in fascination as the mist began to glow brightly. Cynthia shivered and she now watched me with awe and fear in her eyes. The glow increased and the manacles suddenly began to crumble away like dry mud that has been struck by a hammer. Cynthia fell forward, and I manifested so that I could catch her before she hit the ground.

"Can you walk," I asked urgently. "We need to get you out of here, but I can't manifest for long. It's too costly."

"I can walk," Cynthia said with a grimace as she righted herself and shuffled towards the open trailer door. "When I get my hands on those hyenas!"

"Not today," I told her curtly as I returned to my incorporeal form. "You have some broken ribs, I think. I know you'll heal quickly, but I didn't rescue you so you could get captured again. You'll get an opportunity real soon to strike back. I promise."

Cynthia's shoulders bunched up in stubbornness, and she seemed to go through an internal struggle.

"Mumfasa agrees with you," she said finally. "Where do we go?"

"You get up front and drive this truck away," I said guessing that Mumfasa must be the name of the cat fury that shared Cynthia's body. "There's a dead zombie up there. Just push it aside."

Cynthia blanched at this, but she nodded and got moving. I waited until she had driven away, making sure that no one would pursue her. A hyena did indeed emerge from the open service door; one instant she was a beautiful blond dressed in black hot pants and a sports bra, the next she was a streaking spotted hyena. Her clothes were shredded as she made the near instant transformation. I caught her with a concentrated banshee wail before she'd gotten ten paces down the road. I know it wasn't fair, but in war those who fight fair suffer unnecessary casualties. The blast did to her body pretty much what her transformation had done to her clothes: shredded it. It wasn't pretty. The zoo was going to have a hell of a time cleaning the blood stains. I should've felt a lot worse about what I did, but God help me, I didn't. This was one of the bitches that mutated my poor lions.

I waited an additional thirty seconds to make sure that there were no other pursuers. I kept my eyes averted from the stain that I'd made of the hyena stripper. The last thing I needed was more reminders of what a monster I'd become. It's fortunate that when ghosts go to sleep we don't dream. If I could dream, I knew that I'd have nightmares about myself turning into a horrible beast. Once I was sure that Cynthia had made her escape, I launched myself back into the sky and headed for the Solitude.

The Solitude is an elegant two story English colonial home that belonged to John Penn, the grandson of Philadelphia's founder William Penn. The box like house was now an administration building for the zoo and was surrounded by gardens and zoo habitats. I was flying over the Peacock Pavilion when the house came into view. I knew right away that things weren't good there. As if to confirm my worries, the sounds of gunfire rang out once more coming from North of the house in the direction of Bear Country. A moment later there was an explosion that told me Nathaniel had joined Brianna and Frank. That put my mind at ease a little. The thought of Frank and Brianna having to confront a mutated grizzly by themselves sent a shiver through me. Nathaniel could handle the forces of chaos even better than I could though.

I landed on the roof of the Solitude and let myself pass through it until I reached the floor below where I tethered myself. The top floor of the manor was a nightmare of death and destruction. Whatever had passed through here had torn the unlucky zoo staff to pieces and had flung furniture around as if they were matchbox toys. I didn't find a single living person. The ground floor was even more horrifying if that can be believed.

There was no living person on the first floor, just a lot of bloody meat; it was so messy that it was hard to believe that the gore represented what had once been living people. My stomach churned and I wanted to vomit. Crawling into a dark hole and hiding forever seemed like a good idea too, but I couldn't do that, and ghosts don't vomit. I followed the trail of mayhem to another service lot in the Southern part of the park. It was painfully obvious that the enemy had taken what it wanted from the Solitude and made its escape.

I flew North till I reached Bear Country where I found Brianna, Frank, and Nathaniel finishing off a mutated polar bear. The poor creature's normally huggable face was marred by a kraken beak and a green eye in its forehead. All around my three friends lay piles of dead bears of all types. Whatever the outcome of the war we were fighting against chaos, the blow it had struck today against innocence, against the soul of God's creation, would reverberate through time and space. This attack was a message that everything that we cherished and anything that we held sacred could and would be corrupted or destroyed.

"Did you get Bruno?" I asked as soon as I'd landed among my friends. They all looked haunted and weary.

"No," said Frank. "They fucking took Bruno and set these bears on us. If the fucking wizard hadn't shown up when he did, Brianna and I would have been torn apart. There were too fucking many of them."

"Alright," I said as the sounds of sirens started up in the distance. "It's time for you guys to get out of here. I managed to rescue Cynthia, but the Solitude was a wreck. I'll do a fly over the park to see if I can't nab Bruno's kidnappers. Then I'll get a cleanup team in here. We'll meet in Brewerytown as previously planned. It's likely that those taken from here will be taken to where my body is. Arkham Enterprises is our only chance to get a bead on a location before all hell breaks loose."

No one argued with me, and we scattered in all different directions. I did a quick but thorough flyover the park paying particular attention to the service and maintenance lots but to no avail. Bruno and the hyenas were gone. The PPD was on the scene now. The cleanup crew would have to do some quick work. The Ghost Watch maintained a very skilled team of ghosts whose job it was to cover up anything we don't want mortal authorities to know about. This was an aspect of my job that I hated. I was generally vehemently against interfering in mortal affairs, but there were times when it was necessary. In this case, my friends needed to be protected. The authorities would not look favorably on their actions this morning, and they could all find themselves in county lockup if the police found out. The cleanup crew would take care of fingerprints, video, and ballistic evidence. By the time the cleaning crew was done, the PPD would be left with a lot of unanswered questions that would likely result in a concocted story of a mentally deranged individual shooting animals and zookeepers. It was a pretty classic scenario that the public would buy.

Without further preamble, I translated back into Limbo and went looking for the cleanup crew.

30

"Is everything alright?" Nathaniel asked as I appeared in the Brewerytown alley we'd chosen as our meeting place.

"I think so," I said. "Sorry for my tardiness. I had trouble finding the cleanup crew, and then I got caught up in a battle outside the Franklin Institute."

"Did the cleanup crew fix everything?" asked Brianna worriedly.

"A battle outside the Franklin Institute?" asked Nathaniel. "What's going on in Limbo?"

"Cleanup crew reported back to me a half hour ago," I said. "Everything has been sanitized. As far as the PPD knows, none of you were anywhere near the zoo this morning. They even planted camera footage of you at various locations in the city while the attack was underway. As for Limbo, the number of chaos incursions has increased dramatically."

"Can we get this fucking party started?" Frank asked impatiently.

I nodded my agreement. All three of my friends looked tired; the sooner we got this done, the sooner they might be able to get some rest.

"Let's do it," I said and led the way out of the alley.

The city was awake at this hour of course and both vehicle and pedestrian traffic was moderate in this section of town. The good thing about being in a big city is that you really have to work at attracting attention. People are used to seeing multicolored freakish hairdos, scantily clad biker chicks, or two guys making out on a park bench. Compared to the wild sights you sometimes see on the streets, my three friends are relatively common. Frank Cooper kind of messes with this invisible commonality though. He still dresses and walks like a cop, and a certain segment of the population always notices cops. I was going to have to get Brianna to work on that with him at some point, but for our purposes today, being tagged as cops wasn't a bad thing. People wouldn't interfere with us as we went about our business, nor would they call the real police on us.

Once I was sure that no one was taking undue notice of us, I flew on ahead to the front door of the Arkham Enterprises building. I tried to stick my head through the door to get a peek inside before the others arrived, but my face smacked into a coating of mania stone, and I recoiled from the foul ore's touch. Nathaniel looked at me questioningly as he and the others joined me on the landing of the old brewery.

"The interior is lined with mania stone," I said with disgust. I signaled Baron to join us. The gargoyle flew down from the building across the street where he'd stationed himself to watch, he landed besides me. The gargoyle elicited wild eyed stares from passersby's, but like in most cases where the human mind can't deal with what it perceives, they make up something that they can plausibly understand. In Baron's case, people probably saw him as a huge guy in weird SWAT armor.

"Hi Baron," I greeted the gargoyle. "Would you open this door for us please?"

Baron growled his greeting to us and reached for the door's brass handle.

"That's gonna make too much fucking noise," Frank objected

looking around nervously. He clearly thought that Baron was about to rip the massive brass door from its frame.

"Watch and learn," I told him.

Baron held the door handle with one hand and laid his other hand flat on the door. Nothing happened for a moment, then his huge hands seemed to pulse and turn into liquid. Then they melted into the door itself. The door shuttered and we heard the sound of a heavy chain falling to the ground on the other side, followed by a click. Baron withdrew his hands and one of the doors slid open soundlessly.

"Holy fuck," Frank exclaimed in shocked admiration. "That's pretty fucking useful."

Baron growled in pleasure as Brianna stared at his handiwork with envy. Nathaniel didn't seem surprised and would have stepped into the brewery first if I hadn't been paying attention. Calling the wind to lend me speed, I slid into the building ahead of him. I heard him sigh in exasperation, and I could just imagine his stormy grey eyes staring at my backside with a mixture of tempered annoyance and maybe a little lust. I do have a nice ass after all. The thought made me smile; I wished our private morning could have gone on forever.

Forcing my mind back to the task at hand, I scanned the short hallway that I'd walked into, searching for any signs of trouble. There were no immediate guards at hand, nor was there any sign of an alarm having been raised. The front door had been secured with a heavy chain and the deadbolt was thick; the interior of the door had a coat of mania stone painted onto it. It was an impressive array of security except for not having taken gargoyles into account, but then again, most people don't know about the gargoyle's transmutation capabilities. The interior floors were made of black and white checkered rubber tile, while the walls were finished in oak paneling. To the right of the door was an unoccupied mahogany desk with a laptop computer resting on it. The walls were covered with poster advertisements for various beers made at the brewery. As I moved down the hall to get a look at the larger room beyond, Brianna slid into the leather chair at the desk and began to tap keys on the mobile computer. Frank took up a defensive position near her while Nathaniel and Baron followed me.

The room beyond the short entry hall was cavernous, encompassing nearly the entire length of the building except for a bank of offices on its Western side. The space was mostly open except for a small portion of it being devoted to cubicle work spaces. There was a staircase going to the upper floors in the Northeast and Northwest corners of the room. As we entered, a single vampire strode across the open floor towards us. The blood sucker's aura was all wrong though. There were black smears and Mountain Dew green mixed into its normally pure scarlet hue.

"You ever see that?" I asked Nathaniel as the vampire approached. Baron growled in warning, and I prepared to pounce on it. It moved with liquid grace, not hurrying or showing any signs of fear. It was male with a tall lithe body, and a handsome face framed by a goatee and black eyes. It was wearing black slacks and a blue button up shirt opened casually down to mid chest. I wondered if it meant to speak to us. Maybe it was confused as to who we might be or perhaps it was waiting for us to let down our guard long enough for it to gain the advantage through a sneak attack.

"No, I've never seen this before," Nathaniel said. "Careful."

I decided that it planned to strike us first while our guard was down and so I resolved to strike before it could; I'd strike when it got to within twenty feet of us. Unfortunately it struck when it was twenty five feet from us. It raised a hand towards us and made a shooing motion. The air in a twenty foot radius around us shimmered, and suddenly I was plummeting towards the ceiling as gravity reversed itself. I immediately tethered myself to the floor falling back three feet to the ground, but Nathaniel and Baron weren't so lucky as they fell onto the ceiling head first. The vampire raised his hand again and then closed it making it into a fist. His gaze was locked onto the sprawling Nathaniel who was trying to regain his equilibrium. A bubble of opaque darkness suddenly engulfed the wizard, and I saw him claw at his throat, clearly trying to catch his breath.

As the vampire turned its attention towards me, rage and desperation filled me. Not Nathaniel I howled internally. As the vamp raised his hand towards me, I let loose with my banshee wail. It struck the vampire full on and shredded him into a mist that was blown half way across the room. The chaos infused creature that remained was apparently unaffected by my sonic attack.

The thing that had possessed the vampire was a being of chaos, not a demon. It was an oozing ball of jelly filled with the blood of its victims. It had no discernable face, though there were many eyes of various colors that would appear and disappear randomly all over its bulbous body. It floated in the air and wielded dozens of tentacles, each with a fanged mouth that cried piteously to be fed. The only reference that I had for this mind numbing horror was Japanese anime. I'm a stinking ghost, a bad ass banshee who kills demons in my spare time, and this fucking thing scared the living shit out of me. What could I do against a monstrous being that could survive my banshee wail and had power over gravity?

The roaring of Frank's big ass gun snapped me out of my stunned terror, and I looked around to find that he and Brianna had entered the huge room. Frank was wild eyed as he let fly his entire clip into the thing. It was fortunate that I'd made sure to bring back celestial steel ammo from Limbo. The bullets tore gaping holes into it, and when the fifth one struck, the jelly monster exploded in a shower of blood and opaque chaos ooze. Baron and Nathaniel plummeted back to earth; this time it was natural gravity that yanked them down onto the floor. The bubble that had enveloped Nathaniel popped on impact, and the wizard rolled onto his back gasping for air that now rushed into his lungs. I ran to his side, desperate to make sure that he was alright.

"Are you ok?" I asked lamely, wishing that I could hold him but not daring to expend the power in case another of those things should be nearby.

"I'll be fine," he coughed. "Just as soon as I can get more air. Damn it, I didn't expect that."

"What the hell was that thing?" asked Brianna in a quavering voice.

"A fucking star lurker if I had to guess," said Frank sounding pissed off and terrified at the same time.

"Yes, a star lurker Ooze Horror from outer space," replied Nathaniel, who was slowly getting to his feet now. "They are pretty rare, very powerful, and hard to kill. I guess celestial steel is Kryptonite for them. I'll have to catalogue that. It was fortunate that you provided Frank with more of that ammo."

"No fucking kidding."

"I want more of that stuff when you get a chance Veronika," Brianna said.

A noise at the far end of the room caught our attention and we all turned in time to see three more vampires emerge from one of the offices. Their auras were exactly like the first's.

"Those aren't like that other one right?" Brianna asked in a pleading voice.

"I'm afraid so," I said drawing my katana and long knife.

"I'm ready this time," Nathaniel said grimly. "Baron your job is to keep them off of me. Veronika, use your wail to take out their meat suits. The body protects the lurker beneath from any harm. Frank, you hold your shots till Veronika takes off their masks. Brianna, provide fire support for Frank. I'll counter the worst of their spells."

I didn't wait for the vamps to come to us. I called the wind to me and sped towards them, flying at a six foot height and gathering suppressed rage as I went. The vamps scattered using their own supernatural speed to get far apart before I could hit the entire group with my banshee scream. I was forced to choose one of them: a female dressed in an elegant executive's suit. I let loose with my sonic scream when I was a mere three feet from her as she was running for the cover of the nearby cubicles. She leapt straight up just as I screamed, and the attack missed her. She came down on my back as I passed through the space where she'd been a millisecond earlier. While she should have passed right through me, the chaos creature within her sent its tentacles through her flesh and latched onto me.

As soon as the tentacles grabbed me, their little mouths began to suck power out of me. A wave of dizziness threatened to send me careening out of control, but through sheer force of will I ignored the feeling and began a rapid vertical ascent. I hit the ceiling at full speed, passing through it easily until the vampire smashed into it too. The tentacles were torn away from me, and I flew through the floor above without the extra rider. As soon as I cleared the floor, I somersaulted in mid air and dove back through it in hot pursuit of the falling vampire who was still clearly stunned by the impact with the ceiling. I let loose with my banshee wail before she hit the ground, turning the air around me into a bloody haze. The lurker halted its falling descent effortlessly, and it crooned in pleasure at the blood shower it found itself in. The pleasure was short lived however as I plunged into the mist and drove both katana and knife into its gelatinous form. It screeched in surprised agony and tried to grab me with its tentacles again, but I evaded them and stabbed it some more. I had to strike it three more times before it finally fell to the ground in an oozing puddle.

Meanwhile the other two vamps had circled around my friends coming at them from two different directions. The big muscled guy was pointing a finger at Frank, and a black beam of chaos energy shot from his hands toward the detective. Nathaniel roared a single unfamiliar word and a bright blue dome of energy suddenly appeared over my three friends. The beam hit the dome and the shield seemed to get a little less bright, but the black beam vanished without hurting anyone. The other vampire, a male in a silk suit, began to chant and the outlines of a portal began to form three feet away from him. I shot towards him knowing that whatever gate to chaos he was opening we wouldn't like what came out. I hit him with my banshee wail as he was saying the name *Yog-Sothoth* over and over again. As with the other vampires, his body was obliterated into liquid meat. The star lurker that was left behind continued the chant in a hair raising trill that formed words and chilled the blood. Nathaniel dropped the shield, and Frank unloaded an entire clip into the lurker; it took four shots to pop it this time.

The third vampire tried to envelop Nathaniel with another airless bubble, but the wizard countered the spell by shooting a bolt of lightning from his outstretched hands. The bolt pierced the bubble that was forming around him and continued on to strike the vampire in the chest, sending it flying twenty feet away where it landed in a writhing heap. The wizard strode forward ten feet and struck the vampire again with a second bolt of electricity as it tried to stand up. I flew in above Nathaniel and struck the vampire with a banshee wail as it was once again trying to get to its feet. As soon as the lurker became visible in the wake of the vampire's messy demise, it shot a beam of dark energy towards Nathaniel who sent a baseball sized globe of molten fire at the oncoming beam. The fire ball exploded upon impact with the chaos beam and everything within ten feet of the blast was burned to ash. Everything except me and the lurker of course. The chaos creature was stunned long enough for me to get within reach of it, and I got two good stabs into it before it suddenly vanished out of thin air.

I stared at the spot where it had been in stunned surprise and wondered where it had gone. A gasp of fear brought both Nathaniel and I around to find that the lurker had reappeared next to Brianna and had grabbed onto her with several hungry tentacles.

31

"No!" Frank shouted in anguished fear as he tried to position himself in such a way that he could shoot the thing without hitting Brianna.

Though in obvious pain, Brianna maintained her composure. She shifted into ferret form, surprising the lurker with the sudden loss of mass. I called the wind to me, and in a blink of an eye I was across the room threatening the lurker once more. I slashed and severed the tentacle that still held Brianna, and the ferret leaped away from the monster with a frightened squeak as she ran for cover. The lurker uttered some words that seemed to make the very foundations of creation tremble, and it suddenly began to grow. It grew until it was the size of a bus. Hundreds of beak-like maws with needle teeth began to appear and disappear all over its gelatinous body. Baron attempted to get in close to the thing, but the chaos beast batted the gargoyle aside as if he were a rag doll. The unfortunate gargoyle was sent flying across the room to crash in a heap of thrashing stone limbs.

"Holy fuck!" Frank swore.

"Your telling me," I agreed and turned a questioning gaze on Nathaniel. I wasn't too worried about Baron. The stone gargoyle had survived worse beatings than what he'd just taken, so I was fairly sure that he would be fine. "Have you ever seen a lurker do this? How do we kill it?"

Nathaniel shook his head in negation. His stormy gray eyes were regarding the mammoth chaos beast with a mixture of interest and horror. The thing's thousands of mouths began to chant in a booming shrill screech that put us all to trembling.

"Yog, Yog, Yog-Sothoth!"

The beast's massive tentacles began to whip around, smashing up the large room's scant furnishings and making the structure shake. I yelled to the slowly rising Baron to stay away, and Nathaniel put up another shield dome over all of us except Brianna who was nowhere to be seen. A tentacle smashed into the dome, and Nathaniel stumbled as the shield quivered and dimmed for a heartbeat. The tentacle paused, and an eye suddenly opened on its surface. It studied the shield closely for a moment, and then a mouth appeared below the eye and it began to lick the ward's surface with a blackish, swollen tongue. More tentacles drew in closer, mouths formed on their ends, and they all began to shriek in unison while the first tentacle mouth continued to lick the magical surface of the barrier.

"I'd suggest getting the fuck out of here, but I'm not leaving without Brianna."

"The ferret can take better care of herself than we can at the moment. But we can't leave this monstrosity loose in the city. Veronika, do you have any ideas?"

I turned to stare at Nathaniel in dismay.

"Who's the wizard here, me or you? I don't know anything about these monsters. I could try to blow it up with a full dispersal blast of my banshee wail, but that'd probably bring half of this historic building down around us. I doubt that the siren's song will work. Other than those, we've got my sword and Frank's bullets. How bout you use fire on it? Most things hate fire."

Nathaniel shook his head no. The giant monster was beating on one of the outer walls, threatening to bring the building down on us.

"I'm the only one that can protect us, and keeping this ward up is hard enough. You'll have to make it go away Veronika. Try one of the mist tricks you told me about, the ones you used during the war for shadow Philly."

"Whatever you two are going to fucking do, do it fucking soon before this blob brings the fucking building down on our heads!"

"I can't do any of those tricks here. I need fog to do them, and most of it has burned off by now."

"I can conjure as much fog as you need."

"You can?" Chunks of the ceiling were beginning to rain down around us now, though they bounced off of Nathaniel's ward, leaving us unharmed.

"Yes."

I watched as the wizard squatted down in front of me. He withdrew a small pyramid from his duster. I stared at the artifact in surprise because it seemed to be made of both celestial steel and devil's iron. It had an eye etched into all four sides of its surface. After setting it on the floor in front of me, Nathaniel then drew a chop-stick sized wand, also apparently made of celestial steel and devil's iron, and tapped the pyramid three times. He then began to chant in his arcane language. The giant lurker continued raging; its tentacles smashed relentlessly into the shield dome. I noticed with concern that blood was beginning to trickle from Nathaniel's nose. Every blow on his shield caused him to flinch. I was certain that any other person would have broken by now, but not Nathaniel.

"I'll try the vortexes then."

A thick fog began to pour out of the pyramid and quickly filled the dome around us. I immediately began to call it to me, willing it to form into hundreds of deadly vortexes.

"That's fucking cold," Frank complained, rubbing at his arms and looking very uncomfortable in the magical mists. "It feels like someone is dancing on my fucking grave."

"You're feeling the energies of the world of the dead. The artifact is pulling mist that Veronika is used to working with, and it's doing so without weakening the veil between our world and Limbo. Of course, it's still not good for the living to be exposed to Limbo's energies. We'll probably both lose a few years off of our lives."

"Then why the fuck are you exposing us to it?"

"Would you rather be eaten by the lurker today? I figured what's a few years compared to dying now?"

I ignored their banter and continued to call more mist and form more miniature tornadoes, filling all available space in the shield bubble while making sure to leave ample breathing space for my friends.

"Drop the shield," I shouted to Nathaniel once I'd made as many of the vortexes as I could safely contain in the confines of the dome. "I want the two of you to fall back and take shelter."

With a sigh of relief, Carter released the shield, and before the lurker had time to react, I launched my tornadoes at it. The first volley I sent against the nearest tentacles. I then continued to pull more fog from Limbo, making more vortexes while sending wave after wave of the tornadoes at the chaos beast. The creature went wild with rage as multiple vortexes tore several of its limbs off. I perceived quite quickly however that the lurker was too big to be hurt very badly by the small vortexes; most of the tornadoes that hit the huge gelatinous surface of the monster were dispelled without doing any significant damage. They did keep the thing from destroying us, but that was just a momentary distraction. As my mind raced to come up with an alternative plan, the intuitive and impulsive part of me was already in motion. Not fully understanding why I was doing it, I began to pull the vortexes into me.

The power that began to fill me was mind numbing. I felt myself growing and becoming something new. I laughed with joy as I pulled more mist into me. I was now as large as the lurker. I could see in all directions around me, and my head was nearly touching the ceiling. I knew that a simple little touch from me could tear the beams and flooring around me asunder. I noticed Nathaniel and Frank gaping at me from where they'd taken shelter in the corner stair well. Only Brianna eluded my three hundred and sixty degree vision. Off to one side I saw that Baron was clapping his stone hands in glee and was barking wildly at me.

The Lurker attacked first, its tentacles slashing and striking deeply into me. Without a thought, I tore them to shreds. I was the mist and the wind: nothing could hurt me. The lurker's mouths began to chant, and a bubble of airlessness cut me off from the source of the fog. As I began to shrink rapidly, I desperately willed all of the celestial steel on my body, my weapons and armor, to become bits of shrapnel which I scattered along my whirling wind form. The steel shrapnel struck the bubble's edge with the force of an F5 tornado and it burst. I pulled fog into me once more and launched myself at the lurker, enveloping it with my mighty winds. I filled its mouths and eyes with my deadly celestial steel projectiles. Even in the face of the storm, the lurker defied the laws of order and maintained its chaotic form. Like any storm that encounters a mountain, I began to weaken. I'd hurt the lurker badly, but it refused to be destroyed. Rage filled me, and I let loose with a tightly focused banshee wail. What can I say? Despite the risk involved, the banshee's wail was still the best tool in my arsenal.

For just a moment, it looked like the lurker was going to withstand the wail of a twenty foot tall banshee; it paused for a moment, a look of confusion crossing its thousands of eyes; then it shook itself like a dog, and just as I thought it was going to attack again, it flew apart in a shower of ooze that left a three inch puddle across the entire room. Though the building shivered at my wail and pieces of masonry fall from the ceiling, it didn't fall, proving that it was indeed capable of withstanding a nuclear blast. And just like that it was over. I squelched the vortexes within me, released the fog, and promptly fell to the floor in exhaustion. I felt as though I'd run a marathon with a car strapped to my back.

Nathaniel walked across the room and waved his wand at the pyramid which stopped filling the room with fog. He then picked up the artifact, put it into the pocket of his duster, and finally ambled over to me. I felt his warm, glowing hand on my shoulder and almost immediately started feeling better as power flowed from him into me. I tried to push him away, worried that he'd overextend himself, but he stubbornly maintained his hold on me until I was nearly fully powered again.

"Stop. You're tired. I don't want you expending all of your energy on me."

"Hush. This actually doesn't cost very much. It's another trick from Franklin, most of us thought it useless knowledge. It's called the ghost battery spell."

32

"THAT WAS SOME FUCKING COOL SHIT!" exclaimed Frank as he picked his way through the sludge to stand a few paces away from Nathaniel and I. "Those tornadoes weren't fucking working so you made a bigger one, and made yourself a giant inside of it. When your clothes and weapons shattered into blue shrapnel, you looked like a fucking badass naked diva queen. That was a fucking sight I'll never fucking forget."

"What about this sight, Franky boy?" called Brianna from across the room. She was standing in the doorway that the vampires had come from; she was totally naked and had a sultry come hither look on her face. "If you ever want a piece of this again, you'd better forget the diva. Now come and check out what I've found."

She turned and with a suggestive shake of her ass disappeared into the office. Frank was first to move. He had a leering smile on his face. Apparently he was having a good day with all the naked women around. Nathaniel helped me to my feet and we followed Frank, hand in hand, the wizard continuing to feed power into me. Baron followed us making waves in the slowly receding slime left by the super lurker.

"Could you really see me in the vortex?" I asked Nathaniel.

"Yup," he answered with a glint in his eyes. "Twenty feet tall, a true Amazon queen with your black hair flying wildly in the wind: It was quite a sight."

"I thought I'd become the wind," I said embarrassed. "I could see all around me. I could feel everything. I wasn't actually naked was I?"

"Oh yeah you were. A twenty foot tall goddess in the buff. What a sight," he grinned at me then turned serious. "That was an impressive display of power. You would have been a wizard on Master Franklin's level I think, though the Order's outdated views on training or even finding women with the gift would've limited you."

My embarrassment vanished replaced by surprise and pride.

"Really! But I don't do magic or anything like that."

"What do you call controlling the mists?" He asked. "You make yourself invisible with it, you make tornadoes out of it, and you make yourself bigger and faster with it. I'd call that magic, wouldn't you?"

"I thought that that was some unique power I have as a banshee," I protested.

"No," Nathaniel said firmly. "It's magic. The fact that you can wield it so effectively without knowing what you are doing shows how disciplined a mind you have."

"But I don't use arcane words. I've never studied magic, so how can I use it?"

"Words are meaningless in the use of magic, they only help focus the mind," he answered. "Imagination and will are what matter in spell crafting. If you can imagine it and then make it happen through your will, then you've used magic."

I stared at him dumbfounded. I did that all the time. It couldn't be that simple, could it?

Before we could talk about it any further though we arrived at the doorway that Brianna and then Frank had disappeared into. Looking in, we found a large office with a desk in one corner, a paper covered table in the center, and a bulletin board sized map of Philadelphia covering one wall. Frank was standing in front of the map staring at it while Brianna was sitting at the desk punching the keyboard of a desktop computer. Nathaniel and I joined Frank at the map and I immediately noticed the dark pins dotting the city. There were four large black ones, one at Byberry, another in Penn's Landing marking the spot where Jezebel's was located, one here in Brewerytown, and the last at Fort Mifflin. Dozens of smaller black pins were scattered about the city, but they all had one thing in common: they were pinned on a cemetery. Baron remained in the doorway watching us and the main room.

"Do we know what the pins represent?" I asked no one in particular.

"They're all locations where Arkham Enterprises has a contract to build using their newly patented alloy with their unique architectural style," Brianna answered pointing towards the table. "It's all there."

"Contracts and blueprints," said Frank. "Looking at this map though, I can't see any pattern. Why all these cemeteries?"

"That's because there isn't one" Brianna answered. "I just fed this info into Quantico's mainframe; it says there is no pattern."

Both Frank and I turned to stare at the still naked young woman. Her fingers flew over the keyboard almost faster than I could see.

"Quantico!" Frank exclaimed. "Don't fucking tell me you hacked into the CIA's computer network."

"Of course I did," she replied innocently. "They've got the best computers in the world, except for maybe Israel's intelligence services. Why would I use anything else for this important matter?"

"She's got a point," I told Frank.

"I know what's going on," said Nathaniel grimly. He was still staring at the map. His body was completely still, and the look of dread on his face scared the hell out of me.

"What?" Brianna asked fingers pausing on the keyboard as she gave the wizard her full attention. "I've checked the FBI and NSA main frames as well, they all agree, there is no pattern."

"There's no pattern that logical beings or their machines could understand," Carter answered. "We are dealing with chaos and it doesn't operate logically. All of these chaos element structures are simply dimensional anchors. Their size, location, or architectural style is irrelevant. They simply need a certain number of them scattered about the city. Judging by this map, I'd guess they have enough."

"Enough for what?" I asked in the silence that followed his words. None of us wanted to hear the answer; we all knew that it would be terrible.

"They're going to bring the black city here," Nathaniel answered simply.

We all gaped at him in uncomprehending astonishment.

"What the fuck does that mean?" Frank finally blurted into the heavy silence.

"It means no more Philadelphia," Nathaniel said turning to face us, his stormy eyes blazing with intensity. "The black city will switch places with our fair city of brotherly love. Philly will be moved to the chaos plane where its people will be devoured by creatures of chaos. The black city will take its place on the Delaware River. The Great Old Ones will have a portal to this world once more. It is likely that the entire planet will become a play ground for chaos within five years and a wasteland within ten. This is the beginning of the apocalypse: mankind's final doom."

Once again we all gaped at him in horror.

"Is that really possible?" asked Brianna in a small voice, the computer completely forgotten now.

"Yes," said Nathaniel. He turned back to look at the map.

"They will need a very large sacrifice in order to pull off something of this magnitude, but I think they've come up with an unconventional method of doing so."

"The shifters," I said with sudden insight.

"The shifters are the rocks that get the avalanche going. They will be used as sacrifices to raise the dead from all of these graveyards," he answered waving his hand at the map. There were a score of pins set on cemetery locations throughout the city. "The zombies that rise will provide the final massive sacrifice needed to power the dimensional shift as they attack and feed on the populous of Philly."

"Holy shit," Frank breathed. "This is fucking crazy."

"They're going to cause a zombie apocalypse in order to fuel an even bigger apocalypse," Brianna moaned.

"But we've taken measures to prevent them from accessing enough souls to raise their zombies," I objected. "I'll get the Governor to get every ghost out of the city if need be."

"It doesn't matter," Nathaniel shook his head. "You can bet that Delilah is providing them with all of the darklings they will need."

I wanted to deny this, but I couldn't. We knew that darklings had entered the city in large numbers and that they'd hidden among the chaos sites. We'd expected some kind of attack from them, and they'd obliged our assumptions a few times, but I now realized that it had just been for show to keep us blind to their true goal. Delilah was going to sacrifice her own people to achieve revenge.

"Is there anything we can do?" I asked Nathaniel desperately.

"I'm not sure," he answered thoughtfully. "I need to get back to the temple. I'm fairly sure that Franklin foresaw this event and left instructions. I just don't recall seeing mention of this kind of threat."

I nodded in agreement thinking back to the prophesy that Franklin had left behind for me. Something clicked in my head at the recollection.

"The answer's not at the temple," I told Nathaniel excitedly. "It's at Franklin Court."

"Let's go," said the wizard without questioning my intuition. His faith in me made me love him even more.

33

FRANKLIN COURT IS TUCKED AWAY down an alley between Market and Chestnut streets in Center City within America's most historic mile. The site is now an empty courtyard except for a steel frame ghost house marking the location and dimensions of Franklin's house. The historical site features an underground museum where some of Franklin's inventions and other items are displayed. Normally in the middle of the day the historical site would be full of tourists, but not today.

Shortly after leaving Brewerytown, Nathaniel had placed a call to the Mayor's office and had been immediately connected to the Mayor himself. Without preamble, Nathaniel had asked him to have Franklin Court and the surrounding alley completely cleared. The Mayor had agreed to do so without asking a single question though his voice betrayed his displeasure. I'd wondered if The Order had that much political clout or if the Mayor simply owed Nathaniel a favor. The wizard had answered my unspoken question by telling me that the Order did have that much political power in certain quarters and that the Mayor himself owed him big time for freeing him of vampiric influence, so the answer was both. How the Mayor was going to get the National Park Service, a federal agency that managed historical sites like Franklin Court, to agree to Nathaniel's request was his problem apparently.

Parking in the historical mile district was too much of a hassle for us to try to get closer, so we left the cars in a nearby parking garage. When we arrived at Franklin Court, we found that the Mayor had been true to his word; a police cordon had indeed been set up on each side of the alley. The PPD officers had let Nathaniel and the rest of us pass through, clearly having received prior instructions on the matter.

We left the police cordon behind us and entered the courtyard proper. I sighed wistfully as we passed under the eaves of the ghost house. Although I'd used an absolute ton of power in the past few hours, I wasn't nearly half as drained as I should be thanks to Nathaniel and Franklin's ghost battery spell. Still, being in this place made me think of home on the other side of the veil where Franklin's house still stood and was my haunt now.

I wasn't surprised when Nathaniel produced keys that actually fit in the lock of the basement museum door. I was betting that his keys worked on every lock of city property and maybe more. We went down into the museum and began to search for clues. I realized right away that the space was laid out differently than mine in Limbo; most of the modern site had been constructed in the recent past and was not part of the original complex. I started with the rooms that I knew existed in Limbo and found the place where the two floor plans diverged. I pushed my hand through the cement wall at the location, and six inches in I found what had turned the museum builders away. A celestial steel wall or door blocked further access. I called the others and within a few moments everyone was assembled around me.

"It's a fucking blank wall," Frank exclaimed after looking around.

"There's a celestial steel barrier six inches in," I said.

"Fucking great," Frank swore. "What are we supposed to do now, demolish the wall of a historical site?"

"If that's what it takes to stop that black city from coming here," Brianna replied fervently.

"That won't be necessary," Nathaniel said. "Veronika and I will go check it out while you two wait here."

We all stared at him dumbly for a moment.

"What? You can walk through fucking walls too?" Frank finally asked.

"Anyone in spirit form can walk through walls," Nathaniel answered with a smile. "You just have to know how to untether your soul from your body. Of course, it's wise to have a good guide that can help you get back."

"Are you saying you can do astral projection?" asked Brianna in wonder.

I stared hard at the wizard as if he'd grown a second head. Was there no limit to his power and his ability to surprise me?

"Franklin called it ghost walking and made it a requirement that every arch mage be able to do it. It's part of the final testing."

"Fucking Franklin had his hands in everything!" muttered Frank.

"Thank God he did," I said fondly. "How much time do you need to do this Nathaniel? Any special instructions for us?"

"It'll take a minute or so," he said as he sat down on the floor and rested his head against the wall. "I just need to go into a deep mediation, and then I'll be able to slide out of my body. Frank and Brianna won't be able to see me because I won't have the power to manifest like you can, Veronika. Both my body and spirit will be very vulnerable to outside forces. Veronika and I will be able to communicate normally though. Frank and Brianna, you must guard my body, and Veronika will be my spirit guide and protector, got it?"

We all nodded and the wizard closed his eyes and seemed to instantly fall asleep. It took less than a minute for Nathaniel to slide out of his body. He had a golden aura and his stormy eyes flashed with pleasure as he extended his hand and I took it.

"It's done," I told the others while I turned back to the empty wall and extended my hand towards it. "I'm gonna open a way through the celestial steel. I'm untethering now, so you won't be able to see me anymore Frank. We'll see you soon."

I became fully incorporeal. I pushed my hand through the wall once more, and when I encountered the celestial steel barrier I willed it to flow aside so that Nathaniel and I could pass through to the room beyond. As usual, the steel obeyed my will and a sizable area was opened for us. I stuck my head through the wall to get a glimpse of what lay beyond. The room was similar to my basement in Limbo, and like my first time on the other side, the area was flooded in a blue glow. Piles of raw celestial steel lay heaped on the floors just like it had in Limbo when I'd first discovered the basement. I stared at it stunned until Nathaniel squeezed my hand in worry. I pulled my head back and looked at him with excitement.

"There are piles of manifested celestial steel ore on the other side," I told him.

"Interesting," he said without a hint of surprise. "Let's go see what else the old sage has left us."

I led the way through the wall and we immediately began to explore the rooms beyond. They were all filled with piles of celestial steel ore. I paused long enough at one of the piles to make sure that I could still shape the ore even though it had become more than spirit metal. I could.

"What is this stuff?" I asked Nathaniel as I stared at it in wonder. "How can it exist in both the living world and Limbo?"

"Franklin wondered about it also," Nathaniel answered. "He speculated that it was the stuff that the universe is made of. Other grand masters have theorized that it is the essence of God, though myself I think Franklin would have scoffed at that."

"So he believed that celestial steel is what everything is made of at its subatomic level or something?"

"Yes, but he would include the spirit as well. Spirit steel has both physical properties and spiritual properties."

We continued this discussion for a few more minutes until we came to the final room. As in Limbo, Franklin had left a message scrawled on the wall in celestial steel.

On that night, the dead shall rise to devour the living,

And the spirits of Limbo shall hold back their tide,

The black city cometh with its gods of old,

In its wake the bells of chaos shall toll,

The counter stroke shall fall,

Liberty's Bell must lead,

The chorus of city bells at midnight's fall,

Only then shall the Death Toll end.

We remained silent for several minutes while we both read and reread the cryptic prophecy and tried to decipher its meaning.

"This is incredible," I finally said breaking the silence. "How could he know this stuff?"

"I don't know," Nathaniel replied, the awe in his voice echoing my own. "He was a rare man of unparalleled talent and power, but how he could have foreseen these events with such a high degree of accuracy is beyond my understanding."

We fell silent once more, each of us pondering the prophecy and the mystery that was Benjamin Franklin.

"So," I said. "It seems that I must bring Limbo's army across to defend the city from the zombies. This stash of celestial steel will help us arm all of the free souls who can manifest here. I'm going to have to get back to Limbo ASAP. The Governor is going to take some convincing."

"We're also going to need your help stealing the Liberty Bell," Carter said in a matter of fact tone.

I gaped at him again.

"The prophecy is clear," Nathaniel went on. "Liberty's bell must lead a chorus of the city's bells at the stroke of midnight in order to prevent the dimensional shift. I think what Franklin is revealing here is that the black city's bells play a major role in its ability to accomplish the dimensional shift. I'm sure you'll never forget the sound of those nightmare bells. The Liberty Bell will lead the counterstroke: it will be a battle of the bells if you will."

The memory of the terrible city and its tolling nightmare bells sent a shiver through me.

"But the Liberty Bell is cracked," I objected. I suddenly wondered if the enemy hadn't had their own prophecies and taken action years ago so that we couldn't counter them when the time came.

"That's a myth conjured to keep the bell safe," Nathaniel answered. "It is a fairly well known fact in the circles of power and mysticism that the Liberty Bell is a powerful artifact. The bell was removed for its own protection."

"Then why do we need to steal it?" I asked. "Call the mayor again."

"The Liberty Bell was placed under federal protection. The Secret Service is an entirely different entity than the National Park Service. Moving them will require much higher level involvement," Nathaniel said. "Given some time, we could use the Order's contacts with the President and he'd lend it to us, but time is something we don't have. We can't risk running afoul of bureaucracy. We're going to have to steal it."

"Frank's gonna love this one," I said sighing. Could my life get any more complicated? I had to get my body back before Delilah turned me into a Mountain Dew Zombie, I had to convince shadow Philly's leaders to bring the whole army into the living world to fight against zombies, and I had to steal the Liberty Bell; all of it in one night!

"Help me back to my body," the wizard said. "You can go back to Limbo and meet us back at the temple in two hours. I'll work with the others to devise a plan to get the bell."

I nodded my agreement and numbly led him back to his body. Saving the city was the top priority. We couldn't let chaos get a foothold in the living world. This meant that there was a better than good chance that I could become Delilah's slave. If I couldn't get to my body this night, I was going to have to make sure that I met my final death before the necromancers could reanimate me. Considering the nature of the coming battle, I was guessing that I would find plenty of opportunities to sacrifice myself for the cause. The thought made me sad; I had just found love, but this only made me more determined not to become a monster.

The others peppered Nathaniel with questions as soon as he awoke from his mediations, but he silenced them with a hard glance and then turned to me.

"I know you must be feeling despair with regard to your body," he said, taking my hand in his. "Do not lose hope. We will stop Delilah."

"Saving the city is our top priority," I told him, fighting of tears. "Nothing else is as important."

"I agree," he said softly. "But remember that where there is love, there is hope, and I love you Veronika Kane."

Tears began to stream from my eyes, and I was glad that I hadn't manifested so that the others could see me. With love comes hope, I thought, but sometimes bitter loss as well.

"I love you too Nathaniel Carter," I said and kissed him softly on the lips. He tried to wipe the tears from my face but I pulled away and began to translate back to Limbo. "I'll see you in a few hours."

34

SHADOW PHILLY WAS IN absolute turmoil. Three chaos armies had invaded the city emerging from the mania stone structures at Byberry, Jezebel's, and Fort Mifflin. Adding to the threat was the advance of a darkling and specter army from Pittsburgh led by none other than Black Maria herself. Black Maria was a bad ass shadow reaper that had nearly ended our revolution prematurely last year. She had the power to shape devil's iron and souls; everyone was afraid of her and for good reason. Now it seemed as though she was ready to take revenge on us for having defeated her the last time she invaded the city. There was also the possibility that Delilah had maneuvered her into attacking us so that there would be plenty of angry ghosts around to be taken when the necromancers performed their zombie raising rituals in the living world. Either way, Black Maria's presence only served to plunge shadow Philly deeper into chaos.

As I approached Independence Square, I found it totally cordoned off by a full battalion of the army. The captain in charge gave me a quick update on the situation and let me pass through without question. A second unit of more elite troops ringed Independence Hall and Old City Hall. I was let through after a more thorough inspection which included the use of a siren to make sure that I wasn't actually a darkling in disguise.

Once through the security, I made my way up to the second floor of Old City Hall where I was directed to a conference room where the Governor was meeting with aides and other officials. Guards were stationed at the conference room doors; they were part of the Governor's elite guard unit under Bridget's command. As I approached, they opened the door for me. The room beyond was large and featured a celestial steel table and chairs. Governor Rachel sat at one end with Bridget hovering at her back. On her right sat Speaker Jully, and to her left sat Jonus. Melanie occupied a seat next to Jonus while Amber sat next to Jully. Other officials occupied the other seats at the table though most I didn't know very well.

"We can't fight on so many fronts," Anton, the leader of the opposition party in the Assembly, was saying. "We must pull back and defend Center City."

"You heard the Marshal," Jully snapped back. "Falling back will only delay the inevitable."

"So what? Are you suggesting that we turn tail and run? Are you saying we should abandon the city?"

Judging from the weary looks on the faces of many of the ghosts in the room, this was an ongoing argument that everyone was tired of hearing.

The Governor cleared her throat and all eyes turned to her. She was looking at me with a placid look of expectation on her face.

"Let's hear from the good Captain Kane. Perhaps she can shed some new light on our situation."

All eyes turned to me, and I noted with trepidation that many of those gazes weren't friendly. I hated politics; at least on the battlefield you know who your enemies are.

"I have important information Governor," I said with a bow

of the neck in her direction. "But I request a private audience with you first. The information is extremely sensitive in nature."

"I object," minority leader Anton barked before anyone else had a chance to respond. "This is a war council. Anything the captain has to say can be said here."

The Governor studied me for a moment then stood. Her expression was hard as she focused her blazing blue eyes on Anton.

"Veronika Kane has served this city at great personal risk. I trust her implicitly. If she wants a private meeting, then by God she'll have one. I'll decide what the council should know after I talk to her. That is my right under the Emergency Powers Act which I now invoke. Grand Marshal, would you join the Captain and I in my office please?"

The look that the minority leader shot me was of pure hatred. The man's attitude baffled me. What had I ever done to him?

The Governor led us into her personal office where she took her usual seat behind her celestial steel desk while Jonus and I sat in seats across from her. The Governor would have left Bridget outside the office, but I nodded to her letting her know that I was ok with the banshee being present in the meeting.

"So, is there anything you can tell us that will help us in this situation?" Governor Rachel asked.

"Yes," I said. "But you won't like it."

"That's not surprising," Jonus interjected. "You're always at the heart of the most complex and dangerous problems; there's no reason to think this one will have an easy solution. I'd be happy with one that doesn't involve us getting annihilated though."

"Agreed," said the Governor.

"In order for us to win the city we must first abandon it," I said.

The two of them stared at me, a mixture of chagrin and disbelief marring their angelic features.

"You've been spending too much time with that wizard," the Governor said flatly. "I've heard that their first language is riddles. Care to give us an English translation?"

"Sorry," I said with a grim smile that neither of the luminaries returned. "The true battle for Philly's survival will be fought in the living world. We must abandoned Limbo, move our entire population into the living world, and join the fight there."

This time even the unflappable Bridget joined the Governor and Marshal in gaping incredulously at me.

"Are you insane?" Jonas finally exclaimed. "Even if we could pull something like a mass translation off, we'd be ceding the city to Black Maria. We'd lose everything we've worked for."

"And that's why I said that in order for us to win the city we'd have to abandon it first," I said. "The battle cannot be won on this side. If we stay and fight, we will all be pulled into zombies during a mass ritual. Our enemies want us to fight. They need us to fight. If we do what they want, Philadelphia will be overrun in a zombie apocalypse, and then the black city of chaos will dimensionally shift to take Philly's place. What will happen to our city on this side, not even Nathaniel can predict, but chaos would at the very least be a close neighbor. We have to get out of the ritual's way, and staying here isn't an option."

I paused a moment to give them a chance to speak; they remained silent, too stunned to reply yet.

"We found a prophecy from Benjamin Franklin himself that indicates that Limbo's forces must fight the zombies in order to prevent the apocalypse. Our intervention will give the bells of liberty a fighting chance to ward the city from the dimensional shift."

The room remained silent for nearly three minutes before the Governor finally spoke.

"If anyone else but you had brought me this news, I'd need a lot more information and assurances. I'd still like them, but I'm feeling your urgency. How much time do we have?"

"We expect the zombies to begin their rampage at around nine this evening. That leaves us with about six hours."

"So Black Maria has been maneuvered into providing the souls necessary to raise the dead?"

"Yes," I answered Jonus. "And Delilah has prepositioned plenty of her own forces in the city to provide more souls in case something goes wrong. She'll sacrifice her own people to make this happen. The enemy will have no lack of souls for its zombies. The only question is whether we'll add to the stinking pile by fighting the wrong battle."

Jonus nodded in understanding. No one in the room was the least bit surprised.

"We're going to have a hell of a time getting the city back once Black Maria takes it," Jonus said. "The ritual won't take out her entire army. Necromancy is very random, and it isn't likely that they'll have enough sacrifices to take a whole army. Black Maria will be weakened to be sure, but with us gone she'll still be in control of the city at the end of the day."

"We'll worry about that when the time comes," answered the Governor. "One problem at a time. The problem we need to deal with now is how to pull off a mass translation."

"Take minority leader Anton's advice," I said. "Pull everyone back to Center City. Nathaniel is going to teach me, Quinn, and a few of his men how to make translation gates. Once we've learned the technique, Quinn and the others will teach everyone else in the Spec Ops division."

"Can this be done Marshal Jonus?" the Governor asked.

"If the translation gates do what I think they do," he answered. "Then, yes."

"Ok then, let's do it," the Governor said. "Keep the plan secret. Quinn and a few others can be added to the need to know list. Everyone learning the translation gate should be taught in a secure area and told to keep it quiet. Veronika, I'll be joining you and Quinn in living Philly to learn this gate technique from the wizard. Once we're done, you can return to your duties with the Watch. We'll need them to help with an orderly evacuation. Jonus, can the army hold the chaos forces back long enough for us to do this?"

Jonus nodded.

"Since we aren't going to try to hold the entire city from Black Maria, I'll pull all of our troops off the borders. The incursion at Penn's Landing is the one that poses the most risk, so I'll reinforce our defenses there. Byberry has a good bit of distance between it and our center. We'll make them fight for every inch using urban guerilla tactics. Fort Mifflin should be easiest to hold back since it's a relatively small base."

"I'm sorry Governor, but I will be needed in the living world very soon. Melanie should continue to act in my stead. I have to help Nathaniel steal the Liberty Bell."

Again everyone stared at me.

"What…? Don't look at me like that, the bell's an artifact. We need it in order to prevent the black city from accomplishing its dimensional shift," I said defensively. "We're going to return it when we're done with it, I promise."

"I see now why heroes do so poorly at day jobs," sighed the Governor. "Very well. Melanie has been doing a splendid job in your absence. She's got a solid head on her shoulders, no pun intended. Now let's go learn how to make these translation gates so that we can get things moving."

35

I TRANSLATED BACK INTO the living world just outside the Grand Masonic Temple and immediately went in. The place was heavily warded, but Nathaniel had attuned me to the defenses a few hours ago when I'd brought the Governor and Quinn's team for the translation training. I found the group in the Grand Master's office; Brianna was sitting in Nathaniel's high backed chair with Frank and Nathaniel looking over her shoulder at the computer screen in front of her. Both Nathaniel and Brianna saw me enter but neither said a word. Feeling benevolent towards my detective friend, I tethered myself to the physical world in front of the door where his roving eyes constantly returned too. For once, he saw me without jumping out of his skin.

"What are you guys looking at?" I asked by way of greeting.

"Floor plans of the fucking Liberty Bell Center," Frank answered, clearly not in a good mood.

"Did you know that abolitionists were the first to call it the Liberty Bell?" I asked conversationally, recalling facts from my own several school trips to the Center.

Frank just glared at me.

"Our friend's sense of humor died when I told him that we would be stealing the bell," Nathaniel said with a smile of his own. "Of course, like the little thief ferret that she is, Brianna's reaction was quite different."

The woman looked up from the computer, her green eyes dancing with excitement.

"No one has ever stolen such an icon before," she said eyes darting back to the display in front of her. "The bell weighs over two thousand pounds and has formidable security around it."

"It's fucking impossible I tell you," Frank said between gritted teeth. "We would need a crew of big time experts to pull this off. It would take millions of dollars to hire the fucking people we need, and it would take a few months of recruiting and prep time."

"No time for that," Nathaniel said. "We're going to have to rely on magic and supernatural power for this job."

"Do you have a plan?" I asked the wizard.

"Absolutely," he said with a twinkle in his stormy gray eyes. "I'll take out the electronic security with a spell that mimics an electromagnetic pulse. Do you think you could get a siren to handle the human guards?"

"Probably," I answered. "I'm sure Amber would love to join us on our grand adventure; it'll probably be more fun than fighting zombies. We've pulled off an ordered retreat and are holding the chaos forces at bay. Black Maria's forces continue to advance, but they aren't in any hurry. The enemy doesn't appear to have a clue that we're up to something. Soon we'll abandon Limbo in a mass translation tide. Our forces will then engage the zombies as they rise. Thanks to Nathaniel's training, all of Philly's ghosts will be on this side of the veil in a few short hours. I'll ask Amber to join us then."

"Fucking great! A zombie horde is gonna rise while a ghost army manifests so that it can battle the other undead. All we need now is for fucking Cthulhu to come and crash the party."

"That about sums it up," answered Nathaniel.

"How are we going to move the bell once all of the security is overcome?" asked Brianna.

"Veronika is going to move it for us," the wizard answered.

I stared at him in consternation. How the hell did he expect a ghost to move a two thousand pound bell?

"How the fuck is she going to do that?" asked Frank, and then a wide smile spread across his face as a light bulb went on in his skull. "You dirty dog. She's going to do the diva queen thing again, eh?"

"Yup," said Nathaniel with a nod. "No sense leaving all that mist in Limbo Veronika. While you were gone, I did a bit of research, and I think I can teach you how to store the mists as energy for yourself. The stored mist can be used for restoring your power and for fueling spells like the vortexes and the diva magic."

"What are the mists?" I asked liking the idea that I might be able to put some in my pockets as it were.

"They're a visual representation of negative magical energies. Ghosts channel negative energy to both sustain themselves and to fuel their supernatural powers including the ability to use magic."

"Cool," I said. "How come we mostly see it in cities, and there's hardly none in the wilderness areas? We theorized that it had to do with the number of violent deaths in the city compared to the countryside."

"No. The mist is drawn to human ghosts, so it collects where ghosts can be found in abundance. It's as simple as that."

"What about the other bells?" Brianna asked.

"What other bells?" I inquired.

"The prophecy mentioned that the Liberty Bell would lead a chorus of the city's bells," she replied. "Is that going to happen magically, or do we have to make that happen too?"

"We should assume that we must make it happen," answered Nathaniel. "Can you get some ghosts detailed to the city's bells Veronika?"

"Marshal Jonus won't be happy about that. It will take a large number of our most powerful ghosts to ring the bells. Manifesting strongly enough to move physical objects takes power. Last I knew, there were something like seven hundred churches in the city."

"Three hundred twenty three with bells in them," Brianna replied.

"This needs to happen Veronika," Nathaniel said earnestly. "Otherwise everything else could be in vain."

"I'll take care of it," I said sighing heavily.

"Do you remember how to do the diva thing?" the wizard asked quietly.

"It's very easy," I told him. "You call it magic, but all I do is imagine it and then will it to happen and it does."

"And that is why you are a scary, powerful ghost," said the wizard as he came around his desk holding a hand out to me. "I've also figured out a way to track down your body, let me show you."

An hour passed by as we finalized our plans for the Liberty Bell heist, and Nathaniel taught me both how to track my body and how to store mist energy. It took another full hour to suck up and store all of the mist that I could contain. It was a freaking ton! The power coursing through me was unbelievable.

"A storm like no other is building," said Nathaniel, looking up as if he could see through the temple's ceiling. "It's fitting really. Nothing epitomizes chaos like bad weather. I hope we're ready for it."

"I hope so too," I said and kissed him goodbye. I needed to make one more trip to Limbo to pick up Amber and to tell Jonus about the church bells.

36

IT WAS NEARLY EIGHT PM by the time I was able to rejoin Nathaniel and the others at the Masonic temple. The historic structure had become headquarters for our side by then. Governor Rachel and Shadow Philly's leadership had arrived at six in the evening to begin the long wait. I had recruited Amber to join the Liberty Bell operation and then spent several hours shaping the celestial steel that was left hidden in the Franklin Court museum. Once I finished that, I'd joined the rear guard in Limbo to see how the fight was going. The enemy seemed content to drive us back without trying to overrun us; they were really only interested in keeping us penned in the city. By the time they realized that we weren't doing anything like what they expected, it was too late for them to crush us. The mass evacuation was nearly complete by the time I left, and the final withdrawal was left in Jonus's capable hands.

I was shocked to find how much conditions had changed in living Philly while I was gone. The temperature had dropped by nearly twenty degrees and the wind gusted above fifty miles per hour. The sky was thick with clouds, and a driving rain had begun to fall. It was as if a hurricane had struck the city. I wasn't surprised to find the radio on as I entered Nathaniel's office where the wizard had graciously given his desk over to the Governor of Philadelphia's ghosts. Melanie, Jully, and Bridget were present as were Frank and Brianna. They were listening to the radio; the worry was clearly visible on everyone's faces. The weather man was talking about the unprecedented nature of the storm, the fact that it had suddenly appeared out of nowhere, and that it seemed to be stationary right over the city. People were warned to stay indoors and away from windows; they could expect flooding and damaging winds. As if to punctuate the seriousness of the warnings, the lights flickered on and off for a few seconds and went out completely. The Order was prepared for this however, and the temple's generators kicked in a minute or so later. When the lights came back on, everyone breathed a sigh of relief.

"Are the bell teams in place?" I asked Melanie in the silence that followed the loss of power. We'd decided that the Ghost Watch would take on the task of being bell ringers while the army fought the zombies.

"Everyone is in place," Melanie said nervously. "I should be out there. I feel useless here."

"Welcome to my world," said Governor Rachel. "But a leader must be in a position to coordinate her forces. Your people know where you are and how to reach you if they need too. The confusion of the field is a bad place to maintain communications when the troops are as spread out as ours are."

"But I'm a banshee. This is a waste of my abilities," Melanie complained stubbornly.

"We don't need banshees ringing church bells," the Governor replied. "Believe me, I plan on using all of you banshees against the zombies as needed, but I don't want the enemy getting a bead on you early on so that they can assassinate you. You'll get to fight, but I'll be using you tactically to best advantage. You'll go in quick, accomplish your task, and disappear."

"That sounds good," I said approving of the tactic.

"Quinn's idea," the Governor said. "I hope you don't mind that I commandeered your familiar. Sebastian is with Quinn. When the banshees are needed, he'll be bringing the word."

"I know Sebastian is as eager to help as I am," I said.

A sudden feeling of vertigo hit me, and I nearly fell. I was suddenly lying in another room; black robed figures were chanting around me. It lasted only a second and then I was back in Nathaniel's office. The wizard was by my side; his softly glowing hands were holding my shoulders steady as I shuddered. Everyone in the room was staring at me with concern.

"Have you over extended yourself?" asked Governor Rachel, a worried rebuke in her eyes.

"She's used a lot of power over the past few days," Nathaniel answered for me. "But I've kept her sufficiently charged. This is something else."

"Yes," I replied, shaking myself and taking a determined step away from Nathaniel. "The enemy has begun the ritual. Soon the dead will rise, and it would seem that Delilah plans on raising me with them."

Everyone in the room stared at me, trying to make sense of what I was saying. Looks of terror and genuine concern for my well being filled their eyes. Brianna rushed forward to comfort me while Nathaniel stood stunned; his stormy eyes suddenly looked hollow and frightened.

"How do you know this?" Governor Rachel asked.

"Nathaniel taught me a spell that allows me to find my body," I replied. "As soon as I got back on this side of the veil, I activated it. Nothing happened until now. It was as if I was in my body, and I could see everyone around it. There are a group of necromancers, including the old crone and Delilah. They've also got a shifter that they intend to sacrifice."

"Could you tell where they were?" the Governor asked. "We'll send a strike team to stop them."

"They're at Fort Mifflin," I replied.

Nathaniel was staring at me, a look of sudden awe in his eyes. "What?" I asked.

He looked around the room as if wondering who he could trust. He turned a questioning eye to me.

"Speak freely," I said. "I trust everyone here."

He nodded slowly.

"This is very dangerous information," he began. His gaze fell on each person in the room; the look was demanding and hard. Even the Governor, a mighty luminary, blanched under that stormy gaze. "The spell I taught Veronika is one that was left behind by Franklin. By all accounts it shouldn't have worked the way it just did with her. She should have been able to sense the direction in which her body lay, nothing else."

"Perhaps she did it wrong," said the Governor. "She's not a trained wizard after all."

"Veronika is a natural talent of incredible power," Nathaniel said shaking his head. "I'm positive she didn't do it wrong. There's no way she should be able to see through the eyes of her own corpse, at least not until they've broken her down into her essential salts and reanimated her."

The room was silent for a moment.

"Is that what she said?" Speaker Jully finally asked. "I thought she was describing a vision or something. Was she actually seeing through her body's own eyes?"

Nathaniel turned to me, his eyes questioning.

"Yes…," I said slowly, thinking back to the feeling of vertigo. Actually it hadn't been vertigo at all; it was as if I'd suddenly been pulled somewhere else, or even in two places at the same time. "It was like I was really there, actually in my body."

"We don't have time for this shit," Frank suddenly burst out. "If we're going to help her, we have to get fucking moving now."

"I agree," Nathaniel answered. "But even if we left an hour ago we probably wouldn't reach her on time in this storm. Not even the ghosts will get there in time. Veronika is the only one who can save herself now."

Both Frank and I stared hard at the wizard. What was I supposed to do in the two or three minutes that was left to me?

"Are you saying she can use her body as a conduit to travel through?" the Governor asked. "Can she just appear at the location of her body?"

Wild hope surged in me at this thought. If it was possible, I could travel to my body in an instant and then blast everyone around me with my banshee wail.

"Not exactly," Nathaniel said dashing my hopes. "Something even more amazing and powerful. She can possess her own body."

"That's impossible," both Speaker Jully and Governor Rachel said coming to their feet in denial.

"Why would I even want to do that?" I asked. A sudden sense of hopelessness filled me, and my eyes filled with tears.

"It's not impossible," Nathaniel shot back. "It's just impossibly rare. It's not wrong of you to take possession of your own body Veronika, especially if someone else is going to use it for their own evil ends. If I'm right, then fate has marked you as not only a banshee and a wizard, but also as a lich."

"What's a lich?" asked Speaker Julie.

"Isn't that a fucking wizard who gives his soul up for fucking immortality?" asked Frank.

"There's no time for explanations," Nathaniel said, turning to me and taking my hands. "Do you trust me Veronika?"

"Yes," I answered without hesitation.

"Good! This is the only way that I can think of that will allow you to save yourself," he said earnestly. "You are going to take possession of your body before they can finish their ritual. This will automatically cause their spell to fail as they won't be able to bind your spirit since it will be tethered to your body already. You will however be vulnerable; if they kill you while you're in your body, you will be utterly destroyed. You will be supernaturally strong and quick, you'll still be able to use your banshee powers and your magic, but you will be easier to kill than in your current form."

"This is madness," Governor Rachel said. "And it smells of necromancy. It sounds like she'll be some kind of vampire or zombie."

The wizard wheeled around to face the Governor, anger marring his features.

"This is a thing of creation," he said through clenched teeth. "It's her body. If God has given her the gift of using it even after death then she should use it rather than become the pawn of evil. Would you call what Christ did to Lazarus necromancy?"

"Of course not," Governor Rachel retorted angrily. "That was a divine miracle. Are you saying this is some kind of resurrection rather than reanimation? Would she be a living person again?"

"She would not be living again, though by all outward appearances she would seem to be," Nathaniel answered. "It is a form of resurrection though. The Bible is replete with the stories of God's champions returning from the dead. It is a gift that can be used for good or for ill, and I am certain that Veronika will not use it for anything other than good. Now Veronika, go! Will yourself into your body. Allow yourself to go."

I desperately wanted to take time to consider my options, but a sense of urgency filled me. If I didn't do this now, I was going to be Delilah's bitch.

"I'll meet you at our prearranged meeting place," I told my friends and then shut my eyes to concentrate on my body.

"If you leave your body," I heard Nathaniel say as I began to slide away. "Be sure to hide it well or leave it under guard. Once you do this, you will forever be connected to it, and those with the right knowledge could use it against you."

"This is like a fucking D&D game, except it's real," were the last words I heard as my soul shot through time and space like a stone being flung from David's sling shot.

37

MY AIM WAS TRUE. An explosion of sensory information threatened to overwhelm me. The stone table I was lying on was cold and uncomfortable, and the lights of hundreds of candles burned my eyes as they opened for the first time since my death. The smell of animal musk, blood, sweat, and sandalwood combined to create a pungent odor that made my nostrils itch. The sound of chanting combined with the howling of the wind outside, and the angry grunts and growls of a nearby beast were defining. Add to this the sensation of my moldering skin, muscles, hair, bone, nails, and other tissues all regenerating at a rapid speed. The feeling was at once like having millions of ants crawling all over you and the itch that you feel when a cut is healing only ten thousand times more pronounced. I literally felt my hair growing out of my scalp pushing the dead stuff out and then flowing down my back till it reached the level which it had been at when I'd died. For a moment, it seemed like my body was covered in scales as the flesh regenerated and new skin pushed the rotten stuff aside. As the skin finished repairing, I felt my heart start to beat and blood began to course through newly formed veins. I shook myself and the dead stuff fell away revealing a strong, pink, naked body beneath.

Although I suddenly felt very alive I knew deep down that I wasn't. Living is about more than just breathing: the body and soul are entwined as one. In my case however, my spirit was merely possessing my body. I could feel the tethers that tied me to this vessel. Even though I was in my body, it felt like I was controlling it like a puppet.

"Is it done?" asked a voice to the right of me. "Is she mine?"

There were only a few people chanting now where there'd been dozens just a few moments ago. My blurry vision began to clear as my eyes regenerated, and I saw that I was in one of the bunkers of the old Revolutionary War fort. I was now sitting on a gore splattered stone table. The old crone, whose hand I'd severed at the Christ Church Burial Ground battle, was standing a mere foot away from me with an ebon knife held in her good hand. She was gaping at me as were most of the other necromancers; at least a dozen of them stood around me in a circle. Delilah and a reaper stood behind the necromancers near where my head would have been when I was lying on the table. Delilah stared at me, a maniacal smile on her face. She was obviously oblivious to what had just happened. Off to my left, a huge bear was chained to another alter. The creature was bleeding from a nasty gash in its throat, and a knife wielding warlock stood over the bear poised to reopen the rapidly regenerating wound. I could see that the fury spirit within the bear was getting low on power, and once that happened, it would not be able to continue its self healing.

Before the brown robed old witch could reply or do much else, I grabbed her by the throat. My body moved with blazing speed without me having to call on the wind. The witch's eyes bulged as I began to squeeze, and I was shocked when the sound of breaking bone and cartilage announced that I'd crushed her wind pipe. Knowing that she would suffocate in a matter of minutes and therefore no longer posed a threat to me, I nonchalantly flung her aside. The hag sailed across the room and smashed into a wall. The sickening sound of flesh impacting against stone was accompanied by the sound of more breaking bones. Nathaniel wasn't kidding when he said I'd have supernatural strength and speed. This was downright scary stuff.

"Stop!" Delilah roared. Her face was now contorted in rage. "You are mine to command. You will move and attack only when I tell you too."

"Wow, Darth Delilah, it seems like your Jedi mind tricks aren't going to work on me this time, so you can save your breath and kiss my ass."

I let loose with my banshee wail, striking a group of necromancers who were backing away towards the door. They were all instantly eviscerated, and the wall behind them was blown out. The room was suddenly filled with the rush of the howling wind, and everyone in the room was lashed by driving rain accompanied by human gore from the sorcerers that I'd just annihilated. The chamber was plunged into darkness as the candles were snuffed out. My ghostly senses compensated however, and I was able to see as if looking through night vision goggles although the world appeared in blue phosphorescence rather than green. Delilah stared at me, open mouthed, apparently still unable to comprehend the situation. She began shouting but was drowned out by the storm. I smiled wickedly at her as I leaped off the table to land standing before the acolyte assigned to killing the bear.

The kid, he seemed to be roughly my own age, was clearly blinded in the face of the furious storm, but he sensed my presence and swung the knife at me. I could have admired his courage and tenacity if it weren't for the fact that he was trying to slaughtering a helpless creature. For all I knew, this guy could have been involved with the zoo massacre. I caught his wrist and with a sharp twist, broke it. The knife fell to the floor, and as he opened his mouth to scream, I punched him. The blow caught him dead center, and his face imploded in a shower of blood and bits of bone. The kid fell like a ton of bricks, bone shards having been shoved into his brain, killing him instantly. I grabbed the heavy chains that were wound about the bear, and with a single, powerful heave, I snapped them. I pulled a length of the chain free while my left foot probed for the fallen knife. When I found it, I used my toes to flick it into the air where I caught it with my free hand. I then flung the knife at a terrified cultist, catching him in the throat.

Delilah's reaper was moving towards me, black sword raised in challenge. Delilah was concentrating, her lips moving in a barely perceptible whisper. Since the chain was going to be useless against the reaper, I pulled some of the stored mist in me and formed it into a ball of energy. I launched the bolt of grey mist at the ghost, and it reacted by throwing up a black shield around itself. The mist bolt struck the shield and immediately started to devour it. I shot two more bolts into a wide gap in the reaper's shield, and the mists began to disassemble the reaper itself. Just like that it was over. I'd never had an easier time against a reaper. They were near the top of Limbo's food chain after all.

Delilah completed her spell, and a ghost cage made of chaos energy went up around me. The witch had apparently taught the darkling that useful spell, and now I wished I'd killed her more slowly. I reached a tentative hand to one of the magical bars and pulled away quickly when an overwhelming sense of intense depression slid over me. I stared hard at Delilah, letting all of the menace that I could muster show in my steely gaze. Delilah just smiled like a long suffering mother who was punishing her child for wrong doing.

"I don't know how you defeated the reanimation ritual," she said making an odd gesture with her hands. "But I will do it myself since everyone else is so incompetent."

The air around her shimmered and the storm itself seemed to pause. Four shapes out of some B horror movie began to coalesce around her. They were tall, maybe nine feet, and skeletally gaunt.

They had a humanoid shape to them though their necks ended in a headless stump. Their faces, twisted things with four eyes, no nose, and a gaping circular maw with no apparent teeth, were located on the chest and back, though which was which wasn't clear. Their joints were constantly shifting so that either side of them was the front at any given moment. Worst of all were their voices; they sang, and the sound they produced was both unimaginably revolting and so beautiful that it made you want to weep in awe.

"Put her in there," Delilah ordered, pointing to some boiling cauldrons that I hadn't noticed, they were in the corner of the room. Those must be the chemicals they used to break the body down to its essential salts. I wondered for a moment why they hadn't done this to me already. What had they been trying to do? I didn't dwell on the mystery for long however, for the four horrors turned their full attention upon me. Their song was now directly focused on me.

I felt them trying to slide their wills into me, to possess me. Their songs caused a lethargic feeling to come over me, and I felt myself relaxing under their brilliantly choreographed chaos song. I could now understand the vision of chaos that they longed for. Only through strength and natural selection could true power and freedom be achieved. Why should a being of my power be limited by rules set down by those weaker than me? God was a mere figment of imagination; a dream conjured by the weak to control and pacify the strong. I must throw off the shackles that bound me to the decrepit of society and embrace my strength and dominance. The way to do this was to leap into the boiling vat where I'd be broken down into my true essence; only then would I be reforged into the weapon that I was meant to be.

I took a step towards the vat, and Delilah made a gesture that banished the ghost net. The horrors' song hadn't affected me in the way that she'd imagined though, and I immediately began to belt out the lyrics to *The Show Must Go On* by Queen, countering the chaotic song. Though the song of the chaos horrors was potent, my own siren's song power seemed to be a foil to their ability to dominate me. I swiftly untethered myself from my body and shot out towards Delilah. I continued to sing, and the creatures seemed confused by the entrance of an unfamiliar song. Delilah panicked, seeing her death in my eyes; she fled, translating back to Limbo, before I could reach her. Unfortunately circumstances dictated that I not pursue. There was too much at stake here to let vengeance distract me from the real mission at hand. I instead turned my fury onto the singing fiends. Their confusion inspired me to sing a medley of Queen songs from the *Bohemian Rhapsody* to *Another One Bites the Dust*, moving on to *Legs* by ZZ Top, and a montage of songs from Night Ranger, Bon Jovi, Def Leppard, and AC/DC. The creatures went from complete confusion to mimicry, seeming to have fallen completely under my spell instead. To test this theory, I laced my song with a strong desire that the creatures attack each other. It worked spectacularly.

The horrors tried to outperform each other in brutality; their clawed hands ripped into each other and chunks of flesh and acidic blood flew around the room. Surveying the carnage that I'd wrought, I knew that I should feel remorse or disgust, but I felt nothing. I'd slaughtered people with my own hands; my brain should be shutting down or at least trying to get away from the reality of it all, but there was nothing: no coldness, no anger, no rage. There was no emotion at all. I didn't have time to wonder at my own lack of feeling; it was time to go. I re-tethered myself to my body and went over to the bear who was now a naked man.

"Hi Bruno," I said self consciously. I was stark naked like him. I helped him rise and led him towards the opening that I'd made in the bunker wall. The storm was still raging. "I'm Veronika, a friend of Brianna Martin's. I can carry you if you're feeling too weak."

The shifter was watching the chaotic brawl of the singing

horrors; they were in an entangled pile of thrashing limbs on the bunker floor. They continued to sing the song I'd given them, and the spell held even though I was no longer singing. They were totally oblivious to us as we made our escape.

"Holy shit," Bruno muttered in a deep voice. "What the hell did you do to those things? Those fuckers made all of my bears go crazy with their song. I tried to fight them, but they got into my head and I couldn't move. Next thing I know I wake up here surrounded by these freaks and then you pull all that crazy shit. Who the hell are these people? And what the fuck are you?"

"There's not enough time to explain everything," I told him as we finally made it into the stormy night. "I'm a ghost, and more importantly, I'm a friend. I've got a lot of work to do tonight; otherwise the entire city is going to go on a trip that no one wants to be a part of. I need you to trust me and do what I say."

"I can feel your fucking tits on my arm," Bruno said mildly, bringing a furious blush to my face; it was the first emotion I'd felt since taking control of my body. "They feel nice and firm. You expect me to believe you're a ghost? Shit, if I knew ghosts felt so good, I'd have gone out and found me one a long time ago. Better than a blow up doll."

I was so embarrassed that I almost let go of the shifter, if only to get some space between him and my breasts. He was leaning heavily against me. Closer scrutiny of him convinced me that his fury had mostly healed him already. He was playing up his injuries in order to get a free feel and he was getting a freaking hard on to boot! I had to suppress a flare of rage that could only have ended with me body slamming the piggish man. This was no time to lose control. The man was just acting like most men would in his situation. Liking the feel of a woman didn't mean that he was a rapist like Freak. Freak again, why did everything about men come back to that slime? Nathaniel was my man now, and I apparently still needed his help in healing me from what Freak had done to me. I needed to give this guy a break; he was just playing around. It was a bit unnerving how my emotions were suddenly all over the place: non-existent when it came to hardcore violence and still crazy when it came to sex.

"You don't need my help buster," I told him and pushed him away from me. He went tumbling almost ten feet away and landed in a puddle. I ran over to help him back up, mortified at having forgotten how strong I was now. "I'm sorry. I forget how strong I am."

"Damn woman!" Bruno said looking up between my legs instead of at my preferred hand. "You are one sexy mamma. Are you a damn vampire or something?"

I yanked the shifter to his feet so he wouldn't have the pleasure of that view anymore. I had to get some clothes on.

"I'm a lich," I told him. "I'm a ghost that can possess my own body, and if you don't stop staring at me like that I'm going to throw you into the Delaware."

He looked into my face for the first time and smiled.

"Sorry honey," He said. "You can't blame a guy for enjoying the scenery when it's right there in front of him, especially when that scenery is so fine. I've heard of you, I think. Veronika Kane right? One of the young ladies who was killed by that Tormentor serial killer last year?"

"That's me," I answered with a pang of sorrow. Though life had gone on, and I was doing important things that the living could barely imagine, I was separated from my friends and family, and I could never go back. "We need to get to somewhere safe, and then I've gotta go."

"Alright," said the shifter looking around at our surroundings. "This is Fort Mifflin if I'm not mistaken. We aren't too far from the airport. Let's go take shelter there."

"I'll get you there safe," I told the shifter. "But I've got other business I've gotta take care of tonight."

Bruno nodded in agreement and looked around at the structures that surrounded us. He pointed towards one that looked intact, but unfortunately it was also black as night and bore a familiar non-Euclidean architecture.

"Maybe we should take shelter in there until this storm blows over," he said taking a step towards it. "I'm not sure we'll be able to find our way to the airport under these conditions."

"No!" I said sharply, stopping him in his tracks. "That building belongs to those alien monsters fighting it out in the bunker. There might be more of them in the vicinity. We need to get the hell out of here."

Bruno looked around nervously; he was clearly eager to avoid encountering the singing monsters again. I tried to call the wind to me so that I could fly, but nothing happened even though there was plenty of wind riding with the storm. I wondered if the nature of the storm, chaos induced as it was, was preventing me from using the wind. On a whim, I sat down and untethered myself from my body. I called the wind and it answered, bearing me into the stormy night. My body was powerful, but apparently flying wasn't on the menu of super powers available to me in my physical form. Oh well, a girl can't have everything.

"Well I'll be!" exclaimed Bruno, who was looking straight up at me. He bent over and waved a hand in front of my body's eyes and then straightened back up to look at the real me. "That's not something you see every day. Can you fly us home? I reckon you've got the strength to hold me even in my bear form."

"That's what I was just testing," I told him. "I can only fly in my ghost form. The body doesn't fly."

"I guess we'll have to hoof it then," he said with a shrug.

38

THE ISLAND THAT FORT MIFFLIN had originally been built on was called Mud Island, and the torrential down pour was causing it to live up to its name. The driving rain obscured our vision as we slogged our way Westward, at least we hoped it was West. We were relying on Bruno's animal instincts and hoping that we'd soon come across Fort Mifflin Road. The island had long ago ceased being an island as the water between it and Philly was dredged and filled until it was part of the mainland on the Philly side. The fort had been one of the country's longest active military bases having been built in 1776 and finally decommissioned in the mid 1960's. The base had sustained the worst artillery bombardment of the Revolutionary War with some 250 plus defenders having been killed during a month and a half long siege. During the Civil War, Fort Mifflin had primarily served as a prison for prisoners of war. Most of the fort's structures had survived to some degree or another, and money had been poured into them in the last few decades for historical preservation purposes.

I was relieved when we reached the outer walls of the fort; the pitted white surface of the historic fortification was the only remaining bulwark of the original 1776 base which served as a testament to unyielding persistence in the face of oblivion. These walls were all that remained standing from the British siege of 1777; all of the other original buildings had been rebuilt in the decades and centuries that followed. The place had long been rumored to be haunted, and as I passed through it this night, I knew the rumors were true.

We were a mere ten feet past the outer walls when the wind and rain suddenly subsided. There wasn't a gradual slow down of the storm or a lightening of rain to a drizzle; it just suddenly all stopped. An eerie silence blanketed the whole city, and a thick mist began to rise from the ground and rivers. The normally glittering night skyline of Philadelphia was a dark silhouette on the horizon.

Bruno and I stood frozen, stunned by the sudden cessation of the storm. Our senses were trying to make sense of the change. A new sound rose to torment the night. At first it was like the moan of the wind through a tunnel, but the moans soon grew too loud and distinct to be mistaken for wind.

"What the hell is that?" asked Bruno, a primordial fear making his voice quaver.

"Zombies," I answered grimly. "You'd better shift now. I think your bear form will fare better against zombies. I saw the road over that way before the mist obscured my sight. We'll follow it to the tunnel where we'll find friends. Let's get moving."

Bruno didn't argue. One minute he was a giant naked man, the next he was a huge grizzly bear. He took the lead; his lumbering gait setting a pace that he couldn't have matched in human form. In life I wouldn't have been able to keep up with the galloping bear either, but as a lich, I didn't have any problems at all. Even though my heart beat and my lungs pumped out air, and in theory my muscles were only able to support certain activity levels before weakening, I found that feeding the negative energies of Limbo into my limbs fueled my body and allowed it to go far beyond its normal capacity. The energies restored and rejuvenated my muscles, heart, and lungs, keeping them healthy and strong even when they should have failed me. I found also that I was connected to the earth in a way I'd never experienced before. I could feel the worms and other living things crawling through and upon it. Though I couldn't be sure until I had more time to test it, it seemed that this new earth sense extended to somewhere like a half mile around me. I could feel the dead rising from the earth, and their every shambling step was known to me. The black sore that lay upon the earth, the nearby chaos monument, blazed in my mind as the earth trembled in agony at its touch. I felt the wound open and the cancerous monsters within pour out into the night. The second battle for Philadelphia had begun in earnest now.

I caught up to Bruno and with a nod took the lead. I used my new found earth sense to avoid the majority of the zombies; more than two hundred of them had risen in the vicinity. At one point, Bruno and I plowed through a group of eight zombies. My senses told me that trying to avoid this group would put us in danger of encountering a much larger group. The eight zombies were too far decayed to be effective against supernatural combatants like Bruno and I, hence the battle was quick and messy. Bruno was a wrecking ball; his huge body slammed into the group and trampled three of them into uselessly crawling horrors before any of the others could react. I followed in his wake, using speed and finesse to tear off an arm here, a leg there, and smash a lunging head with a powerful side kick that shattered the zombie's skull. Once through, we kept on going, not bothering to finish them off. They would follow, and our friends could deal with them.

We reached the tunnel and found that battle had been joined here already. A regiment of Philly free souls was fighting in formation against a horde of chaos spiders and zombies. I led Bruno into the fray, letting loose with my banshee wails while the grizzly bear kept the monsters off my back. We cut a swath through the enemy's rear and within moments won free to our own front line. Daniel, the regiment's commander, and my banshee sister Catherine greeted me once I'd passed through our ranks to the rear. The luminary and banshee were being held in reserve; they commanded from the back ranks where they had a full view of the battlefield.

"I need to get to Center City right away," I told them without going into the usual small talk. "The problem is that I can't do it quick enough in this body. I need you to make sure nothing happens to it while I'm away."

They both stared at me in confusion and I sighed.

"Look, I have to make this quick," I told them. "It turns out that I'm a lich as well as a banshee. It means I can possess my own body. Problem is that I can't fly while riding in it. I need to get to the Liberty Bell Center or what you're doing here won't mean a thing. If anyone who knows what they're doing gets a hold of my body while I'm not in it, well…let's just say it won't be good for me. Sorry to saddle you with this, but I need you to make sure no one gets a hold of it. I'm leaving it under Bruno's protection, but I need you to keep him safe as well."

Bruno growled and I felt certain he was telling me not to worry about it. Daniel seemed troubled by my revelation, apparently not sure of the morality of what I'd become, but he nodded his understanding. Catherine looked intrigued and assured me that my body would remain safe. Wishing that I had another alternative, I lay down, untethered myself, and without a look back, I called the wind to me and leapt into the sky and sped my way towards Center City.

39

THE FLIGHT BACK TO CENTER CITY proved to be far more challenging than what I would have liked. The night hags had returned in large numbers, and I found myself unable to avoid encountering them. A series of vicious aerial battles slowed my progress to a crawl until I was able to team up with a unit of Quinn's special forces aerial combat brigade. Though this helped me move along more rapidly, I was frustratingly aware that I was already behind schedule, and time was continuing to tick away. Still the night hags flew about in swarms that slowed our progress and all but destroyed our ability to communicate with units scattered across the city wide battlefield. The only thing saving our butt at this point was that Nathaniel had imbedded an acolyte or knight of the Order into every one of our units, and all of them were equipped with cell phones. Of course, the storm had caused the system to be mostly ineffectual as cell towers and power stations had suffered damage. The adage that no plan survives completely after first contact with the enemy was proving annoyingly true.

After a particularly long and vicious fight, I brought the

company I was traveling with to an exasperated aerial halt. Since our enemy was kind enough to provide us with fog, it was time to use it against them. Taking up a position in the center of the company where I was protected while I worked, I began to call the mists to me. As they did in Limbo, and as they'd done in the Woodland Cemetery, the mists came to me. It was like being a drain sucking up all the nearby water, all of the fog rushed to me and began to swirl around me. Having seen this before, my men began to drop out of the sky, but with a pang of adrenalin stirring fear, I saw the night hags doing the same. They'd seen me do this too and they were reacting appropriately. Anger surged in me and I filled the super vortex with a will of its own. I gave it a singular purpose: seek out the chaos creatures and destroy them all. I willed the winds to be my instrument of annihilation against the enemies of creation. I briefly considered sending the tornadoes against the zombies as well, but they were too similar to living people, and they had spirits in them. Would the winds distinguish between the zombies and living people or my own ghostly friends? The chaos things were unlike anything in this world or in Limbo, so I decided to send the vortexes against the chaos only. The zombies would be handled by the armies of creation, both the living and the dead.

The giant funnel cloud that hung over Philly broke into thousands, if not millions, of vortexes that boiled away from me when I let them go, and they scattered across the city hunting their prey. I imagined what people at home were watching; an unnatural storm had struck the city ending without warning in a blanket of fog that cleared away and formed into giant tornado that hung over the cityscape for several minutes, then it broke apart into thousands of smaller tornadoes and scattered about the city doing relatively little damage. It was going to be the weather story of the century. I waited for a few moments until my men rejoined me. They relayed the news to me; the vortexes were doing exactly what I'd willed them to do. The chaos forces were being decimated. That was good news since we'd really counted on fighting only the zombies. The chaos forces were supposed to be busy in Limbo. We should have anticipated their ability to react quickly to our own maneuvers. After all, they'd been ahead of us all along the way thus far.

The skies being relatively safe once more, I sent the company of flyers off to assist in the myriad of battles taking place throughout the city. I continued my flight towards the Liberty Bell Center. Independence Mall and its surrounding historical buildings including Independence Hall, Old City Hall, Congress Hall, and the Liberty Bell Center among others finally came into view, and I breathed a sigh of relief when I saw that everything appeared to be quiet. There were no battles being fought in the immediate area which Nathaniel had assured us would be the case due to the heavy warding spells placed around the historic mile by The Order.

As I landed near the bathroom building on the Northwest corner of Chestnut and fifth streets, a ferret chittered at me from the shadows of the building and darted inside before I could reply. Before I followed after the ferret, I took a good long look at the target of tonight's mission. Liberty Center lay just a couple hundred feet away from me. Flood lamps illuminated the glass, stone, and brick building. Its architecture was a strange blend that melded the grandeur of nineteenth century architecture with a modern style of sophistication culminating in three distinct architectural elements; an outdoor columned arcade, an extended rectangular exhibit hall, and a tapered vault like chamber housing the bell itself. It had opened in 2003 replacing the adjacent pavilion as the new home of the Liberty Bell. The area around it was quiet now, and I hoped that it would remain so. Across the street from it lay Independence Hall; its belfry would be our destination soon enough.

I stepped through the wall of the restroom building roughly where I judged the men's bathroom to be. Since the living complement of our team included two men and just one female, we'd decided that the men's room was the safest for avoiding a potential scene. Men are less likely to get bent out of shape if they find a woman in their bathroom than the reverse. It's a safety thing for women of course, and most men probably wouldn't care about finding a female like Brianna in their bathroom anyway. I found my friends huddled around the wash sink area. Frank was watching the door, at least he was supposed to be doing so; instead he was watching Brianna as she dexterously pulled on her black cat suit. Nathaniel was chatting quietly with Amber, and the young siren was listening raptly to the wizard. I saw that Nathaniel was holding Amber's hand, a golden glow surrounded him, and I was immediately jealous even though I knew the wizard was merely acting as a battery and recharging Amber's power. They both turned to me as soon as I phased through the wall. Brianna winked at me and shook her ass suggestively in Frank's direction as she wriggled into her cat suit. The detective remained oblivious to everything around him except the semi nude shifter.

"How did it go?" Nathaniel asked as he moved to greet me. He took my hands in his own. The soft glow around him began to brighten, spilling visible light into the whole chamber. He gave me a quick kiss and looked me over. "We were getting worried."

"About fucking time you got here," complained Frank, Nathaniel's glowing aura clueing him in on my presence. "You're a fucking half hour late. Hanging out in the john isn't my fucking idea of fun."

"Hush Frank," Brianna told the detective. She slunk over to stand before him her breasts still bare and stared up at him with what I could only guess was a sultry gaze. "Give Veronika and Nathaniel a minute or two of privacy. I could use your help getting this thing on, and you might as well be useful since you've forgotten to keep an eye on what's going on outside."

There was no way that the petit former CIA agent and ferret shifter needed help getting into her skin tight outfit, but I gave her a nod of gratitude for running interference.

"I'm fine," I told Nathaniel. I was enjoying his touch and was thankful for the power he was filling me with. "There were complications. The chaos forces figured out what we were up too and sent their armies out to join the zombies."

"Damn," Nathaniel cursed, his stormy gray eyes blazing with frustration. "I should have anticipated this. Azathoth's avatar is directing this whole operation. It is older and vastly more cunning than any of us. This is a dangerous game we play. We should expect that he'll have figured out the threat of the bell as well. There will be trouble."

I nodded in silent agreement.

"What about your body? Where is it?" the wizard asked turning an inquiring gaze back to me.

"It's fine," I assured him. "It worked just like you said it would. It was freaking amazing. I'll give you more details later, but for now you just need to know that I left it with Bruno, the bear shifter. Catherine and Daniel are also there at the tunnel."

"I wish you hadn't left it," Nathaniel said, a worried look passing over his features. "You are very vulnerable now."

"I know," I sighed. "But there wasn't any choice. I can't fly while tethered to my body. If you think I'm late now, imagine how long it would have taken me to get here via normal traffic."

Nathaniel nodded his understanding and with an effort pushed the worry out of his posture.

"Did I hear you say Bruno was safe?" Brianna called to me. She was now fully dressed and facing our way. Frank was peaking through the door, keeping an eye on the outside.

"I wouldn't say he's safe, but he's safer than when I found him chained to an alter with an acolyte bleeding him to power a ritual. The important thing is that he was alive when I left him with the regiment assigned to hold the Fort Mifflin tunnel."

"That's great news," Brianna said with a smile. "I hope Martin is as lucky."

"Hey," called Frank. "Something's going on out there!"

We all rushed to the bathroom door to get a glimpse of what

was going on outside. Rather than take up space the living needed in order to see, I just poked my head through the wall and looked around. At first I didn't notice anything out of the ordinary, but then I saw the cracks in the brick laden space that surrounded the Liberty Bell Center. The earth began to buckle in the Southwest corner of Market and Fifth streets including in the very street itself. The quiet of the historic district was shattered by explosions of stone and dirt followed by the moans of rising zombies. A quick glance around showed me it was happening in other areas of Independence Mall as well.

"Holy shit!" exclaimed Frank. "More fucking zombies! They're clawing their way out of the fucking concrete!"

"I thought this area was supposed to be safe from this stuff!" I yelled at Nathaniel after pulling my head back inside. "Now we're going to have to fight our way into the Center."

"The known cemeteries are warded," Nathaniel replied with a grimace. "We can't account for every burial ground in the city, especially if they weren't marked."

There weren't a whole lot of reasons to not mark a grave site: mass murder would be one of them, and slaves sometimes were unceremoniously dumped in mass graves in the nation's early days. Whatever the case, it seemed like we were going to have to deal with at least a score of zombies from two different sites.

"Here's that trouble you were expecting," I told Nathaniel grimly. "Let's hope that this is the worst of it. Let's go get the bell."

40

WE EMERGED FROM THE RESTROOM building and moved quickly and as silently as we could manage towards the Liberty Bell Center's main entrance which lies on the North side facing Market Street. The zombies became aware of us almost instantly despite our attempt to sneak past them, and both groups made a beeline for us.

"I'll handle this," I told my friends. I called the wind to me as I rushed forward at supernatural speed to meet the group that blocked our path to the Liberty Bell Center's entrance.

The thought that these zombies used to be slaves who were buried in unmarked graves fueled a fury that grew in me as I approached the unfortunate creatures. It wasn't fair that people who had endured a lifetime of indignity and suffering should have it visited upon them again in death. The fact that these bodies were now possessed by darklings did nothing to allay my righteous indignation; rather it increased it.

When I was a mere three feet away from the lead zombie, I let loose with a powerful blast of my banshee wail. I made sure to angle my body so that no nearby structures or monuments would be affected by the destructive sonic blast. The entire group of zombies was instantly obliterated.

"Jesus Fucking Christ!" Frank swore as the group caught up to me. He stared at the carpet of bone fragments and gore that was settling to ground at my feet.

"Get going!" I yelled at everyone turning towards the second zombie group coming up on our rear. "Get Amber to where she can deal with security."

Still fueled by the wind, I sped away and destroyed the second group of unfortunate zombies before my friends had a chance to move three feet. Without pausing, I raced through the cloud of zombie gore that resulted from my attack and circled the long building to make sure no other threats lurked in its shadow. The plan we'd worked out earlier in the day was for Nathaniel to deal with the electronic parts of the building's security system while Amber dealt with the living security guards with her siren song, and finally I'd snatch the bell in Diva form; then we'd all skip across the street to Independence Hall.

I met the others at the front entrance where Amber had already charmed the guards. Surprisingly, the young banshee was singing the peppy *I'm Alive* by Celine Dion which seemed like a strange choice considering the circumstances, but I wasn't gonna argue with an artist. Watching her dance and sway as her magical voice tugged at even my emotions, I felt sad for what the world had lost; Amber could have reached superstardom if her life hadn't been stolen from her. I was grateful that she was able to use her gifts for good even if it was in death. She was playing a starring role in a battle that would save the world from chaos. Under the force of her will, the guards opened the doors for us and we passed into the long exhibit hall. Nathaniel had apparently already hexed the electronic security systems. He'd said earlier that he'd be able to do it in a mere second or two.

The exhibit hall was long with a dozen or so narrow floor to ceiling windows on either side. The history of the bell from its creation till its final placement in this building was laid out in this room told through a myriad of audio and visual displays. Amber continued to sing drawing a small crowd of security personnel and nightshift employees who danced and capered about her oblivious to what was going on around them. Nathaniel and I led the way down the center of the hall heading for the bell chamber at the other end. Frank and Brianna followed five paces back walking side by side. We were just a little more than half way down the hall when the building suddenly shook and the sound of a thousand chandeliers being shattered followed. Amber continued to sing but pulled those under her spell closer together into a corner of the hall. The rest of us raced for the bell chamber.

The bell chamber was much smaller than the exhibit hall though its ceiling was much higher. The Liberty Bell swayed in the room's center, and it hung from what was said to be its original yoke. It was encased in a glass prison for its own protection. Beyond the bell, the Southern wall was one gigantic window that provided an incredible view of Independence Hall across the street. The huge bullet proof window now lay in shards as the horror that had smashed through it lumbered towards the Liberty Bell. The thing was nothing like anything I'd ever seen or imagined in my worst nightmares. It had the shape and movement of a giant gorilla, and it stood nearly fifteen feet tall. At first it reminded me of King Kong, but its other horrific features overwhelmed that impression. The beast had three heads on its shoulders: one looked like an ape's head, another like a lizard's, while the last was clearly that of a giant insect. Even worse, there were heads and faces protruding from nearly every inch of the things body. They were of all shapes and sizes, some looking recognizably human or animal, but most were alien and monstrous to behold. There were heads in the palms of the monster's hands and on every single one of its knuckles. The heads moved and undulated separately from the movements of the creature itself giving it a dizzying appearance of being covered by a swarm of undulating critters. One feature that all the heads shared in common was at least one oversized mouth with vicious looking teeth, and most of the faces were sporting multiple mouths. The chaos monster's aura was a nasty combination of red and vomit green.

"What...what...the fuck...is...that?" stammered Frank. He and Brianna were shrinking back from the thing; both were clearly ready to bolt in terror.

"It's a gibberer," answered Nathaniel calmly. He spoke one of his nonsensical arcane words and his golden aura spread to envelop the terrified detective and shifter. The bubble of gold seemed to calm our two friends both of whom stood straighter and raised their weapons towards the new threat even as their hands still shook.

"No, my friends," the wizard said to them. "This is beyond you. Go tell Amber what is happening and withdraw from the building. Have her bring everyone along. We don't want collateral damage here."

The gibberer suddenly stopped in its tracks on its way to the bell and turned towards us as if just noticing us. Every mouth on its body opened and began to shriek and gibber. Frank, who had seemed prepared to argue with Nathaniel's instructions, turned and bolted for the exhibit hall with Brianna right on his tail. The aberration began to stalk towards us. I gathered my rage and will, preparing to slam it with the most powerful banshee wail that I could muster.

"Don't bother," Nathaniel said. "Its gibbering acts like a shield. It's impervious to almost anything we can throw at it including sonic attacks."

"What do we do then? Should I go diva?" I asked the wizard.

"No," he answered with a shake of his head. He began moving away from the oncoming monster, angling to the right. "I don't know how to hurt it let alone destroy it. Let's ping-pong it till we can come up with something. Go left."

The gibberer suddenly charged forward, and calling the wind

to me I did likewise. In a single instant I let loose with my banshee scream while drawing my katana. The gibbering turned to hideous laughter rolling out of a thousand throats, and my wail shattered as if it were a wave encountering a sea wall. My forward momentum carried me to within five feet of the gibberer whereupon I suddenly felt myself being pulled towards it by an unseen force. I tried to put on the breaks, but it was as if I'd suddenly been caught in a tractor beam. I lashed out with my katana and stared in horror when one of the faces extended its mouth far beyond what it should have been capable of. My blade flew into empty space and the mouth snapped shut; its teeth sheered through the celestial steel sword as if it were made of butter. The mouth opened again less than a millisecond later, and the rest of my katana and arm were pulled towards the hideous maw. Though I struggled with all my might, I couldn't get free. The pressure of being pulled in by all of those mouths was threatening my cohesion, and I suddenly knew that my being a ghost wasn't going to save me against this thing. It could devour me as easily as it had done my celestial steel blade. Panic filled me, and I began to attempt a translation back into Limbo, but even that final retreat was denied to me as the gibberer's power prevented me from sliding into the world of the dead.

As all hope left me, I suddenly slammed into a wall of force and just as quickly as the sucking force had grabbed me, it vanished.

"Get out of there!" roared Nathaniel and calling the wind to me I did just that and fled to the left side of the chamber.

I looked back at Nathaniel and saw him staring the gibberer down. His stormy gray eyes were blazing and sweat was pouring down his face as he focused all his will on the shield that he'd thrown up around the gibberer. The abomination was sucking at the shield as it had done to me and pieces of the shimmering magic were actually being peeled off and sucked into it. It was obvious that the shield wouldn't last long, but it had done its job and given me the chance to get away. The impending fall of the shield meant we had to come up with a plan very quickly. Fleeing wasn't an option; if we did so, we'd lose the bell and any chance we had at saving the city. I looked around the room desperately looking for something that we could use to fight this chaos monster. My eyes came to rest on the Liberty Bell for a moment but there was no help there. Azathoth had sent the minion best suited for eliminating the bell as a threat. The gibberer was likely impervious to the bell's power. It was probably going to feast on it when it was done with us.

As Nathaniel's shield began to implode, and I failed to find anything of use, my father's teachings intruded on my frantic thoughts.

"When fighting a more skilled and powerful opponent, remember that his greatest strength is often his greatest weakness."

My eyes shot back to the gibberer. Its greatest strength was clearly it's thousands of mouths with their ability to protect it by gibbering and their offensive traits of sucking and devouring pretty much anything. Did those mouths need to breathe? Probably not. Nathaniel had told me that most of chaos's creatures were formed and normally lived in places without an atmosphere. But what about water? Could the thing be drowned? The water should at least reduce the effectiveness of its gibbering powers. There was a pop as Nathaniel's shield finally gave way and the wizard staggered as if struck. I wanted to run to him, to see if he was alright, but I had to trust that he was as tough as I was; it was the only way we'd survive.

"Nathaniel," I called to him as the gibberer cackled in delight, apparently savoring the taste of Carter's magic. "Can you conjure water? A lot of it?"

The wizard looked over at me. His stormy eyes were subdued, tired, and afraid.

"Go! Get out of here! I'll buy you some time."

"There's no time for this shit!" I roared at him as the gibberer took a step towards him. The abomination paused and looked back at me. It stared in indecision at both of us. "Get your bad ass wizard self up and fill this damn room with water or we're both dead."

Without waiting for a reply, I pulled some of the remaining stored mist in me and willed it to form a shield around the entire bell chamber. The gibberer gurgled in pleasure and immediately went to the edge of the shield to inspect the new obstruction.

"I can't do this all day," I called to Nathaniel as I replenished the mist that the gibberer was siphoning from the shield with the shrinking supply of mist stored in me. There was a sudden change in air pressure, and just like that the entire room was filled with brackish water. I almost lost my shield as the sudden surge of pressure against it increased dramatically; where the gibberer had sucked on a single area, the water now pushed against the entire shield. I managed to hold the shield up though and soon found that I could do so without much effort. The water wasn't attacking and neither was the gibberer, and the pressure had stabilized. The water was too murky for even my eyes to penetrate for any distance beyond ten feet, and I was unable to see if Nathaniel had taken any action to protect himself; I flew towards where he'd last been to make sure he was alright. It felt weird flying through water as if it were air, but the liquid had no affect on my ghostly body. I spotted Nathaniel almost in the same spot he'd been in. A golden globe surrounded him and he waved at me questioningly. I gestured for him to hold on and went to see what was happening to the gibberer.

My father's words could not have been more correct in this instance. The gibberer's thousands of mouths had naturally sucked in all the water that it could hold. The thing was still twitching, but it was clear that it was rapidly drowning. I waited until it stopped twitching and waited some more until I could see its prone form begin to disintegrate into nasty muck. I released my mist shield and the water cascaded outward flooding the entire building in a few feet of water. I sighed in relief when the gibberer continued to puddle into a mound of mud. Splashing footfalls told me of Nathaniel's approach. The wizard looked exhausted, but he had a broad smile on his face.

"What in the name of creation gave you the idea to drown it?" he asked shaking his head. "It's brilliant. I would never have thought of it, but it's so damned obvious."

"My dad gave me the idea," I said smiling sadly. I missed him so much. I wish I could tell him how so much of what he'd taught me had saved my unlife. The sound of an approaching motorcycle brought my attention back to the smashed wall sized window that looked towards Independence Hall. I knew that midnight was rapidly approaching.

"We'd best get moving," said Nathaniel, his attention also having been drawn to the noise of the city outside. "Do the diva thing and we can get on with this."

All over the city, sirens were wailing as the zombie apocalypse reached its peak. Philly's ghost army was going to keep the majority of the public safe from the undead assault, but some were going to get through; a lot of people were going to die this night, and the PPD was likely going to bear the brunt of it as they responded to emergency calls.

"Is there a plan B?" I asked quietly. "I used up almost all of the stored mist to pull off that big ass shield. I don't have enough to go diva."

"That's going to be a big problem," said the wizard turning towards the bell. "It will take too much time for me to power you back up or to even use the arkose device to pull mist from limbo. We just don't have enough time. I can't imagine how we're going to move it."

"Can we sound it from here?" I asked.

Nathaniel shook his head in negation.

"Symbolism and faith add greatly to the power of any magic," he answered quietly. "Ringing the bell from Independence Hall is a must. Without it we're screwed."

"What do a wizard and ghost want with the Liberty Bell?" someone with a deep, resonate voice asked from behind us. The hint of amusement in the voice made the sudden intrusion less threatening than it would have been otherwise.

41

NATHANIEL AND I SIMULTANEOUSLY whirled around to face the intruder. A man stood confidently at the broken wall sized window. He was a big man, taller than Nathaniel, and with a far broader build. He was built like a freight train; probably a bodybuilder I mused. He had long chestnut brown hair that was braided into dreadlocks. His eyes were also brown, but unlike his casual posture, they danced about looking for any signs of trouble. They revealed the soul of a hunter. His face was angular with a strong jaw that was covered by a neatly trimmed mustache and goatee. His nose was straight and his eyebrows were full but not bushy, and his eye lashes were to die for. He wore a pair of tight black jeans, a brown polo shirt with only the bottom button done up, black bikers boots, and a black leather duster. The hilt of a sword protruded from over his shoulder, and he held a shotgun nonchalantly in his right hand. It was pointed at the ground at the moment. He looked handsome, but there was something odd about his aura and his shadow which said that there was more to him than his handsome appearance indicated.

His aura was slate gray with bubbles of red and green twining through it. Gray wasn't a color I'd seen in an aura before now, and it hadn't been covered in any of my trainings with Delilah or Nathaniel. Red auras usually signified demons, but green was shifters; the combination left me puzzled as to what this guy's true nature was. What really put me on alert though was the man's shadow. He was standing in the flood lights that illuminate Independence Mall, and the shadow that he cast suggested that he was literally a giant with a single horn on his head. The earrings that dangled from his earlobes and the rings he wore were unmistakably made of devil's iron.

"I just took out your master's gibberer," I told the man, stepping forward and preparing to blast him with a banshee wail. "Get lost or I'll make a puddle out of you too."

The man tensed; the amusement vanishing from his features as he took my threat seriously, but to his credit he didn't panic or move in any way that would be considered threatening. The air around him went cold though, and the rage that seethed within him was visible in his hard eyes. His aura was now menacing: the red bubbles in it pulsed angrily.

"I don't have a master, ghost girl," he rumbled in reply. "I wander these streets of my own will, though admittedly I have strayed into claimed territory. Death stalks the night, and I found myself desiring to join the battle. Fear not young ghostling, I think we are allies this night."

I stared at the man in consternation.

"Who the hell are you?" I finally blurted out.

"I am Alrik Solheim, at your service youngling," he replied, and then shocked me by actually bowing his head to me in a sign of respect. Where in the hell was this guy from, and what century had he crawled out from?

Nathaniel stepped to my side and put a hand on my shoulder.

"I haven't seen you around before Alrik," he said, a hint of warning in his voice. "Are you new to Philadelphia?"

"My apologies master wizard," the big man said, inclining

his neck in deference to Nathaniel as well. The hint of threat that had been in his voice when he'd addressed my own threat against him was gone now, and he deliberately avoided making eye contact with the wizard. "I have been in these parts for over a century, though I've not lived here in more than a decade. I've been back for nearly a year now."

"What the hell is going on here?" I asked Nathaniel, beginning to get annoyed. "We're on a time crunch here."

"This entire city is my territory," Nathaniel told Alrik, his voice having gone cold. "Alrik here is a troll Veronika. They are kin to the First Born. You are probably more familiar with the Germanic and Celtic fairy legends though. The trolls are a Nordic people, exceedingly rare these days since Beowulf hunted them down to near extinction. The few that remain are usually mercenaries employed by the Twilight Court."

I stared at Alrik incredulously. This handsome hunk of a man was a troll? A glance at his monstrous shadow convinced me that Nathaniel wasn't pulling my leg. The fact that Beowulf had been a real historical figure and not just a legend from English literature shouldn't have shocked me either, but it did.

"Aren't trolls evil?" I asked tensely.

"I could ask the same about ghosts and wizards," Alrik answered caustically. "If the wench is done wasting time master wizard, I would be honored to offer you my service."

"Wench!" I screamed and charged right up to him. Up close he was even bigger than he looked from twenty feet away. I saw that my assessment of his bodybuilding physique wasn't incorrect either; this close I could see his six pack abs pressing against his tight shirt. He'd reactively raised the shotgun to point at my head, but I ignored it as I stared up into his angry eyes. "You'll take that back or God help me I'll blast you into oblivion."

"I'd do as she says if I were you," Nathaniel said quietly. "You've made a grave mistake here Alrik. She's not merely a ghost, she's a banshee."

The big man blanched and took an involuntary step back, his

tanned features going pale. He stared at me, weighing me with his deep brown eyes, trying to determine whether Nathaniel was speaking the truth. Judging from his reaction, he knew exactly what a banshee was capable of doing.

"We could use his help Veronika," Nathaniel cut in. "Trolls are incredibly strong. I'm guessing Alrik could carry the bell."

The troll suddenly went to one knee and bowed his head in submission to me.

"I beg your pardon Most Terrible Maiden of Battle," the troll intoned. "I swear that if you let me live, I will serve your present need to the best of my power."

I stared at the man in chagrin. He'd just called me a wench and just as quickly he was bending the knee to me. I looked back at Nathaniel for direction.

"Among the old Norse religion of which most trolls still adhere to," Nathaniel explained. "Banshees are the Celtic equivalent of the Valkyrie: warrior women who serve Odin and are tasked with selecting the greatest of warriors from the living. The chosen of the Valkyrie join the ranks of the einherjar who will fight at the last battle of Ragnarok. There is no greater honor or omen for a Viking than to come face to face with a Valkyrie. The chance to actually serve one is beyond contemplation, is it not Alrik?"

"It is both an honor and a mighty omen though my people would not deign to serve Odin."

Wow, and just like that I'd become a warrior woman out of Norse mythology with a troll servant to boot. My unlife was sometimes cooler then all heck.

"Ok Alrik, you can help us move the bell," I said finally, and the troll raised his head and nodded his agreement "Helping me is going to put you in a lot of danger. I've got some powerful enemies who are trying to destroy the city. And if you wish to be an ally of the Ghost Watch you will need to rid yourself of the devil's iron trinkets that you carry, and you'll need to assure us that you will always act benevolently towards humanity."

"I will aid you this night," the troll replied with a nod of his head. "Ragnarok hasn't arrived yet, but clearly the doom of this city is at hand. This night we are allied due to a common foe. As to your demands concerning my blood iron, that will not be possible. Jotunheim has its own bands who will fight at Ragnarok. It may be that at the final battle we will find ourselves on opposite sides of the field. Let us be about this quest."

I watched Alrik as he lumbered towards the Liberty Bell. He moved with a grace that belied his massive size. I respected his bluntness and honesty; he would help us because it was in his best interest to do so now, but that might not always be the case. I judged that he wasn't someone who would hurt people because he liked it. He would do it for a purpose though, as long as it aligned with his moral code. And that was what set this monster apart from all the other monsters that I'd dealt with over the past nine months; this one did have a moral code that guided his decisions and actions beyond what his simple desires might be. I felt certain that he would act in a way that was counter to his personal interests if his moral code conflicted with most of his goals.

Whatever the future held for us however, tonight we had to save the city. Ragnarok and the rest of it could wait for tomorrow.

42

THE HUMAN SKIN THAT ALRIK wore vanished as the troll's fist made contact with the bullet proof glass that protected the Liberty Bell. The glass shattered under the impact of the troll's supernatural strength, and the nearly ten foot tall warrior reached in and grasped the bell. Alrik had long black hair that flowed down his ridged back, his eyes were completely black like a dog's, and he had a single sharp horn that protruded from his forehead. His skin was leathery looking and was emerald green, his huge muscles rippled with every move that he made, and I wondered if the Incredible Hulk had been inspired by a troll sighting. He was still dressed in jeans, biker boots, a polo shirt, and a long, black leather duster. The hilt of his great sword peaked out from behind his left shoulder. I expected him to tear the bell free from its mounting, but once Alrik had both hands on the artifact he paused, his brows pinching in concentration. About ten seconds later there was a popping sound as the bolts that held the bell fastened to its original yoke suddenly tumbled to the ground. Alrik smiled with satisfaction and with barely any effort pulled the bell free and hoisted the one ton brass bell over his shoulder as if it were a sack of potatoes.

"Let's go," he growled, and without waiting for us, he strode towards the broken window and Independence Hall beyond it.

"Hey, wait up greenie," I called, leaping into the air and speeding after the troll whose long strides were taking him towards our final destination at a rapid speed.

Just as Alrik was about to cross Chestnut Street an explosion of magical energy rocked him back, and he almost fell. A roiling black cloud of chaos formed in the middle of the street, and bolts of freezing fire lanced outward from it. A giant with black skin, red eyes, red mane, and a kingly bearing stepped from the cloud. Two other slightly shorter giants with paler skin followed at the first ones heels. All three of them towered over Alrik. The first giant stood at nearly seventeen feet tall while the other two were approximately fifteen feet tall. They were all clad in battle garb: chainmail hauberks, steel gauntlets and vambraces, greaves, and steel boots. All of their protective gear was complemented by their deadly looking weapons.

"Give me the bell troll!" boomed the lead giant, its massive hand reaching towards the Liberty Bell.

Alrik nimbly hopped back out of the giant's reach, and instead of dropping the artifact and reaching for his sword, he grasped the bell by its neck and waved it about threateningly. The leading giant stepped back in consternation while its two companions fanned out to either side so as to come at Alrik's flank.

"Do you know who I am?" the giant bellowed, reaching behind him and grasping the hilt of his sword. He drew a devil's iron great sword that was wreathed in cold black flame. "I am Surt, black god of the Jotunns. Give me that bell Alrik, and I'll guarantee you a spot at my side when Ragnarok comes."

"Don't believe him, Alrik," panted Nathaniel as he ran up to stand on Alrik's left flank. "This is Azathoth's avatar, the One with Many Names, all of them black. He doesn't care about Ragnarok or any of our beliefs except for how he can manipulate them to his master's own ends. All he cares about is bringing chaos, and right now that means stopping us from getting the bell in place to save the city."

The giant threw back his head and laughed. Center City actually shook so terrible and full of power was his mirth.

"You are a fool wizard," Surt said. "I don't subvert religion, I create it. The Jotunns are my true children, and someday soon they will feast upon the flesh of men."

"Troll's are not Jotunns," Nathaniel shot back. "They are of the Nephilim, the first children of man and angels. Don't listen to this foul creature Alrik. You are a child of creation not chaos."

"My kin were hunted by servants of the Christian god unto extinction," Alrik said bitterly between gritted teeth. My heart sank at this pronouncement. How were we going to get the bell back if he turned on us? "And where was the mighty Surt and the rest of your precious Jotunns when my people were fighting for their very survival? You did not offer us your aid then, and we didn't expect it from your kind. I care nothing for you or the Christians, but I have made this city my home and have sworn to assist the Valkyrie for this one night. So step aside."

"Kill them!" Surt raged leaping forward and swinging his flaming sword in an arc that would cleave through Alrik and Nathaniel both in one fell swoop.

Alrik raised the Liberty Bell and to my horror parried the great sword with it. There was a clang as the bell and flaming blade met. Surt's impressive sword exploded into useless shards, and the bell's brass skin broke away in chunks revealing a gleaming bell made of celestial steel beneath. Surt cried out in pain and fell back, but Alrik pursued him, swinging the bell as if it were a war hammer. He connected with a powerful upswing that caught the giant in the left shoulder. The sound of shattering bone was accompanied by the bell's own song of battle. Surt groaned and then collapsed in on himself, dissipating into mist before Alrik could club him in the head.

Meanwhile, I flew in on the smaller giant on Alrik's right flank as it closed in on the troll. I let loose with a banshee wail and was pleased to find that the giant didn't have the same resistance to sonic damage as many of the chaos monsters had; the blast tore it apart leaving only a shower of black gory mist in its wake. Nathaniel dealt with the other giant on the left flank, striking it with several bolts of fire that left it crumpled in a smoking heap in the middle of the road.

"One thing before we go," the wizard shouted over the roar of approaching sirens. He came to me and placed a glowing hand on my shoulder, mumbled a few words, and a burning heat suddenly filled me. "Now we can go, we have twelve minutes left."

"What did you do?"

"I buffed you."

"Excuse me?"

"It's an MMO term. It means I gave you some mojo that will make you more powerful against chaos creatures. Your screams should cut them down more easily now."

"What's an MMO?"

"Never mind, run!"

43

Alrik and Nathaniel broke into a run. The bell didn't seem to slow the troll at all and he managed to keep an easy pace just ahead of Nathaniel. I called the wind to me and sped ahead of the both of them looking for more signs of trouble. Frank and Brianna emerged from the shadows to join us while Amber moved to intercept the arriving cops so that they didn't interfere with us. Independence Hall loomed before us, it's figure was brightly lit but closed; I could see no enemies lurking in its shadows. Nathaniel took out the electronic surveillance and security systems with a single word hex, and Alrik opened the door by simply touching the handle and concentrating. Amazingly, the locks turned themselves and the troll simply pushed the door open.

As we were climbing the steps of the bell tower, a wave of chaos energy hit us, and we were suddenly standing on the black stairs of a massive domed building. The steps were made for a giant: each one was nearly ten feet high and thirty feet wide. Looking upward, I thought I saw a pair of glowing green eyes looking down at us before they winked out. A massive bell dominated the upper reaches of this domed room, and a pang of fear shot through me as I saw it begin to move.

And just as suddenly as we'd found ourselves in that black tower we found ourselves back in Independence Hall.

"The shift is beginning," Nathaniel said in the terrified seconds of silence that followed. "The two cities are coming into alignment. We need to get up there."

As if to punctuate his words, a faint sound of distant bells seemed to reverberate through the very stone and steel of the city, and it buried itself deeply into our very souls. The tolling of those bells sent a shiver of terror down all of our spines. It carried the promise of everlasting horror and chaos. In our minds eye we all saw what was coming: an elder god who cared nothing for life, and who was so alien to humanity that we were nothing more than cockroaches to it. The entire citizenry of Philadelphia experienced the nightmare vision of this gigantic tentacle god, and behind it an even darker and more sinister force lurked. I guessed that the undefined menace behind the elder god must be Azathoth, the God of chaos. Just the thought of him made me want to tear my eyes and tongue out. If we failed in the next few minutes, we not only doomed ourselves but also all of humanity to death in a world of ever growing chaos.

The sounds of the bells passed as did the vision, but with their passing came the chaos spiders. They poured down the stairs from above and up from below. The momentary phasing of the two cities must have allowed them to cross over. I prayed fervently that this was a targeted strike at us and not a city wide invasion otherwise the streets would run red this night, and Limbo's harvest would be great indeed.

"I've got these," Alrik boomed as he lunged up the stairs swinging the Liberty Bell as if it were a flail.

Nathaniel and I turned to the swarm of many eyed giant spiders crawling up the walls and bounding up the steps towards us. The wizard raised his staff and a bolt of lightning shot from it and struck an oncoming spider. The creature screeched then plummeted to its final death below. I targeted one of the spiders and sent a controlled burst banshee wail at it, obliterating it in a shower of black gore, while doing no collateral damage to the building. My banshee wail had never been more effective against a being of chaos. Hurray for Nathaniel's buff! Seeing what we had to contend with made me glad that Frank and Brianna had elected to stay with Amber to offer her protection.

A glance over my shoulder towards Alrik convinced me that the troll didn't need our assistance. He was making steady progress upward; the pile of broken spiders that now littered the stairs attested to the troll's deadly prowess. Confronted with their inability to overwhelm us, the spiders began shooting their webs in order to slow us down. Alrik simply ignore the incredibly sticky webs, powering his way through them as if they were made of silk. Luckily, the troll also seemed to be immune to the insanity that the strands of webbing could induce in the minds of people and ghosts that came into contact with it. The webs were a much bigger threat to Nathaniel and I, and they'd already proved that they could hold a ghost. The wizard dealt with the threat by putting a warding shield around us. The shield moved with us, but it did slow us down. This wasn't too much of a problem however, because we were covering Alrik's back and therefore could afford to lag a little behind.

Alrik had reached the landing at the top of the belfry when the city was once again wracked with a planar shift and we once more found ourselves in the black domed tower. This time however, there were chaos beasts waiting for us: thousands of them. I screamed in fear and rage as chaos frogs lashed me with their serrated, madness inducing poisoned tongues. The banshee wail took out a half dozen of the chaos creatures in a cone sized area in front of me. Nathaniel let loose with balls of fire that shot from his outstretched hands one after another as he moved his arm in a strafing motion. The building shook with every explosion of the wizard's fire balls, and scores of chaos beasts were annihilated with each blast. Above us, Alrik roared in fury as dozens of chaos beasts threatened to pull him down.

As the bell above us prepared to toll once more, the troll howled a battle cry and leaped straight up swinging the Liberty Bell in a mighty arc. The celestial steel artifact of the American Revolution struck the massive black bell that was one hundred times its size and weight, and with a soul jarring clang the chaos bell shattered upon impact. Every remaining chaos beast in the tower began shrieking and thrashing about in agony as the mighty black bell came apart in a shower of deadly shrapnel. The two cities shifted as the shards fell towards us in a deadly down pour. The shift saved Nathaniel and I, but I saw Alrik get struck by many sword sized shards before the translation was completed.

Back in Independence Hall once more, we found that all of the spiders invading the bell tower were dead. The chiming of distant bells and the horrible visions were also absent this time. A groan from above brought Nathaniel and I around to see that the mighty Alrik had fallen to his knees. We sped up the stairs to the troll's side, finding that his leather duster was torn to ribbons and green blood poured from a dozen deep gashes and scores of smaller cuts. A mortal human would have been unconscious and dying from the wounds the troll had sustained, but as I reached a comforting hand out to him, I saw that the wounds were already rapidly healing. Apparently the stories of troll regenerative powers weren't incorrect.

"Give me a moment," Alrik said gruffly shaking off Nathaniel's hand but allowing me to touch him with a hand that I made solid at the expense of a little power. "By Loki, that hurt!"

"If we hadn't shifted when we did you could have been killed by the falling debris," Nathaniel said, his stormy gray eyes flashing in anger. "What in the name of creation possessed you to try such a foolish stunt? You could just as easily have destroyed the Liberty Bell, and then where would we be?"

A shiver ran through me at the thought. The line between hero and foolhardy risk taker was separated by mere luck in many cases, and this was certainly one of them. My recent experience with things made of chaos alloy was that it had a tendency to break celestial steel. The Liberty Bell had certainly proved its specialness this night.

Alrik grunted as he rose and hefted the bell. He was bleeding still, but his body was repairing the damage at a rapid rate. I wondered what cost would have to be paid for such use of power. He'd probably have to eat five whole cows or something like that.

"I saved your asses wizard. The only thing that matters is that it worked. It's better to be lucky than good, in my case I'm both," Alrik blustered. He suddenly guffawed and turned, hefting the bell so that we could see it. "Look here, it really does have a crack now."

Nathaniel swore as we both stared at the crack that now marred the smooth blue steel surface of the bell. It seemed to be in the exact spot as it should according to the historical records.

"Don't be so uptight wizard," Alrik said with another laugh as he swung around and headed for the bell chamber. "The Norn would call this fate. The bell will work as it should."

"Who knows what damage has been done to the magic," Nathaniel muttered darkly.

"It will be ok," I told him taking his hand and squeezing it. "We couldn't have done this without him. I think we might have been goners if he hadn't done what he did. They were waiting for us."

Nathaniel sighed and nodded, the tension left him.

"You're welcome," came Alrik's voice from within the bell chamber. He was really getting full of himself. When we entered the room we found that he'd already put the Liberty Bell down and was working at removing the current bell from its place using the same method he'd used with the Liberty Bell. Once the bell was removed, he picked up the Liberty Bell and placed it up into its proper place. His eyes closed and he seemed to go into a trance. I stared in awe as new bolts seemed to flow out of the existing material and fuse the bell into its housing. I realized that Alrik must have a gift similar to my own celestial steel shaping except his appeared to encompass a wider range of materials; it was similar to what the gargoyles could do. "It's ready now."

"And not a moment too soon," Nathaniel said as we began to feel the distant chiming of chaos bells reverberating through our souls once more. "Quickly, begin the tolling!"

Alrik grabbed the nearby rope and began to pull on it vigorously. A beautiful sound rose up drowning out the sound of the bells of chaos, and within seconds it was answered by a chorus of the city's bells. It started in Center City and worked its way outward as outlying areas became aware of the signal to begin sounding the bells. Over it all, the magical sound of the Liberty Bell could be heard, and it seemed as though it took the ringing of the city's bells and harmonized them into something grand: a symphony of bells never before heard upon the earth. The entire city shook as the bells of chaos tried to intrude with their discordant sound, but liberty's bells rang forth across the entirety of the City of Brotherly Love and drowned out the tolling of chaos. I sprang into the air and passed through the ceiling of Independence Hall, flying high so that I could get a view of the entire city. Philadelphia was blazing with lights. Everyone was awake and the power had apparently been restored. Hundreds of emergency lights flashed everywhere; the city's entire first response teams seemed to have been called out. It seemed like everyone was outside now, and they were gazing around in bewilderment and awe at the battle of sound that was taking place. I saw that there were still battles raging but most of these were contained and the majority of the fighting was over. The zombie apocalypse was largely under control.

As the bells of chaos fell silent, the city shook as a howl of rage and agony threatened to overwhelm the city's bells. The Delaware River near Penn's Landing began to boil, and I saw a massive head with a huge gaping maw and thrashing tentacles break its surface. The thing was huge, maybe the size of a ten story building, and I instinctively knew that one of the elder god's had crossed over; it was the statue from the black city. I sped towards the Masonic temple where I found the Governor and five other banshees waiting.

"Sisters," I said without preamble "Follow me. An elder god is rising, and we're all that's left to stop it."

To their credit, my sisters followed me without question though they all looked terrified. The Governor said she'd send us what aid she could muster as quickly as possible, and Sebastian was dispatched to inform Nathaniel and Alrik of where I'd gone. Without further discussion, I led my sisters off to confront the rising elder god.

44

THE ELDER GOD WAS STILL MIRED in the river when I was finally able to lead my sisters to the scene. The city bells were still tolling, and apparently they'd prevented the monster from being able to fully cross over to the living world. The thing was struggling mightily, causing huge waves to crash onto both sides of the river, but for the moment it was stuck. Seeing our opportunity, I gave my sisters a signal, and we all came together to hold hands in a flying line with me at its center. We paused midair for a moment then as a group dove towards the mammoth god and simultaneously let loose with our banshee wails. The last time we'd combined our sonic attacks in combat, we'd destroyed an entire army and leveled a few city blocks.

The elder god was struck full on in the face; its eyes exploded in a shower of green gore, but other than that, our combined blast seemed to have little effect on it. The beast roared in rage, and its tentacles lashed out. My sisters and I broke formation and scattered to avoid the attack. Unfortunately, Angela failed to evade one of the tree trunk sized appendages, and she was snatched out of the air and held in a crushing grip that had no trouble holding onto a ghost.

Bridget and I were at her side instantly as she writhed in agony and was pulled towards the god's gaping maw. Bridget had her sword drawn and was hacking at the thick limb holding our sister, but although her celestial steel blade was biting into the blackish green hide that covered the creature's body it was clear that she would neither be able to cut through the tentacle nor was it causing the monster enough pain to cause it to release Angela. All of our other sisters darted about the god's head, blasting it with sonic screams, except Amber who had joined us on our way from the temple. The siren was trying to lull the beast with her magical song, but even that had no perceptible affect. The god continued to blindly lash the air with its remaining three tentacles, forcing all of us to take evasive action and keeping us off balance.

I waved Bridget aside as Angela was pulled within a few yards of the monster's hideous mouth. She was screaming in terror and begging us to set her free. Bridget dove out of my way, and I blasted the tentacle with a focused wail that blew through the limb and sent Angela plummeting towards the river below. She was still entangled in the severed limb, but I was confident that she could make good her escape now. Unfortunately for me, I let my guard down for a moment and took a riposting blow from the heavily bleeding limb that I'd severed. The strike stunned me and sent me careening a hundred feet to crash through a nearby building on Front Street. I picked myself up slowly and flew back through the building's ceiling thanking God all the while that I was a ghost. That blow would have pulverized a living being.

As I reached the rooftop and surveyed the unfolding battle I was dismayed to see that more of the god had risen from the river, and it seemed to be gaining purchase despite the fact that the city's bells were still tolling. The Governor had been true to her word though; ghostly troops were flowing onto the scene and launching themselves at the behemoth, but I could see that there was little any of us could do to truly hurt the thing. As I wracked my brain for a plan, I dimly became aware of a steady chanting. Looking around I spotted a cluster of robed figures on a nearby rooftop. A chill went down my spine and I instinctively knew that whatever those figures were up too it wasn't good for us.

I moved quickly towards them finally hearing the words they were chanting as I came in closer.

"Ph'nglui mglw'nafh Cthulhu R'lyeh wgah'nagl fhtagn," they intoned over and over again. I had no idea what they were saying accept the name Cthulhu, which had been a name mentioned several times by both Nathaniel and Frank. From what I'd understood, it was an important god of the chaos pantheon that Lovecraft had prophesied about. A shudder ran through me as I realized that the elder thing in the river must be this Cthulhu and these cultists were helping it get through.

A battle cry rang out, and Alrik was suddenly leaping through the air to land in the midst of the cultists, his huge devil's iron great sword sweeping in an arc that cleaved three acolytes in a single swing. The chant faltered as the troll spun in a deadly circle, every swing and slash resulting in the bloody death of a cultist. One of the fanatics was quicker than the others; his tall gaunt form moved gracefully to avoid the troll's cleaving blade. Alrik growled at the man and stalked slowly towards him. He was the last of the chanters. The man raised an arm and a green beam lashed out and struck the troll full in the chest. Alrik flinched then came to a complete stop. His muscles seeming to go lax, and his sword fell from his grasp.

"You meddlesome dog," spat the cultist as he strode towards the troll. "Your Twilight Court assured us that they would remain neutral in this battle. They will pay dearly for what you've done. You, I will give to the Great Cthulhu."

The man's hood fell away revealing long blond hair that I instantly recognized from the incident at Byberry. This was the necromancer named Curwen, and he was in my sights. He never saw me coming as his full attention was on Alrik. I blew him into dust with a point blank focused banshee wail. It was an anticlimactic ending for the evil necromancer of a bygone age, but monologues were for movies, not real battles. If I can help it, I never let the bad guy get a word out. It's just healthier that way.

Alrik sighed and shook his head as the charm left him after Curwen's demise. He looked around for the cultist and spotted me instead. He nodded his thanks and picked up his sword. Turning back to the battle I saw that Cthulhu had stopped rising, but now only the lower half of him was mired in the river. The elder god had its huge hands free to help it in battle now. Four beams of white light suddenly sprang from the Penn's Landing shore striking Cthulhu in its torso and head. He roared in rage and swept the shore with a mighty hand, several buildings collapsed in the attacks wake and luminaries were apparently swept from their vantage point. Lightning began to smite the angry god and I saw Nathaniel standing on a nearby rooftop, his arms were raised to the sky.

A grunt from Alrik brought my attention around to the troll. The Viking monster had picked up a green stone idol of Cthulhu that had lain at the center of the cultists' pentagram which had gone unnoticed by me until now. The thing was grotesque, and it appeared to weigh a lot more than it should for its one foot stature. That or the thing was draining the strength out of the troll. I surmised that it was probably both.

"Don't touch that," I said to the troll. "Who knows what it will do to you."

Alrik grunted again as he hefted it as if to throw it, and then to my amazed shock he did exactly that. The idol sailed through the air straight at Cthulhu and struck the elder god between its empty eye sockets. Cthulhu actually mewed in surprise, and then screamed as the idol imbedded itself in its forehead. The water around him boiled once more, and the great Cthulhu began to sink. The elder god was pulled back into its own realm kicking and screaming the whole way. It only took a minute.

"That's twice I saved you little Valkyrie," the troll harrumphed as he loomed over me, watching Cthulhu's head finally disappear below the surface of the Delaware River.

"Indeed," I said seeing no point in arguing about whether he'd saved the city and not me specifically. "You are a true hero Alrik Solheim. I'm honored to have had you on my side, at least for tonight."

Alrik nodded in satisfaction.

"The Twilight Court was maneuvered into a truce with this cult. They hadn't wanted to make the agreement, and so they called upon me as my actions wouldn't break their pledge. As king of the Trollheim, I am an independent ally of the Court. They cannot be held responsible for my actions."

"Huh…It seems that this Twilight Court found a convenient loophole," I said. "Are you the Twilight Courts hatchet man? I've never met anyone from the fey courts. Perhaps you can introduce me to the appropriate officials sometime."

"I'll introduce you to the Princess Mors Morta sometime soon," Alrik said with a mischievous smile crossing his handsome features. "It will be most enjoyable to see what you make of each other."

"Hmm…," I agreed, getting the feeling that the troll was laughing at an unspoken joke that I was somehow a part of.

"I must go," Alrik said bowing to me and striding to the edge of the building. He swung himself over the edge and began to climb down like a monkey; his hands sunk through the brick of the building's facade but left no trace of his passage. The city's bells continued to ring sounding the call of victory. I turned away from the troll and went looking for my friends, fearful of what the death toll had been for both the living citizens of Philly and the ghostly population of the city.

Epilogue

IT WAS NEARLY A WEEK LATER, and I'd finally had time to come back to living Philly to spend a night of amazing passion with Nathaniel. I was resting quietly next to him as gray light began to show through his bedroom curtains. His breathing was light, and I suspected that he was still sleeping, though I couldn't be completely sure. I was lying against him, comfortably spooned so that his body could give me the power I needed to sustain full manifestation for the whole night. My physical body was downstairs under heavy ward. I've noticed that my emotions are weird and that I'm not me when I'm using my body. I've spoken to Nathaniel about this phenomenon, and at his suggestion I'm limiting its use until we can figure things out.

I mused quietly on the events of the past week as a cloudy, rainy day dawned over Philadelphia. The death toll had indeed been high both for the living and the dead. Nearly a thousand people had been killed in the battle. The PPD blamed most of that on the freak storms and the rest on gangs trying to take advantage of the chaos that followed in the wake of the storms.

We lost almost two hundred ghosts during the battle, and more in the ensuing days. The unprecedented destruction to the city's graveyards was also blamed on the freak storms as were the mass hallucinations that had half the city's population claiming to have seen zombies and ghosts. The psychiatric community was unanimous in its diagnosis that the entire city had fallen under a type of mass hysteria as a result of the terror caused by the freak storms. Perhaps the most dangerous thing to have come out of the events that struck the city was that it had put Philly on the supernatural radar in a huge way. Philadelphia, in a single day, had become a major point of interest for every preternatural being on the planet.

The theft of the Liberty Bell and its subsequent finding in Independence Hall left authorities scratching their heads and all kinds of conspiracy theories grew from it; most of them were against the government and its policy of moving the bell from its proper place in Independence Hall. Strangely, the bell had been found in perfect condition; the brass covering its true nature was back in place when it had been discovered. Another mystery involved all of the city's bells tolling at once during the night's trouble. An investigation found no evidence of this event actually happening even though everyone in the city had heard them. Once again, the event was chalked up to mass hysteria and a trick of the wind and rain whipping through the city's steel canyons. Of course it didn't help that Governor Rachel had our clean up teams wipe out the most obvious evidence of supernatural incursion: the city video surveillance system. Still, there were dozens of amateur videos popping up on the internet that taken as a group painted a pretty accurate picture of what had truly happened. Someone had even managed to get a shot of Cthulhu rising out of the Delaware River. Most people dismissed this stuff as a hoax, like Bigfoot or alien sightings, but the number of people who had suddenly become aware of the true nature of the world had increased significantly.

As for us ghosts, we faced a very real problem with Black

Maria having invaded and occupied our city. Jonus convinced Governor Rachel that there was no better time than now to liberate Pittsburgh, so the entire lot of us rode the Amtrak train to The Steel City, phased back into Limbo, and set Black Maria's massive slave population free. The token force that she'd left behind was swept away, and the city was liberated in less than an hour. We then marched to the Celestial Fields and liberated the valuable mines. Black Maria rushed her forces out to stop us, but with six banshees in the vanguard of our army, she stood little chance against us. In a short but vicious battle we defeated her army, but unfortunately the shadow reaper herself escaped. We were able to return to Philly where we easily drove out the force that Black Maria had left behind. With our home back in our hands again, we finally got to get some rest, though the next few days were busy as we worked to get things back to normal. Many of the living casualties from the Battle of the Bells had been harvested by Black Maria's forces, but fortunately we were able to rescue them. The result was that our population actually increased despite the losses that we'd suffered. Pittsburgh established its own free government, and our two cities became fast allies, agreeing to a joint operation of the Celestial Fields. Control of the mines was going to change things dramatically for us as it would aid our economy and give us control of a vital commodity in Limbo.

The Styx Cartel remains a problem; they managed to slip into the shadows and continue to hide among us even after we reclaimed the city. We still don't know what their true goals are, other than to establish a new world order. Reverend Creed was the highest level member or the organization that we knew about, but despite all of our efforts to find him, he eluded us. Even now, the Cartel remains a definite threat that is the cause of much anxiety in shadow Philly's government. The mania stone buildings remain a problem as property rights in the living world protect them from our wrath. We haven't yet figured out how to deal with them, but something is in the works.

As for myself, I returned to being Captain of the Ghost Watch. My friends returned to their normal lives too. Brianna Martin found herself second in command of the Philly shifter pack under Bruno the bear. The pack's former leader had unfortunately been sacrificed as were many other pack members. It was going to be a time of regrouping for the pack; both Bruno and Brianna were committed to having the community be more involved in the supernatural goings on in the city. Their neutrality policy under the old leadership was over. Frank Cooper's detective business took off as the city's population grew more aware of the hidden world. He and Brianna were a hot item and they continued to work together closely. Nathaniel also found himself in great demand, having proved himself one of the most able wizards in North America. This wasn't a detriment to us of course since I could pretty much go to him wherever he was, and we planned to continue working closely together to protect humanity from the monsters that preyed on them. As for the troll, Alrik Solheim, he was someone that I was going to have to keep an eye on. I had a feeling that his heroic actions during the Battle of the Bells were only the tip of the iceberg. Nathaniel believed that besides demons, the fey were the next most likely preternatural beings to be drawn to the city by the recent display of supernatural power. If this is borne out, I was guessing that Alrik would rise to be an important figure, but would it be for good or ill?

Nathaniel elicited a groan of pleasure from me as he put an arm around me and cupped a breast in his warm hand. His teeth nibbled at my ear and I felt his manhood come fully awake against me. Gold energy flowed over us, and I groaned with pleasure. Damn, who knew being a ghost could be so good, and with that, all thoughts of the past week and what lay ahead left me as I melted into the embrace of my wizard lover.

ABOUT THE AUTHOR

Robert Poulin was born and raised in the New England state of
Connecticut. After spending his late teenage years in Boca Raton
Florida, Robert moved to upstate New York where he lived with
his uncle Wilbrod Poulin and attended the State University of
New York at Plattsburgh. After earning a Bachelor's in Political
Science and a Master's in Teaching, Robert went back to Florida
where he taught Social Studies for a few years. After returning to
Northern New York, Robert took a job with the North Country
Center for Independence: a disability rights and advocacy organizations. Robert has worked for NCCI for thirteen years and is
now the Executive Director. *Wail of the Banshees* is Robert's first
novel; he has been a huge fan of fantasy and science fiction since
second grade when he discovered *The Hobbit*. Urban fantasy in
particular has become Robert's favored genre in the past decade.
Robert has been legally blind since infancy, but thanks to a mom
that encouraged independence, hard work, and a healthy dose of
dreaming, the disability has mostly just been an inconvenience.

About the Editor

Jaimee Finnegan grew up in Keeseville, NY. She was first introduced to the beauty of the novel in her youth by her 4th grade teacher who instilled a love of reading in her. Since then, she always dreamed of working with literature. Whether it was writing or reading she always found herself drawn to the written word. Jaimee went on to attend SUNY Plattsburgh and graduated with a Bachelor's degree in English Literature. She enjoys editing any sort of piece that comes her way whether it is from old college friends or new friends that she meets along the way. This will be the first published piece that she has edited. Jaimee still lives locally in Keeseville, NY happily surrounded by her supportive friends and family.

ABOUT THE COVER ARTIST

Hannah Carr has always had a love of books and has even bound a few of her own, but this is the first time she has designed a book cover. Most of her commissions have been tattoo designs and paintings, so working on a piece to be mass produced while still maintaining an intimate, hand crafted feeling was a new kind of challenge for her. Hannah received her Bachelor of Fine Arts in Metalsmithing and Jewelry Making from Maine College of Art. She is currently living and working in Cadyville, New York.